STAR REVELATIONS

A NOVEL

C000166067

STEVEN PAUL TERRY

Steven Paul Terry/Hero Acts LLC

StarRevelations.com | Info@HeroActs.com

Printed in the United States of America

This is a work of fiction. Names, characters, places, and incidents are a product of the author's imagination. Locales and public names are sometimes used for atmospheric purposes. Any resemblance to actual people, living or dead, or to businesses, companies, events, institutions, or locales is completely coincidental.

Star Revelations/Steven Paul Terry. -- 1st ed.

ISBN 9798761653856 Print Edition

To all the warriors of light in this world and others...
And to all who are on their way to becoming one...

Our birth is but a sleep and a forgetting:
The Soul that rises with us, our life's Star,
Hath had elsewhere its setting,
And cometh from afar:
Not in entire forgetfulness,
And not in utter nakedness,
But trailing clouds of glory do we come,
From God, who is our home.

-Wordsworth

PROLOGUE

I t is a future time in a distant world. A woman sits on an elegant chair arranged by a fountain in a courtyard surrounded by a sumptuous garden. She is dressed in a silvery robe and her long blonde hair lies draped over one shoulder. She appears to be in her mid-forties but is many years older, and those who know her consider her strikingly beautiful.

Birds and insects flutter among the blossoms. In the distance, majestic spacecraft streak silently through the sky. The ambiance is one of harmony and balance, between human and nature, between individual and society.

The woman knows that such peace and balance are not by accident, that nature itself is always in a state of entropy, that humans are disposed to fear and violence. But her people have learned how to rise to and maintain themselves at a higher level of being, above ignorance, greed, hypocrisy, vindictiveness, and prejudice. She knows there are dark forces within the galaxy keen on disrupting her kind's way of life and interrupting their message of faith and progression.

She is one of the chosen messengers of a special communications group called Secret Transmissions Allied Response (STAR). She receives telepathic messages through the chasm of time and space, calls for help from a faraway planet named Earth, specifically from a group of people gathered at a place known to them as Mt. Shasta.

The messages are frantic and the distress they evoke is immediate and visceral.

Help us, there is a bomb...

Many will die...

We are waiting...

You are our liberator...

On her lap rests a small open book; as she receives these messages, she thinks of a response and its words appear on the blank pages.

The bifurcation of your world has begun...

Control and Fear or Love and Freedom...

Dystopia or Utopia...

Your choice...

Part I
MESSAGES

CHAPTER ONE

*You might think you know what I am doing, but it goes beyond
anything you imagine. You don't know I am borrowed from
another galaxy, from another time. I arrived shortly after you
detonated the two atomic bombs in the middle of your last century. My
work of infiltration, subversion, and transformation began immediately.*

The woman stumbled over the uneven ground, dazed, confused.

Thoughts trickled into her head.

Where am I? What is going on?

She realized there were cold, wet stones beneath her bare feet.

What happened to my shoes?

Through a veil of pain, she tried to discern what appeared around
her, but her eyes couldn't focus in the dawn light because a fog
blurred the details.

A chill poured over her skin, and when she hugged herself for
warmth, she discovered that her clothes were ragged and torn. When
she brought up one hand, she noticed blood smeared across her
fingers.

She heard waves lapping against rocks. A humid mineral smell
filled her nostrils.

The ocean?

She turned to the sound of the surf and saw, on the water's edge, a large, unusual formation of rocks, shaped like a pyramid. In the distance, past the rocks, she noticed a light shining through the mist. This light was also unusual in the way its reflection cast a strange trail of sparkles across the water.

What is that?

For a moment, she stared, transfixed, then realized she'd been holding something in her hand. As she brought the object closer to her eyes, she saw her bloody fingers gripping a small red book with a silver pinecone embossed on its cover.

She realized someone was behind her. The abrupt presence startled her, and she dropped the book. Just as she was about to turn around, the stranger said, "Get their attention before it's too late."

On the nightstand, a cell phone chirped and vibrated.

Diana Willis jolted awake. She groped for the phone. Through bleary eyes, she read the caller ID: Larry Reynolds. Senior Production Editor at West Coast Broadcasting. Her boss.

She glanced at the time: 5:01 AM.

Diana spent a moment trying to talk herself out of answering. She let her mind transition from last night's pleasant memories—a date with a Deutsche Bank investment manager, and way too much partying — to the harsh reality of another day at work.

She fumbled for the switch on the table lamp. In the abrupt glare of light, she blinked the sleepiness from her eyes and threw off the bedcovers. Sitting up, she drew her knees close and regarded the phone as it kept chirping and buzzing. A call from Larry at this time of the morning spelled only one thing: *CRISIS STORY.*

Her thumb hit the phone's answer button.

"Hi, Larry, what's up?"

He blurted, "We've got a fire drill." Despite the urgency, Larry sounded upbeat. The man thrived on calamity.

"And?"

"Seven thirty AM meeting. You. Maggie. Gabe. My conference room."

Diana swung her legs off the bed. "Can I get a heads up?"

He laughed. "Not over the phone." That was his way of telling her the news was a red-hot emergency. So red hot he could only share it face to face.

Interesting. And maybe, just maybe, worth getting out of bed at such an ungodly hour.

"See you there," she said.

"Awesome." He clicked off.

Diana set her phone down. Her nose wrinkled as if she were a wolf sniffing distant prey. *Another hunt.*

She slept in an oversized t-shirt, which she peeled off on her way to the bathroom. Moments later, she slipped into exercise clothes and unrolled a yoga mat on the floor. She ordered, "Alexa, yoga routine twelve."

The little speaker on her nightstand answered. "Good morning, Diana. Yoga routine twelve."

The lights adjusted for mood and Alexa began guiding Diana through the routine's asanas and Pilates moves. When she held warrior's pose, the floor-to-ceiling window changed from opaque black, like a sheet of obsidian, to transparent. From this vantage, thirty-six floors above street level, she watched the morning darkness fade away and the fog envelop the Golden Gate Bridge. Lights from the bridge and the pulsing arteries of traffic diffused through the diaphanous haze. Across the bay, dawn's bronzed illumination outlined the hills of Marin, and for a moment, the world hovered in that brief magical interlude between night and day.

After years of practice, Diana's morning ritual clicked with the precision of her favorite Rolex watch. At 5:35, flush with sweat, she had completed her morning exercise.

She said, "Alexa, shower. Regular temperature. Brew coffee."

"Shower started," Alexa answered. "And for coffee, latte, or regular?"

"Latte."

"Latte started."

From the kitchen, the overhead lights flickered on and the coffeemaker gurgled.

"Commute to West Coast Broadcasting?" Alexa asked.

"Yes. Six forty-five pick-up."

"Valet summoned. Your car will be waiting."

Diana returned to the bathroom and quickly jumped into the shower. By 6:05, she had dried and styled her hair, applied makeup, and was ready to get dressed. "Alexa," she asked, "what's the weather forecast?"

"Partly sunny. Current temperature, fifty-three degrees. High today, seventy degrees. No precipitation."

Thus informed, Diana padded into her bedroom-sized wardrobe closet, wasting not one movement, spending not more than one second necessary in selecting and putting on her clothes, a suit-dress ensemble in navy blue with an ivory silk blouse and a scarf tie in regimental colors. Next, she headed into her shoe closet, itself the size of a bedroom, albeit smaller.

At 6:23, fully dressed and expertly coiffed, she walked into her kitchen, where a steaming latte waited. She sipped the latte for the caffeine kick, then munched on a fresh banana and downed a fruit-protein smoothie. As she finished the latte, she gazed out her window and watched the thinning tendrils of fog drag from the bridge as the early morning light washed over the bay.

Typical Larry, she thought, *keeping the details of some juicy emergency close to his vest, and making me wonder what in the hell kind of hoops I'm going to have to jump through for another Diana Willis exclusive. No matter, I'm ready.*

Even as she worked to keep her mind clear, her spirit compressed like a spring ready to hurl itself into the task at hand.

At 6:42, she was finished with breakfast and collected her purse, phone, tablet, and computer into her leather briefcase. She paused in front of a full-length mirror by the entrance. She appraised her reflection—shoulder-length blonde hair, of medium-tall height, fit, smooth complexion. At 36, she still possessed a fashion model's good looks—and made certain she was outfitted to the last detail. Today she wore diamond stud earrings. She pivoted to check herself from behind and glanced at her beautifully toned legs. Diana liked to turn heads and keep them turned her way.

But sometimes those heads turned for the wrong reasons. As the lead journalist and anchor of the megahit TV news show *World Primetime Now,* she had plenty of haters.

Next, she ticked down the checklist taped to the mirror:

Wallet? *Check.*

Phone? *Check.*

Computer? *Check.*

Homework? *Check.*

Attitude? *Check.*

Though this ritual cost her a full minute of precious time during those hectic mornings, the delay centered her. It was like the countdown before the launching of a rocket. Or the tensing of muscles before delivering a knockout blow. Whatever the metaphor, she was on the path to conquer the day, and nothing would stop her.

Then, as she was about to step from the mirror, her gaze remained transfixed on her own eyes—radiantly green, as though light shined from them instead of into them. It was as if there was more to her than even she knew, another personality imbedded within? But how was that possible?

This awareness brought with it a sense of dislocation—but a dislocation from what?

Diana felt herself off balance and tipping to one side. When shifting weight to regain equilibrium, she looked away and broke focus with the mirror. That spell—or whatever it was—was broken, and the urgency of the day flooded through her, washing away whatever uncertainties had poked at her.

Stepping quickly, she exited her condo and made her way to the elevator. Her phone chimed that her car was just arriving. In the basement parking garage, as she stepped out of the elevator, her Mercedes AMG Convertible rolled close and halted. The young valet hopped out of the driver's side and held the door open.

Thanking him, Diana tossed her briefcase onto the front passenger's seat. Her phone synched with the car's audio system and tuned to Star 101.3, which was playing the song "Atomic" by Blondie. She turned up the volume, and once behind the wheel, steered toward the exit ramp.

Already at this hour, trucks and other cars jostled for position on the crowded street. The high-rises towering around her kept the scene in shadow. This was San Francisco, and traffic crawled along at a walking pace. The four-mile drive to West Coast Broadcasting took thirty-one minutes. But all the while, the city teemed around her like she was in a giant machine. A machine, she liked to imagine, that was hers to control.

On the way to work, a commuter bus had stalled, clogging traffic even more than usual, and that delay put her five minutes late. Arriving at West Coast Broadcasting, Diana passed through the security checkpoint in the underground parking garage and steered toward her parking spot.

Her phone chimed, and a text appeared on its screen.

She glanced at the phone. Suddenly, movement flashed in the corner of her eye.

Looking up, she locked eyes with a man in front of her. Panicked, she jammed on the brakes. His piercing blue eyes didn't register surprise. Instead, they beamed with empathy.

Before she could roll down her window to apologize, a thought flooded into her mind. *Be careful.*

He stared at her intensely for a moment before continuing toward the elevators.

She watched him walk away in astonishment. She felt like he looked familiar, though she couldn't place him. He looked to be in his mid-fifties with a pleasant enough, well-sculpted face. He appeared as if he worked here: nicely attired in an expensive suit. She guessed he had to be one of the midlevel executives working in some department in the building.

She shrugged off the incident and was about to proceed toward her parking spot when she reflected on something. This car had a sophisticated anticollision system. It should've detected the man, and both slowed and warned her. But the car had done neither.

Diana scanned the instrument panel. Everything looked okay.

This was odd. Very odd.

At 7:25, Diana exited the elevator of the fortieth floor in the West Coast Broadcasting Building, a recently acquired subsidiary of Great Global Media, itself controlled by Grand Mount Equity, one of the largest equity firms in the world. Maintaining her resolute pace, she entered Room 4012, Larry Reynolds' executive conference room.

Maggie LaClair and Gabe Mendoza were already at the table, but Larry's place remained vacant. Maggie was in her mid-forties and wore loud prints to camouflage her expanding middle. Large colorful bangles of jewelry drew attention from her wrinkles. So, she was vain. Who in this business wasn't? Her amber eyes followed Diana.

Gabe's olive complexion was freshly scrubbed and his macho pompadour glistened, still moist from an early morning workout. Dark eyes gazed from a square-shaped face. His custom-made suit emphasized a trim torso. He was handsome enough, and he knew it. Diana knew he checked her out at every opportunity.

She exchanged pleasantries with Maggie and Gabe. Neither offered a clue why they were here so early. Diana mused that the three of them were a talented team, the company's good luck and hers that they happened to be working here. As Diana took her seat, Larry Reynolds entered through a private door that led from his office and eased into the large executive chair at the head of the table.

Larry looked every bit his sixty-three years, dark hair thinning and silver at the temples. A paunch settled against the bottom of his tailored white shirt, and his suit coat draped too snugly against his broad, fleshy shoulders. An athlete's body gone soft by decades behind a desk. But whatever the toll of time and drama had on his physique, his steel-gray eyes radiated intelligence and cunning that burned just as brightly as when Diana first met him, fourteen years ago.

He set a portfolio on the table, then said, "Glad to see everyone here," as if the rest of them had a choice. "Is the door locked?"

Gabe jumped from his seat and verified that it was.

Diana fished a tablet from her briefcase and readied her stylus. Maggie and Gabe also had their tablets on the table.

"You won't need to take notes," Larry said. He pressed a button on a keypad embedded in the table. One panel in the wall lit up with the face of Dan Talbot, Global Media's CEO, and now their top boss. Thin lips smiled from his pink, pulpy visage. Burst capillaries from too much wine and sun stained his slack cheeks and enormous nose. Beady eyes glinted from slits beneath bushy eyebrows.

Diana's nose crinkled again. *Early morning disaster meeting. Dan Talbot. This is going to be juicy.*

Larry panned the table. "I don't think I have to review Talbot's escapades."

Maggie smirked as if to say, *no you don't. We all know.*

Diana couldn't think of a recent time when Talbot wasn't sidestepping a catastrophe of his own making. The man had insatiable ambitions and equally insatiable appetites. Diana recounted the episodes of sexual harassment and blatantly inappropriate behavior. Like the Ivy League intern whom he had offered a full-ride scholarship, in exchange for the full ride she gave him between her young legs. Or the Parisian waitress/exotic dancer he kept shacked up in luxury digs billed to the company tab. Or the Irish media analyst he consummated trysts with on corporate executive jets. Those were only three examples out of dozens.

For Talbot, Great Global Media was his private piggy bank and brothel. Legal expenses to keep his entitled fat ass out of hot water had their own line account in the corporate budget. Why Great Global Media kept him around remained a mystery to her. So after all that he'd done, if Dan Talbot was the subject of today's meeting, then he must have stepped in it big time.

Larry began. "Our competitor, Apex Real Media, is about to break the story that Dan Talbot has been accused of conflict of interest and sexual harassment."

To the latter part of what Larry just said, Diana went, *huh?* Sexual harassment, no big deal. Talbot might as well have that printed on his business card. But conflict of interest?

"So, they caught Talbot with his hand in the cookie jar?" Gabe asked.

"I'm afraid for his sake it's more serious than that," Larry replied. "It was a quid pro quo for advertising dollars."

Diana shook her head in mild disgust. Apparently, it wasn't enough for Talbot to satisfy his wanton desires on the company dime. He needed to line his pockets.

"In what way?" Maggie asked.

"That's not why I brought you here this morning," Larry explained. "Not directly anyway." He pressed another button on the keypad. A map of Columbus, Ohio, replaced Talbot's image. "I need you and Gabe to head ASAP to Columbus, Ohio."

"What for?" Maggie asked.

"It's a counterattack that'll air on your show." Larry opened the portfolio and passed out file folders and memory chips. "You're to meet with local whistleblowers who claim to have the goods on city officials colluding with Apex Real Media."

Sensing a move of corporate skullduggery, Diana asked, "ARM?"

"Indeed," Larry chortled. He hated Apex Real Media. "Apparently, the city and Apex have been burying reports of water contamination to protect their holdings in municipal government bonds."

Actually, Diana thought, *the water contamination is old news.*

She flipped through her folder. The documents were mostly reprints of media accounts, confirming her assessment. *But the Apex twist is new.*

But how new? And how extensive was it?

"Larry," she began, "what exactly is the connection?"

15

He pointed to her folder. "We've reconstructed the paper trail. It's all right there. The city water services are owned by Green Planet Industrial Resources, itself a sister corporation to Apex Real Media within the Basel-Brussels United corporate umbrella. When Green Planet learned that they'd cut too many corners and thus contaminated the city water supply, they brought Apex in to provide media cover. Which included bribing city officials to go along with their strategy. And funding legal muscle to strong-arm whistleblowers into keeping quiet."

Something that elaborate couldn't sneak past Great Global Media without them noticing. The thought prompted Diana: "When did we learn about the Columbus-Apex collusion?"

Larry grinned at her, acknowledging how quick she was to connect the dots. "I'm not at liberty to discuss when we learned about Apex's crooked dealings."

"So we've been sitting on the story? Waiting?"

"This is spin control?" Maggie pressed. "We're deflecting public attention from Talbot's problems to this Columbus-Apex water issue?"

Gabe chimed in. "Saving Talbot's butt while we deliver a haymaker to the competition?"

"It's prime-time news." Larry's grin deepened. "We're doing our duty as the Fourth Estate."

Diana wondered who had thought of this twisted Machiavellian scheme. Maybe it had been Talbot himself, sensing the opportunity for a political smokescreen while he scuttled off center stage. Unscathed. Again.

She shook her head in bemused admiration of the crafty, gluttonous letch. That's why Talbot kept floating to the top, despite whatever toilet bowl he found himself in. He knew how to play corporate politics like a champion.

Gabe thumbed through his folder and whistled. This assignment was beyond juicy. A talented journalist could set himself up for years on this story alone.

"While you are both boots on the ground in Ohio validating what we know and digging up whatever else is relevant, Diana and I will strategize an exclusive with Talbot."

Larry rapped the table. "You should have all the information you need to get a jump on this. If you need help, your file has the contacts to get help. Make me proud."

The three journalists closed their folders. Diana clipped the memory disk to a ring inside her briefcase, then tucked the folder inside.

Gabe was first out the door, Maggie at his heels, looking back at Diana with a glare of envy.

Larry stood up. "Diana, let's move to my office."

CHAPTER TWO

The trials and tribulations of this work have me traversing the neutral edge between light and darkness. I transform pain into power, and as a catalyst for expanding human consciousness, I am waking those of you who are ready.

One of those is a prominent, beautiful, and mind-controlled television star who has lost her way and forgotten what she came here to do. This is a high-stakes rescue requiring everything I know.

Diana closed the door to his office and approached Larry. Her colleague's part in the urgent plan to get Apex Media was full steam ahead, and now what did Larry have up his sleeve? This deft maneuvering was so typical Larry, but Diana trusted him because so far, he had always done right by her.

He pointed to the seat closest to his.

Taking the chair and placing her briefcase on her lap, she asked, "There's something more about Dan Talbot that you want me to look into, isn't there?"

Larry chuckled. "How did you know?"

"A hunch."

"Hunch?"

Now it was her turn to chuckle. "I wouldn't be the lead journalist and anchor of your number-one news show if I wasn't able to smell a red herring from a mile away."

"Red herring?"

Diana smiled. "The Columbus story."

Larry fixed his eyes on her, and his demeanor chilled several degrees. "You're to meet with Dan Talbot," he said stiffly.

"When?"

"This morning."

Diana's thoughts stalled. "A video chat?"

"No. Face to face. Just you and him."

"Where? Here?"

"No, no," Larry said. "In Great Global Media's San Francisco headquarters building. You'll meet him in their C-Level suites."

"What's this about?"

"Talbot is in serious trouble. I'd like you to get on his side. Spin control works both ways. We get the dirt on Apex Media, and meanwhile, we find a way of making our dirt smell like perfume instead of manure. As far as West Coast Broadcasting and its viewers are concerned, Dan Talbot remains a man of integrity."

Diana tightened her lips. If what Larry had just briefed them on about Talbot's shenanigans was true—and it was—Diana had her work cut out. It hadn't bothered her in the past to dance to the company tune, this ability to bend the facts and twist reality. *This time, something was different.*

Talbot had crossed the line, and he deserved to be smacked hard for his transgressions. Not dismissed with a handshake and sent away with a big bag of money.

Diana collected her briefcase. "Tell our disgraced CEO that I'm on my way."

◆ ◆

A company chauffeur drove Diana to the Great Global Media building. A lobby receptionist was waiting for Diana and ushered her to the executive elevator. On the way up to the C-Level, Diana fumed over the injustice of how they treated Talbot with kid gloves. The man and the word integrity didn't belong on the same page. Hell, Talbot and the word integrity didn't even belong in the same building.

She recalled a line from an old war movie. *Ours is not to question why; ours is but to do and die.*

Diana regarded the security camera in the upper corner of the elevator. She saluted and said, "Aye, aye, sir."

She'd been in the Great Global Media high-rise before it acquired West Coast Broadcasting, but this was her first visit to the C-Level. The elevator chimed, and the door opened.

She had given little thought about what to expect. When she gazed upon the C-Level lobby, it took her aback with astonishment. A fountain gurgled and splashed water into a low, glassed-in pond. Visible through the transparent sides, rare saltwater fish darted among delicate anemones and exotic coral. Degas and Gauguin paintings, originals for sure, decorated the marbled walls. Above her, light sparkled from a dazzling chandelier the size of a compact car. This lobby alone made a five-star hotel look like a shack. Equity money from its holding company bought all this.

A trim, elegant Asian woman stepped from behind a desk that appeared to have been sculpted from ice. Her sleek jet-black hair blended into her designer black pantsuit. Her accessories included Lalique art deco jewelry (had to be original) and Yves Saint Laurent heels. She looked so perfect that Diana scrutinized the woman to make sure she wasn't a hologram. The woman extended a hand. "Diana Willis, I'm Kathryn Chang. Welcome," she said, as if the C-Level was on another planet. "Mr. Anthony Briscane is waiting."

When they shook hands, her grip was warm and firm. Human, that was a relief.

Who was this Anthony Briscane? Diana said, "I thought I was meeting with Mr. Talbot."

Chang didn't reply as she led Diana out of the lobby. On the way down the hall, all the doors were closed but one. The nameplate on that door said, *John Herald, Executive Liaison, Media Relations.* Out of curiosity, Diana glanced inside, and to her amazement saw the same man she had almost run over earlier in the West Coast Broadcasting parking garage.

He looked up at her. They locked eyes, and the same flash of recognition from earlier washed over her. But from where did she know him?

She was about to ask when Chang insisted, "Ms. Willis, Anthony Briscane doesn't like to be kept waiting."

Diana made a mental note to return and speak with this John Herald. This was twice she had seen him by coincidence. He gave her another warm smile and a nod.

Chang cleared her throat. "Ms. Willis."

Diana nodded in return to this mysterious man, then spun on her heel to catch up with Chang.

When Diana met Anthony Briscane, what came to mind were the words "oily weasel." His rounded face sharpened to a point, and his ears were set a little too high on his head. The gel in his wavy, fashionably unkempt hair appeared greasy. He was about her age and dressed well enough in a tailored double-breasted suit, but the way his beady eyes kept shifting about her person gave the impression he was looking for a chance to steal her pocketbook.

Chang made the introductions, then departed.

"I'm Mr. Talbot's chief of staff," Briscane explained. When he and Diana shook hands, his grip was clammy and limp. He pointed toward a red leather love seat and an armchair arranged around a coffee table sculpted out of blue alabaster and veined in gold. The gesture drew attention to his diamond cufflinks and diamond-encrusted Cartier watch. He swiveled onto the love seat. Diana sat in the armchair and noted that it was so ornate that it wouldn't have looked out of place in the Vatican.

Briscane leaned forward, close enough to bring a whiff of his cologne. At least he smelled nice.

"My apologies for the mix-up in communications," he said, "but Mr. Talbot was detained."

"Detained? Arrested?"

Briscane rolled back into the love seat and laughed an unctuous guffaw. Though there was much off-putting about Briscane, there was also something familiar about him. The tiny detail pricked at Diana, but when she asked herself about him, her memory came back blank.

Briscane's laugh faded, and he answered, "Of course not. What I meant was that he won't able to meet you here."

"So I'm wasting our time?"

"Not at all. This allows me to fill you in on some important background information."

More spin thought Diana.

"First," Briscane lowered his voice to a conspiratorial tone, "and this is strictly confidential, to be released only by the Great Global Media legal department…" He paused.

She said, "Go on."

He leaned even closer. "Strictly confidential." He pantomimed locking his lips and throwing away the key.

His flippant gesture annoyed her. "I understand. Go on."

Briscane glanced about the room, then gazed at her. He licked his lips. "Mr. Talbot is going to resign. He's doing so to spare Great Global Media unwarranted bad publicity."

Diana felt herself recoil a bit. She thought Talbot would engage in a corporate scorch-the-earth campaign to save his hide. Either the case against him was too strong, or he was finally surrendering to the inevitable, a decision no doubt lubricated by a payout worth millions.

If she shared this, Talbot's imminent departure represented a significant scoop. But according to her contract, she had to abide by the corporate rules, so mum's the word until later.

"So that's it?" she asked.

"Not at all. Mr. Talbot would like an interview with you to set the record straight. This afternoon is possible. He's staying at the Grand Marquis." Briscane whisked a card from his breast pocket. "Here's my business card. Security at the hotel will be airtight. But my card should get you through, no problem."

Diana glanced at the card and tucked it into her briefcase.

"One more thing." Briscane raised a finger. "And what I'm about to tell you is deep background."

"About Talbot?"

Briscane leaned into the love seat. "No. It's about a bigger scandal."

"Internal to Global Media?"

"I'm afraid so. Do you know a man named John Herald?"

Diana answered, "No," then remembered the man from earlier.

Before she could amend her reply, Briscane said, "He's a very high-placed executive in our western bureau. He even has an office just down the hall. You passed right by it."

Something tugged at Diana's nerves, something that told her not to trust Briscane until she understood his motives.

To verify that they were referring to the same person, she asked, "What's his title?"

"Executive Liaison, Media Relations."

"And what's he suspected of doing?"

Briscane waved his hands. "There's nothing to suspect. He's in it up to his neck."

"In what?"

"All kinds of trouble. He's been meeting with various competitors and spilling corporate secrets."

"Why?"

Briscane shrugged. "Money? Other opportunities? Why do people dodge the rules?" He leaned forward again. "That's what we'd like you to find out. What has he done, and why?"

"So, our meeting," Diana circled a finger to encompass the space between her and Briscane, "is not about Talbot but John Herald?"

Briscane nodded.

On her way to the elevator, Diana noticed that John Herald's door was closed. She wanted to see if it was locked or if he was in, but Chang urged her to keep going.

Diana reflected on the irony that Briscane and John Herald occupied offices practically next door to one another and yet there appeared this gulf of suspicion between them. What was that saying? *Keep your friends close and your enemies even closer.*

When she arrived back at Larry's office, Diana called Maggie's cell phone. After Maggie answered, Diana said, "Keep me updated there in Columbus."

"What's going on?"

"I've been sidetracked. Corporate."

Maggie remained silent.

"You there?" Diana asked.

"Yeah, I'm here," Maggie snapped. "How come Gabriel and I get sent on this Apex Media wild-goose chase while you get a meaty assignment?"

"You're on no wild-goose chase. What you can dig up is important."

"All right." Maggie's voice softened. "Anything you can share about your new assignment?"

"Let me clear it through Larry."

"That high up? Let me guess—"

Diana cut her off, "I'll get back to you," and hung up.

She entered Larry's office. He read the anxiety on her face and spoke into his desk intercom. "Hold my calls."

As she took the leather chair in front of his desk, Larry folded his hands together and studied her from his executive chair.

"I've never seen you this wound up," he said. "What exactly did Briscane tell you?"

Diana regretted not being better at hiding her emotions. She didn't feel so much wound up as off-kilter. Something was not right in this business between Talbot, Briscane, and John Herald. Perhaps Briscane sending her after John Herald was another play of misdirection to keep attention away from Talbot.

Before Diana said anything, Larry commented, "When I first met Briscane, what came to mind was *grifter*."

She chuckled. The humor loosened her a bit. "He told me that Talbot is going to resign."

Larry opened his hands. "Old news."

"Since when?"

"Legal came down and told me and they need a major spin on this." He arched an eyebrow. "So, how?"

Diana noted Larry was mentioning nothing about John Herald. Why? The phrase, *wheels within wheels* came to mind.

"Diana?" It was Larry.

She blinked. "Sorry. I got lost thinking about our next steps. Where were we?"

"We were discussing Talbot's departure."

"Yes," Diana tipped her head as her thoughts came back to speed. "We could fall back on the old line, that he's resigning to spend more time with his family."

Larry quipped, "More like to spend more time with the nanny."

"Here are some of my ideas," she offered. "We could say that he's going on a sabbatical. Maybe tour the Third World to champion various causes. Climate change. Clean water. Rural education. Maybe he can say that he's felt constrained by corporate policies and needs to see what he can do as a private citizen."

"I like that." Larry pursed his lips, pleased. "A few well-placed photo ops. Around African farm wells, Indian rice fields, that sort of thing?"

"Exactly! He can afford to toss some of his money around like confetti. What he spends on legal fees alone could build fifty elementary schools in Brazil."

"Any inclinations about how he'd feel about this?" Larry asked.

"We'll soon find out. I'm meeting him this afternoon at the Grand Marquis. I'll float the idea past him."

Larry furrowed his brow as he considered her plan.

For her sake, Diana had more on her mind than saving Talbot's reputation. She wondered about Larry's true allegiances. He had diverted her to see Talbot. At that meeting, she instead met Briscane, who diverted her again, this time after John Herald.

She knew Talbot had Briscane on a leash, but was Larry colluding with them?

Diana hoped not. Larry was one shoulder she could lean on during the rough-and-tumble that was high-level corporate politicking. If she couldn't trust Larry, then she might as well walk the plank.

Then there was John Herald.

She got a different vibe from him. She didn't get the sense that he was a threat to her, but that they had a connection she couldn't yet decipher. Who was he, anyway? Was he doing something underhanded, as Briscane had stated? That vibe told her no.

But intuition wasn't enough; Diana needed to unearth for herself the truth about John Herald.

Briscane had told her to scope him out, but he didn't say how. For that, Diana would fall back on what had gotten her this far as an ace journalist.

Her cunning and daring.

CHAPTER THREE

*T*he controlling dark forces have done their job well. They have stopped her, turned her to their side, and made her do their bidding. I have already penetrated their inner sanctums and have collected information and begun influencing decisions. This is mostly in the economic and political realms, but also in the media.

Anthony Briscane helped himself to coffee from the carafe on the table, well aware that his every move was being scrutinized by the three other men in the room: General Wayne Carcano, former commander of the US Space Force, tech industry titan Reginald Deighton, and billionaire oil magnate Sheikh Ahmed Kaddar. They had gathered here in Room 1211 of the Grand Marquis Hotel, as a way-stop before continuing to the Bohemian Grove, a secretive retreat of the world's elite in Monte Rio, north of San Francisco.

Carefully, Briscane stirred in sugar and cream and then took a slow, luxurious slurp from the porcelain cup. His guests were supremely powerful men, yet ironically, they were helpless without individuals like him, underlings who didn't balk at doing the dirty work that kept people like them seated on their private thrones.

Satisfied that they had waited long enough, Briscane withdrew a tablet from his briefcase and laid it face-up near the center of the table. His brow knit as he summoned the tablet using a telepathic command. A column of sparkles beamed from the screen and materialized into a hologram of Diana Willis, from her upper torso to the top of her head.

"This is who I met this morning," he said. "I'm sure there's no need for an introduction."

Carcano and Deighton regarded her image and nodded appreciatively.

Kaddar narrowed his eyes. "Quite fetching."

Carcano asked, "Was this the first time you'd met her?"

"It was. And my impression of her confirmed what we suspected."

Briscane projected another thought and in the air beside Diana, images from her infancy, childhood, and career flashed in rapid-fire succession.

"Does she know?" Carcano pressed.

"Of her past?" Briscane shook his head. "But with every passing day, she's coming into her powers again and remembering what happened."

"What do you mean?"

"She's becoming more amenable to telepathic intrusions again, as she did during the remote viewing experiments, years ago."

"How do you know?" Carcano furrowed his brow.

"That's my job." Briscane tapped his temple. He kept his tone bland to hide his contempt that his bosses didn't show any amazement or incredulity. They considered his telepathic powers little more than a trick, one useful for their ends, and Briscane little more than a servant.

"It's established she can receive telepathy," Kaddar noted. "But can she transmit?"

"Not yet."

"Then when?"

Briscane helped himself to another sip from his coffee. "Soon."

"We expect something more definite than 'soon,'" Kaddar reprimanded.

"I have my reasons," Briscane replied.

"Tread carefully, Mr. Briscane," Kaddar added, "we can replace you."

Briscane let the sheikh's veiled threat wash over him. Considering the task ahead, who would replace him? Now, more than ever, these three needed him.

Carcano leaned forward. "She has been very useful to our agenda all these years. We got what we needed. Now she must die."

"Let me show you something," Briscane said as he thought-projected another command to the tablet.

The image of John Herald replaced Diana's. Carcano recoiled uncomfortably. Briscane expected him to hiss like a vampire reacting to a crucifix. He asked, "General, how do you know John Herald?"

"When I directed Project Stargate, Herald was a team supervisor."

Stargate had been an above-top-secret effort to test and develop remote viewing—spying using clairvoyant methods. When its existence was finally disclosed to the public, what had accompanied the announcement was a caveat that the exercise was an example of pseudoscience at its worst and a gross waste of time and money. But that was misinformation. In reality, they had ended Stargate because the subjects were too precise in what they saw, and what they saw was more than they should have—including the CIA's most notorious secrets. No walls were thick enough to prevent remote viewing.

Briscane explained, "Diana Willis is bait to draw out John Herald. As long as Diana is alive, Herald cannot go away."

"What's the significance of this John Herald?" Deighton asked.

"He was a loose cannon," Carcano explained. "While at Stargate he had a habit of straying outside his mission boundaries."

"Then how did he end up in Great Global Media?" Deighton asked.

Carcano cleared his throat. "You know the CIA has infiltrated many areas of society, the government, Silicon Valley, and the media. It's a policy we've pursued since Operation Mockingbird."

Briscane reflected on what Carcano just said. Operation Mockingbird was the CIA's extensive program to infiltrate and influence the media, not only abroad but also in the US. They used an unwitting Diana Willis as part of this.

Deighton raised an eyebrow. "And Herald is part of this group?"

"Yes," Carcano replied, "they planted him in Great Global Media to steer the news according to our instructions. The problem is that he's getting too close to matters outside his focus, just as he did with Stargate and another program he led later."

"So you don't trust him?" Briscane pressed.

"I consider him a LIMDIS Level Sigma Threat," Carcano announced.

Deighton and Kakdar sat up. Such a threat implied terminate with extreme prejudice.

"And how is our plan coming together?" Carcano asked.

34

"Like clockwork. I've convinced Diana Willis that Herald is the mastermind behind the troubles that brought down Dan Talbot."

"And you're sure she's after him?"

"I'm positive. She's got the personality to pick relentlessly at the loose ends of what she's been given and then come to her conclusions."

"But we want to make certain that her conclusions are the ones we want her to have," Kaddar said.

"Which are irrelevant," Briscane replied. "Because she's following a trail of breadcrumbs right into our trap. Whatever misgivings you have about Diana rediscovering her powers will soon vanish."

Briscane eyed the others around the table. "But time is short. With every passing day, her latent powers are slowly awakening. I can't predict when she'll make the connection and—"

"And the sooner," Carcano interrupted, "we act to make sure she never connects with her past, then the better for all of us."

"I have that under control," Briscane replied. "When John Herald leaves the Great Global Building in his helicopter, Diana will be on board." Briscane paused dramatically. "The two of them will never arrive at their destination." He projected another command and Diana's image disintegrated like glass shattering.

"Don't underestimate John Herald," Carcano said. "From my experience with him in the CIA, I discovered that he's wily and perceptive."

"That won't help him because he has no clue what awaits. As for his altruistic legacy," Briscane held up a thumb drive, "I thoroughly corrupted every database that refers to him. I will smear his reputation beyond hope of redemption."

Deighton steepled his fingers and stared at Briscane. "I'm delighted to hear that. But I can't stress enough how important it is that we... *you*...stop Diana Willis and John Herald. They are the biggest threats to our plans."

Not just plans, but schemes, Briscane mused. Schemes of world domination that would blow the minds of the most ardent believers of conspiracy theories.

"It will happen. Today." Briscane finished his coffee, the epitome of self-control, of pathological aplomb. "Everything is in place. When Diana boards John's helicopter, she will have signed her death warrant. She and your LIMDIS Level Sigma Threat will be no more."

When Diana Willis turned onto 3rd Street toward Moscone Center Garage, a police checkpoint blocked the road. Dozens of protesters milled along barricades that stretched down the street. Their handmade signs said: *Down With Corporate Greed! Stop Mining in Indonesia! End the Surveillance State!* Heavily armed riot police watched in boredom.

At first, Diana wondered the reason for the protest, then remembered that executives from the SEU—the Super Economic Union— were staging a conference at the Grand Marquis, hence the need for such tight security.

Diana drove to the checkpoint. A police officer leaned toward Diana's Mercedes. She scrolled down her window and presented her press credentials. The police officer used a card scanner to read Diana's badge. He said, "Park in Moscone Center, Garage. Then proceed on foot." The police officer gave a hasty wave and Diana veered into the parking garage. Minutes later, she walked along 3rd Street to the hotel, where people queued at a screening table flanked by police and security guards.

Diana checked her watch. She hadn't been given a set time to meet with Talbot, but she chafed at standing in line like some kind of peasant supplicant. This was no time to be polite, so she shoehorned her way to the front of the line. A reporter from the *Chronicle* was trying to argue his way inside. Diana leaned between him and a guard by the table and offered the business card Briscane had given her.

Upon reading the card, the guard made a call over the radio clipped to her shoulder. A reply buzzed in her earbud. She returned the card and, clasping Diana's arm, ushered her through the door and around the metal detector. "This way, ma'am." The treatment was so preferential that no one bothered to check her briefcase or purse. As she stepped inside, she could feel the dagger eyes of resentment from those stranded in line behind her. But too bad.

She hadn't been impressed with Briscane when she met him before, but the way his card allowed her to ease through security made her reappraise his station in the corporate world. *That guy has juice.*

Scores of well-dressed and well-heeled people milled inside the sumptuous lobby in an ambiance that reeked of privilege. Several of them tossed glances her way, but she wasn't certain if the reason was that they recognized her or that they—both the men and women— were giving her the once-over.

Large flat-screen monitors erected between the statues and planters cycled through presentations of corporate humanitarian programs— clean water, micro loans to small farmers, free vaccines—while never mentioning collusion between governments and corporations regarding under-the-table deals involving taxes, monopolies, and infrastructure contracts.

Don't be so cynical, not everybody is a crook, she chastised herself. She, too, was a cog in the Great Global Media machine, but that didn't mean she had her hands dirty.

Then, up ahead, John Herald, like he'd been conjured from the air. Taken aback by the coincidence of seeing him again, she stared at him. He moved at a brisk pace along the periphery of the lobby, deep in conversation with two other men. She hoped that he'd look up to recognize her, but he and his companions kept walking, turning down a corridor where they vanished from view.

Curiously, she felt a bit frustrated, as if she expected him to acknowledge her.

She stopped and scoped out the lobby, wondering what to do next. Meet with Talbot, but where was he? She gazed up to the ceiling of the lobby, an enormous atrium that seemed part aviary and part Mediterranean palace. The Grand Marquis towered above her forty-eight stories.

Her mind stuttered as if her thoughts were becoming disconnected. The sensation nudged her off balance, and she clasped a nearby statue to steady herself. A thought entered her mind. The thought was as clear and definitive as if she'd heard it: *The quiet war has begun—ready or not.*

What war? Why is it quiet? Ready or not for what?

The thought had pierced her consciousness like a flaming arrow. What did it mean? Why did she perceive it now?

Suddenly, another interruption broke her line of thought. It was her phone vibrating with a message. Caller ID announced: Anthony Briscane

She mused suspiciously, *how did he get my number?*

His text said: Room 1211

Okay, she thought, we're to meet there. Diana regained her bearings and spotted the corridor leading to the elevators. Showing Briscane's card got her through a phalanx of guards. Hurriedly, she stepped into an elevator and pressed the button for the twelfth floor. At her destination, she exited the elevator and had to pass through yet another cordon of guards.

A female guard, fit as a Pilates instructor, but wearing a police shield on her ID badge—and with her sport coat bulging over a pistol underneath—stepped forward to greet Diana. Afterward, the policewoman spun on her heel. "This way."

They continued resolutely over ornate carpets and past exquisite miniatures decorating the walls. At Room 1211, another guard stood beside the door. The policewoman escorting Diana knocked on the door. It opened to reveal Briscane's oily, smiling face.

"Ms. Willis, please come in." He acknowledged the guards with a curt nod and closed the door behind her.

They entered the parlor of a suite, the large room as opulently appointed as the rest of the hotel. A large, ruddy-faced man was sitting at one end of a leather sofa. Rising to his feet, he extended his hand.

Dan Talbot. His immense paw of a hand swallowed hers. Though he towered over her, his demeanor was more like a friendly bear.

Briscane made the introductions. "Mr. Talbot, it's my pleasure to introduce Ms. Diana Willis. She's the reason West Coast Broadcasting's *World Primetime Now* is number one in its field."

Talbot looked down his wide, fleshy nose at her. "It's my pleasure." He pointed to a chair. "Please, sit. I appreciate you making time to see me."

His behavior wasn't what she imagined. Instead of being imperious and condescending, he was rather charming.

"And get your side of the story," she said.

"One of many sides, I'm sure. You know how it is in these situations. There's her side. There's my side. And then there's the truth."

She hadn't expected this candor, and she warmed up to Talbot. In her mind, she'd pictured him as a scheming, greedy tyrant. She expected his gaze to rake her body with a lascivious stare as intrusive as an X-ray. But his eyes remained on hers as if she were the only person in the room and his expression was benign, friendly.

He gestured to the armchair facing the sofa. "Please." As he took his seat on the sofa, he began, "What do you think of all this security? It's a bit much, no?" He chuckled. "So many guards and guns. I wonder if what's driving such security is the paranoia all these entitled bastards feel about being so goddamn rich. Maybe they fear that the great unwashed masses will storm the castle, torches and pitchforks in hand, and confiscate their treasure." Talbot's eyes twinkled with delight as he laughed.

"Perhaps," Diana replied, uncertain what to say.

"Why you're here, Larry Reynolds tells me you have some ideas for my…uh… rehabilitation."

"Yes, we hashed out some options. I haven't yet elaborated on them because I didn't know in what direction you'd want to proceed."

She was pulling her laptop from her briefcase when he interrupted her. "No, I hate computers. Can you explain it by jotting it down?" Talbot snapped his fingers at Briscane. "Anthony, could you fetch Ms. Willis a writing pad."

"I have one here," she said, scrambling, feeling like she didn't want to disappoint Talbot.

"Very good," he replied, and settled against the cushions. Briscane perched himself on an arm of the sofa.

She checked her notes on what she and Larry Reynolds had discussed. When she suggested Talbot adopt a school in Africa, he perked up.

As Diana talked, she expected either Talbot or Briscane to bring up the subject of John Herald. But neither man did, which she found curious. Didn't they know he was in the hotel?

When she finished presenting her ideas, she said, "That's all I have for now. But if you give me a day, I can prepare a more detailed proposal."

"No, please, don't bother." Talbot gestured for the notes. "Let me review these, and then we can meet again to outline our next steps."

Talbot stood, and this told her he adjourned the meeting. He folded the notes and slipped them inside his sport coat. "If you don't mind, I need to freshen up."

Diana stood and collected her briefcase and purse to leave.

Just as they reached the door, Briscane said, "I hope you haven't forgotten about John Herald."

She glanced in the bathroom's direction, where Talbot had disappeared, and noted that Briscane had taken this moment to mention John Herald. "Actually, I thought you had."

He offered her a thumb drive. "This will point you in the right direction." He added empathically, "We need the truth quickly."

Diana took the thumb drive and considered it. "How does Talbot figure into this?"

"Are you familiar with Bohemian Grove?"

"If I wasn't, I have no place as a journalist. I'm certain a lot of the men here in the hotel are on the way there."

"And so is John Herald."

She never figured John to be the consummate insider, yet to attend Bohemian Grove, he had to be well ensconced among the rich and powerful. "He's going to be there?"

"Undoubtedly."

Briscane tilted his head and knit his brow ever so slightly as he stared into her eyes.

In a flash, Diana glimpsed John hustling to board a helicopter. Then the image vanished as abruptly as it had appeared. She figured it was her journalistic intuition showing the way. She would intercept him on the helipad atop the Great Global Media Building.

Now it was up to her to determine what John Herald was up to. She would need to break protocol and return to her former investigative prowess.

Would this be as easy as it used to be?

CHAPTER FOUR

*T*he quiet war is upon you. I am planting in those of you who have receptive minds that what is apparent is not, and what is not apparent, is. The price you pay for freedom is constant vigilance. So be discerning and question your assumptions. Some of you do that; most do not.

After Anthony Briscane had given Diana the thumb drive, she hurried back to her condo, eager to learn the truth about the enigmatic John Herald. Once home, she inserted the thumb drive into her laptop and began her investigation.

Aware that she was sleuthing through deep-background stuff on Herald, she hadn't bothered to tell anyone what she was doing, not even her boss, Larry Reynolds. Whenever she dropped down a rabbit hole of research like this, she never knew where she'd end up. There was the possibility that Reynolds—Mr. Integrity himself—might be implicated in Herald's schemes. What would that mean to Reynolds' career and reputation?

Briscane's thumb drive contained a secret dossier on Herald and his whereabouts since his time in the CIA and then with Great Global Media. On the surface, his activities were consistent with a high-level government plant within corporate media. He had attended the expected conferences and retreats, making connections with the appropriate corporate and government movers and shakers (foreign and domestic), no doubt ensuring that what moved would shake in the right direction. Although his motives were not obvious, since it wasn't apparent on whose behalf he was acting at the time—the CIA or Great Global Media—she hadn't stumbled into anything sinister.

Then, as she paged through files, she sat up, fully alert.

Nothing sinister until now.

When she clicked on the new file, it brought up an unusual screen that offered a portal to another network, one that resided with an entity called D-O. By checking the server links, Diana saw this network lived not only above Great Global Media, or its parent company Grand Mount Equity, or even at the highest corporate level with Comerat Holdings, *but above that!* They named this highest level, Davos-Outil.

Although she had never heard of Davos-Outil, Diana experienced a rush of adrenaline that gave her a stronger buzz than any jolt of caffeine. It was as if they had given her the secret password to Ali Baba's cave of stolen treasures. She lived for opportunities like this, when hidden doors cracked open and let her tiptoe into a labyrinth of mysteries.

The screen presented many folders, but the first one was the only one that mattered immediately: John Herald. When Diana clicked for information on the folder, the dialogue box showed this folder lived at the nexus of links connected to all the lower-level networks. Each of these tapped into extensive international databases spanning the fields of administration, finance, and security. What Briscane had given Diana was a keyhole into everything that Davos-Outil and its subsidiaries had on John Herald.

She took a moment to reflect on what this meant. Corporations worldwide had taken a keen interest in Herald. Why? He wasn't another Steve Jobs who could make them richer than they already were. Herald had to be up to something significant to make this assembly of billionaires worry.

When Diana clicked on the first link, it opened to a slideshow folder featuring photos of John Herald. He was socializing with people Diana recognized as high-placed individuals who had been in some kind of scandal: financial, political, or sexual. The photos were captioned with excerpts from media articles outlining the associated public outrage.

She saw Herald in an office, deep in conversation with Senator Lloyd Hammerstein during the congressman's trouble with the IRS, when they discovered he'd listed trips to Thailand and his stays in Bangkok brothels as tax-deductible expenses. Herald's involvement was that he'd acted as "tour guide" for the senator on these trips.

And there was Herald with Gauri Pritam, the wealthy dowager who had been enmeshed in a scandal that shorted Credit Delhi, the Central Bank of India, when the national green-tech industry collapsed and thus almost bankrupted an entire subcontinent. Here, Herald's blind trust had somehow enriched itself to the tune of millions of dollars while tens of millions of Indians saw their savings and investments wiped out.

In another series of photos, Herald hobnobbed with the Emir Qualqazzi of the Federated Arab Commercial Alliance, who had been caught laundering drug money for heroin cartels and paying bribes to Interpol. Herald's connection was that he had coincidentally chartered the airliners used to transport the drugs, and that his contacts within Interpol included a long list of his pals from the CIA.

Some images were of Herald beaming at the camera while at posh clubs or in ritzy digs at opulent hotels. But in others, someone had surreptitiously taken the photos from far away using a telephoto lens, or from odd angles—usually from overhead—as if from a ceiling camera or a micro-drone.

The slideshow ended with Herald in the company of barely legal young women in expensive though not wholesome settings—as in casinos, on the decks of luxury yachts with drinks in hand, sitting around a glass table festooned with lines of...was that cocaine? In the last photo, Herald soaked in a hot tub with three ingenues. One of them appeared to be sitting on his lap, and no one in the picture was wearing clothes.

Diana cracked a smile at this last image. Something about these photos wasn't right, especially the last set with the party girls. The tableau of incriminating photos could be a grand attempt at a smear job on Herald, and Diana was experienced enough to be wary of computer-generated fakes. Not that these were, and not that they weren't. When she had the chance, she would ask Herald point-blank about these photos, and then she would decide if they were genuine or not.

What triggered her suspicions was that given Herald's scandalous deportment in so many venues, why hadn't the authorities acted on him? Did he have dirt on these tycoons? What leverage could he possibly have that kept these corporate coyotes off his back? And why was Briscane so interested in Herald now?

Further complicating her thinking about Herald was that she couldn't shake that intense connection she felt whenever she was in proximity to him. What was that about? It was as if something deep within her brain was opening to Herald. Was this feeling an omen?

Or was this her sixth sense, her intuition braiding together clues that bypassed her conscious mind?

She couldn't ignore the evidence. John Herald was neck-deep in backroom dealings worthy of the most paranoid of conspiracies. As a hard-nosed journalist, Diana couldn't let these strange feelings influence her search for the truth.

Briscane hadn't given her this task to amuse her. Herald appeared to be at the center of a global web connecting a plethora of hidden agendas and underhanded negotiations.

Diana glanced at the clock on her screen: 1:12 AM.

She blinked at the clock, surprised at where the time had gone. When had she started this inquiry? Around 5:30 this afternoon. Before diving into the files on the thumb drive, she had promised to limit herself to a quick peek, then dinner. Seven hours had passed. She yawned. Though she was hungry, more than anything, it had wrung her brain dry, and she was ready to turn in.

But her determination to find out what Herald was up to wouldn't let go. One more file, she promised herself.

The next file opened to a flight plan Herald had registered with the FAA, showing him departing from the helipad at Great Global Media's headquarters and following a course over the northern California coastline to Monte Rio. She didn't need to look up the significance of Herald's destination. It was the exclusive and secretive Bohemian Grove.

Whose helicopter was it? She saw it was a CT-11 executive transport model. There was only one passenger listed on the manifest and that was the pilot: John Herald. He was a helicopter pilot? She reviewed the flight plan to see who owned the helicopter, but all she noted was the aircraft registration number. For its type, the CT-11 was a large machine, a crew of two with seats in the passenger cabin for eight. If John Herald was the only one on board, why take this helicopter with so many empty seats? The manifest mentioned no cargo. Was he picking up passengers at Bohemian Grove?

She recalled the thought she'd had with Briscane in Room 1211 at the Grand Marquis Hotel and of the fleeting image of Great Global Media's rooftop helipad. She'd never been there, but the details were remarkably crystal clear.

The flight plan showed Herald planned to depart at 6:45 AM—sunrise.

To understand what Herald was doing, she would somehow stow away aboard his helicopter.

Having decided this was the next step, Diana surrendered to her fatigue. If she was to catch Herald before he took off, she'd have to get up and out the door by 4:30, in a little over three hours. All right, she told herself, she'd fix herself a snack, select her clothes for the next morning, set the alarm, and then go straight to bed.

But as the adrenaline rush of the hunt faded, so did her resolve, and she got sleepy. Eyelids growing heavy, she nodded off.

Then she shook her head and fought to remain awake. She had tasks to complete before she could allow herself to rest.

Where did this weariness come from? It was as if someone was commanding her to sleep through a kind of remote hypnosis.

Then a gray static blossomed in her mind, and everything turned black.

🌰🌰

Diana saw herself as if she were a kind of spirit and looking down upon a teenage girl sixteen years old, a girl Diana knew that, in the past, was her.

Diana sank toward the young girl and slid into her, their bodies fusing into one. In that instant, Diana perceived the loud drumming reverberating through young Diana, a tribal beat that stoked the most primitive of urges.

She wore only a robe, her long blonde curls tucked within its hood. She stood to one side of an outdoor stage dominated by an enormous stone owl forty-five feet tall. In the center of the stage burned a fire, and in a circle around the flames, other teenage girls danced—all of them naked. The girls moved in a syncopated erotic choreography, kicking and swaying.

Darkness surrounded the stage, and the fire illuminated dozens of masked faces transfixed upon the dancers. Though she couldn't see the faces, she could sense their collective lust and anticipation as if the dance was a prelude to an orgy of violation.

Young Diana asked herself where she was, and she immediately knew the answer: at the annual retreat of the world's most powerful men—the Bohemian Grove.

Fear and despair gripped her, and she held fast to the collar of her robe. How did this come to pass? Had someone kidnapped her? Why her?

She grew weak and queasy. The stones beneath her bare feet were cold and unyielding, as if a metaphor for her impending fate.

A man dressed in a Roman emperor costume—toga, sandals, and golden laurels—sat on a throne at the base of the giant owl. His eyes glittered through the holes in a simple mask covering the upper part of his face. He cradled a scepter, which he tapped against one hand in rhythm to the drumbeat. Then he pointed at one dancer, a slender girl with long brunette hair. From either side of the stage, two large men in Roman legionnaire costumes marched to the girl and grabbed her from behind. She did not resist. They easily lifted her and heaved her off the stage, her limbs flailing helplessly. For an instant, her lithe body floated airborne, where it glowed like a delicate porcelain figurine. Then from the audience, outstretched hands scrambled to catch her, and in the next moment, they lost her in the murk. It was as if she were a scrap of meat tossed to hungry wolves.

The man on the throne aimed his scepter at young Diana. A pair of rough hands appeared from behind her and tore the robe off her shoulders, exposing her nude body. They pushed her onto the stage, and she felt the audience's collective rapacious stare. She staggered a step, then as she straightened, allowed the tom-tom beat to take over her psyche. To her right, the fire's illumination shimmered up and across the magnificent stone edifice and made the monstrous owl appear alive. In that moment, she shrank before it and her consciousness shriveled into a hard little ball, divorcing itself from the impending horror. Her brain numb, she joined the circle of dancers, mechanically kicking and shimmying like a mindless wind-up doll.

Maggie LaClair waited in the lounge of the Grand Marriott Hotel in Columbus, Ohio. Since Larry Reynolds' early morning briefing, she'd been on the move, jetting from San Francisco to Columbus while constantly calling, texting, and emailing as many potential sources as possible. Their rival, Apex Media, had revealed a chink in their corporate armor, one that, on behalf of Great Global Media, she was keen to exploit. Opportunities like this didn't happen often enough.

When Maggie arrived in Columbus shortly before noon, she hit the ground running. Like other hot-shot journalists, she thrived on the adrenaline rush. But she was only human, and as the time was after nine in the evening, she'd reached the point of diminishing returns. Better to turn in and get ready to storm the barricades at first light. But her nerves still buzzed with the thrill of the chase, and she had energy for one more escapade.

About an hour ago, Gabriel Mendoza had texted her. He would meet her here to share notes and plan for tomorrow.

Out of the corner of her eye, she saw him enter from the lobby. His normally sharp appearance looked a bit disheveled, as if the rough-and-tumble of his day had left him ragged.

Gabe perched himself on the barstool beside Maggie's and dropped his briefcase. "Have you heard from Diana?"

Maggie waved her cell phone. "She is in the thick of things with Talbot but wouldn't tell me specifics."

"What about Larry Reynolds?" Gabe asked.

"He reminded us to stay focused," Maggie replied, as she signaled the barkeep. "How about joining me for a drink?"

Gabe waved her off. "Not yet. I've still got work to do."

"Oh?"

"One of the city's chemical techs is going to call me," he explained. "About yet another twist in this disaster." He fished his cell phone from inside his coat and laid it on the bar. "Seems that Green

Planet was tweaking the fluoridation of the water supply. This entire scandal appears to be a diversion to draw attention from what was really going on."

"Which was?"

"Introducing more than fluoride, but other EDCs—Endocrine Disruptive Chemicals."

Maggie cocked an eyebrow. "Enlighten me."

"EDCs interfere with the body's hormones. They can inhibit the development of your body."

"Why would Green Planet do that?"

"That's the million-dollar question," Gabe replied. "When the tech calls, I hope he supplies appropriate answers." Gabe gathered his phone and briefcase. "I'm going to take the call in my room for privacy."

Maggie wasn't ready to call it a night and didn't want to spend time alone at the bar. "What about dinner?"

Gabe shook his head. "Don't have the time. I'll order room service."

Maggie could've volunteered to join Gabe, but he had a handle on what he wanted to do. For her sake, Maggie had had enough for the day. Prying information out of her contacts was an enjoyable challenge, but grueling. She needed to unwind and start fresh tomorrow.

A stiff drink would be a good start. She ordered an Old fashioned. As she enjoyed the first sip, in the mirror behind the bar she caught the reflection of a woman checking her out. The stranger was a blonde, and for an instant, Maggie imagined it was Diana.

Maggie turned around, and the blonde was not shy about making eye contact. Her face was fuller than Diana's, and her features softer.

The expression in her eyes was more than friendly, and Maggie recognized a come-on.

She took her drink and approached the blonde's cocktail table. She looked like the white wine type but was instead treating herself to a martini. The woman wore a dark pantsuit, the top of the blouse unbuttoned enough to display inviting cleavage. Her jewelry was expensive, but not gaudy. The diamond on her wedding ring glittered like an inviting beacon. Mind no marriage vows. Just as Maggie was going to ask if she could sit, the blonde pushed the chair out with a foot clad in a designer shoe.

Maggie tingled with anticipation. She set her glass beside the blonde's. This would be the start of tonight's last escapade.

CHAPTER FIVE

Certain aspects of human consciousness and wisdom were more advanced in your distant past. I could attest to that after many assignments and identities in your world. Knowledge is power, and the Controllers are manipulating and suppressing that knowledge, telling you, you are at the height of science and technology, but these are false gifts. This is part of this quiet war: a campaign of deception.

The Grand Marquis Hotel.

While Diana was reviewing the background information on John Herald, he stepped onto the escalator, descending toward the banquet hall level. His destination: the reception dinner sponsored by Great Global Media for this year's Crypto-Confederation Technology conference. The event was black-tie formal, and he was dressed accordingly.

When he stepped off the escalator, a young woman guided him through a security scanner. Herald proceeded toward a table, where they gave him a name badge decorated with a hologram of the conference logo.

Two security agents in matching black suits flanked the entrance into the banquet hall. Each agent wore an earbud, and despite their relaxed postures, it was obvious they were armed.

The maître d' stood outside the double doors into the banquet hall. He intercepted Herald and glanced furtively at his name badge. "Regretfully, Mr. Herald," the maître d' said, "you've missed the receiving line."

"Oh dear, that is a shame," Herald replied, sounding contrite. He'd deliberately arrived late so he could avoid the patronizing ritual.

The maître d' opened one door slightly, and he and Herald slipped in. The hall rumbled with a cacophony of conversations, punctuated by hearty laughs. The maître d' escorted Herald to his table. Except for those who queued at the bar at the back of the hall, most of the 150 guests were already seated and picking at their salads. The conference executives sat at the head tables arranged on the dais. The dinner's toastmaster was Reginald Deighton, and beside him sat the keynote speaker, Jeff Kennedy.

As he made his way across the room, Herald returned waves of acknowledgment. While outside, Great Global Media and Apex Media were locked in guerilla warfare; during this conference, their corporate heads were as chummy as fraternity brothers.

When Herald was seated, with a curt nod he acknowledged one of his tablemates, Sheikh Ahmed Kaddar, but the billionaire seemed more focused on his comely partner, a stunning brunette in a daringly revealing and clingy gown. At the adjacent table sat General Wayne Carcano, whose uniform glittered with rows of military decorations. Because of his silvery crewcut and athletic build, he could be mistaken for a varsity football coach.

On the dais, Anthony Briscane scurried behind the guests at the head table, whispering into their ears. Herald wondered how much of this was Briscane coordinating last-minute details, or if he was making a show of how important he was. Herald pretended not to notice when Briscane pointed him out.

The dinner proceeded in its expected manner. After the salad, they brought the entrees out—Herald chose sea bass—with latke-potato medallions and steamed vegetables. He skipped dessert.

As they served coffee, Deighton began the evening's program. He acknowledged guests, especially Senators Aston Floyd and Maryanne Bastien, and a raft of California politicians, whose contributions of taxpayer money had made the conference possible. After assorted guests had taken their turn at addressing the crowd, Deighton returned to the microphone.

He thanked all the other speakers and then began, "Ladies and gentlemen, though tonight's featured speaker needs no introduction, I'd be remiss not to mention his accomplishments and his contributions to our society. His name will become enshrined alongside the industry's other legends, such as Thomas Edison, Henry Ford, Steve Jobs. It is my honor to introduce our special guest, the founder and CEO/President of Second Eden Technologies, Jeff Kennedy."

A chorus of applause echoed in the hall as Kennedy rose from his chair. Deighton waited for him at the lectern, where the two men shook hands and slapped each other on the back. All eyes were on Kennedy. Wide shouldered and trim, with a full head of coppery hair and ruddy features that glowed against the stark black and white of his tuxedo, he radiated intelligence, energy, and boundless charm.

He thanked Deighton, the guests, and this opportunity to share his thoughts. He made a self-deprecating joke, and good-natured chuckles rippled through the audience.

57

After the obligatory preamble, he gripped the edges of the lectern and his posture became commandingly firm, as if to emphasize the seriousness of his speech. Pundits and academics alike crowned him as one of the most resolute hands on the world's tiller, and they rumored that what he said tonight would be a glimpse of where the future was headed. His pronouncements blew with gale-force power through industries and stock markets.

Kennedy cleared his throat and cast a measured gaze across the room.

"If I could encapsulate the mood of our world, it would be in two words: uncertainty and hope.

"Two opposing moods, for sure, but relevant to each of us and our constituents.

"What breeds the uncertainty is the fog of tomorrow's unknown. We are all familiar with the adage penned by Robert Burns, 'the best-laid plans of mice and men,' etc. Try as we might, we have yet to develop a crystal ball, and the most we can be sure of is that the future offers no guarantees.

"Despite the promises of politicians"—Kennedy traded smiles with the senators—"and bureaucrats, all well-meaning for sure, and industrialists, plus bankers, our world still stumbles along, hobbled by environmental challenges, pollution, waste, overpopulation, and the demons of violence and corruption. As a species, as soon as we solve one problem, we create two more."

He paused for laughs.

"Ever more powerful drugs created to accelerate healing and ease pain have brought about waves of addiction. Automation has swept away the drudgery of menial work, increased the efficiency of the workplace many times over, but in its wake has left millions unemployed. A world of have-nots breeds resentment and despair that do no one any good. People without meaningful livelihood have no stake in their communities, and to draw upon another quote: 'Idle hands are the devil's workshop.'

"To be sure, at times we seem to grope through a world of shadows. But take heart in this, the brightest of lights casts the darkest shadows.

"Now on to *hope*. What shines the brightest are the opportunities we can leverage through our technology. Two hundred years ago, we used steam power to remake our world. Then it was electricity, chemistry, and the internal combustion engine. After that, computers and a greater understanding of the symbiotic relationship between society and artificial intelligence and advanced technology.

"But one major challenge is the perception that the compensations of this new society are not fairly distributed. What we are dealing with is a matter of perception, which is no trivial matter. People who perceive themselves as happy feel connected, empowered, and validated. Yet other individuals, in identical circumstances, if perceiving themselves to be unhappy and frustrated, are prone to all kinds of mischief and fertile ideas that cultivate contrary behavior.

"That bright light I just mentioned is the yin and yang of AI and AT, that is, artificial intelligence and advanced technology. You in the media and those of us in my industry, together we must aim to reeducate the masses through electronics—the AI part, and through drugs—the AT part. It's an approach that will leave little to chance. As you in the media improve our messaging, we'll see that our light will burn brighter even as the shadows shrink away. You here tonight are the champions of this better alternative world, which through your efforts will be made more efficient, peaceful, productive, and profitable."

Kennedy paused for a drink of water, then continued, "The naysayers will protest, asking, 'What about choice? What about the free will of the individual?'

"To that we say, people will have a choice. They will be free to choose what we offer. Our notions of personal liberty are holdovers from the time when the state and industry were extraordinarily flawed institutions. Thanks to modern media, working with AI and AT, we can coordinate government and commerce into one seamless enterprise, providing an efficiency far above what our forbearers would've dreamed possible. How can anyone question the wisdom of oversight that is plugged into a global network of information that sees all, knows all? Freedom of speech, freedom of assembly, freedom from unreasonable search and seizure are quaint holdovers that mean nothing today when we can control and monitor anything and everything. Clinging to the notions of liberty is as outdated as insisting the world is flat. We must dedicate ourselves to removing the last impediments to progress. We, and you in the media, know what's best. Our message to the world is: Trust us with your security. Trust us with your livelihood. Trust us with your future."

After the speech, the audience gave a standing ovation, and Herald used the commotion to excuse himself. He knew well that his premature departure made him conspicuous, but no matter, he was used to being watched.

He left the Grand Marquis Hotel and summoned a taxi, arriving shortly in his home on Alameda Island. To an observer, the use of a simple key to unlock his front door might have seemed backward and low-tech, but in reality, the door was fused shut until his presence caused the mechanism to open the metal cocoon encasing his apartment.

Herald stepped into his bedroom and opened a large cigar box resting on his bureau. From the cigar box, he removed an assortment of odds and ends—cuff links, a couple of gold watches, fountain pens, a silver case for business cards, various coins—and set them on the bureau. He relaxed to synch his vibrations with those of the box. The air inside the box shimmered and a small book materialized. The book was made of red leather with a silver pinecone embossed on the cover. He paused a moment to consider what he was doing. This seemed like such a primitive gambit, passing along the contents written in this book, ink on paper, but it was vital information no matter the means of transmission.

Clasping the book, he set it aside and returned the objects he'd removed to the box.

Herald collected the book and slid it into a padded envelope. Next, he changed out of his tuxedo and into casual clothes. Now to wait. He made tea and, as he sipped, reflected upon the immediate future for himself and Diana Willis.

Their enemies were powerful and well entrenched in government and business. But Herald had one crucial advantage, the most important advantage of all—surprise. He was always one step ahead of his adversaries and no matter how substantial their resources, they would react to what he just did, not to what he was going to do.

Through deft moves, some small, others large—and as he considered this, he bounced the envelope in his hand—he kept his rivals off balance and guessing.

Time to go.

When Herald returned to the front door, he slipped into an overcoat, one with an inside pocket large enough to unobtrusively hold the padded envelope. After he stepped outside and locked the door, his security system all but hermetically sealed his apartment.

What amazed Diana this morning was how muscle memory had guided her through the morning's routine. It wasn't until she was fully dressed and pouring a cup of coffee that she realized she was at last wide awake.

Images from last night's dreams lingered ghostlike in her mind. What most disturbed her about these phantom images was not the images themselves, but that the dreams were more like repressed memories floating into her consciousness.

How was this possible?

As a teenager, had she danced naked on the stage at the Bohemian Grove retreat?

It was too fantastic, too bizarre, too obscene.

Suppose it had happened? When? She scoured her memory, looking for a time in which such a thing would've been possible. Nothing?

A chill ran through her, and she sipped hot coffee to warm her nerves.

She respected her intuition enough to listen to the growing tingle of suspicion brought on by the surrounding events. She couldn't quite put her finger on the immediate danger, yet the alarm pulsed like a radar warning.

Whatever this danger, it had to do with what Briscane had assigned to her. Was he the danger, or was it John Herald, or was it from getting trapped in their competing machinations?

Diana took a deep breath. All her career, she hadn't just survived but prevailed against the odds by being agile and drawing upon her wits and fortitude. Who knew what would develop soon? To protect herself, she had to safeguard Briscane's thumb drive and its trove of secrets.

She returned to her bedroom and opened the middle-left drawer. After tossing aside her rolled-up socks and leggings, she pressed the bottom of the drawer to reveal a shallow false bottom, just deep enough for the thumb drive.

The morning developed without incident. Diana double-checked the FAA flight planning and confirmed that John Herald had not revised his flight plan.

After arriving in the Great Global Media headquarters building, she rode the elevator to the twentieth floor and got out, the highest she could get without special clearance. Now to get to the roof, another twenty-six stories above.

Urgency nipped at her nerves. Down the hall, she heard a clatter. Following the noise, she discovered a maintenance man struggling to pull an overloaded dolly through a wide door into the service area. Diana helped him hold the door open and noticed a placard on the wall: *Authorized Access Only*. An adjacent card reader prevented unauthorized entry.

Aha, if she could sneak past the door, she'd be inside the security area. The maintenance man thanked her for the help, looking surprised that a white-collar type like her would even bother. There was a second door behind him, one marked *Service Stairs*.

Diana watched him retreat down the hall, dolly clattering, and let the door close, only to catch it with the toe of her shoe. She waited a moment until she heard him round a corner. Then she pushed the door open and slipped through. Continuing past the door of the service stairs, she entered the stairwell and girded herself for the climb, long but doable for someone in her fit condition. She paused before starting the climb and pulled out her cell phone to text Maggie and Gabe Mendoza: Will be out of touch for a few days.

CHAPTER SIX

To find the truth, sometimes you must lose everything, including your mind. That can be good because the way you use your mind is flawed and you on earth rely on it too much to discern the truth.

You see your world with two eyes, but I see it with three. It's time to open your other eye and there, beyond your mind, is a truth detector. It can pick up on the subtle inconsistencies of lies and deceptive subliminal messages. That truth finder is what the Controllers want to block. That is what you must protect.

A terrifying bedlam engulfed Diana. The noise swirled around her like she was in a tornado. Panicked, heart racing, she screamed and—

Sat upright in bed. The scream died in her throat.

What now surrounded her was a quiet as profound as the deafening sound had been an instant before.

She blinked and took stock of where she was. Warm, bright light flooded the room. She recognized the windows, the curtains, the surrounding bed. She was back in her luxury condo, dressed in her sleeping clothes—loose t-shirt and boxers—safe, comfortable. As she gathered her wits, the panicked sensation evaporated. Her heart rate eased.

Breathing easily, she relaxed. *What kind of dream was that?*

"Diana," someone called to her.

She turned and saw Maggie LaClair sitting beside her bed. Diana stammered, "W—what are you doing here?"

"I'm helping."

Diana noticed a bottle of medication on her nightstand. "What's going on? How did I get here?"

"You collapsed," Maggie said.

"What? *What?*" Diana groped for answers.

"Yesterday morning—" Maggie began.

"Hold on," Diana interrupted. "I've been here since yesterday morning? Collapsed?"

"Let me explain. You collapsed in the stairwell of the Great Global Media Headquarters."

The memories came back. Diana saw herself stepping off the elevator on the twentieth floor and heading for the stairwell leading to the rooftop helipad. She remembered the urgency of her task. To catch John Herald before…

Before what?

"A guard monitoring a security video saw you fall," Maggie said. "He called the paramedics, and they rushed you to the hospital."

"Hospital? Then what am I doing in my home?"

"The doctor said you had collapsed from stress and exhaustion. She felt that in such circumstances, being in a familiar environment would be best."

"Me?" Diana asked. "Collapsing from stress and exhaustion? Impossible. I'm in excellent health."

"I'm only relaying what the doctor said."

"I thought you were in Columbus working on the water assignment."

"I was. Gabe uncovered something interesting. However, when I heard what had happened to you, I rushed back here right away."

"Then who brought me here?"

"I did," Maggie replied. "I'm the one who undressed you and put you in those sleeping clothes."

Diana blushed. "Thanks." But the way Maggie was looking at her implied there was more to the story of her collapsing. Diana said, "I'm picking up that something else happened."

Maggie leaned closer and put her hand on Diana's bed. "I'm afraid so. John Herald's helicopter crashed."

"Crashed? How? Where? When?"

"Yesterday morning. Soon after takeoff."

"And John Herald?"

Maggie shook her head. "So far, there's no sign of him. But according to witnesses, the helicopter smashed into the ground and exploded."

"Oh, God." Diana clutched her throat. The panic returned, now as creepy as icy claws raking her nerves.

"There's a lot of chaos in Great Global Media," Maggie said. "Seems that Herald was exceptionally crucial to many high-level corporate operations."

Diana raised a hand. "Give me a second. There's a lot I have to process."

A torrent of thoughts cascaded through her mind, but the one she latched onto was John Herald. What was her interest in him? She pictured Anthony Briscane. He had assigned her to investigate Herald. Why?

Because of his alleged involvement in underhanded dealings. Which she had confirmed. *More or less.* What she had was Briscane's thumb drive of circumstantial evidence.

Then there was John Herald himself. In the last two days—why did it feel like over two days had passed? Diana and Herald kept crossing paths, and every time they did, the connection between them kept getting more intense. This was another reason she was curious about him.

Diana regarded Maggie and waited for the obvious question. *What were you doing in the Great Global Media building?* But Maggie didn't ask. Her doleful eyes remained on her coworker. Maybe Briscane had sent out a memo. After all, she was working on a secret assignment for him.

Maggie grasped a remote from the nightstand and aimed it at the wall flat-screen TV. She cycled through the program menu and clicked on *GGM TV Now!*

The program showed a video of a ragged column of smoke lingering over a line of trees. The video next showed the smoke from another perspective with a caption of Mt. Tamalpais State Park Area. Site of helicopter crash.

The video transitioned to an aerial view, either from another helicopter or a drone, as it hovered over the smoking wreckage of a helicopter in pieces. Flames licked the surrounding brush.

Seeing the smashed remains of Herald's helicopter brought back that awful icy sensation. It had crashed along the coastline and along the flight path he'd filed with the FAA. Engrossed by the horrific spectacle on the video, Diana struggled against a wave of disbelief. "What happened to John Herald?"

The screen showed a man in a ball cap and a light jacket pointing toward the distance. The caption read: Helicopter Crash Witness.

The man explained, "I was on my way to work when I looked out the window of my truck and saw the helicopter like it was in trouble. Smoke was shooting from the middle part and it started spinning around before it dropped below the tree line and I lost visual. Then I heard a loud boom and saw this fireball rise from behind the trees."

The video switched to a slender brunette holding a microphone and speaking to the camera. She was standing outside, against a backdrop of fire trucks from the Marin County Fire Rescue, emergency lights flashing, firefighters dragging equipment into the brush.

The woman said, "Efforts to contain the fire continue and considering the recent rain and fog, the team captain says he's confident the flames will not spread beyond the crash scene. However, none of the passengers, including the pilot, have been located—"

Diana mused, the only passenger had been John Herald, the pilot. So where was John Herald? That his body hadn't been found meant there was hope he remained alive.

But that hope wasn't enough to dampen the foreboding. The video again showed the smoldering wreckage. How was it possible for anyone to have survived that without getting blown up or burned to death?

The only reasonable possibility was that he'd been thrown out when the helicopter was spinning. But how high and how fast had it been spinning? She imagined it would've been like being thrown out of a speeding car that was plunging over a cliff. What were the chances of surviving that? And since he hadn't been located, that meant that if he had survived being catapulted to the ground, he would've been lying injured and in great pain for over twenty-four hours. She felt the sting of irony in that he might have lived through the crash only to die of neglect.

Diana thought *I was supposed to be in that helicopter.* She pieced together what had happened to her. She was on her way to the roof-top helipad of Great Global Media when she had collapsed suddenly from stress and exhaustion. All right, she reflected, the day before she had been working full throttle and slept but a few hours. However, that routine was nothing new to her. She was used to such demanding work surges. And she didn't remember even so much as a hitch in her step when she left her condo and arrived in the GGM building. The climb up twenty-six stories of steps hadn't even winded her.

It had amped her to learn what she could about John Herald and confirm what Briscane alluded to: that Herald had his fingers in a lot of corrupt pies.

But there was something else.

That connection between him and her. She kept circling back to that thought.

Which nurtured a belief that the more she found out about Herald, such information would exonerate him and, even more pointedly, point any scandal back at Briscane.

That latter thought she couldn't prove, but the hunch nagged her like a fly buzzing in her head.

And one more thing.

That dream.

Of her about to start dancing naked on an outdoor stage at the Bohemian Grove. The image brought bile to her throat. What had prompted that dream? And why now?

Diana knew dreams happened when the subconscious was trying to make sense of something else in your life. But what?

So many questions and so few answers.

She again noticed the TV and her GGM colleague. "We wait for investigators from the National Transportation Safety Board. Hopefully, they will sift through the many questions surrounding the mysterious crash and the even more mysterious whereabouts of John Herald and bring us answers. This is Prissy Jameson, GGM Now News."

Maggie pointed the remote at the TV. "Is there any more you want to watch?"

Diana said, "That's enough."

Maggie clicked off the TV and handed Diana the bottle of meds. "The doctor said that when you wake up, to take one of these."

The prescription on the bottle read: *Normafon: muscle relaxant. One capsule every eight hours.*

"Now that my thoughts are coming back, I don't feel that bad."

"The doctor recommends that you take it easy for a couple of days."

"Yeah, but there's so much—"

"The world spins without you, Diana, remember that."

"Okay, if I wound up here the way I did, then I need to take care of myself." Diana rattled the bottle. "I promise."

Maggie stood. "Now that I've seen you come to and that you look okay, I'll be off."

Diana extended her arms. "Maggie, thanks so much."

Maggie slid onto the bed, and they hugged. Maggie held tight for a moment that bordered on uncomfortable. "I'm so glad that you're all right. You gave me quite the scare."

"I'll be fine." Diana glanced at her phone on the nightstand. "You're just a call away."

After Maggie left, Diana decided against taking a pill and opted for herbal tea. She rose and sat on the edge of the bed. She felt a little stiff, but nothing that required medication to relax. She padded into the kitchen and a moment later, made herbal tea, and sat by a window with a steaming cup of mint-chamomile to gaze upon San Francisco and the bay beyond. Mist from a midday rain settled upon the city, muting the colors, turning the lights of traffic and the animated billboards into colorful smears. The distance faded into a gray haze. The scene had the serenity and understated beauty of an Asian tonal painting.

But neither the view nor the herbal tea brought calm. Disjointed thoughts tumbled through Diana's mind, like the pieces of a broken jigsaw puzzle. No sooner had she grasped one piece than another one pushed it out of her mind's eye. There was John Herald. The helicopter crash. Her unexplained collapse from exhaustion.

This last thought disturbed her. She had collapsed from exhaustion? Impossible. Not her.

She'd prove it to everyone. After setting the cup on the table, she made her way to the center of the room, announcing, "Alexa, yoga routine twelve."

Alexa adjusted the lights and played soothing music.

Diana assumed the first asana, warrior pose. But as her muscles flexed to hold her steady, her balance shifted, and she stumbled. *Strange.*

72

When she resumed the stance, she not only felt off balance but weak and light-headed. She realized perhaps she was suffering residual effects from the stress and exhaustion.

"Alexa, end routine."

Diana retrieved her teacup. On the way to the kitchen, she got more than light-headed, dizzy in fact, and stopped to brace herself against the wall. *Okay, maybe the doctor was right.*

Deciding to get some rest, she returned to bed. Even after she laid her head on the pillow and closed her eyes, the disjointed thoughts returned, vivid and chaotic now. It was as if she stood inside a brightly lit kaleidoscope, the wild pattern of thoughts shifting and re-shifting.

Restless and frustrated, she thought maybe she needed the meds. She grasped the bottle of Normafon and shook out one tablet, then downed it with a swig of water. A chemical caress pulsed through her body, and her muscles softened. The mental kaleidoscope dimmed and blurred, and Diana felt herself melting into unconsciousness.

Diana moved through a cloud. Or maybe the densest fog she'd ever walked through.

A diffused light surrounded her. Slowly, as she materialized from the vapor, she noticed a young girl about eight years old walking ahead of her.

Tangles of blonde hair draped the collar of the girl's blouse. She also wore jeans and tennis shoes and proceeded at a rushed pace.

Diana perceived herself as floating toward the girl, getting closer, seeing herself pass into the girl until she was looking through her eyes. She and the girl were one.

The fog vanished. Diana was right behind a man and woman strolling along a country road lined with nicely kept houses, the landscape bathed in mild sunlight. The man and woman looked in their late thirties and were dressed in casual clothes.

She felt no threat from them, quite the opposite in that their presence comforted her. They headed off the road toward a cottage in yellow stucco laced with green ivy. The sky was such an intense blue that Diana remarked to herself that the surrounding colors were almost garish, as if from a comic book.

A row of pavers led from the street, passing a large black mailbox that was carefully labeled in handwritten script: *Starnowski*

She reread the name, feeling that it tugged at her subconscious.

The man and woman urged her forward. They strode over the pavers around the side of the house, through a steel gate in a stone wall, and entered a backyard garden overgrown with flowers. Planters encircled a large patio slab. The man took a seat on the concrete bench at one end of the patio. The woman reached into a bucket by the bench. She retrieved two large pieces of chalk, one green, one red. She pitched the green one to Diana. Together, they sank to their knees and drew a diagram for hopscotch.

Diana went first, hopping and skipping. Then it was the woman's turn.

They both laughed, but it sounded muted, as though something muffled her hearing. Then, as Diana was about to play again, the woman addressed the man using a clear and distinctive voice. "Joseph."

Abruptly, the world dissolved from around Diana except for her and the man and the woman. She sensed memories flooding from them into her, memories that coursed from pleasant to terrible. At that moment, she could see across the landscape of time, from the past to the future. And she realized who this man and woman were. She whispered, "Father. Mother."

They turned to her, smiling benignly. "Alexandra."

Diana's eyes popped open, and in a flash, she was fully awake. Taking a moment to center herself, thankfully, she was back in her condo.

Gasping, she sat up and tapped her chest to settle her breathing. Warm sweat beaded on her forehead, and her face felt hot to the touch. What was causing this? Why was she whipsawing from reality to dreams and back to reality like this?

While she was awake, this last dream clung to her mind like tendrils of fog. She felt unmoored, as if she were now someone else.

Like who?

She swung her legs off the bed and rushed to the bathroom. Upon entering, the lights brightened automatically, and she stared into the mirror above the sink.

Dumbstruck, she staggered backward, thumping against the wall before she caught herself.

She remained transfixed on her reflection, because it wasn't her gazing back, it was the little girl from the dream.

Astonished, she whispered, "I'm Alexandra Starnowski."

CHAPTER SEVEN

When you remember your dreams, they are not dreams. They are messages. Sometimes answers come to you in ways that only you can understand. It is most important to have a clear mind to receive and understand the message.

The CT-11 helicopter lay on its side, the fuselage a shattered, smoldering wreck. During the crash, the helicopter's rotor blades had hacked through the surrounding brush like gigantic machetes before gouging into the dirt and breaking apart. Smoke and steam lifted from the circle of blackened, soggy grass that defined the perimeter of the crash site within the narrow clearing.

Two rough-terrain fire trucks prowled the southern side of the site, the water cannons on top of the cabs swiveling from side to side like hungry snouts. Firefighters stomped through the grass, using shovels to tamp down any lingering flames. A group of techs in HazMat coveralls stepped gingerly around the scattered pieces of the helicopter, documenting the scene with cameras and cataloging the debris. Overhead, two small surveillance drones hovered.

Hikers and other curious folk wandered from the north down a trail that emptied into the clearing. They clustered along a yellow plastic tape labeled *Crash Site Investigation - Keep Back* that stretched across the trail. Chatting among themselves, they pointed and snapped photographs and videos on their smartphones.

Diana made her way down the trail, dressed in a pair of casual pants, a short jacket over a loose blouse, hiking boots.

When she reached the crowd at the tape, she tried to step through, but the people wouldn't budge. She kept repeating, "Excuse me, excuse me," but no one moved. It was as if they couldn't hear her.

A badge with her press credentials hung from a neck lanyard. Even when she held up the badge, the others wouldn't even so much as acknowledge her. She sidestepped to the left, hoping to get past the end of the tape where it had been tied to a tree. But another group of hikers blocked her way, held in position by a deputy sheriff.

"I need to get through," Diana raised her voice to the deputy.

Ignoring her, the deputy made a call on a radio.

Diana tapped the shoulder of a woman in front of her. But the woman, like everyone else, didn't respond. Diana tapped again, harder. The woman's body was solid and very real, and Diana saw how her fingers wrinkled the woman's jacket. So, Diana was physically here. But no matter, the woman didn't respond.

Diana walked back along the line of spectators, feeling oddly disconnected from the scene. To determine if she was dreaming, she rubbed her eyes and tugged at her hair. It all felt real. She bit the inside of her lower lip until it hurt. All real.

She regarded the people along the yellow tape and wondered why everyone acted as if she was not here. Then she felt someone's gaze. Diana scanned from left to right, and at the far right side of the tape, a plump, older woman was staring right at her. The woman appeared at loose ends, what with her baggy clothes and vintage down vest, and strands of hair dangling from under a knit cap.

Their eyes met, and Diana knew she had made a connection. *At last*, she thought, *someone who might give me answers about what's going on.*

She passed behind a knot of people who blocked her view of the woman. Then, on reaching the other side, Diana discovered that the woman had vanished.

"Where did she go?" Diana asked aloud, frustrated, angry. *What the hell am I hallucinating?*

The onlookers rustled with excitement. In the middle of the crash site, three people strode toward the helicopter. Diana recognized Prissy Jameson, who was accompanied by a cameraman and a sound tech. They halted and set up a shot with the wreck of the helicopter and the fire trucks as backdrops.

Microphone in hand, Prissy faced the camera and began reporting. "Prissy Jameson, *GGM Now News* live on location…"

Diana shouted to her, but it was as if the air swallowed her words. She could hear Prissy, but Prissy couldn't hear her.

"Make way," announced a newly arriving deputy, who hustled down the trail. Behind him crept an off-road ambulance, emergency lights flashing. The crowd parted, surging against Diana, pushing her back, yet still not acknowledging her.

Her phone pinged, and she fished it out of her jacket pocket. It was an alert over the Great Global Media news feed: Breaking news, Body close to helicopter crash site.

Has to be John Herald. She looked back at the wreck. *Close to the crash site? Where?* When the ambulance rolled past her, she slipped behind it, hoping to get closer to the helicopter. Once the ambulance entered the perimeter, she showed her badge to the deputy. But as before, he acted as if she didn't exist. He pulled the yellow tape taut in front of her and ordered everyone to keep back.

People crowded in front of her again, and she rose on tiptoes to see over their heads and shoulders.

Her phone chimed with an incoming text.

It was Larry Reynolds: I need to meet you.

Finally, she thought, breathing a sigh of relief. *Someone knows I'm here.* She typed back, When?

Your place. An hour.

Why at her home? How about I come to the GGM offices?

Absolutely not. You need some rest.

Even though she was at the crash site, this request made sense. Considering the topsy-turvy state of her world, she needed rest.

Diana gathered her thoughts. This was so strange. On the one hand, she was in a place where no one acted as if she was here. And on the other, Larry Reynolds was texting her.

As Diana dropped her phone into a jacket pocket, she glanced back to the crash site. The plump woman was back. Staring at her.

Diana stepped toward her, shouting, "Wait! Don't move."

A gaggle of onlookers walked in front of Diana, blocking her line of sight toward the woman. In vain, she tried to push them aside and when they had passed, the woman was gone.

Diana returned to her condo. Traffic delayed her, and while hoping for a shower and a nap, she didn't have time, nor did her mind let her rest. She kept seeing that mysterious woman. And what was going on with everyone else, acting as if she wasn't there?

She made herself a cup of strong coffee to hold her over until the meeting with Larry Reynolds. He arrived on the dot as promised, the doorman alerting Diana that he was here and was sending him up. Reynolds wore his business suit, showing he had just come from work. Diana apologized for her appearance, as she had hoped to shower and change.

Reynolds shrugged. "What are you talking about? You look fine."

She offered him a seat on the sofa and a drink, his choice. He accepted the seat and declined the drink. Diana stared at him, wondering why he was interacting with her, unlike the people at the crash site.

"I'm here to fill in the gaps about Dan Talbot," he said.

"Okay," Diana replied, though she remained curious why Reynolds had not asked about her reactions to John Herald's crash and death. To her, Dan Talbot was old news.

Then why was Reynolds here? He must have something else on his mind. If all he wanted was to chat about Talbot, he could've done that over the phone or on a video chat.

"Talbot wants to set up some meetings, have you start on his strategy for 'public rehabilitation.'" This last in air quotes.

"Yeah, sure," she replied, catching her flat tone, then perking up, "I mean, gladly."

"Good. Good." Reynolds coughed. "Which segues into another reason I'm here."

Diana smiled to herself. *Here it comes.*

"My concern is, are you well enough to get back in the saddle?" Reynolds asked.

"What do you mean?"

"Great Global wants to air promos about your return to *World Primetime Now.*"

The announcement stunned her. "Of course," she replied. "You want me back in the saddle, you only need to say when."

"The worry is that you're still a little... I don't know how to say this." Reynolds glanced at the ceiling, then at her. "Out of sorts?"

"You've got nothing to worry about." Diana sat straight and squared her shoulders. "You want me in the anchor's chair of *World Primetime Now,* I'm there."

Reynolds clapped his hands. "Good. I'm glad to hear that." He stood.

"That's it?" she asked.

Laughing, he asked, "You returning to the airwaves isn't enough?"

"No, no, that's not what I meant. It's just so sudden."

"Then we're all set, Diana," Reynolds said. "We'll start the promo campaign tomorrow."

"When do you need me to come in?"

Reynolds gave one of his avuncular smiles. "We've got plenty of stock footage, so don't worry about the promo video. We'll schedule a meeting for later."

After Reynolds left, Diana stood staring at her front door. Dozens of thoughts crisscrossed her mind. Dan Talbot. Her collapse. Maggie

LaClair. John Herald. The helicopter crash. That weirdness at the crash site. The mysterious woman. The strange dreams. And now Reynolds' offer of a speedy return even though she had only been gone a day.

This is so very bizarre.

But first things first. She had promised herself a shower and a change of clothes. And depending on how she felt after that, perhaps a nap.

Later, in the shower, water splashed over Diana and rinsed away the last traces of body wash. Closing her eyes, she lifted her face toward the spray from the showerhead.

The tiles beneath her feet shifted, and she jerked in surprise.

The sound of the splashing water became a thunderous roar, like she was at the bottom of a waterfall. And she was spinning, light and dark rotating around her. Her mind jolted in panic, as if at any second she was going to die. The noise became deafening like the world was ripping apart.

The light brightened into a blinding flash.

Diana slipped and smacked her head against the tile wall of her shower stall. The noise faded to the soft gush of water raining over her.

She settled on one knee, the water dripping off her body, and regained her balance. The blow rattled her nerves, but she realized she was okay.

She grabbed a towel and dried off, then stepped carefully out of the shower. After slipping into a favorite robe, she headed to her kitchen for a cup of tea.

Anthony Briscane was sitting on the sofa, arms stretched across the back, legs extended.

Upon seeing him, she froze in shock, then flushed with anger. Her robe was not much longer than a miniskirt and, with that being her only garment, she felt almost naked, violated. She clutched the lapel of the robe. "What are you doing here?"

Briscane sized her up with his shiny, weasel eyes. "What do you mean? You invited me in, remember?"

"No, I don't—"

He interrupted. "How else could I be in here if you didn't let me in?"

His question stumped her. *This is a secure building. How did he get in?*

"You buzzed me in from downstairs and said to wait while you took a shower." Briscane stood. It was then that she noticed his business suit was blood red. She did a double take. And then there was the creepy feeling of this slimy bastard skulking around her place while she was naked in the shower. She winced from a shiver of disgust.

"I've come to discuss John Herald," he said. "If you wish, I can come back another time."

She re-cinched the belt of her robe and again clutched the lapels, making sure they were tightly closed. "Now is fine, since you're already here."

Briscane walked past her, across the room to the large picture window, looking down upon the city. The glass was perfectly clear and from Diana's perspective, the sight created the illusion that Briscane was floating in the air, the illusion more surreal because of his red suit.

He kept quiet, looking up to the left, to the right, toward the bay. While he admired the vista, she retreated to her bedroom, locked the door, then changed into casual clothes.

Returning to the front room, she saw Briscane had remained at the window. She studied the back of his head, the cut of his suit across his shoulders. Although he had treated her with deference, there was something about his flattering, oily manner that set her teeth on edge.

Finally, he said, "It's an amazing view."

"It's why I bought the place," Diana replied.

He turned to face her, and for a fleeting moment, Diana mused that if the window hadn't been there, she would've pushed him to the ground thirty-six stories below.

"What do you think of John Herald?"

"I was just getting started looking into his past." She added, "I was at the crash site when I learned the search team found a body. His, no doubt."

"Yes, and burned beyond recognition." Briscane went *tsk, tsk.* "Based upon the personal effects, they say it was Herald, but have to wait for DNA tests to be certain."

Burned beyond recognition. Diana became ill as she contemplated what that meant. She'd seen other burn victims before. They were shriveled knots of charred flesh and bone—fingers and toes, noses roasted off. But what bothered her now was how she remembered John Herald. His charm, his robustness, his vitality.

Now he was gone, replaced by an incinerated mass of burned meat. She hoped his death had happened quickly.

"Are you okay?" Briscane's question snapped her to the present.

"I'm still coming to grips with Herald's passing," she answered. "I guess this is the end of my investigation of him."

Briscane smiled at her, trying to be charming, but the result was like grease being squeezed from his pores. "Not at all. I need you to keep digging. We need to determine once and for all the extent of his dirty dealings and crimes. While he might be gone, his accomplices are alive and well."

"Who are...?" she asked.

Briscane opened his hands. "Throughout corporate. Who do you think? Do you want me to supply an organizational chart?" He pantomimed holding something small between his index finger and thumb, which she interpreted to mean the thumb drive.

"That's unnecessary." Diana reached for a bottle of water she'd placed on an end table. Talking with this creepy toad had made her want to rinse her mouth of the icky sensation that he brought, and if he didn't leave soon, she might have to take another shower.

"I want you to ask Maggie LaClair to help."

"Why her?" Diana replied. "I can handle this."

"Two sets of eyes are better than one."

"I can manage. Maggie has her hands full with what she and Gabe uncovered in Columbus."

The light in Briscane's beady eyes sharpened to needlelike points. A palpable malevolence replaced what little charisma he possessed. "No, I insist. Maggie is to help you. End of story."

CHAPTER EIGHT

To help free the television star, I left my impartial space and entered the deep recesses of her past and memories in her unconscious mind. This world of the unconscious is one of your most powerful influences because you are not aware of its influences until it surfaces.

This is where the Controllers are staging their quiet mind war.

Wake up! It's not as it seems.

The man ran through the dark woods. He dashed headlong through the brush, bashing recklessly through branches, making no attempt for stealth. The breath came out of him in panicked gasps. He tripped over roots and rocks, gathered himself, and continued his desperate race to escape.

Behind him, the beam of a flashlight slashed through the murk, its harsh illumination rendering the landscape as frightful tangles.

On and on the man continued, groping, stumbling through the darkness.

He crashed against a tree and clung to it. He held his breath, hoping that his pursuers had lost him. Waiting through several heartbeats and hearing nothing behind him, he stepped lightly and proceeded forward.

A shot rang out.

Sharp pain pierced the man's back as if they had skewered him with a red-hot poker. The pain turned ice-cold, and he dropped to the ground as his life ebbed away.

Night vanished, like a fog yielding to the warm sun.

The young Alexandra stepped through the woods, now bright with sunlight. As she emerged from under the shadow of a tree, holding pinecones she had collected, she spied a man lying on his belly. At first, she thought he might have lain down, but because of the askew position of his arms and legs, it appeared like he had been knocked over.

She paused and waited for him to stir. When he didn't, she felt the faint ring of an alarm, and that ring shrieked louder when she walked closer. Something about him looked very familiar. Too familiar.

An even darker spot stained the back of his dark coat. A pistol lay at his side. Had he shot himself? In the back? How was that possible?

Her heart seized in trepidation, and she slowly, carefully, crouched beside the man.

She placed the pinecones on the ground and grasped his shoulder and rolled him to his side. When his face came into view, it was instantly recognizable. It was her father, Joseph.

Diana clutched her throat, certain that she had just been screaming.

An instant ago, she had been in the woods. Now, where was she?

The room was dark. She was sitting in a wide luxurious bed, sumptuous bedcovers gathered around her. All about the room, her dress and underwear, and a man's clothes were strewn on the floor and furniture. She peeked beneath the bedcovers and saw that she was naked. Glancing to her left, she noticed torn condom wrappers on the nightstand.

Light spilled into the room from the direction of the foyer. She heard water running. Slipping quietly out of bed, Diana crept to the foyer and looked through the open bathroom door, the source of the light. A man was in the shower, his back to her, steam fogging the glass walls of the stall.

What was going on? Okay, judging by the discarded clothes and the used condoms, she knew exactly what had gone on. A hotel hookup. But what hotel? What day was this? And who was he?

Diana retreated from the foyer and dashed about the hotel room, collecting her clothes. She slipped into her panties but didn't bother with her bra and hose before sliding into her cocktail dress. She stashed her bra and hose in her purse, then made sure she hadn't forgotten her phone, watch, wallet, keys, or anything else. Stiletto heels in hand, she tiptoed through the foyer, eased quietly out of the room and into the hall.

Diana and Maggie LaClair were in Larry Reynolds' office, briefing him on their projects. Diana had just handed him a summary of her proposed report on Dan Talbot. Reynolds' large gray eyes swiveled across the printout, but his expression remained plain. This was weird for Diana, as she had rushed to this meeting straight from the hotel and hadn't had time to change out of her abbreviated cocktail dress. To keep the gossip down, she'd covered up with a borrowed sweater. Her boss would've normally shared a barbed comment about such a mismatched outfit.

Reynolds inhaled deeply and placed the summary on his desk. Diana still couldn't get a read on him. She had busted her ass putting that summary together and stepping through the bullet points of her recommendations for his rehabilitation. Talbot had gotten himself into his mess; she was going to get him out—on Great Global's dime.

"Well?" she asked impatiently.

Reynolds rested his hand on the summary and cleared his throat. Not a good sign. Her breath hitched.

"Whose idea was it for an interview with him at an orphanage?" he asked.

"Since I'm the only one working on this project, it was mine," she answered.

His expression remained inscrutable. This was a new affectation; she used to read his face as if it were an open book.

"Okay," he said, his expression still blank. "I'll send a copy of this to editorial, and they'll start scripting the program."

"Great," she replied, relieved. With all the recent craziness in her life, she couldn't take anything for granted. She waited for Reynolds to fill in the details about tonight's program, but he turned to Maggie. "What do you have?"

She scrolled through her tablet. "Quite a bit. Gabe and I uncovered a good amount of what Apex Media has been covering up." She leaned toward the speakerphone on Reynolds' desk and keyed the buttons. The tone cycled as it connected the call, and Gabe's voice rose from the speaker.

Maggie and Reynolds said hello. Diana tried to sound enthusiastic, but since tonight was her return to *World Primetime Now,* she couldn't wait to get started on the program. Reynolds prompted Gabe for his report.

"I dug deeper into municipal records," Gabe said. "I found evidence confirming that the city's testing of their water supply found EDCs far above legal limits. I also discovered where the city manager's staff signed off on those exceptions to water regulations."

"And you have copies of those documents?"

"I have both the documents and the control numbers to prove they aren't bogus. With those numbers, we can retrieve the original reports from the city's archival system. And I found more evidence of irregularities. It was like peeling an onion, one layer after another."

"What irregularities?" Maggie asked.

"Very high levels of fluoride," Gabe said. "Unusually so. Many of the analysis reports were—"

"I'm sure you did a thorough job," Reynolds interrupted, "but I need you to drop that and focus on the Apex Media story. Meaning look solely on the collusion between Apex and the city government."

"Isn't that what I'm doing?"

"No, you're straying into things we can't stop or control."

"Larry, it isn't our job to stop or control anything."

"But don't you want to hear what he found?" Maggie asked.

Reynolds looked at Maggie as he spoke into the speakerphone. "Gabe, I need you to focus on the Apex story."

"Larry, this *is* the Apex story." Gabe's uncertain tone showed his confusion.

Reynolds added, "You've gone outside the original scope by looking into the water treatment situation. Remember, what you and Maggie were supposed to investigate was Apex Media's collusion with the municipal government."

"Which led straight to this." There was no mistaking the frustration in Gabe's voice. "It's all braided together."

"Then I need you to unbraid it and stick to the assignment I gave you."

The phone went silent, and a tense awkwardness set in. After a moment, Reynolds said, "Gabe, you there?"

"Yeah boss, I'm here."

"I need you to tell me you're dropping the water treatment story."

There was another awkward pause.

"Gabe?" Reynolds' voice had an edge to it.

"I'm dropping the water treatment story."

"Excellent. I need you to stay on track with the Apex story. It's going to be our lead later this week, so I need you to stay on task and keep focus."

"Is that all, Larry?"

"For now."

"Aye, aye, captain."

"Gabe, listen, you're a fine reporter with a lot of potential. But even the best of us needs to know when to toe the line."

"Anything else?" Gabe larded the question with sarcasm.

"That's it." Reynolds punched the End Call button.

Diana studied Maggie. It had been her story, and now Reynolds was all but quashing it. Maggie's eyes were lost in introspection.

After a moment, she let out a long breath, her shoulders sagged, but she kept quiet.

Diana's thoughts turned to Gabe. He was more than a fine reporter and someone who cared deeply about his craft. Reynolds couldn't spin Gabe in circles for long before he went somewhere else. And Reynolds' handling of the entire episode wasn't typical for him, either. Any other time and he would've sicced Gabe and Maggie on Apex Media's misdoings like a pair of attack dogs. But it was like he was someone else, only pretending to be Larry Reynolds.

From the periphery of her hearing, Diana sensed a growing noise, like a distant train gaining on her. Suddenly, the noise cascaded over her. The terrible racket drenched her with mind-numbing turbulence. She had the sensation of being pressed against a chair as it spun round and round. Through a window beside her, she glimpsed an aerial view of the ground rushing up to meet her.

Then, blackness.

Something warm dripped from her nose.

A voice called from far away. "Diana."

The voice got louder. Closer. It was Reynolds. "Diana, are you all right?"

She came to and realized that she was still in his office. She felt another warm drip from her nose and looked down to see blood spattering on her notepad. Embarrassed, she scrambled for her purse.

Reynolds handed her a box of tissues. "Diana, are you sure you're okay?"

Confused and still light-headed from the sensation of spinning around, she wiped her nose and looked away. Obviously, she was not okay.

"Everything checks out," the specialist said. Her smock was embroidered with *Central Medical Center*. "Your blood work and eye test, hearing test, all look good."

Diana felt fine, so the news wasn't surprising. Her nosebleed could've been from stress, or that her nasal passages had temporarily dried out. "Or" the specialist offered delicately, "picking your nose."

Diana cringed, embarrassed. "No, of course not."

The specialist tapped her tablet. "We've scheduled you for an MRI. Nurse Wyeth will see you there."

Nurse Wyeth was a flaxen-haired Amazon who escorted Diana to the MRI department on the hospital's second floor.

Since Diana arrived at the center in her cocktail dress, she had changed into an appropriate, though even more revealing, examination gown. Moving carefully to maintain her decorum, she climbed onto the MRI table and lay down.

She was of a divided mind about what she wanted to learn. On one hand, she didn't want the scan to find anything and, as a result, she'd be declared to be fine. But she also wished that the scan would find something, a definite anomaly the doctors could point to and announce that thanks to modern science, they could fix her problem, whatever it was. Hopefully, the hallucinations and strange dreams would then stop.

She relaxed, confident that medical technology could cure her.

The machine clicked and hummed, and the donut housing of the RF coil passed over her. Many people freaked out from the procedure, but Diana didn't mind. It was less invasive than a mammogram or a pap smear.

Diana sank into the moment and her consciousness floated, first through darkness, and then toward a flickering yellow light. The light intensified, and she sat on a laboratory table, the flickering light coming from an overhead bank of fluorescent lamps. She was now the same young girl again and dressed in drab overalls. Clips in her hair held wires against her scalp and connected these wires to a computer.

A man in a rumpled blue suit handed her a drawing pad and a pencil, then adjusted a blindfold around her eyes.

Diana pressed the point of the pencil against the pad and remained still. She let her mind open like a window, as she'd done many times before. She waited.

A picture developed in her mind like an image on film. She drew a building, first the walls, then the roof, the doors, and windows. The building had strange but interesting lines—lots of swooping curves—and its image was very distinctive.

In the room next to the laboratory, a man stared at a photo of a building, the exact building she was drawing.

Diana returned to her condo, the MRI tests negative. So, for all this time she had missed from work, her tests showed she was normal—in perfect health.

However, she had time to return to her office and get ready for tonight's show. Her heart racing in anticipation, she picked through outfits in her closet. Fashion pundits would scrutinize her dress and use that to prognosticate her fortunes as television's premier "news magazine" show anchor.

Her phone chimed. Larry Reynolds. She answered, chirping with enthusiasm. "Larry, I'll be there in an hour, plenty of time to review the program's notes."

"About that," he replied ominously. "Right after you left, corporate called and asked about you."

"Why would they call?"

"Well," he drawled, "when you checked in at Central Medical, their staff alerted HR."

"What!" Diana shouted. "What gives them the right?"

"Corporate has every right to know. It's that fitness clause in your contract, remember?"

"Yeah," she replied, resigned but not at all happy. "So you're postponing the segment?"

"Not exactly."

"Killing it? Listen, Larry, I did a lot of work and—"

"Diana, we're not killing it. We're still running it as tonight's lead."

"B... b...but..." Diana's thoughts spun in a tight circle.

"Anya Sullivan is tonight's anchor. Maggie is helping her." Reynolds segued into how corporate was deeply concerned about Diana's health and that it was for the better...*blah, blah, blah.*

The headshot of the raven-haired beauty burst into Diana's mind. Sullivan was sexy as hell and sharp, but she didn't have Diana's investigative chops. And Dan Talbot was Diana's story. Reeling off balance, Diana dropped onto her bed. Just like that, they had pulled the rug right from under her feet.

Her spacious condo shrank around her. It seemed like the entire building was ready to collapse on top of her. She pictured her health and her professional life crumbling into ruin, and there was nothing she could do but watch helplessly. Her stomach heaved, and bile washed up the back of her throat. She scurried to her bathroom and threw up.

CHAPTER NINE

*I*n your world, the dark forces from several other worlds use managers, known as "Controllers," to implement systems and procedures to keep your world functioning and under their control. They have blocked contact, isolating you from other worlds, and created a different, nefarious agenda.

A sister world that once hosted and then defeated these same Controllers sent one of their own to wake you up, so you can rise and stop the subjugation before it is too late.

Diana lounged on her bed, heeding Larry Reynolds' advice that she remain at home and take it easy. Resigning herself to the inevitable, she switched on the flat-screen TV facing her bed and relaxed to watch tonight's show of *World Primetime Now*. Though they'd shunted her aside, for the time being anyway, she wished the show success in the ratings since soon, hopefully, she'd be back center stage. The credits sparkled in dramatic tempo to the award-winning theme song. Diana hummed the catchy tune.

The camera focused on Anya Sullivan. She appeared composed, elegantly coiffed, and fashionably dressed. Her shapely legs were demurely crossed at the ankles and tucked under her chair. Her large brown eyes were locked on the camera. Diana had to admit that

Anya captured that rare gift of looking sexy, smart, and trustworthy. Diana smiled, expecting the journalistic hammer blows Anya was about to deliver against Apex Media.

"Hi, I'm Anya Sullivan," she began, "and welcome to *World Primetime Now*. Later this week, we'll be returning to our coverage of Dan Talbot's departure from Great Global Media."

Diana smiled; her story on Talbot was still in play.

Anya continued, "Tonight, in our lead segment, we're going to focus on breaking developments in the Apex Media-City of Columbus, Ohio controversy." One corner of the screen showed downtown Columbus overlaid with the Apex Media logo.

Controversy? Diana straightened, a tiny alarm going off in her head. Based on what Gabe and Maggie had shared with her, what Apex Media and the city of Columbus had done was no controversy but an out-and-out scandal.

"We begin our story by reviewing the misunderstandings in the deals between Apex Media and the municipal government."

Misunderstandings? It was collusion, plain and simple.

"We've documented evidence in that Apex Media took part in the city's erroneous accounting concerning the municipal water supply."

Erroneous accounting? The scandal was more than that. Diana listened, waiting for Anya to mention falsified test results and the impacts to public health. Instead, all that Anya recounted were issues regarding funds exchanged through misplaced receipts and inaccurate invoices. What should've been a monumental exposé of corruption had been deflated into a simple and banal tale about sloppy accounting.

Diana glared at Anya's image on the screen. *What?*

What Anya was relating was not even close to what Diana, Maggie, and Gabe had presented to Reynolds.

They had surely tuned in to the program. What was their reaction? Diana reached for her smartphone on the nightstand to text them and discovered that its screen was shattered.

She stared at the phone, shocked, confused at when and how it had been broken.

Gabe Mendoza watched *World Primetime Now* from an armchair in his hotel room. Anya's tame account of the report he had given to Larry Reynolds left him reeling in bewilderment, then frustration. And those low emotions fell to outright disgust when Anya announced that the follow-on story would reveal the trade secrets of professional dog grooming. *Dog grooming! Is that what his story would segue into?* What Gabe handed over to Reynolds was journalistic dynamite. His report should've blown Apex Media to smithereens, and instead, what the public received had all the impact of a Nerf bat.

Gabe grabbed his phone and texted Maggie: What happened? The story is not true. Whose side is GGM on?

Expecting an immediate reply, he turned off the TV and palmed his phone. A minute passed. Why wasn't Maggie replying?

Impatient and roiling with anger, Gabe decided on the next most logical course of action. He would drown his woes with alcohol.

The hotel bar resembled any other bar of any other hotel in the price range, plush leather seats arranged in groups to give the illusion of privacy, while tall stools lined the bar counter. Shelves of liquor stood in front of a mirror, which reflected the patrons and the two barkeeps dressed in the hotel uniform. Flat-screen televisions hung from the ceiling, several tuned to sports channels and one to news.

Gabe was working on his second scotch-and-soda. His thoughts churned on how, even to an insider like himself, journalism was a game. He swallowed the booze, enjoying the way it burned on the way down; it was like drinking liquid penance.

An older gentleman asked if the adjacent stool was taken.

"Help yourself," Gabe replied, though there were plenty of empty stools scattered around the bar. Out of reflex, he performed a quick study of the stranger.

For a guest in this hotel, the man was slovenly dressed and needed a shave. His shirt looked made of cheap polyester and with its garish yellow and green stripes, didn't come close to matching his gray sports coat—flecked with stains—or his tattered jeans. His dirty cross-trainers looked ready to fall apart at the seams. Overall, Gabe noted, this stranger appeared as if he had lifted the ensemble from a donation bin at the Salvation Army. Because of the ragged, salt-and-pepper hair, Gabe guessed the stranger to be in his mid-sixties.

The stranger signaled the barkeep and asked for a Manhattan. He kept quiet, which Gabe understood to mean that he wanted time alone.

When the Manhattan arrived, the stranger cupped the glass in one hand and looked at Gabe. "I think they think we are stupid."

"What do you mean?" Gabe replied, surprised by the abrupt outburst.

The stranger pointed to the closest TV and then to Gabe's smartphone. "The messages broadcast to us are being manipulated in many ways and by multiple means. It's all done to create artificial realities everywhere, and so things are not what they seem. We are allowing ourselves to be controlled, mostly subconsciously, and the ones who think they are not being fooled are the ones who are easier to fool." He sipped his drink. "Liars control the truth. You can get anyone to believe anything if you want to. We are being brainwashed, and it doesn't help that we allow ourselves to become addicted to the media and its fanciful trappings."

Gabe stared at the stranger and thought about the coincidence. Here he'd been stewing in resentment, and this man plops beside him and expresses exactly what had been gnawing at him. Gabe held up his glass and wondered if the alcohol was making him hear things. Perhaps. And in that case, maybe he needed to hear more. He rattled the ice in his empty glass. "Barkeep, another one."

He turned to the stranger and continued, "What you are saying is true." He counted the fingers on his left hand and then splayed the fingers to the stranger to illustrate his point. "Exactly five corporations, or to be more precise about it, five international conglomerates control the media. Television. Radio. The internet. Print. Social media. They gather all those venues under the corporate leash. Sure, there are smaller independents, but the large outlets marginalize and throttle them. Whenever one of them makes a splash in social media, for example, they are bought out or denounced as 'fake news' and thus purged."

The stranger withdrew a plastic ballpoint pen from inside his sport coat and drew inter-connected circles on a napkin. "It's worse than that." He looked around. "The number of people who control those corporations could fit in this room. The mainstream media set the agenda for our society, and it would be difficult to overstate the power in their hands."

Gabe sighed. "What we need are more alternative streams of communication to counteract their stranglehold. But like I said, the corporations not only control the media but also the venues available to the public. You say something they don't like, and they'll cancel you."

The stranger said, "True. The only way we are ever going to shake off the control they have established is by winning the information war." He swiveled on his stool to focus attention on Gabe. "We are in the middle of a quiet war. It's a war with silent weapons of deception and literally a constant battle for hearts and minds," his eyes opened wide to express his intensity, "and beyond."

The words "and beyond," echoed in Gabe's mind as if they were an omen. "I hear you," he replied. "But I'm stuck. My company, West Coast Broadcasting is now owned by Great Global Media, which is owned by one of those conglomerates and one of the largest investment firms in the world, and they micro-manage everything we present."

The stranger nodded. "Like I just said."

Gabe anchored his elbows on the bar counter. Despite his down-at-the-heels appearance, the stranger radiated trust and confidence, and Gabe felt free to share what was on his mind. "Let me tell you what's eating me." Gabe raised a glass to the TV screen. "At my job, I discovered while on assignment into corporate-municipal corruption that a city government has been manipulating test results to hide that its water supply is being contaminated with high amounts of fluoride and other harmful chemicals. That made me think. Why? I thought fluoride in the public water supply was a good thing. If so, why cover up what you're doing? That's…" Gabe let the thought hang.

"That's what?" the stranger asked.

Gabe fortified himself with a belt of the fresh scotch-and-soda. "Not what, but when. That's *when* I did a little research into fluoride. Thanks to what the media tells us, we believe that fluoride is good for us. It strengthens our teeth, plus the amount in our water is not anywhere near harmful."

He set the glass down and locked eyes with the stranger. "But this is what I've learned. Fluoride is a toxic chemical that can accumulate in the body and brain, causing harm to enzymes and producing serious health problems, including neurological and endocrine dysfunction. It can lower IQ, interfere with the kidneys, damage the thyroid, and may increase the risk of developing Alzheimer's disease. It's practically a lethal poison."

Disgusted, Gabe shook his head. "We're not just drinking and bathing in it, it's packed into our toothpaste, our food, the nonstick finish on our cookware. We're not being told the truth about its dangers. Rather, they keep the truth from us."

"As I said, liars control the truth." The stranger turned the cocktail napkin over and sketched the outline of a human head with its brain. "Have you heard of what it does to your cognitive thinking?" He tapped the tip of his pen against the center of the brain. "They have proven that fluoride stunts mental development in children and it reduces the production of hormones needed for male and female fertility."

Gabe cupped his glass and relished its icy touch. "If fluoride is so bad, then why do 'they' allow it?"

The stranger again tapped his pen on his sketch. "Have you heard of the pineal gland?"

"Yeah, it's in your brain somewhere."

The stranger held up his right hand, clenched into a fist except for his little finger. "The pineal gland is between your left and right hemispheres and is tiny, maybe this big." He used his thumb to show the size along his extended pinky. "But its value is enormous to your development and health. It's part of your endocrine system and secretes melatonin, which you need to regulate your circadian rhythms—meaning your sleep cycles—and your sexual health."

The stranger capped his pen and returned it to his pocket. "But above all, the pineal gland is often known as the third eye and allows us to perceive beyond our normal senses, and even into other worlds and dimensions. They call it the sixth sense. And it's at the pineal gland where fluoride interferes with these abilities."

"How does that happen?" Gabe asked.

"Because of fluoride, the pineal gland is calcified, and that weakens the mind-body-spirit connection. Sure, you hear the same, see the same, but your brain cannot process those stimuli and, more importantly, connect the dots. Of all your body's systems, the one most affected by fluoride is the pineal gland."

"And that's done deliberately?"

The stranger raised an eyebrow. "What do you think?"

Gabe looked away and leaned away from the bar counter. He'd come here to draw a curtain of alcohol between himself and the world, and despite his two previous drinks, he seemed sober and clearheaded. "What can you tell me about EDCs?"

"You mean Endocrine Disruptive Chemicals?"

"Yes."

"Why do you ask?" the stranger pressed.

"Besides fluorides, they also pumped EDCs into the water supply that I investigated."

"Those also enter the water supply through runoff containing fuels, fertilizers, soap, detergents, and fracking," the stranger explained. "They affect the thyroid gland, which affects growth and the way your body reacts. But the worst of the EDCs are phthalates, which are ubiquitous in many plastics."

Gabe replied, "I've read studies that proved phthalates are harmless, or at least not the threat some make them out to be."

The stranger chuckled. "And who do you think paid for those studies?"

Gabe knew the answer. His mind went *Aha!* What he had done with the Apex Media-Columbus story was connect dots the corporations did not want connected. Their advertising money ruled everything. Although Great Global Media and Apex Media were sworn competitors and keen on driving each other out of business or buying each other out, they had a vested interest in maintaining the status quo. He'd been sent to report on a simple story about people's hands being caught in the till, and what he'd discovered was evidence of a massive coverup involving fluoride and EDCs, all done with the intent to both dumb down and reduce the human population, if what this stranger said was true.

The stranger added, "Let me tell you something that many people don't know. The Nazis put fluoride in the water in the concentration camps to keep their captives docile and compliant and therefore easier to control. This is all about control. They don't want us to realize what is really going on. They want us suppressed, unable to resist, and of course, having less of us makes it easier to control. There are many ways we are being controlled and manipulated. Introducing fluoride and EDCs into our water is one of many ways. When we realize we are being controlled, things will change.

"Eventually they want to control our physical movement, and reward those who comply, and punish those that don't with suffering. One trail leads to Eden."

"You mean Second Eden Technologies?"

"Who else?" the stranger answered.

The avalanche of revelations stunned Gabe, and it took him a moment before he could ask, "Who are the 'they' you are talking about?"

"They are sinister and behind everything. I think we can group them into what we call Controllers."

"Controllers?" Gabe rejoined. "Sounds like conspiracy theory stuff."

The stranger replied, "Or perhaps conspiracy fact."

"How can it be fact, and how can this be proved to be true considering all the many conspiracies out there?" Gabe asked.

"Do you know that *the term conspiracy theory was invented by the CIA to prevent disbelief of official government stories and now, of course, that strategy is used by the CIA-controlled media to* shut up skeptics by branding them conspiracy theorists?"

"No, I didn't." Gabe looked at the televisions hanging behind the bar and then at the stranger, who gulped what was left in his glass and swiveled on his stool to gaze intently at him. "The greatest conspiracy is that no one knows these Controllers are hanging on to their power by a thread. They use teams to develop propaganda and create wars to keep us distracted and numbed to inaction. They do this so we don't realize that if the thread breaks, they would lose their power. Young man, we have to change our thinking from these doubts, these fears, and these concerns as they are but a distraction from the truth. We must think from the standpoint of the eternal truths, that we are sovereign and have the sole right to rule ourselves. We have to be careful about how we program our subconscious mind, or let others do our thinking for us."

The stranger's words unspooled in a slight slur. "You want to know the truth? Then go to the source of the truth, and you will know."

The stranger slapped money on the bar, then slid off the stool. He stood and suddenly poked Gabe in the forehead.

At the touch, Diana flashed through Gabe's thoughts. The stranger's face appeared to contort, as if changing into the visage of another man. Gabe blinked, feeling that the scotch had at last caught up to him.

The stranger scanned the room like he was searching for something. He nodded as if finding what he was looking for, then turned once more to Gabe and said, "Wake up! It's not as it seems. There is only one way out of their great web."

"How?"

"First, we must stop the hypocrisy!" With that, the stranger staggered toward the men's room.

Gabe sat confused and pondered what the stranger meant. And was it a coincidence that he had appeared when he did? For all they had discussed and the bond they had established, Gabe had never once thought to ask the stranger's name.

Reading his watch, Gabe decided it was time to turn in. He paid his tab and, feeling the need to relieve himself, proceeded to the men's room. There, he'd reacquaint himself with the stranger and get his name and contact info.

But when Gabe stepped into the men's room, he was alone. How could this be? He'd been watching the door all this time, and there was no way for the stranger to slip out unnoticed. Gabe checked the stalls, and to see if there was another exit, but there wasn't.

The stranger had vanished.

CHAPTER TEN

You could think of us as a kind of intergalactic secret agent. My colleagues on assignments in other worlds can also materialize at will and be in multiple places at the same time. Let me begin to reveal how.

On one of my earlier assignments, I helped one of your famous poets with his works. He then wrote, "you are not a drop in the ocean; you are the entire ocean in a drop."

You exist in this ocean of energy, made up of the same energy as you are. Through observation and research, it is proven that everything in the universe is a vibrating frequency of energy, which then combines with the energy of similar frequencies to create the physical world or your perceived reality. Atoms are in a constant state of motion, and depending on the speed of these atoms, things appear as solid, liquid, or gas. Therefore, everything around you is not solid things, but forms made up of pure, vibrating energy—all connected.

A state of absolute terror engulfed Diana. She jerked her head from side to side, trying to comprehend where she was and what was happening. The noise was deafening, a tornadolike roar of turbine engines and whirling rotor blades. She comprehended enough to realize she was in the back of a helicopter as it spun around, out of control, mere feet above the ground, seconds from crashing. Centrifugal force pinned her to the corner, and she struggled to climb into a nearby seat and buckle in. That was the only action that could save her from certain death during the impact.

A bright light appeared on the right and it seemed to pulsate, holding steadily close to the spinning helicopter. The door beside her slid open, and for a miraculous instant, the helicopter stopped spinning. Hearing a voice shout, "Go! Go!" she lunged out the door.

The momentum flipped her through the air and she slammed on the ground, landing on her back. The blow knocked the breath out of her and as she gasped for air, her heartbeat slowed from a break-neck tempo to a sluggish *thump-thump*. But it wasn't her heart rate that had reduced speed, but time itself.

She gazed at the belly of the helicopter as it hovered above her, backlit by a bright light. The helicopter's rotors pinwheeled in slow motion, the individual blades slicing in front of the light to produce a staccato strobe effect.

A figure leaned over her, the silhouette of a man haloed by the flickering light.

The scene was beyond surreal. First, she was in the out-of-control helicopter. Then she hurled herself to safety. Now the helicopter seemed frozen above her as time decelerated to the speed of dripping molasses. And there was that pulsating light, then the appearance of this stranger.

A man's voice wafted through her mind, and she knew the voice belonged to the stranger.

"Wake up! It's not as it seems."

She blinked. The man was gone. She gulped and inhaled. Her heartbeat sped up, and the helicopter's rotor blades blurred to normal speed. The helicopter zoomed out of view.

A tremendous *boom!* shook the air and the ground. An enormous fireball and clouds of smoke roiled across the sky. The heat and pressure of the blast washed over her and pushed the odor of burning jet fuel up her nostrils.

The fire was about to engulf her, and she'd scrambled onto her hands and knees to crawl away when the scent became that of alcohol.

That of the alcohol encountered in a doctor's office. The abrupt shift in smells jolted her thoughts.

Then it was as if her mind had been stuck and was now knocked free.

She had the sensation of a giant sucking sound surrounding her, as though she were being torn from the fabric of time and space itself. It was as if she was being dragged along a tunnel through curtains of memories.

Of her parents from childhood, smiling at her as she whisked by.

Then she was holding pinecones in the dark forest when she saw her father, Joseph, on his side, dead.

But before the reaction to that terrible revelation sank in, she was sitting on a laboratory bench, a harness of wires clipped to her hair, the metal connections cold against her scalp.

But as she looked around to determine where she was, bright lights shined in her face and she was dancing around fires on a stage, moving to the harsh primal beat of drums as cool night air prickled the skin of her naked body.

As she recoiled in horror, she found herself at her anchor desk, facing a teleprompter and a bank of video cameras. The horror morphed into surprise, then anticipation and pride as she was about to start another broadcast of *World Primetime Now*.

Then she was flung forward in her safety belts as she jammed on the brakes of her Mercedes. John Herald strolled in her path, aware but unperturbed; continuing on his way, he glanced at her, saying, "Be careful."

She exhaled in relief that she hadn't run him over and when she looked up, she was back in her condo, that creepy Anthony Briscane in a creepy red suit talking to her about his obsession with a thumb drive.

When she was about to tell him to get lost, he became Larry Reynolds and she was with him in his office at Great Global Media, Reynolds behind his desk, her staring at him.

As Reynolds talked, his voice became feminine and the light in the room changed and suddenly, Reynolds was now Maggie LaClair.

Maggie was also talking to Diana, but what Diana heard was a voice in her head that emphasized, "The quiet war has begun, ready or not."

Diana was about to respond out loud, "What do you mean?" when she realized she was back at the crash site, watching the plump woman who had been watching her in return.

Suddenly Diana moved in a new direction. Instead of being dragged backward, she was on her back, on a platform rolling in the direction the top of her head was pointing. She was on a gurney, tugged along by people in scrubs as she glided beneath a ceiling lit by fluorescent lamps.

The illumination in the corridor got brighter and brighter until the light fused into one luminescent ball, floating right over her. The light grew points, so it resembled a star. The light remained fixed for a moment, then grew and expanded. Diana heard, "Get their attention before it's too late." But the voice was faint, like an echo fading into the distance.

The light above her collapsed on itself, shrinking ever smaller until it compressed into a white dot that vanished to blackness.

The sucking sound ceased. Diana popped her eyes open. She stared at a ceiling, a checkerboard pattern of acoustical tile and square light fixtures. The smell of medical alcohol returned, though not as strongly as before. Something beeped to her left. Turning her head toward the sound, she noticed she was in a hospital bed. She lifted her left arm and discovered an IV taped to her skin. They had cinched tight a plastic cuff with an electronic sensor to her wrist. Her gaze continued from the cuff to a monitor on a nearby rolling cabinet. The monitor's display showed her vitals and beeped in tempo to her heart rate. A female nurse stood by the door, which was closed, and she was busy entering information onto a data tablet.

Diana flexed her arms and tried to stretch, but she felt both tight and weak, as if her joints had stiffened and her muscles atrophied. Her gaze swiveled in all directions as she tried to figure out where she was.

In a hospital. But which one? And why?

Seconds ago—*or was it years*—she had been thrown out of a helicopter just as it was about to crash. But she had survived, and a mysterious stranger had appeared to tell her to wake up.

The memory made her blink. She was definitely awake.

But between when that stranger vanished and now, it was as if Diana had been pulled through layers and layers of dimensions that evoked memories she didn't know she had.

As she struggled to sit up, weary, confused, clumsy, her bedcovers rustled. The noise drew the attention of the nurse.

She turned to stare at Diana, dumbstruck, as if witnessing the impossible. Without a word, the nurse set her tablet on top of the monitor and groped for an intercom by the door. Eyes fixed on Diana, she spoke into the intercom, "Dr. Turner, room 314. Stat."

Who was Dr. Turner? Perhaps he would answer her questions. Diana continued to scope out the hospital room. Cabinets lined one wall. Oxygen tanks and high-tech electronic consoles stood on trolleys. A television—turned off for now—hung from another wall.

The door swung open. The nurse stepped aside. A doctor hustled in, his black skin a dramatic contrast against his white physician's smock. The ceiling lights reflected momentarily across his receding hairline and his spectacles. His astonished expression told Diana that something was very wrong with her situation. But what?

The name Dr. E Turner on his ID badge confirmed he was the Dr. Turner the nurse had just summoned. He took cautious steps toward her, as if worried she remained in a very delicate state and a wrong move could send her spinning back into critical condition.

The nurse offered him the data tablet and whispered in his ear. His gaze was still riveted on Diana. He nodded and swiped the tablet, then studied the monitor. He handed the tablet back to the nurse and stepped closer.

"Diana Willis," he said.

She gazed at him, puzzled that he called her by that name. Instinctively, she replied, "No, I'm Diana Star," and hearing her own voice surprised her.

"Diana Star?" The doctor glanced at the nurse. The two leaned close and whispered for a moment. The nurse made a note on the tablet and showed it to the doctor. He nodded and turned back to Diana. "How do you feel?"

The answer escaped her. She did not understand how she felt, or how she should feel. Outwardly, she felt stiff and fatigued, but inside it was as if her consciousness was assembling itself bit by bit, like her memories were tiny pieces of magnets pulling themselves together.

"I'm not sure," she answered.

Turner's expression softened with compassion. "That's understandable. For you see—" He cleared his throat. "You've been in a coma for almost two months."

Diana wasn't shocked. Her mind remained too scrambled to contemplate what it meant to be in a coma for such a long time. She scrolled through her memories, going back and forth, back and forth, until she landed upon the moment when she was in the Great Global Media Building to find John Herald before he flew off in his helicopter.

Was it the same helicopter she had escaped from?

All of her new recollections washed back on her, and she shut her eyes to hold them at a distance and remain in the present. For a moment she hesitated before opening her eyes, worried that she might yet again tumble through Never-Never Land.

Thankfully, this time, when she opened them, Turner was still in the room, looking right at her.

"What happened?" she asked, raising her arm to show him the plastic cuff on her wrist.

"I'm afraid I'm not at liberty to answer," he replied, and began backtracking to the door.

"Then who is?" she insisted, her voice filled with frustration.

Turner yanked the door open and, as he pivoted out, he pulled a phone from his smock pocket.

After he left, Diana stared at the nurse but didn't press her for answers, as she didn't appear to be any more forthcoming than Turner.

Diana let her head settle on the pillow and wondered if she was back on the terra firma of her reality, or was she drifting again through more imagined space?

She listened to her heart's beep on the monitor as she stared at the ceiling, marveling at the insignificant quotidian details within her perception. The dimpled acoustical ceiling tiles, the dead bugs inside the dull white panels of the light fixtures. The distant hum of air conditioning. The murmur of voices in the outside hall.

The door opened abruptly. Turner reentered, accompanied by two men. They wore dark suits, and their name badges had a pale green tag attached, labeled *Special Admittance.*

"Diana," Turner said, "this is Special Agent Cal Brock of the FBI."

The taller, more handsome of the two nodded.

"And Tony Serani of the NTSB."

"NTSB?" Diana asked.

"National Transportation Safety Board," the portly and shorter man replied.

The two men radiated a serious manner, as if they were here on urgent business. Brock turned toward Turner and the nurse. "We'd like some privacy."

The doctor grasped the nurse by the elbow and steered her toward the door. Brock and Serani remained quiet as they waited for the door to close.

Serani retrieved a small device from inside his sports coat and clipped it to his breast pocket. "I'm recording our conversation." He touched a button on the device and a small red light on the front flashed on. Serani said to no one in particular, "We're in Central Medical Center Hospital, room 314, with Diana Willis. She is awake and appears coherent." Then he addressed her directly. "Dr. Turner shared that you've been in a coma for fifty-six days."

"Apparently," Diana answered. "But my name is Diana Star."

Both men appeared confused.

"You are Diana Willis," Brock asked, "the TV presenter of *World Primetime Now*, correct?"

She nodded and wondered what was going on. After hesitating, both men seemed to brush this aside and continued.

"I don't suppose you remember much," Brock said.

"I remember a lot."

Brock and Serani traded surprised looks, but when Diana elaborated, "It's just that what I remember doesn't make much sense," the two men exhaled in frustration.

"Is that bad?" Diana asked. "Good?"

"Neither. We'd like you to remember as much as you can," Brock said. "But I need an explanation why you say your name is now Diana Star."

"I don't know where to begin. Perhaps if you tell me how I got here and then we can proceed from there."

Serani nodded. "Sounds like a plan. You were found staggering along a beach several miles from where the helicopter crashed in the Mt. Tamalpais park area."

"So, there was a helicopter crash?" she asked.

Serani arched an eyebrow. "You don't remember?"

Diana massaged her forehead as if she could dislodge her memories into a coherent whole. "I remember some details from the helicopter. I thought I was going to die when I fell out at the last second. Then…" She hesitated, worried that the next thoughts—of the helicopter pausing in slow motion above her, of the mysterious stranger—were but figments of her imagination.

"A hiker found you on the beach," Brock said. "She thought you had fallen from a nearby cliff as you were covered in blood."

"When my people—" Serani began.

Diana interrupted him. "Your people?"

"From the NTSB," he continued. "When they arrived at the crash site, they found several of your belongings in the wreckage's vicinity, showing you had been on board before the crash."

"So, I was in the helicopter?"

"You were. A video surveillance camera from the rooftop helipad on the Great Global Media Building recorded you getting on board just before takeoff."

Diana shook her head. The memories were at first hazy and the more she dwelled on them, the sharper they came into focus.

First, exiting the stairway door onto the rooftop heliport and halting a second. From that open vista, the panorama seemed limitless, the city fusing with the green hills and ocean. She expected to see a fireguard watching the helicopter, but there was none.

The helicopter had already started, the turbine engines blaring, the rumble from the rotor disk, the fierce whirlwind from the blades rustling her clothing and hair. The nose of the helicopter faced away from her and she used this opportunity to dash under the tail boom. From another assignment, she was familiar with the CT-11. An emergency exit at the rear of the fuselage allowed access to the passenger cabin. The tail rotor spun menacingly past her head.

The engines roared, and the helicopter grew light on its wheels. She had but seconds to scramble on board before it took off. *Now! Now!*

She rushed for the exit door and snapped the latches. The door swung down, stopping its arc with a taut retaining cable. The door had rungs of sorts, which she grasped and used to pull herself up until she could put her feet on the door.

She passed through the hatchway in a stoop. The cabin seats were empty. At the far end of the cabin, on the other side of a bulkhead, she saw John Herald sitting in the pilot's seat, his figure silhouetted by the sky beaming through the canopy frame.

The helicopter swayed upward. She wanted to sit in one of the plush leather seats but worried that if she moved forward, Herald would notice her.

She crouched, hauled at the cable to secure the exit door, and sighed in relief for being such a good stowaway.

After that, she couldn't remember much of the helicopter trip except for the terrifying moments just before she was thrown out and the subsequent crash.

"Somehow, miraculously," Serani said, "you had been ejected at the right time and the right place."

"If I was at the right place," Diana countered, "I wouldn't have been on the helicopter at all."

"But you were, and it was a miracle you survived," Serani replied.

"Which leads us to the matter at hand." Brock took a step forward.

There's more? Diana tried to scoot up in bed but found that she was too weak to move easily.

"The helicopter pilot was John Herald," Brock said.

"That's correct."

"But we have not found his body," Serani added. "Neither at the crash site, and in the eight weeks since you've been in this coma, anywhere else. He's vanished."

John Herald's body hadn't been found? But she remembered being told. By whom? She recalled it had been Briscane, the time he was in her apartment. Wearing the bizarre red suit, the devil's costume. Or had that happened? Had it been a dream from her coma?

"Something wrong?" It was Brock, looking right at her.

Diana pressed her fingers against her temple. "Sorry. It's that coming out of the coma, my mind seems full of cobwebs." She barely knew what had happened to her, much less to John Herald.

"Understandable." Brock nodded. "His disappearance is one of the biggest FBI mysteries in years," he continued, and advanced another step toward her bed. "So, the questions are, Diana Willis—Diana *Star*, what happened to John Herald, and why were you in the helicopter with him?"

Part II
MISSIONS

CHAPTER ELEVEN

You must realize liars control the truth. They are going to target your awareness so that you remain unaware. The silent weapons that the Controllers use are keeping you undisciplined, ignorant, confused, and distracted. They know that you co-create reality based on what your mind believes to be true and real. So they tell you what they want you to see and hear. It is done so gradually, so slightly, that the change in your behaviors and perception is unnoticeable. If you don't know that you have been programmed, it is because you have been programmed. That is what they want. That is their primary weapon in this quiet, imperceptible war.

Sunlight streamed through partially opened curtains and into a low-lit room. Two large ceiling fans swirled a blend of dust and cigar smoke in this light. The room was stately and expansive. A large and long table filled most of the room. On a dark wood-paneled wall hung several paintings, and on the opposite wall was a series of built-in shelves containing old leather-bound books, military artifacts, a moon rock, and an unusually colored crystal. Spotlights in an alcove illuminated photos of General Wayne Carcano with the President of the United States of America and other world leaders.

At the far end of the room, around a fireplace, were large red leather wingback chairs. Carcano was sitting in one of these chairs, holding a tumbler in one hand and a large cigar in the other. Instead of a uniform, he wore casual clothes, attire that didn't blunt his usual powerful, commanding manner.

He growled, "We need to move forward. Diana Willis shouldn't have survived, and Briscane knows this changes everything for us."

Reginald Deighton was standing a few feet away and paused his conversation with Jeff Kennedy. The dozen other men in the room suddenly quieted and moved in closer.

Carcano placed the tumbler on the end table beside his chair and sat upright. "She served her purpose like the others have all these years, and we got what we needed from her as one of our programmed media representatives."

"What's next?" Deighton asked.

Carcano took a big puff of his cigar. "Willis is one of Briscane's and as her main handler, he will trigger an alternative plan to slow her down. This will turn the world against her. She must be discredited."

A tall, slender, bald, and serious-looking man with a narrow thin-lipped mouth and heavy, black-rimmed glasses abruptly interjected, "Intelligence is tracking Herald."

He was the only one who abstained from drinking or smoking. He was standing back from the rest of the group but moved in a little closer as he continued. "How he disappeared or even survived such a crash is mysterious. We think he may have been able to save Willis before the aircraft went down. The FBI is investigating, and I will make sure they keep after Herald and stay within their boundaries. Intelligence thinks they know where his secret documents might be, and we will try to get them. We must consider all options."

Carcano moved forward in his chair, picked up his glass, swigged the rest of his liquor, and rose to attention like he was addressing a formation of soldiers. "Gentlemen, we know the stakes. We have stopped this many times before with all the resources we have available to us. I made it clear to Briscane and I want us to understand too, that if she gets her powers back and reconnects with her past, everything we've been working for will be over."

Carcano paused, put the cigar into the ashtray, and then looked at each of the other men before continuing. "We cannot let that happen under any circumstances. Do I make myself clear?"

A collective nod and murmurs of assent circulated among the other men. Carcano noted that Nemer Indarte, the bald, slender man with those unusual features, had quietly slipped out of the room. Throughout his military career, Carcano had met few men who disturbed him with their underlying cold-blooded menace, as if they were carnivorous insects in human form. He rebuked himself that monsters like Nemer Indarte were necessary for his purposes. He let the chill pass, then leaned toward Deighton and spoke in a muted voice. "We have another problem to take care of."

The words *Diana, wake up. It's not as it seems* filled her sleeping mind again. For three consecutive nights, the stranger's voice haunted her dreams.

She jerked her body as she felt a warm hand squeezing her shoulder, then awoke in her hospital room.

A nurse stared at her. "Miss Willis, Agent Brock is here to see you again."

Diana blinked and kindled her thoughts. She was still in the hospital. It had been eight days since she had risen from her coma. Being comatose for many weeks had caused her muscles to atrophy. Her physical recovery had gotten easier with each day, but it seemed as if it was going to take a long time to get strong again. Her routine comprised electrical muscle stimulation, Pilates-type exercises, assisted walking, water and breath therapy, and a regimen of good nutrition.

Because of her celebrity status, her recovery was all over the internet and mainstream media. Great Global Media hired Kelly Foster, a public relations assistant, so that when Diana was not in physical therapy, she could get help with interviews, updates on her social media accounts, and catching up on the news that had transpired over the last nine weeks. Great Global Media and *World Primetime Now* reported on her recovery and their ratings skyrocketed. One news article, Diana Willis - TV Darling Survives Death, caused another media stir, and her social media accounts reached into the millions. Media outlets offered her special deals for an exclusive interview as soon as she was well enough. However, GGM had forced her to decline them all because of her contract. Her show would get exclusive rights when the time was right.

This newfound fame mattered little. It was her mental state that worried Diana the most. She was apathetic and somewhat depressed, and she had this gnawing feeling in her solar plexus that something was not right. What were these strange and fragmented memories now lodged in her mind? It seemed like there were two Dianas. She was as surprised as her doctor and FBI Agent Brock when she said her last name was Star and not Willis. It was even stranger when she signed a medical disclosure as *Alexandra Diana Star.*

Diana grimaced from pain as she reached to the bedside table for a notepad and pen. As part of her recovery, her psychologist suggested she write down as many memories as she could when they entered her mind. The vivid and strange procession of déjà vu since coming out of the coma had been the catalyst. The sensation of the giant sucking sound surrounding her, as she was being dragged along a tunnel of fragmented recollections, was something that lingered in her mind.

What do these strange memories mean? Did I die and then return? And where is John Herald?

It seemed both significant and yet very confusing. "Wake up! It's not as it seems!" had been haunting her in this recurring dream. She made notes before she forgot. As she thumbed through her notepad to find a clean page, she was drawn to one of the twelve numbered circles she had created around these memories. She read what was inside circle twelve:

I remembered the illumination in the corridor getting brighter and brighter as I was being wheeled on the gurney. I remembered the light fused into one luminescent ball, floating right over me. It was so mesmerizing to see the light transform into a star and watching as it remained fixed for a moment, then grow and expand as I heard, "get their attention before it's too late."

The note prompted these thoughts. *Why was the voice faint, like an echo fading into the distance? The same voice in my dreams. What was the significance of the light collapsing on itself and then shrinking ever smaller until it compressed into a white dot that vanished? Whose attention am I supposed to get, and why? What does it mean, before it's too late? Too late for what?*

A knock at the door startled her.

"Come in."

The door opened, and Agent Brock walked in. "Good morning, Ms. …?" He grinned. "Willis? Star?"

"Diana is fine." She sat up in bed, warmed by his presence. He seemed sincere, trustworthy, and equally important, someone—she suspected though she didn't know how—whose help she might someday need.

He walked toward the chair beside her bed. "How is the recovery going?"

"A little stronger every day." Her gaze scanned the room, and she sighed. "The staff has been very helpful and I couldn't ask for a better doctor. But I want to leave and go home. They want to move me over to a special center temporarily, but I insisted we can do the recovery at my home."

They locked eyes for a moment, connecting until a text alert from inside Brock's jacket startled them. "Sorry," he muttered as he unbuttoned his suit jacket and retrieved the phone. Reading the message, he frowned and typed a quick response. "Something's come up so I can't stay as long as I wanted." He slipped the phone back into his jacket and pointed to the chair. "May I sit?"

"Please."

Brock pushed the chair closer to the bed and sat. "I wanted to update you on two discoveries in the investigation and ask for your help again with anything else you can remember." He readied a small notebook.

Diana asked, "Have there been any developments with John Herald?"

Brock looked up from his notebook. "I shouldn't be telling you this, but you may get a visit from another investigator outside of the bureau. It gets complicated, but all I can say is that Herald may have been an intelligence officer and his investigation is being handled separately."

"Intelligence, as in the CIA?"

"Yes, or one of the other agencies, I don't know."

"Can you give me a name?"

Brock shook his head. "I don't know."

Diana believed him, but as to the rest of what he had just shared, she wasn't as shocked as she was aggravated. "You are telling me that John Herald, Executive Liaison of Great Global Media, is possibly a CIA officer or something else like that?"

"I can't say anything else." He hesitated as if he wanted to explain more, then lowered his eyes to the notepad. His tone changed, becoming official. "The flight plan revealed that Mr. Herald was heading towards Monte Rio, and it appeared to coincide with the annual event at Bohemian Grove. Did you know that was where you were going?"

The question faded, replaced by the primal beating of drums. Diana was on a stage and bright lights shined in her face as she danced naked around fires.

"Diana?"

Brock's voice broke the trance. She blinked away the image and regarded him. It disturbed her how easily she could slip into these hallucinations. "Sorry, what were you asking?"

"About John Herald." Brock's manner was considerate and patient. "The flight plan of his helicopter."

Diana massaged her temples. "There are so many unusual and disconnected fresh memories in my head. I'm sorry, I don't know more than what I told you previously."

"Diana, I understand this has been a terrible ordeal for you. I want to be as transparent as possible here. That text message I got a few minutes ago was from my colleague leading the NTSB investigation. There is some evidence that shows the crash may not have been an accident, but possibly an act of sabotage. What we don't know is if the target was Mr. Herald, you, or both of you."

The news rang through Diana, making her feel brittle. She whispered, "Why would anyone try to kill me?"

Brock leaned close and lowered his voice. "Why, indeed? If it was sabotage, to what end? You are alive, Herald presumed so, so what are the saboteurs up to now? That is why you must stay vigilant."

"You mean I'm in danger?"

"We have to assume so."

"From whom? Why?" The questions were loose shards tumbling with the rest of her broken memories.

"I wish I had those answers." Brock clasped her wrist. His grip was firm. "We'll continue to protect you. The local police have posted a sentry and hospital security has added guards."

Diana took all this in. These strange dreams seemed as real as her true memories. The helicopter crash. This second name, Star. Now guards and perhaps a second attempt on her life. All of which had to do with this mysterious man, John Herald. Why did her life seem like a hall of crazy mirrors?

Brock retracted his hand and glanced at the wall clock. "I have to go. But before I do, there's this one important detail. From the witness transcript of the crash site, the interview with the hiker who found you unconscious on the beach. The hiker told us, 'I knew who she was right away. I recognized her as young Alexa. Alexandra Starnowski was her name.' What's this about?"

Brock took out his phone and scrolled to a photo of the hiker. Diana immediately recognized her as the same plump woman she had seen staring at her when she was in the coma during the memory flashback of being at the crash site. Diana let the shock pass before she could speak. "Did she give her name?"

"Sally Mund. Do you know her?"

Gabe Mendoza was asleep on the sofa in his small East Oakland studio apartment. He hadn't shaved or bathed in days. On the floor lay an empty bottle of cheap vodka and a greasy pizza box amid a clutter of paper printouts and scribbled notes. The mess extended to a wooden coffee table and the kitchen counter.

On the other side of the room, next to an enormous pile of books, hung a giant whiteboard arrayed with Post-it notes. He had organized the display into three sections and across the top, written in bold black pen, were three words: WHO, HOW and WHY. He'd placed most of the notes in the HOW section and included Poisoning our bodies, Nano Domestic Quell (NDQ), media propaganda, school system brainwashing, divide/conquer, astroturf, fake wars, and debt.

In WHY there were only three notes: Population Control, Survival of the Fittest, New World Order.

In the WHO section, there was a large question mark on a solitary note. Then in the section titled Only One Way Out, a single card hung, quoting those words uttered by the stranger, Stop the hypocrisy.

It had been over two months since Gabe had met the mysterious old man in the Columbus hotel bar. Gabe continued drinking that night and got so hammered that the police had to be called to the hotel. They charged him with disorderly conduct. He'd spent the night in an Ohio jail and then appeared in court where he paid a fine. The repercussions didn't end there. His employer, Great Global Media, promptly fired him.

His colleague, Diana Willis, had defied death and had disappeared into a coma for many weeks, and that did not make things easier for his mental state. What he had learned about the coverup regarding the Columbus water contamination scandal alarmed him, for he was certain that he was unraveling the threads of a grand conspiracy. Since then, Gabe had gone into an alcohol-fueled tailspin as he lost faith in his profession and his humanity.

Recently, Gabe had heard that Diana had regained consciousness and was now in recovery. Soon, he'd go see her. After he'd learned something useful.

A loud text alert jolted Gabe from his sleep. A headache clanged through his skull, and he grimaced in pain. He fumbled for his phone, groping through the litter on the table and the floor, then eventually found it under him, wedged between the folds of the sofa cushions. Caller ID: Maggie LaClair

Gabe sat up, the message clearing his head with a gust of optimism. Finally, a way forward. He clicked on the message and it read: We need to talk.

CHAPTER TWELVE

You instinctively feel that something is wrong, but because of the nature of these weapons of mass distraction and deception, you cannot rationally express your feelings or handle the problem with intelligence. You can't cry for help and do not know how to associate with others to defend yourself against it.

Your television star must realize this before it's too late.

Murray Sims tipped the bag of Doritos over his mouth and shook the bag to dislodge the last of the chips. Fragments spilled onto his face, and he brushed them off his chin, then off the front of his shirt. As he moved his corpulent bulk, the executive chair groaned beneath him and his belt pinched his enormous gut, now more bloated than normal. He plucked a can of Pepsi from where it rested in the cupholder affixed to the arm of his chair. At some point, he'd have to do something about his weight. Or so his doctor had advised him.

He knew junk food was not about nutrition; it was specifically engineered to release dopamine for a feel-good rush. Murray was okay with that. Eating junk food helped him cope with night terrors, and if getting fat was a by-product, then so be it.

Murray slurped the drink, then belched, the loud burp easing the strain about his waist and the associated discomfort. He took a moment to survey the array of computer screens facing him, each of them a fountain of digital information. He placed both large, doughy hands on an expansive keyboard. Besides having memorized a plethora of keyboard shortcuts that reduced the motion of his hands and fingers, through sensors he could also control his suite of computers via an assortment of finger waves, nods, and voice commands so that his physical movements during the day were at an absolute minimum.

He spent most of his waking hours in this small, windowless room. Food and drink arrived via delivery, his only real human contact with the outside. But Murray didn't mind. Years ago, he'd withdrawn from normal society, becoming an electronic hermit, which allowed him to interact with the world on his terms.

Murray Sims was a hacker extraordinaire. He'd earned such a reputation that the powers of the world recruited him to do their dirty sleuthing, which Murray reveled in. He could burrow into any network, no matter how secure, via any connected device transmitting to the internet, and these days, you'd be hard-pressed to find a device not linked to the World Wide Web. Banks. Cell phones. Home security. Webcams. Cars. Fitness wrist bands. Coffee makers. He'd once gained entry into government secret archives through a toaster in their break room!

A pop-up alert on one of his screens got his attention. He deftly slid a window on his screen to the right and opened a new text window that contained an encrypted message titled HTFS Required. Murray opened the message.

New Target - Hack, Track. Now.

Set up Full smear later. Wait to pull Trigger. File attached.

He clicked on the file and snickered to himself when asked for a password. A couple of keystrokes to bypass security, and he was in. The file automatically arranged itself into sections across the primary screen in front of him. Diana Willis's photo was top center. Her image astonished him. *Diana Willis? What would his clients want with her, aside from the obvious fleshly desire?*

Murray paused a moment to reflect on Diana. She was one of the most beautiful women in the world and the object of many masturbatory fantasies, Murray's included. Until now, he'd limited himself to images of her that were publicly available. With this assignment, they had hired him to peek into every aspect of Diana's life and gawk at what he saw.

He flushed with anticipation and sweat beaded on his forehead. His response to such nervousness was to eat, and so he scooped Skittles into his mouth. He chewed noisily and washed the candy down his throat with a guzzle of Pepsi. The sugar rush jolted through his blood, energizing him.

Alert and on the hunt, he scooted closer to his desk and leaned over his keyboard. He waved a finger over Diana's visage to capture it for facial recognition. "Search Diana Willis," he commanded.

Several internet sites popped up immediately. *TV's Miracle Darling* and *Diana Willis back from dead* were the first two that filled the screen. He navigated through the articles and zoomed in on several photos of her. He then clicked a site that secretly published naked pictures of celebrities and opened those of Diana. There was only one set as she was especially modest, not one of those media types who visited public topless beaches and then feigned outrage when the ensuing photos were published.

His eyes widened in delight as he studied the images of her nude body, taken from a roach-drone that had crawled into a hotel bathroom. Her body was exquisitely toned and formed, flawless in every respect and from every angle. But there was nothing erotic about the images. She was a woman caught unawares in the ordinary routine of undressing for a shower, then toweling herself dry afterward.

A pang of guilt wormed through Murray. The embarrassment was uncharacteristic for him and he wondered about the reason, considering he'd experienced no similar qualms when peering through the other electronic keyholes he had access to. In fact, whenever any woman caught his fancy, he'd make it a point to see what she looked like naked and what carnal pleasures she dabbled in. But for Diana Willis, it seemed like a violation.

He closed the site and then clicked a link inside the encrypted file, which opened a subfile that elaborated on the specifics of the smear campaign they ordered him to orchestrate. *Business is business*, he debated with himself. If Diana had drifted into his client's crosshairs, that was her problem. *Still.*

Murray read the list of requirements and realized this would require a familiar smear formula, one he had developed AI software for. He had used it previously multiple times, and his genius for hacking and using technology to plant fiction and outright lies in the media and internet made him a go-to gun for hire for this slander. He had been successful so far in being able to compartmentalize his feelings and opinions about the people whose credibility they asked him to undermine. However, with his latest target, Diana Willis, something caused him to hold back.

Then he thought about how much his client was paying him. His value was in not only his technical skills, but his ruthlessness in using them. What did he owe Diana? What had she ever done for him? Did she really think that as a celebrity, what he was about to unleash would never happen to her?

Thus bolstered about the mercenary demands of his vocation, he swigged the rest of his soda, and with a two-word command and quick touches to the screen, he activated the smear campaign AI software. He would wait for the signal to pull the trigger.

Buckle up, baby, here comes your hacker daddy!

In the meantime, Murray keyed strokes at rapid speed and seconds later, he was observing Diana Willis on a Pilates reformer in front of her physiotherapist. *If I'm in*, he comforted himself, *then I'm in all the way.* For now, the office camera was the keyhole into her world.

Anthony Briscane cracked his knuckles and sat back from his laptop. He had just finished sending the encrypted message to his secret contractor. Working for the Controllers—with Carcano at the helm—meant that Briscane was to maintain a veil of deniability between himself and those criminals he hired. Though they'd never met, Briscane knew this contractor was Murray Sims, an obese excuse for a human being, more Jabba the Hut than a person. Somewhere in the digital world, Sims had ensconced himself like a barnacle, where he filtered streams of data and then ejected code that infected the rest of the world like poisonous spores.

Truth was, Briscane didn't trust Sims because the fat slob had too much power. He could bore a hole through the thickest walls of electronic security and Briscane feared that one day, Sims might get it into his fat head to see what the Controllers were up to and talk himself into undermining them. Such double-crosses had to be planned for.

But at the moment, Briscane needed Murray Sims and had to trust him.

The Controllers had put Briscane under pressure and there was no choice but to activate a Plan B. The failure of his first plan to take out John Herald and Diana Willis had knocked him down a peg or two. While this setback would be temporary, his mission to orchestrate a smear tactic against Diana and destroy her reputation could not fail.

The background subfile he included did not go into the specifics of Diana's past before her famed career. Those specifics were too explosive. What he offered only alluded to her beauty, and because of it, they had groomed her to be a media darling. That way, she could be controlled and used to report whatever she was told to report. Control of the media and their representatives, like Diana, was one way the Controllers kept the world in their domain, hence their name.

Now that the repressed memories had seeped into her consciousness, she might reveal secrets that could threaten the Dark Forces agenda, for the Controllers were themselves the minions of a larger, more subversive power. Murray must prevent this by undermining her credibility so that no one would believe her if she came forward.

Briscane knew everything was on the line here, and after he hit *send*, he sank back in his chair and took a deep breath. He opened a drawer, took out a portrait of Diana Willis, and propped it up against the screen on the desk in front of him. He gazed at the photo and felt himself sinking into her incredible eyes, a pair of radiant gemstones more captivating than the most precious of emeralds. Briscane shared a secret past with Diana and this past included gaining a power that he kept hidden from the Controllers—the power to traverse the psychic plane and into another person's mind for subconscious suggestion.

Now to see what mischief he could cause.

Diana pulled herself on the carriage of the Pilates reformer, her body sliding back and forth against the resistance provided by her weight and the machine. There had been much improvement in her form and strength since she started this exercise ten days ago.

Her physiotherapist Susan Bell stood to the side, supervising and motivating. "Let's do one more set of ten, Diana."

As Diana started on this last set, Anthony Briscane flashed into her mind. He was shaking his head, and she heard *the quiet war has begun, and you will lose.* Diana faltered during the routine and clumsily stopped the exercise.

"Are you all right?" Bell asked.

"Yes, I...I...had a cramp." Diana massaged her thigh. "It's fine now."

"We'll call it a day, then. It's almost time for your psychotherapy session with Dr. Bowman." Susan helped Diana out of the apparatus.

Diana walked unassisted to the bathroom, where she undressed and stepped into the shower. As hot water cascaded over her body, she reflected on seeing Briscane's face. She remembered him as Dan Talbot's chief of staff. Why had he popped into her mind? What does it mean *the quiet war has begun, ready or not*, and now Briscane says *you will lose*? This was so crazy and confusing.

After drying off, she slowly dressed and stepped back into the room.

Her duties for the day completed, Bell had left. Diana's physical therapy was on track, but it was her mental state that most bothered her. The hallucinations and fragmented memories, especially of reliving the helicopter crash, plus now that weasel Briscane, were a miasma of distress.

Diana gathered up her journal, then left her private room and headed to the office of Dr. Genie Bowman, the psychologist assigned by Great Global Media to help with Diana's recovery. Bowman's credentials were as impressive as her mane of brilliant red hair.

Dr. Bowman waited in one of the small therapy rooms and stood as Diana entered. "Hello again, Ms. Willis, how are you?"

Diana made her way to a plush armchair. She looked at Bowman and considered the history of the therapy. At their first session, when Bowman had asked, *Tell me about your childhood,* Diana's mind went blank. She answered, *I...I...don't remember,* and felt herself stumbling backward. Bowman then asked, *Tell me your favorite memory.*

There were none. Nor bad memories. Nothing.

Bowman had then said that Diana had undoubtedly experienced severe trauma that caused her to blank out her childhood and the later years.

Diana began retracing her life, her career in media, her earlier work as a journalist, and the details blurred. Going past eighteen years, her memories dissolved into a fog and she faded into nothingness. It was as if her present being had stepped out of that fog, fully formed.

Bowman had continued to press with questions that pierced the fog like a powerful searchlight to illuminate a small door in a back recess of Diana's mind. She remembered standing over that tiny hatch, realizing it was the trapdoor above a dark hole. What terrors remained below?

Diana had remarked aloud, "What had been so terrible that I have forgotten my entire childhood?"

"It is possible," Bowman explained. "It's a process called dissociation or detachment from reality. The brain will attempt to protect itself after a trauma."

Bowman took a sip of water. "Our minds are remarkably resilient creations. They have to be to cope with life's setbacks. We have this ability to repress painful memories. Our brains are wired to move on. But this coping mechanism is not perfect, sometimes causing gaps that can erase years. These repressed memories seep into our consciousness, affecting our behavior, our thinking, and our well-being."

"What should I do?" Diana had asked.

"Let them out. Welcome them even."

Diana had felt her skin prickle with fear, as if she were staring into the void of that dreadful abyss and the unseen monstrosities that lurked within. "I...I'm afraid."

"The best disinfectant is sunlight," Bowman had advised. "Now that we know what they are, we'll be ready." She clasped Diana's wrist. "But it won't be easy or without pain."

Diana brought herself back to the present. She offered the doctor a warm smile of gratitude. "How am I doing? Progressing and ready to get past this."

Bowman opened the notebook on her lap and readied a pen. "Are you still having flashbacks and dreams?"

"Yes, constantly, and I write it all down." Diana tapped her journal. "I mix these recent memories with several recurring messages that continue to haunt me."

Bowman glanced at her notes. "So, what you shared were three key messages: 'Wake up! It's not as it seems,' 'get their attention before it's too late,' and 'the quiet war has begun ready or not.' Are there any new ones?"

Diana shared the recent episode of Anthony Briscane popping into her thoughts and who he was. He said, "'The quiet war has begun and you will lose.'"

"Why this man?"

Diana shook her head.

"What do you think of Briscane?" Dr. Bowman asked.

"I don't like him." Diana never liked to speak ill of someone behind their backs, but in this case, she made an exception. "I don't trust him. He's oily and disgusting, like he just crawled out of a grease pit."

Bowman repressed a chuckle. "I know the type." Her voice became serious again. "Could it be that this negative association you have with him is prompted by your memory of the messages?"

Diana pursed her lips for a moment. "You tell me. You're the doctor."

Bowman smiled at the jest. "This last time with Briscane. When you imagined his face, was the message a thought or did you hear his voice?"

"Definitely a voice. His voice. It so rattled me I lost my balance."

Bowman's eyebrows arched upward. "Did you get hurt?"

"No. I was on an exercise machine. When I heard the voice, I lost my rhythm and had to stop."

Bowman scribbled more notes. "We need to keep track of this." She pointed at Diana's journal. "Is there anything else you want to share?"

Diana hesitated. While she understood the need to discuss what she had written, reviewing the memories picked at wounds she didn't even know she had. She opened her journal. "It's a disjointed, confusing collage." She thumbed the pages to a memory she numbered as one. "As I told you the first time we met when I came out of the coma, I remembered a quick succession of flashbacks that seemed to be linked to memories. I think they may be in sequence and trying to tell me something. I keep reading each of these memories to see if they trigger anything more. It's still frustrating, as they seem to be an important link with my past."

"Why don't you share what you wrote and then I want to try something to see if we can access your subconscious mind."

Diana read what she circled as number one. "'I am young, maybe six or seven, and with a man and woman who are smiling at me. I think they could be my parents. I think it is tied to the second memory.'" She turned to the page she had marked as two. "'I was plunging headlong through a dark forest when I saw my father, Joseph, on his side, dead. It happened so fast.'" The memory made her heart race and her throat tighten. She continued to page number three. The swell of emotion pressed tears against her eyes. Her voice quivered. "'I was sitting on a laboratory bench, a harness of wires clipped to my hair. The metal connections felt cold against my scalp.'" Diana shut her eyes and slapped the journal closed. She groped for the box of tissues on an adjacent end table and dabbed her eyes, wiped her nose.

Bowman waited for Diana to compose herself. "Diana, if you're up for it, I'd like your permission to put you into a meditative state and see if you can go deeper into these subconscious memories. It's not hypnosis. Some people go deep right away. We will see how you go and we can take it in stages if necessary. We need to understand more about what is going on in your mind. It might take several sessions. Is that all right with you?"

Diana nodded and sat upright, folding her hands on the journal.

"Put your feet up." Bowman rose from her chair and pushed a cushioned footstool closer to Diana. "Relax. When you're comfortable, I'm going to have you close your eyes."

Diana inhaled deeply and closed her eyes.

"Now take more breaths, deep and slow."

Diana did as instructed.

Bowman said, "Think of the first of those fragmented memories you just shared. When you think of that memory, take another couple of deep breaths, and continue to observe."

In her mind's eye, Diana was right behind a man and woman strolling along a country road lined with nicely kept houses. When Bowman asked what Diana saw, she explained the image.

"How do you feel?"

"I feel comforted by their presence." Diana continued to explore the memory. "Now we are heading off this road toward a yellow stucco cottage. It has green ivy on it. I see a large mailbox." *What is this?* "I can see a name on the box."

"Can you read the name?"

Diana could sense Bowman leaning close as she asked, "Look harder, Diana. What do you see?"

The words on the mailbox were a blur. Suddenly, they sharpened. "Starnowski!" Diana blurted. "It says Starnowski!" She opened her eyes in shock. "This may be why I woke from the coma and said I was Diana Star. Maybe it's short for Starnowski."

Bowman was returning to her chair. She repeated, "Starnowski," as she wrote in her notebook. She brought her attention back to Diana. "If you can, why don't we keep going and see what else you experience?"

The abrupt clarity of the memories electrified Diana like an epiphany. She closed her eyes, and after a few deep breaths, she was where she left off. It was as if her mind was spooling through a video of her life.

She spoke slowly, deliberately. "We have gone through a steel gate in a stone wall, and now we are in a backyard garden overgrown with flowers. The man must be my father. He is seated on the concrete bench at one end of the patio. The woman must be my mother and we are drawing with pieces of chalk, one green, one red. I am using the green one. We are drawing a diagram for hopscotch. We are hopping and skipping. We are laughing. The woman just called the man Joseph. He must be Joseph Starnowski."

Upon saying his name, dread shadowed Diana's mood.

"What else do you see?"

"I am moving closer to these people. I whispered, 'Father. Mother.' They turned to me. They are smiling lovingly. They called me Alexandra." An oh-my-God shock jabbed through Diana. "My name—my name is Alexandra Starnowski."

Diana felt out of breath and gulped for air as she opened her eyes.

Bowman was staring at her with an expression that swung from surprise to amazement.

"Wow Diana, this is incredible." Bowman offered a bottle of water.

"How do I know this is real and not hallucinations?" Diana asked, after sipping the water.

"That's a good question, and one that requires more investigation. We have to find out the truth behind Alexandra Starnowski and your father, Joseph, and your mother. I think the trauma of the accident has opened your unconscious mind and memories are being released."

Bowman made a few more notes in her book. "Do you want to continue?"

"Yes. But I think I know now what the second memory is. My father's murder. I want to skip this and look at the third memory. All right?"

"Yes, we can. We'll keep the same process and look at the third memory you wrote. So, when you are ready, you can close your eyes, relax, breathe and think of the memory. What do you see?"

Diana took some long, deep breaths. *Where can this be?* "I am sitting on a hard laboratory bench. I am wearing a robe and I have these weird wires clipped through my hair and touching my scalp."

"How old are you?"

"I think I am a little older than the last memory. Perhaps eight or nine. They are doing tests on me. I am seeing an intense light. They connected these wires to a large computer."

Who is this? "I see a man in a rumpled blue suit, and he is handing me a drawing pad and a pencil. He is blindfolding me. I am hesitating and not sure what to draw. Now I am suddenly drawing quickly."

What is this? "I am drawing the outline of a building. The walls, then the roof, the doors, and the windows. It is a strange but distinctive design. Another man has just walked in wearing a lab coat. He is showing a picture to the man in the blue suit. They are both looking at my drawing and nodding. They are showing me a photograph of a building."

Oh my God. "This is the same building I just drew. What the hell is going on?"

"Diana, do you see anything else?"

"I am trying to read the security badge he is wearing. It's small. Wait. I can see it. It says National Security Agency. I don't know where this place is. Another man has just walked in and he is escorting me out of the room. I can't see who it is. I am looking through some windows and there are other young children and a few teenagers in the same robes, doing experiments. I can see a large sign on the door at the end of the corridor. Admittance Restricted. They lead me into another room and ask me to wait. They hand me more writing materials."

Diana clutched her wrist. *What is this?*

"What, Diana, what did you see?"

"I just noticed that I am wearing a wristband, and it says Starnowski Alexandra/Monarch G10. I am waiting on my own. The room seems cold, scant of anything except a chair and metal table. I can see a window, but it is dark. Wait. The door is opening and two men are walking in. One of them is taking my wrist and removing my wristband and replacing it with another one."

Diana felt her pulse race and couldn't help but think aloud, "No, no, oh no."

Bowman hovered close. "What?"

The distress exploded from Diana as a scream. She gulped for breath. "The new wrist band says Willis Diana/SG-Remote Viewing L4. They changed my name. What the hell, they changed my identity. That is not my name. I am Alexandra Starnowski. What is Monarch G10 and what is SG-Remote Viewing L4?"

Diana inhaled deeply and kept her eyes closed.

Bowman called to her. "Diana, hang in there a little longer. What else do you see?"

Diana panned her head around as if she was trying to see what was in the room. "The second person in the room is just standing over there staring at me with a creepy look on his face. He is like a guard. The door just opened and an old man in a dark suit just walked in. He is not wearing a badge. I am standing up now."

Oh God, no way. "They are asking me to take off my robe. I am now naked, standing in front of these two men. The older man is standing in front of me, looking at me up and down like he wants to mount me like a whore. The other man is behind me. The older man nodded to the other and then left."

"Do you recognize them?"

The men's faces dissolved into the haze of fading memory. "No." Diana raised her hand. "There is more. A female assistant comes in and is handing me a bright summer dress to put on. I'm now being led out of the room along the same corridor. All the other children are gone. They are taking me out of the building and I am being put into the back seat of a large black vehicle. The same old man is sitting there, but there is also a lady sitting on the opposite seat. She smiled at me. And we drive away."

The image faded, leaving Diana feeling empty. Opening her eyes, she was looking up into the lights and the squares of acoustical tile in the ceiling of Dr. Bowman's office. A sense of violation flooded into her, making her tremble with sadness and loss. She turned her head to catch Dr. Bowman's stare. Diana hugged herself and in a weak voice said, "Was this my childhood? Oh my God."

Murray Sims was in his bathroom when he heard the alert he had been waiting for. The massive system in the adjacent room amplified the sound. *Is that what I think it is?* He lifted his enormous frame off the toilet with the help of a bar installed on the wall. Once upright, he fumbled clumsily as he hauled his pants up and around his seventy-five-inch belly. His excitement at the alert and its promise of treasure made him abandon his attempt to close the zipper. He waddled as fast as his fat body would allow, barely squeezing through the door and back to the systems room.

Come on, baby! He hadn't even occupied his chair when he reached forward and touched a fat finger against an icon on the screen. The window that opened was like a portal into another technological dimension.

"Yes, there she is!" Murray stuffed the last piece of his chocolate bar into his mouth, plonked his body into his extra-wide seat, then watched the words as they appeared on the screen and copied them into a file.

Dr. Genie Bowman, unaware that she was under his secret surveillance, was typing a report and psychological evaluation of Diana Willis—Alexandra Starnowski.

A flash of triumph raked along Murray's nerves. How much would Briscane appreciate this find? Murray was about to chortle in satisfaction when another emotion welled within him.

What was it about this name, Alexandra Starnowski, that seemed so familiar?

So familiar, in fact, that it moved him to protect her.

CHAPTER THIRTEEN

Embrace your memories when they return. Consider them messages from your previous self. Weigh these memories against what is in the present. Your past self will help keep you oriented against the turmoil of the schemes and the false information directed at you by the minions of my enemies. They are powerful and ruthless, but their machinations wilt before the truth. Stay strong. Keep the faith.

Gabriel Mendoza sat on a cheap plastic chair and stared motionless at the wall in front of him. He was sleep-deprived, hungry, and clothed in ratty athletic shorts and a dingy t-shirt, items he had pilfered from a donation bin. His hermit-like existence in this tiny hovel of an apartment was taking its toll. Ever since he'd met that mysterious old man in the hotel bar in Columbus, their conversation had undermined Gabe's perception of the world, setting him adrift on a journey that spiraled downward, his decline accelerating after losing his job at Great Global Media. But as if to prove how crazy he must've been, what most bothered him was not his descent into financial ruin but that he couldn't yet assemble his understanding of the world—reality—according to the map that old man had shared with him.

On the badly scratched wooden floor, an eviction notice stuck out from under one of his bare feet. Next to his other foot were two books, *The World of Cognitive Dissonance* and *Programming the Subconscious Mind,* that lay among pieces of the whiteboard he had smashed and strewn across the floor.

He repeatedly muttered, "What is it?" His eyes widened, and he reached to the floor to retrieve a marker pen and a piece of scrap paper. He wrote frantically on the paper and got out of his chair to approach the wall. With a push pin, he pinned the paper to the wall and stepped back to reflect on what he had written.

The Controllers. Who are they?

They control our minds

Stop the control of our beliefs, thoughts

They control our reality because they control us

We must change our thoughts to change our reality

But how? Reprogram the subconscious.

It then became apparent what he had been doing all this time. What had started on the ruined whiteboard had taken over this entire wall. From ceiling to floor and from corner to corner appeared an intricate collage comprising hundreds of notes, photos, articles, maps, and diagrams. His maniacal focus on conspiracy theories and facts had transformed a barren surface into a masterpiece of research.

Population Control, Eugenics/Survival of the Fittest, Coming New World Order, Poisoning our bodies, Nano Domestic Quell (NDQ), Media Propaganda, School System, Astroturf, Brainwashing, Divide/Conquer, Fake Wars, and Debt Enslavement formed the main angles and sections of this massive design.

His intellectual curiosity made it his obsession, for the truth had been piqued to a razor's edge with the discoveries of the Apex-Ohio water contamination scandal story that eventually aired; it was not only inaccurate but misleading, twisted even. The deliberate false-hoods fueled his desire to find what was really going on and why. Somebody was going to extraordinary lengths to deceive the public. Who was to gain?

While his disillusionment knocked his career props from under him, what kept him going was this quest for the truth.

He plucked a red marker from the elastic waistband of his shorts and beneath what he had just written, added:

There is only one way out

Stop the Hypocrisy

Follow trail to Eden?

What is it?

The face of the mysterious old man again flashed in his mind. He remembered the crazy discussion about the pituitary and pineal glands in the center of his head, creating a third eye as a doorway to other worlds. He also recalled the last thing he had said to him before disappearing: *There's only one way out of this great web.*

Gabe considered with pride what he had just written and scanned the entirety of his work, like an artist who had completed a beautiful canvas or magnificent sculpture.

Am I going mad? He rubbed his eyes, thinking of what this quest had cost him. He had abandoned friends and family. Did any of them wonder what had happened to him? Did he care? Compared to the enormity of what he was uncovering, the answer was no.

As he swiveled his weary eyes across his creation, he was drawn to two photographs under the Media Propaganda section. The images were pinned side by side above an article with a photo of a downed helicopter. The pictures were of GGM executive John Herald and

Diana Willis. He walked over and leaned in to get a closer look. He titled it: What happened to Diana Willis? *and where is John Herald?*

"How are you, my old friend?" he asked as he touched the photo of Diana Willis. "I think I know how to help you."

A sudden thumping on the door startled him from his reverie. He glanced at the eviction notice on the floor at his feet. *Already?*

Maggie LaClair had just finished arranging bouquets of flowers in vases in Diana's condo when she received a text, alerting her of Diana's estimated time of arrival. She was returning home to continue her rehabilitation. Having eagerly volunteered for this assignment, Maggie had spent the past few hours preparing the place for her friend's return. She was glad that Diana was on the road to recovery and felt privileged for the opportunity to get everything ready for this long-delayed homecoming.

Besides making the condo look inviting, Maggie had spent most of her time supervising the delivery and assembly of the physical therapy equipment that now took up most of the floor space in the main living room.

Maggie had known Diana since arriving at West Coast Broadcasting four years ago. Hired initially as a broadcast news analyst, she quickly progressed to the manager of research for the award-winning news magazine show, *World Primetime Now.*

She admired Diana, but the big secret Maggie kept locked tight in her heart was a romantic infatuation with the strikingly beautiful news anchor. From her youth, when she began having "those" feelings, Maggie knew she was only attracted to girls. In her professional life, she kept her sexual adventures discreet, at least around the office.

The first time Maggie laid eyes on Diana it was as if an erotic fire flared inside her. Maggie dreamed, fantasized, lusted over her blonde colleague. She feared in one loose moment, perhaps at a party after one too many glasses of wine, she'd express those forbidden feelings and torpedo both her career and her relationship with Diana.

When Maggie was offered access to Diana's condo, she jumped at the request, seizing the opportunity to explore inside her friend's home, which she perceived as an intimate foray just short of sharing a bed. Before a maid service arrived to tidy up, and the crew bringing the physical therapy equipment, Maggie had stepped through the condo, exploring every nook and cranny of Diana's private space. She not only examined the contents of the bedroom dresser and the closets but lingered in the kitchen, imagining sharing morning coffee after a night of conjugal pleasures. The fantasies of being Diana's life partner made Maggie feel like this place was already hers.

Prissy Jameson from Great Global Media and several other news teams waited anxiously in front of the luxury condominium complex that Diana Willis called home.

When the black Cadillac Escalade pulled into the entrance, the reporters and crews pounced into action. The Cadillac halted, and the driver and Kelly Foster hopped out. The thick-necked driver opened the rear door, his side. While Kelly eased Diana out, the driver hovered protectively close. Diana leaned on a metal cane and straightened. A baggy coat, a scarf, and large sunglasses did little to hide her identity.

Walter Deveron, the building's beefy chief security guard, joined the driver to shield Diana from the crush of reporters. As they shouted questions, Deveron said in his New York accent, "Welcome, Ms. Willis. We're so happy you made it home."

Diana patted his arm. "Thank you, Walter."

Prissy Jameson wedged close and thrust a microphone toward Diana's face. "Ms. Willis, how does it feel to be home?"

Walter raised his hand to bat away the microphone.

Diana grabbed his wrist. "Wait." She turned toward Jameson. "I'm glad to be here, at last. Much has happened and I'm very grateful for the love and support I've received from my fans and my coworkers."

"It's been several months since the crash," Jameson pressed. "What are your plans now?"

A reporter from a rival station shoehorned his way between Walter and the driver. "What are your plans now that Anya Sullivan has taken over your anchor role at *World Primetime Now*?"

Diana turned her head, not toward him but to the building complex as if her condo beckoned. "I wish the best for Anya. What's next for me with GGM? All I've been thinking of is my recovery."

Walter and the driver bulled toward the door, Kelly acting as rear guard. Diana advanced in the pocket, caning her way forward. Beside the entrance, she noticed an unusual-looking, tall man studying her. Because of the way he stood apart from everyone else, she could tell he didn't belong to any of the news crews. Other than his height, he was bald with a pair of thin lips that were the most distinguishing feature of his equally thin, lugubrious face. Round-framed sunglasses obscured his eyes, but that didn't blunt the impression that his interest in her was more than curiosity.

Walter reached for the entrance door, opened it, and ushered Diana inside. The driver stayed behind to ward off the reporters. Diana tossed a glance over her shoulder to look at the entrance windows, but the strange man was gone. Kelly continued with Diana to the elevator.

When the elevator doors closed, Diana felt the symbolism signifying that hopefully, the trauma of the helicopter crash was behind her. She was within her sanctuary. Safe. The elevator began its familiar ascent.

Arriving on the destination floor, she saw Maggie waiting in the open doorway of the condo. Her expression beamed with both joy and hurt at seeing the normally healthy and vivacious Diana creep forward with a cane, Kelly holding one arm and toting a small suitcase.

Maggie rushed to embrace Diana and kiss her cheek. Though Maggie had visited her many times in the hospital, this greeting brimmed with pent-up emotion.

Diana pulled away, smiling. "Thank you for taking care of everything."

At the threshold of her condo, Diana stopped and leaned on her cane. She took a deep breath and scoped out the interior. Flower bouquets filled the space with color and natural perfume. An assortment of shiny exercise equipment waited for her attention. *I have so many good friends.* Tears welled in her eyes.

"Beautiful flowers, Maggie. Thank you."

Kelly placed Diana's bag on the floor.

Diana gave her a kind smile. "Maggie can take over. See you tomorrow?"

"We'll chat then." Kelly dismissed herself with a polite nod.

Maggie shut the door and took Diana's coat, then led her to an armchair.

Larry. Larry Reynolds appeared in Diana's mind, his image clear as a photograph. A few seconds later, when Diana settled in the chair, her phone buzzed from her pants pocket. The image vanished. She answered the phone. Caller ID did indeed announce Larry Reynolds.

She tried not to sound surprised. "Larry, how are you?"

"Just checking in." He sounded upbeat. "Made it home okay?"

"Thankfully, yes. The crazy way things are going, it's a surprise that Martians haven't tried to kidnap me."

"That would be a ratings bonanza," he chuckled, "but let's not jinx your recovery. I'm calling about the possibility of a comeback interview. Call it the Diana 'Miracle.' Would be a nice capstone for my career."

Diana's thoughts stuttered to a halt. "Capstone? Career? What are you getting at?"

"Just between you, me, and the walls, I've decided to retire."

Diana cut her eyes toward Maggie. She was in the kitchen and out of earshot. "When?"

"I'll make the announcement soon enough. Lots of big changes in the studio. People getting shuffled around."

"Leaving like this doesn't sound like you, Larry."

He chuckled again. "Time for this old pachyderm to make his way to the elephant graveyard."

"You're worrying me."

"I've got a lot that will keep me busy, don't you worry." His voice lowered. "Anything else about John Herald?"

"How would I know? Why are you asking?"

"The FBI swooped through the studio, asking about him. It's so bizarre that they never found his body."

Diana turned thoughts about John Herald around in her mind. Was Larry fishing for information? Out of curiosity or on someone else's behalf? Who? Briscane?

"Diana?" Larry prompted.

She answered, "Little about John Herald makes sense."

"Forget that I asked," Larry said. "Enjoy your time home. Relax. Get better and when you're up to it, let's chat about the interview."

"Of course. Thanks for checking in on me." Diana said goodbye and ended the call.

Maggie brought two steaming cups. "I made us tea."

Diana thanked her and took one cup.

Maggie rested her cup on an end table. "I have to tell you something about Gabe Mendoza."

"Gabe," Diana repeated. "How is he?"

"That's the million-dollar question." Maggie's face darkened with concern. "He disappeared soon after your accident."

"What do you mean, disappeared?"

"He came back from the Columbus assignment all stirred up about something. He had been arrested for disorderly conduct after a night of heavy drinking. Larry did what he could to help, but the network's zero tolerance for this resulted in his firing. After that, I lost contact with him."

Diana was about to reply when a swooshing sound spun through her head. It brought to her mind's eye a derelict building, its darkened interior crowded with homeless people. Diana saw herself groping through the gloomy halls, searching for her friend.

She recoiled when someone grabbed her arms and shook them.

"Diana. Diana, are you all right?" Maggie shouted frantically and struggled to keep Diana from toppling forward from the armchair.

Diana realized where she was and sat up straight. She blinked. *What happened? Did I black out or was this a hallucination?* She realized she was panting for breath.

Maggie loosened Diana's collar and rubbed her temple. "You fainted. Should I call a doctor?"

Diana waved her off. "No, I'm fine. Just tired." But the abrupt visions of Larry and then the building with the homeless disturbed her. They both seemed so real.

"What would you like me to do?" Maggie lowered to her knees in front of Diana. They clasped hands.

"Just stay here with me for a while. Keep me company." She didn't want to be alone, not right now.

Maggie squeezed Diana's fingers. "I can do that."

Briscane reached across the desk for his smartphone and dialed a number. He said simply, "Do what you have to do."

As he put the phone down, he opened a drawer in his desk. *Now for the next step in my plan.* He rummaged in the drawer and took out a small photograph. He rubbed his finger over it and then carefully leaned it up against the computer monitor next to the photo of Diana. As he leaned back in his chair, he became very focused on this new image. It was a black-and-white headshot of Maggie LaClair.

Briscane couldn't contain his smile. Diana would never suspect that her inner circle would be turned against her.

Diana lay in bed, rousing from deep slumber and finding herself midway between awake and asleep. She was aware of her heavy breathing, even as that dreadful haunting sound returned to echo in her mind. The details of her bedroom dissolved, and she found herself back on the misty beach; the same ragged and torn garments clothed her blood-covered skin.

Get their attention before it's too late. As the voice faded into the distance, her current surroundings came back into focus.

In the darkness, she scoped out her room. Maggie was gone. She had left after putting Diana to bed.

Diana made out the blurry image of her dresser and, with the images of the beach and the voice still fresh in her mind, she suddenly remembered her secret drawer and its contents. *Briscane's thumb drive. John Herald.*

Yes, she concluded triumphantly, *what was in the thumb drive was the key to these dreams.* Fully awake, she slid out of bed and limped to the dresser. After yanking out the middle-left drawer, she dumped the contents and pressed the bottom of the drawer to reveal her secret hiding place. The void was empty.

This can't be. She ran her fingers into the space. Still nothing. She turned the drawer over and shook it, thinking the thumb drive might be stuck. *Nothing.* Next, she raked through the contents she had tossed aside. Pens. Small note pads. Assorted costume jewelry. Odd coins and tokens. No thumb drive.

Perhaps she had opened the wrong drawer. Moments later, all the drawers lay in a pile on the floor, upside down and empty. Still no thumb drive.

What's going on? She sat on the bed and gathered her thoughts. *My God. The thumb drive is gone.* And there was only one explanation. Someone had taken it.

Diana felt a chill and swaddled herself in the bedcovers. Just when she thought the path toward the truth had coalesced, it had vanished like vapor beneath her feet. Many secrets remained out of reach, out of sight. When? When would she discover what was going on in her life and why? She tried to remain resolute, but the doubts brought fear, and that fear brought tears. She tried not to cry.

Maggie waited in the lobby of Diana's condominium building. She peered through the windows and kept vigil on the cruising traffic. She had made sure that Diana was asleep before leaving. Maggie had taken her time summoning an Uber, still worried about Diana.

Her phone buzzed with an alert. Her ride had arrived. A dark sedan pulled to the curb.

Maggie pushed through the front door, feeling a blast of the Bay Area's infamous cold and humid night air, and waved her phone at the driver. He waved back. Ever cautious, she stepped behind the car to verify that its license number matched what was on the app.

The rear door locks clicked, and Maggie slid inside, the interior brightly lit by the overhead dome. The driver had swiveled around to greet her. "Ms. LaClair?"

"Yes," she replied. Eager to get home where it was warm and dry, she paid the driver little mind except noting that he was bald and possessed an evil-looking mouth.

CHAPTER FOURTEEN

It's unraveling and you are remembering. The game is changing, and we are unlocking some doors to your new reality. Doors that you must choose to open and go through.

The chime of her phone jolted Diana awake. She lay in bed, swaddled within her blanket. The phone chimed again. She rolled to the edge of the bed and sat upright. Though the phone chimed once more, she lingered to study the empty drawers and contents scattered across her floor.

Briscane. It was he who had taken the thumb drive, she was sure of it. But how?

When the phone chimed again, Diana snatched it from the nightstand and answered.

"Ms. Willis?" It was Walter Deveron, the doorman. "You have a visitor. Agent Cal Brock of the FBI."

The sound of Brock's name reassured her. "Yes, please send him up. But tell him to take his time. I just got up."

She didn't bother with her cane and limped to the bathroom to freshen up. When she gazed at her reflection in the mirror, it appeared like she had just crawled out of bed. She ran a brush through her hair and slipped into a long robe that she arranged as best she could to cover her up to the neck.

She was in the kitchen preparing coffee when the doorbell rang. She examined the door video on her phone. Cal Brock waited in the hall outside.

Embarrassed at appearing so disheveled, she inhaled a centering breath and opened the door. Cal Brock regarded her with a warm smile. He was dressed in a sport coat, tie, the lanyard of his ID badge tucked into his coat. His eyes shined with a friendliness that only amped her embarrassment. She clutched the collar of her robe and stepped back to let him in.

"Agent Brock, good to see you. What has happened?"

He scoped out the fitness equipment arrayed across the living area. "Are you doing better?"

"Still overwhelmed," she said. "But I like to think that I am doing better. Thank you for asking."

They made eye contact, and in that silent moment, an emotional spark passed between them. His question was more than professional interest. Diana wanted him to dwell on that sentiment, but when his attention turned to his notepad, she was both relieved and disappointed.

"John Herald is still missing," he said. "Have any other agencies visited you about him yet?"

Diana shook her head.

He asked, "Anything else unusual?"

"Maybe."

Brock looked up from his notepad. "Oh?"

"When I arrived from the hospital yesterday, I saw a strange man outside the building."

The agent cocked an eyebrow. "Strange in what way?"

"For one, he seemed out of place. Everyone else was with the media and he wasn't with them. And the way he was staring told me he was there specifically for me."

"What did he look like?"

"Bald. A white guy about this tall." Diana raised a hand to show his height. "Black-rimmed glasses. Slender, or should I say, trim. The weird part was his lips. Very thin, flat, no curve to them. It gave him a cruel look."

Brock went "hmm," as he jotted in his notepad. "Anything else?"

"Unfortunately, no. I was hurried inside and I was glad to be back home. The only reason I remember him is that he looked so out of place."

Alexa announced, "Coffee is ready."

Diana took that as her cue to offer Brock a cup. On their way to the kitchen, he commented on her limp.

"I'm getting better," she replied. "Which is good as I hate using a cane."

As they huddled around the kitchen counter and enjoyed the fresh coffee, Brock said, "We've had another break in the investigation. The NTSB confirmed more evidence that indicates foul play."

"More evidence?" Diana's eyebrows jumped a bit. "What can you tell me?"

"There was no helicopter engine failure as the engine remained functioning all the way to impact and the rotor blades continued to turn after it hit the ground. It appears Mr. Herald was an accomplished pilot and kept control long enough to get you out. Right before witnesses saw the door opening and you fall to the ground, they said a beam or a flash of light hit the right side of the helicopter. Right after that, it veered to the left and lost altitude. Do you remember seeing a beam or flash of any kind?"

Diana thought hard. "No. All I remember is a sudden jolt."

The memory bloomed in her mind's eye. The deafening, tornado-like shriek of turbine engines and whirling rotor blades roared through her thoughts. She was in the back of a helicopter as it spun around, out of control, seconds from crashing. Centrifugal force pinned her to the corner, and she struggled to climb into a nearby seat and buckle in. That was the only action that could save her from certain death during the impact.

The door beside her slid open, and incredibly, the helicopter stopped in mid-spin. She found herself ejected out the door, somersaulting through the air, and slamming onto her back. With the breath knocked out of her, she gulped for air. She noticed her racing heartbeat slowing to a deliberate cadence.

All time seemed to have slowed. A man stood over her, his form outlined by an uncertain light. The helicopter remained frozen above them. The man spoke. "Diana, wake up. It's not as it seems."

Diana opened her eyes and found Brock standing over her. She lay on the kitchen floor.

He slipped an arm behind her shoulders and helped her up. "You blacked out."

"Sorry. It's been happening a lot." She wasn't so much embarrassed as light-headed.

Brock refilled her coffee cup and pushed a stool closer. After she sat, she sipped the coffee and noticed that Brock studied her with a concerned look.

"Are you okay? Should I call your doctor?"

She waved him off. "I'm okay. These spells are something I have to learn how to control."

"Perhaps the memory of the crash triggers your blackouts?"

She rubbed her temple and nodded.

He cleared his throat. "At some point, we're going to have to revisit how you ended up on the beach three miles away. That is still one of the big mysteries about what happened."

Diana didn't want to sink into another spell and replied reluctantly, "I don't know."

"How has the psychotherapy been going?"

"It's helped to get more clarity about these new childhood memories that have surfaced since the coma. I continue to have strange thoughts and these weird experiences that make little sense. I keep going back to the crash and finding that person telling me to wake up. What if he was John Herald?"

"What do you believe happened to him?" Brock asked, a little suspicious.

"I don't know."

Pursing his lips, Brock tipped his head, meaning he believed her. He set his gaze back on her. "I may have found something important to help you answer some of your questions."

"Really? What?"

Diana leaned toward Brock.

He continued, "I did some further investigation into the name that Sally Mund gave us and what you shared. Alexandra Starnowski. I couldn't find records of anyone with that name born in 1982. However, I found a Magdalena Starnowski, a Polish immigrant born in 1952. Her husband, also Polish, died from a self-inflicted gunshot wound in 1988. His name was Joseph Starnowski."

The news jolted through Diana. *Magdalena Starnowski. Joseph Starnowski! They must be my parents?* Suddenly she was back where she last remembered Joseph Starnowski. She recognized his dark coat and saw the blood spot between the shoulder blades. A pistol lay to his side.

Yet her reaction was not of horror, but of curiosity. *How could he have shot himself in the back? This makes little sense.*

Her chest clenched in trepidation, and she slowly, carefully, crouched beside the man. She put the pinecones she had been collecting on the ground before she grasped his shoulder and rolled him to his side. When his face came into view, it was instantly recognizable. It was indeed her father, Joseph Starnowski.

Diana saw herself as Alexandra backing away, screaming. Then she was back as Diana, in the kitchen, Brock staring at her.

"Another flashback?"

"The same one. I've seen this multiple times and I believe I found my father murdered in a forest somewhere."

"Murdered? The records said suicide."

"In my memory, I see him shot in the back."

"I'll need to investigate further." Brock made a note in his little notebook. "And how do you know it's a forest?"

"Because I am always holding pinecones."

Brock scribbled more notes. He said, "From medical records we know they had a daughter born in 1982 but I couldn't find a birth record. Shortly after Joseph died, the girl was sent away. There was no trace of her in the system after that."

Isn't that daughter me? Diana wanted to ask.

Brock then announced, "Magdalena Starnowski is still alive."

The news whipped through Diana. *Mother?* "Where is she?"

"She's in a residential psychiatric care facility east of LA in the Whittier area. According to records, she has been there for over twenty years."

Diana could only gape in surprise as she considered what all this meant. "I have to see if it's her. And I have to meet Sally Mund. Can you help?"

Brock's mind seemed elsewhere. Diana tried to probe it, wondering what information he was keeping from her.

Then his thoughts came to her, as clearly as if he had spoken them. *You. You. Diana. You are so beautiful.*

She cupped the coffee mug and felt its warmth. No, this wasn't another hallucination. She studied Brock's eyes and what she read in them matched what she had heard in Brock's mind.

With all the strange events in her life lately, she now had three additional complications. One, that her mother might be alive. Two, that Diana was probably telepathic. And three, that Brock was infatuated with her.

A studio tech fastened a wireless mic under Dan Talbot's collar. A makeup artist feathered a brush across his temples and cheeks to smooth his complexion. As he took in the studio's bustle around him, Talbot thought, *Politics is a dirty business*. But it was the world of power and not the pretense of integrity that pulled him into this new career. A recent endorsement from Jeff Kennedy of Second Eden Technologies attracted other benefactors who pumped money into Talbot's political war chest.

It's all about controlling the narrative. And this narrative was that Dan Talbot was the better choice, *no*, the superior choice for the state's governor. Previously, Talbot avoided the limelight since all it did was publicize his many faults. Now, though, he had to hog the limelight, and the only sparkles of media attention that could fall upon his opponent would be to show what an inept clown he was.

The plan was to present Talbot as a man of voracious appetites and ambition, and he would harness that energy for the benefit of the common person. He had lived large and in the governor's mansion, would act large. For the good of all.

The second of the two-part interview with Anya Sullivan on *World Primetime Now* would soon begin. The show would air that evening with a potential viewership of almost twenty million. His chief political advisor Jerry Murphy appeared pleased as he stood off-camera and watched Anya's former boss, and now soon-to-be political candidate, shine. Talbot's candor about his rehabilitation in the first interview turned the tide of needed credibility and popular vote.

Even though Talbot was no longer at the helm of Great Global Media, his influence in the industry continued to make big waves. He understood the importance of the *spin* to change the perspectives of the viewers, and this was going to be no different. Larry Reynolds and his creative team had finely orchestrated, as always, the interview. With five minutes left to go in the interview, Talbot was ready to tape the announcement of his candidacy.

"So, what's next for you?" Anya Sullivan asked as a warm-up question.

"There has been buzz recently in the media that I may run for governmental office." *Buzz, hell. It had been a blizzard of rumor.* "Politics has been something that has been in my focus for a while. Being a self-made, successful entrepreneur"—Audiences lapped up a good rags-to-riches story; it was so American—"and working up through the various ranks of media to the top office has blessed me with many opportunities to learn from the aspiring and dedicated folks inside public service. I believe the people of this great country not only need but deserve a new breed of leadership, and I believe effective governance begins at the state level. I know we deserve much better than what our incumbent governor is doing."

Talbot knit his fingers in a thoughtful, reverential gesture. "After careful deliberation and much counsel from people all over the state of California, I forthwith announce that I am running for Governor of the State of California."

Anya rocked her head back and paused, feigning surprise. Composing herself, she smiled and reached to shake Talbot's hand. "Let me be the first to congratulate you."

Talbot beamed at her. "Thank you."

Just off stage, Jerry Murphy was on his tablet and was sending out social media and promo links across the entire spectrum of mass media. He clicked to an app that managed his candidate's political profile and campaign and added a link to tonight's airing of the show. He emailed his marketing group and sent a separate text to a key spin communicator.

The new candidate for Governor looked at Murphy and saw him offering a reassuring grin and thumbs up.

Agent Cal Brock's dark blue Chevy Impala motored southbound on Interstate 5. Diana sat beside him. They were making excellent progress and were almost halfway to Whittier. His investigation had now taken a new turn. The need to find the truth about Diana's past and the possibility that it was her mother that he had located created the impetus for the seven-hour drive.

Because of this task's urgency, Brock had wanted to shorten the travel time by chartering a commuter airplane. But Diana's medical team had advised that she had better not fly for the near future, not until further neurological tests revealed how rapid pressure changes could affect her well-being. Which justified her newfound fear of flying. For now, she was content to remain safe at ground level.

Brock drew his attention from the highway long enough to glance at Diana where she rested in the front passenger seat beside him. No sooner had they started on the trip than she reclined her seat and laid her head at an angle. He had wanted to listen to the radio but kept it off so he wouldn't disturb her slumber.

She was draped in a long, shapeless coat and had bundled a scarf under her head to use as a pillow. Her legs poked from under the hem of the coat but revealed little skin other than her bare ankles between the cuffs of her pants and the cross-trainers. Her head was turned from him, her hair gathered under a San Francisco Giants ball cap, which gave him a good look at the back of her slender and elegant neck.

Diana stirred and yawned. "Where are we?"

Brock pointed to the dusty, arid surroundings. "The outskirts of Bakersfield."

She blinked out her window and stroked the back of her neck as she said off-handedly, "I'm told I do have a nice neck."

Her comment made Brock wince uncomfortably. Was it that obvious he had been staring at her?

But when she turned to smile at him, it acknowledged that she appreciated the attention. He wondered what to say and then changed the subject.

"If Magdalena Starnowski is your mother, we'll need to confirm that with a DNA test."

Diana remained calm as she explained, "To confirm what I know is already true. There is a vast gap in my life." She touched her forehead. "It's as if part of my mind was erased."

"You're taking this remarkably well," Brock said. "If I found out that my long-lost mother was alive, my father possibly murdered and that most of my past was a mystery, I'd be going crazy."

Diana raised her seat until she sat upright and could look at Brock eye to eye. "I have to get past that. Much is coming into focus about my life and yet much remains a blur. I have to maintain a steady balance or else I'll go bonkers."

Brock chuckled. "It's hard for me to imagine the polished journalist, Diana Willis, going bonkers over anything."

"Still water can hide deep troubles," she replied. "After hypnosis with Dr. Bowman, I did some further investigating when I was in the hospital. I think my past has a connection with some kind of mind control program."

"Mind control?" He looked from the road to Diana.

She kept her gaze forward. "Have you ever heard of MKUltra or Monarch?"

Brock couldn't believe what she had said. Of course, he'd heard of MKUltra and Monarch. But how was it possible that Diana had been involved in either? What he knew about these programs was that they were discredited relics of the Cold War, discarded before Diana had been born.

"Well?" Diana was staring at him.

Brock adjusted his posture and his grip on the steering wheel. "I am familiar with them. Rumor is, the MKUltra program had links to the Kennedy assassination, Oklahoma City bombing, 9/11. I also know that the bureau's investigations into them ended up going nowhere."

Simply talking about this made paranoia shiver down his spine. He squeezed his right elbow tight against his side to verify the reassuring contours of his duty pistol, a Glock 9mm. He scanned his mirrors and studied the vehicles behind him. He peeked upward for an aircraft. A drone. Nothing. Everything seemed so ordinary. Still, cruising alone with Diana through the vast openness of this desolate part of California, he felt suddenly vulnerable.

He asked, "How does John Herald fit into all of this?"

"I don't know. But what I'm told about him doesn't add up."

"Told by whom?"

"Anthony Briscane."

"To be sure, the same Anthony Briscane who worked for Dan Talbot?"

"The same," Diana replied. "But it's not Talbot that I'm worried about. It's the people behind Talbot. The ones pulling his strings. The ones Briscane answers to."

As wide as the landscape appeared around them, the terrain became even more open, with even fewer places to hide. Brock took a deep breath to settle his nerves. "This situation you're in, Diana, may be way bigger than we originally thought."

CHAPTER FIFTEEN

The truth will set you free when you find out who you are and why you are here. But be prepared to see the darkness and light. So, keep on keeping on, as your mission is revealed. You win when you endure to the end.

The deafening roar of a boiler room generator shook Diana as she tried to reach out to the frail woman in front of her. Diana was desperate to save the woman from being sucked into its air intake pump. The woman's lips quivered in terror as she strained towards Diana. Their fingertips touched for an instant, and then she was gone. Diana recoiled in horror as she recognized the woman.

Mommy.

A siren blared over the din of this terrifying ordeal and jolted Diana from her sleep. She blinked in confusion as the car pulled to the shoulder. A firetruck marked Whittier FD rushed past in the blare of noise and smear of flashing red and blue lights.

Brock was looking at her. "Are you all right?"

Several ambulances turned out of a side road up ahead and followed behind the fire crews. In the outside rearview mirror, Diana saw the lights of several other emergency vehicles.

She glanced about. "Where are we?"

Brock read the GPS and pointed past the front of the car. "The Solara Hills Center is a mile that way." Smoke billowed from behind an office complex, but it was not clear where the fire was. Brock turned on his small police radio and adjusted the frequency knob. A woman's calm voice recited a series of codes. "Hold on!" Brock said.

"What?" Diana asked, confused.

Brock stepped on the gas, and tires screeching the sedan darted onto the road. The acceleration pressed Diana into her seat. The car's engine growled as they sped up the road. The cloud of smoke widened and then towered over them. Brock swerved around the corner onto a scene that made Diana's blood turn cold with dread.

Emergency crews sprinted toward the entrance of the office complex. Ambulances and firetrucks crowded against one another. Behind a sign that said *Solara Hills Center*, smoke and flames poured from the building.

Diana gasped, "Oh my God, no!"

A police officer waved at them, and Brock pulled up short in front of a temporary barricade. "Stay here," Brock said and bolted from the car. He waved his credentials and rushed to the cop. Brock signaled that Diana was to remain in the car. He covered his nose and mouth with a handkerchief, then stooped under the barricade and disappeared behind one of the many emergency vehicles.

Across the street, on a grassy lawn, police officers gathered into a safe area people who, judging from their casual dress and robes, were the residents. Diana studied their faces, hoping to find someone who could be her mother.

Did her mother survive? Diana fumbled with her seat belt and climbed out. Sirens and shouts through bullhorns echoed about her.

Heart pumping and energized by an adrenaline rush, she ran limping towards the crowd. Thick, pungent smoke stung her nostrils, and she clapped a hand over her nose and mouth.

A thought rang through her mind. *They did this.*

That was the dream's message. She pulled the front of her cap down to hide her identity. She approached a female police officer who gathered the residents around her.

"What happened?" Diana asked.

"An explosion and a fire," the officer answered, distracted as she continued to motion residents into the safe area.

Diana felt a chill and clutched the front of her coat. "I have to go through. My mother is a patient."

The officer shook her head. "I'm sorry, but you have to stay here, ma'am."

Frustrated, Diana looked for Brock. She spotted him talking with a firefighter in a white helmet, probably the fire captain. All around them, paramedics were attending to casualties on gurneys or laid out on the ground.

The officer in the safe area became distracted by her radio. She pivoted away to better hear over the racket of the emergency vehicles. Diana saw her chance. She ducked under the barricade and hustled towards Brock. The acrid smoke thickened, making her gasp for breath, and she grabbed his arm to remain steady.

A loud crack thundered and from behind the crest of the roof, sparks sprayed upward into the smoke.

Someone yelled, "The roof is collapsing!"

Brock swiveled protectively in front of Diana.

The firefighters backed away. They adjusted the aim of their hoses to cascade water onto the roof. The fire captain announced through a bullhorn, "The building's gone. Contain the fire and keep it from spreading."

Diana watched helplessly as flames licked across the roof.

But something kept her centered. She felt the pressure of a gaze and turned around toward the safe area. From one group, a black male nurse was staring right at her and this thought burst into her mind:

You know the truth!

With the rising of the morning sun, they turned the banks of massive incandescent lights off, as there was now enough natural light for the forensics teams and FBI agents to comb through the ashes of the Solara Hills Center. Diana had been put up for the night in a hotel room, but the hours had stretched into a hellish ordeal as she waited for news about the survivors. Cal Brock remained busy with his FBI duties. When dawn broke and she still had heard nothing, the prospects turned grim that the woman who was likely her biological mother had perished in the fire.

Using her laptop, she had scoured the internet for updates on the fire and then connected into GGM's intranet. As she scanned her personal cloud files, she noticed two unfamiliar documents, titled X56 and X57. She remembered two files with identical names on the thumb drive Briscane had given her. Were these the same documents? Who had put them in her cloud file? Were they to replace the ones on the thumb drive? If so, why?

When she tried to open them, she discovered they were encrypted.

She sent a text to Maggie LaClair: Where are you? Need your help

Out of the corner of Diana's eye, she noticed the cursor on her laptop moving on its own. Someone had control of her computer! She glanced at her webcam. *No way.* She slammed her laptop shut and grabbed her cell phone to call Brock. She realized that they—whoever they were—were watching. And listening. Feeling suddenly vulnerable and helpless, she dropped the phone and curled up on the bed. *They will not stop until I'm dead.*

A knock on the door made her bolt upright. Paranoid, she looked in all directions. The knock repeated.

"Diana!" It was Cal Brock. "Are you okay?"

She rolled out of bed and through the peephole verified that it was Brock. Breathing a sigh of relief, she let him in.

His expression was dark with concern. "We have found five bodies, and all are in terrible shape. The only way we can identify if one is your mother is through DNA."

This practically confirmed that her mother was dead. She held herself firm. Now was not the time to lose control. "Let me get dressed."

Brock acted surprised. "What for?" He reached into his jacket pocket. "I brought an oral DNA kit so you don't have to go anywhere."

Diana let him swab the inside of her mouth. He sealed the sample in a small plastic pouch.

"Let me go with you," she said.

"Stay here for now," he insisted. "You'll be…"

The room spun, and she heard: *The quiet war has begun and you will die.*

The voice reverberated through Diana's mind, booming like a military drum. Her knees buckled, and she collapsed into Brock's arms.

Briscane?

The remote connection to device 357R4Y7 abruptly ended.

Murray Sims muttered, "She knows." He leaned back in his chair, feeling guilty. What he had already done was unconscionable. The more he learned about Diana and his role in her downfall, the treachery burned inside him like acid.

Overcome with resentment, he nervously stuffed a handful of chocolate-covered pretzels into his mouth. There was only one way to redeem himself. Protect Diana, which meant protecting himself as he defied Anthony Briscane and his criminal globalist cohorts.

Maggie LaClair's cell phone was on a coffee table when it chirped and vibrated with Diana's text: Where are you? Need your help

Nemer Indarte read the text. Smiling, he drew his phone from a coat pocket and thumbed, Mission Update. Whittier, Solara Hills Center, Have Removed FBI escort. Now eliminate your target.

Diana Star stared despondently at the remains of the Solara Hills Center. What was left of the exterior brick walls circumscribed piles

of blackened ruin, steam rising from the soaked timbers. The air was heavy with burned wood and chemicals. She couldn't shake the certainty that she had been the intended target of this murderous arson.

On the slope overlooking the Solara Hills Center, a black sedan, its windows darkly tinted, halted and the engine shut off. The driver's window scrolled down, and the square-jawed driver watched through binoculars, focusing on Diana. She was perfectly silhouetted against the ruins. The rear window on the driver's side cracked open, offering just enough clearance for the muzzle of a suppressor on a high-powered rifle.

Diana wandered into the crosshairs, the reticule centered on her upper back, even with the bottom of her shoulder blades. The bullet would sever her spine and tumble through her heart.

The shooter inhaled, tightened his finger on the trigger, and was about to squeeze when a police officer stepped into view and blocked the shot. The cop and Diana seemed to be engaged in conversation. Firefighters and more cops wandered into view.

The driver raised his window and started the sedan, which signaled to the shooter that this attempt had been aborted.

"Ms. Willis."

Diana turned around and saw a police officer walking towards her. "Yes?"

"You need to come with me. It's for your protection."

Diana glanced about. She saw nothing menacing but considering that she might have been the intended target of a possible arson, she followed him across the parking area to the administrative building, undamaged by the flames.

As they walked towards the building, Diana noticed the same male nurse she had seen the previous night staring at her from behind a window. *Who was he?* He dropped out of view. Diana followed the policeman into the building's foyer. Was this a trap?

"Wait here," he said and continued down the hall.

From another door, the same nurse she'd just seen entered the foyer. Diana withdrew, suddenly worried.

But nothing was threatening about the man's expression. His badge read Leon Goodwin. He raised his hand. "Relax. I have something to show you." He offered Diana a single sheet of paper—a drawing of a little girl, standing and looking at a huge bright star in the sky, the figure of another being standing close to her. In the bottom right corner, a small pinecone was drawn.

I drew this. The pinecone. I remember now.

Leon said, "Magdalena had aphasia and couldn't speak, but when you were on television, she would look at this drawing and point."

His words tripped something in Diana's mind. The image of the pinecone registered in her mind as the room spun around her and the walls disappeared into a blur.

Diana was back at the beach. Finding it difficult to breathe, she gasped for air. The familiar sound of the surf and the same large, unusual pyramidal rock formation… The bright light shined through the mist and, as before, pulled her towards it. The wet sand was cool beneath her bare feet.

In her hand, she recognized the red book with the silver pinecone on the cover. She became aware once again of the person behind her. The abrupt presence startled her, causing her to drop the book. As it fell from her hand, it defied gravity and stopped in midair. Her awareness was pulled to the image of the pinecone, which looked like it was now floating in front of her. This was so bizarre, so mind-boggling.

She heard the stranger behind say, "Get their attention before it's too late." But there was a force preventing her from turning around to see who was speaking those haunting words.

Why can't I turn? She grappled with this inability to move and lost her focus on the book. It plunged into the sand in front of her feet.

Someone else was walking towards her. She recognized the somewhat heavyset woman who'd appeared at loose ends, what with her baggy clothes and vintage down vest, and strands of hair dangling from under a knit cap.

She acted as if she was expecting Diana and called out, "Remember me? I'm Sally Mund."

The name plucked at Diana's memories, and she whispered, "Yes."

Sally Mund reached down and retrieved the book from the sand. It was as if the act had removed a pin from inside Diana and she collapsed onto the sand, face down. She lay motionless but could hear Sally calling her name, "Alexa, Alexa. Are you all right?"

A loud thud brought her to the present.

Diana was slumped in a chair, opening her eyes to see the police officer from earlier opening the door.

He rushed at her. "Miss Willis, you all right?"

"Yes, I'm okay," as she looked around for Leon, but he had vanished. She looked at the drawing and wondered how he'd gotten it and why he'd given it to her. How well did that nurse know her mother?

The officer pointed to the door, "Your ride to San Francisco is here."

Diana considered the police officer. "Where is Agent Brock?"

The officer replied, "Who?" then corrected himself. "He's…ah… waiting for you in San Francisco."

Brock would've mentioned that before he left her in the hotel room. Sensing a trap, Diana thought about an escape and noticed a wall sign for a women's restroom in the foyer. "Let me use the bathroom first." She folded the drawing into her pocket, stood, and walked into the women's bathroom.

The officer waited outside. After a few minutes, he knocked on the door of the bathroom. "Miss Willis. You ready?"

Hearing no response, he knocked again. Still nothing. The officer banged on the door again and when he tried to open it, discovered that it was locked.

An elderly man in a custodian's uniform peeked around the corner of the hallway. "Is there a problem?"

The officer jerked on the doorknob. "I helped a woman go in. Then she made a noise and fell," he lied. "I think she's having a stroke. Hurry, unlock the door!"

The custodian limped close and fumbled with the keys jangling on an enormous key ring. He found the correct key, slipped it into the door, and the instant the lock clicked open, the police officer barged past him.

The bathroom was empty, and his gaze latched onto the open window high on the opposite wall. He scrambled to the window and jumped to haul himself to its sill. The window opened onto a narrow loading dock that ran across the back of the building. An asphalt path wide enough for a large delivery truck connected to the parking lot at the left and right. Dense brush formed a wall along the edge of the property. He looked in all directions and scrutinized the brush, but no Diana. Something glittered beneath him. Smashed into the concrete surface of the dock were the remnants of a smartphone.

CHAPTER SIXTEEN

One of your great masters from the area you call Asia, whom I visited several times, once said: "Do not believe in anything simply because you have heard it. Do not believe in anything simply because it is spoken and rumored by many. Do not believe in anything simply because it is found written in your religious books. Do not believe in anything merely on the authority of your teachers and elders. Do not believe in traditions because they have been handed down for many generations. But after observation and analysis, when you find that anything agrees with reason and is conducive to the good and benefit of one and all, then accept it and live up to it."

The black-clad FBI SWAT breacher swung the ram hard into the front door of the small run-down house. The door splintered open. Three SWAT agents stormed through the doorway, hollering to intimidate the occupants. Two agents waited at the back of the house should their target try to escape that way. The SWAT team searched room to room and, finding nothing, backtracked to the front door.

"All clear, premises empty," the team leader said into his headset.

Fifty yards away and down the street, from a scrum of black vans and SUVs, the commanding officer gave the order to his task force, "Stand down."

Cal Brock waited close by, and from the way the SWAT team retreated from the house empty handed, he knew the raid had been a bust. On his way to the commander's SUV, a text on his cell phone distracted him: Diana Willis escaped and missing.

"What is she doing?" He pondered the message and the unsuccessful raid. How was she giving everyone the slip, and why was their intel so bad? This bust would've answered a lot of questions, and all they learned was that they were still stuck on square one.

He got his phone and dialed Diana's number, but the call went straight to voicemail. *Where was she?*

A text appeared. DNA report

The sender was HQ Lab.

He called them back. "Agent Cal Brock here."

The tech who answered gave her name and said, "We just got the results."

"And?"

"I'll send it to your email."

"I'll follow up, thanks." Brock turned to the SWAT commanding officer. "Gotta go. Keep me posted on anything new."

The officer nodded in acknowledgment.

Of course, Diana got away. Murray Sims, several miles away, had viewed the raid through a camera system hidden inside the house, having dispatched law enforcement to this unoccupied and run-down home in what was a wild-goose chase. The excitement took his breath away and made his heart race. Sweat dripped from his forehead onto the keyboard as he continued to control the cameras remotely.

He knew the dark powers, through his handler Briscane, would try to apprehend him as soon as he turned rogue. He suspected he would be framed and jailed to shut him up. Maybe even suicided like others before him.

His clandestine surveillance through Diana's webcam was the trigger that made him remember the beautiful green eyes of Alexa Starnowski.

For years, he had only slept a few hours a day because of night terrors. He never understood their meaning or why they kept recurring. This *remembering* of the green eyes connected him to the trauma of the awful experiments that he and Diana were part of years ago.

He knew all the tricks these Controllers would use to subvert him and the person they had assigned him to track. As an expert in these methods, he now leveraged them for his gain. He had to keep going and support Diana's mission before they tried to smear or kill her again.

It amazed Diana how quickly she could move when the adrenaline kicked in. She had been a fitness fanatic before the accident, and as she ran for her life, she didn't have time to think about her injuries.

She pulled herself headfirst through the open restroom window and dropped onto the small loading dock area behind the administration building of Solara Hills. From there, a quick walk gave way to a jog and within a short time, she was sprinting across the wooded park next to the facility.

She hid behind a large oak tree in a small gully, her heart pounding. She paused a moment to catch her breath and ponder her next moves. Peering back to the remains of the burned building that had housed her estranged mother for so many years, a sense of sadness welled up and made her chest ache. *Why? What's going on?*

The odor of smoke and ash remaining in the air brought a memory so vivid that it drew her into herself.

She was back at the helicopter crash. The door beside her slid open, and she heard a voice shout, "Go! Go!" She lunged out the door. The next instant, she was flat on her back, gasping for breath. Everything had slowed. It was as if a gel had permeated everything, and time proceeded at a sluggish pace. Her heart thumped in a slow cadence. The helicopter glided serenely above her, its rotors stuttering as if in stop-motion.

A man's voice wafted through her mind, a voice she recognized.

"Wake up, it's not as it seems."

Diana blinked and saw John Herald standing over her. The light filtering through the rotor blades formed a pulsating halo around him. She had the sensation of being slightly off, both in the same spot as before and yet feeling apart from it.

John Herald possessed an unreal quality, as if his image were being projected through an aura.

Diana felt with great certainty that she was not dreaming or hallucinating but was immersed in a profoundly altered reality. She raised her hands, examining them, extending her fingers, clutching them into fists, then opening them again, turning her hands in appreciation that she was in corporeal form, that her mind and body were together.

When she parted her hands, she was now on her knees. She heard trees rustling from a breeze. She smelled pine and out of the corners of her eyes, she saw pine trees. John Herald was still there before her, looking serious yet smiling as if to reassure her. He wore dark clothing, matching pants, a jacket of some type, perhaps a sweater underneath.

The location seemed very familiar. Fear pinged down her spine, but the sensation was arrested when John Herald raised and then lowered his hand. But what was of more importance was the book in his hands, of red leather with a silver pinecone on the cover. He tilted the book toward her and opened the cover, displaying the pages.

The first pages were covered in symbols neatly handwritten. Diana squinted at the symbols, realizing they were letters from a strange language. The letters became words, and the words became ideas, and the ideas spoke to her in whispers.

These whispers were likewise in a strange language, whose sound was familiar and comforting. She heard the whispers in the person's voice who had spoken them. It should've been John Herald, but when Diana broke her focus from the book, John Herald was gone!

In his place stood a woman dressed in loose clothing, also holding the red book, wearing a frock coat over a skin-tight pants suit, all made of a silvery fabric. Her hair was silvery blonde, loose, and her long tresses fluttered along with her frock coat as if batted by a breeze. The woman looked to be in her late forties and her expression was serious yet accommodating. Though the woman's lips were not moving, Diana understood that the voice she heard belonged to this woman.

As Diana perceived the whispers, she felt her fingers move as if clutching a pen and writing the words in dictation.

This book in the woman's hands was Diana's journal, her notes from a previous time.

She remembered the book from years ago. She saw herself as a girl of about twelve, clad in simple coveralls, sequestered deep in a chamber of concrete. She recalled the great secrecy she felt at the time of writing in the book; brave, defiant, yet afraid, for who knows what would've happened had they had caught her.

To the right and left of the woman appeared dark shapes, hazy shadows in the vague form of people. Diana's skin prickled with a chill that brought goosebumps.

These were her Controllers in the chamber, the ones who tested her abilities. Memory collided with reality—as if where she was could be considered reality—and she perceived herself both in the present moment and as the girl of twelve. The bloblike shadows floated from beside the woman and surrounded Diana. Fingers pinched her scalp, and she knew that electrodes and sensors were being clipped to her scalp. An extremity extended from one shadow and clasped her wrist—its touch had a texture like cold, dry sand—and turned her arm to expose the crook of her elbow. Another of the shadow's extremities reached toward Diana, pointing a large syringe. As its large needle touched her skin, she looked to the woman, who only nodded, signaling that Diana had nothing to fear.

These are but representations meant to unlock your memories.

Another shadow showed her a photo of a military airfield, with many aircraft neatly arrayed on the tarmac. Diana understood she was to view what was in the hangers and to project her mind into the cockpits of the aircraft. But her mind pivoted upwards, away from Earth, past the moon, to a spot in the distant heavens.

The strange woman hooked a finger into the pages and turned to a new section. The whispers said:

You must remember. What you were told by the others is false.

They have brought you to Earth to complete a glorious mission.

Diana knit her brow. *Brought from where?*

The woman turned the page to another section covered with more of the handwritten text and many small drawings.

We are Secret Transmissions Allied Response, STAR as you will know us, and we are here to help you.

Diana stared at the text and tried to read for an explanation, but the letters were indistinct.

Help who?

The woman gestured to herself and to Diana, then waved her hand to encompass everything outside the compound.

Humans? Diana asked.

Those who believe.

The shadows receded from around Diana, returning to their place beside the woman, then turning into smoke and dissolving.

The unbelievers? Diana asked.

No, they believe in us, but they fear the truth that we—the woman furrowed her brow toward Diana—*that you bring.*

Diana motioned to the book. *That truth?*

A distant muffled *boom!* shook the air. The woman had suddenly morphed to Sally Mund. Then, in the next instant, Sally Mund was gone.

Diana felt as if she was falling into herself, the air making a slight ripping sound as though the fabric of time and space were tearing. She next heard the surf lapping on the shore, which was followed by the salty fragrance of the ocean. Her gaze lifted to an expanse of gray waters and the faraway line of the horizon.

She was at the beach, stumbling over wet stones beneath her bare feet. Her bloody fingers gripped the red book with a silver pinecone embossed on its cover.

The sound of ocean waves crashing onto the beach grew louder, louder still, becoming a deafening thunder. The vista of the beach smeared into a mosaic of hazy colors. She had the sensation of time clicking back a moment, then her vision popped into perfect focus.

Just like that, the surrounding noise became the booming cacophony of rap music from a passing car. Diana reeled in confusion. The beach was gone. The strange woman was gone. There was no helicopter crash. She was back in the park.

Doing what? She remembered the men pursuing her.

She paused a moment and placed a hand over her chest to calm her racing heart.

In her mind's eye, she saw the red book. The silver pinecone on its cover.

It has the answers. I must get that book.

She removed her ball cap and jammed it in the nearby bushes. She raked her hands through her hair. She needed a new disguise if she was to accomplish her next step.

Sally Mund has the book. I must find her. I have to get to Marin County.

"No. No. No." Anthony Briscane cursed. The news that Diana had escaped sent an icy panic wiggling down his spine. Not only had she given the cops at the clinic the slip, but the SWAT team meant to arrest Murray Sims had been sent to the wrong location. Worse, that misdirection was the doing of Murray Sims himself. What Briscane had never considered in his plans was betrayal from within.

This treachery magnified the rest of his problems. He'd been assigned to be her last handler because of his mental abilities to read and control her thoughts and to usher her to her death. But that ability was fading as Diana's memories were awakening. If he could no longer neutralize and reprogram her, then he had no option but to eliminate her once and for all.

The news that Diana had escaped could not have come at a worse time now that they'd lost all trace of John Herald. How had they both survived the helicopter crash? Briscane knew that at the time of his disappearance, Herald had something in his possession that, if found by Diana, would expose the global Controllers, and how they had manipulated and directed the minds of the people of the world for many years.

Even without the discovery of what Herald had, her awareness of her true mission was unfolding, and this would bring Briscane to a terrible end by Carcano's hand.

Briscane couldn't let that happen, not while he still had his powers. He sat down, closed his eyes, slowed his breathing, focused into the center of his head, and sank into an altered state.

A few minutes passed, and his eyes popped open. *I know where she's going.* He sent a text: Willis on way to crash site.

He shut his eyes again and focused back into the center of his head. *There was a great secret. The secret that his mission was hiding. The secret that Diana must never find again.*

CHAPTER SEVENTEEN

*L*et me shed some more light on how my colleagues and I can operate the way we do.

*Some of your scientists I have assisted split subatomic par-
ticles. When they did this, they found the pieces could communicate with
each other. This communication happened instantly, no matter how far
they removed these pieces from each other. This proved that energy does
not need to travel. That it is all connected, and messages and information can be sent instantly.*

*Therefore, a particle vibrating because of the sound of your voice can
affect a molecule inside a star at the edge of the Universe instantly. There
is no time and space. There is no here and there. We are everywhere and
nowhere.*

The sedan cruised along the perimeter of the park. It was the obvious place for her to go. Earlier, the hired thugs inside the car aborted
their first attempt to kill her from a distance. As expert professional
killers, they were trained in the mental game of single-pointed focus,
which made them each as deadly as a heat-seeking missile. Once
locked on a target, they did not stop.

Without her phone's GPS tracking device in play, they would use
a drone to find her. The driver stopped the sedan, drew the small

drone from its carrying case, and powered up its computer. A menu flashed on the remote-control screen inside the carrying case, and he hurried through the start-up sequence. He lowered his window, held the drone aloft, and its four propellers buzzed to life. The drone lifted from his hand and sailed over the park.

Watching the remote-control screen, he manipulated the joystick and flew in search of the target. He spotted a woman about two hundred fifty meters away, walking rapidly from their location. She darted through an opening between the trees. He zoomed in and registered her black jacket and thick, blonde hair. It was her.

A clean sniper shot from this distance was impossible. The driver said, "We'll wait for her on the other side." He locked the drone onto the woman and drove slowly to the opposite end of the park. He'd intercept her when she exited from the other side. As they got closer, his partner retrieved a small .22 caliber handgun from the glove box. The driver slowed, and the shooter slipped out of the sedan, carefully tucking the pistol into his belt, and fluffed his sports coat to hide the weapon.

The shooter traded glances with the driver. Both men knew their reputations were on the line. They'd been paid a lot of money to shut this woman up, and so far, she'd given them the slip. No more mistakes.

This time, he would get close enough to put the gun to the back of her head and shoot until she dropped, then a double tap through her skull for good measure. He hustled from the sedan and stalked her in a diagonal approach, using the brush and trees for cover.

Diana was oblivious to the threat overhead as she continued scrambling through the park. She had to get into town to find help. She realized that even though her phone was destroyed and unable to be tracked, using her credit card would reveal her location. She reached into her pocket and pulled out a small wad of twenties and tens. *I hope this is enough. How do I get to Marin? Does Brock know what's going on? How will he find me?*

Across the street, outside the park, Diana spied an alleyway between some older homes. She had to keep off the major thoroughfares to evade capture and so would need to sneak through this residential area of Whittier.

Taking a deep breath to calm herself, she scoped out the alley to see if this path was clear. She continued her brisk walk towards the town center. From up ahead, she heard the hum of cars. The freeway. She was on course.

Through the lens of the drone hovering above, the driver followed the woman into the alleyway. *Perfect.* She was trapped and as good as dead.

Through his cell phone, he relayed the location of their target to the gunman, guiding him into position about a hundred meters away. From there, the shooter could rush forward for the kill. The driver proceeded to the far end of the alley on an adjacent street to wait so he could recover both the drone and the shooter.

They could not fail their employers.

The drone's remote-control screen flashed an alert. Signal malfunction. The image on the screen Pixelated.

The driver muttered, "Shit." Was this a glitch? He glanced upward to locate the drone and beyond it, noticed a nearby row of communications towers. They must generate interference. Without the drone, the woman might escape. The driver clenched his teeth, frustrated, angry.

The shooter stayed close to the chain-link fence and weaved around dumpsters as he carefully pursued his mark.

Suddenly, a big dog smashed against the fence. The shooter jumped back, panic jolting him. The rottweiler lunged and snarled, spraying saliva from sharp teeth.

The shooter caught his breath, acknowledging that he was safe on this side of the fence, then realizing that the canine's savage barking would alert other dogs and alert the target as well.

He felt a pang of indecision until the command arrived in his earpiece. "Three houses from the end on left. Get her now." He fixed her location and sprinted into the attack.

Farther down the alley, Diana's ears pricked at the chorus of barking dogs, the sound echoing along the alley. The dogs hadn't alerted to her; they had alerted to someone else.

It's them.

A flash overhead caught her attention. She cupped her hand to shield her eyes and adjusted her head until she could focus on what flashed above. A drone.

If that wasn't enough, she now heard someone running towards her. She could hear him getting closer. Then the drone suddenly pulled away. The high-pitched buzzing sound got fainter as it left.

She noticed an opening in the fence. An escape! She crawled through the gap and sprinted into a small backyard. She continued along a tight space between the house and an old shed to the side. The house was being renovated and litter and scrap from inside littered the yard. In the narrow confines between the house and shed, Diana found a roll of musty old carpet and crawled inside.

Taming her fear, she slowed her breathing and closed her eyes. In her mind, she was transported back to the same memory in the woods she'd had before. As she emerged from under the shadow of a tree holding pinecones she had collected, she spied her father lying on his belly. She placed the pinecones on the ground; grasped his shoulder, rolled him to his side, and saw his face.

At that moment, she was no longer Diana but Alexandra.

She backed away, screaming, but this time she saw a man standing at a distance. Someone she had not seen before in her memory. He walked towards her, menacing. She didn't recognize him, in fact, he appeared blurry. She backed away in trepidation, unsure what to do. He bolted toward her. She turned and ran, but he grabbed her and clamped a hand over her mouth.

She wanted to scream, then noticed a stink that made her eyes burn.

What was that smell?

She realized it was the stench of cat urine in the carpet. The absurdity of the moment broke her fear. Her heartbeat slowed. She knew that this time she wouldn't be caught.

The shooter stopped against a wall and peered around the corner. Scanning the junk and trash in the yard, he whispered to his partner, "Where is she? Where is the drone?"

"Lost sight of her. Drone will return in a minute," his partner said through the earpiece.

The shooter stepped into the yard. He knew Diana was unarmed. But where was she hiding? He walked along the outside of the garage, glanced at the roll of old carpet, and walked toward it.

She studied her assailant's shoes when he halted at the end of the carpet. They were black, worn, the stitching coming undone. Why didn't he wear better shoes? Maybe the pay for a hired goon wasn't all that much.

He breathed heavily, signaling his anxiety in contrast to her calm, quiet breathing. A dog began barking along the other side of the wooden fence on the opposite side of the yard. The sound of a door closing and the voice of someone talking on their phone followed.

She watched the assailant's shoes as he stepped away.

Hide or go? Diana knew there was likely a brief window of escape. The sound of the dog and the person on the phone would distract her assailant so she could get away. She turned her head and looked out the opposite end of the carpet to see a tight opening between the fence and the house next door. She lizard-crawled from under the carpet and hustled towards the opening and squeezed through.

As she turned the corner, she noticed a bicycle leaning up against the side of the house. A brown hoodie swayed from a clothesline in the next yard. It looked like the best disguise for now.

All that stood in the way was a flimsy gate that was off its latch. She felt like a cat stealthily eyeing its prey before getting ready to pounce. Her heart hammered. She had little time to think about it. Deftly, she pushed the gate open, ran across the yard, snatched the hoodie, and returned to the side of the house. She flung off her expensive leather jacket, replaced it with the hoodie, pulled its hood over her head, tucked her blonde mane inside, and zipped up the front. She tossed the leather jacket behind a trash can.

Diana mounted the bicycle and pedaled away nonchalantly, so as not to draw attention to herself.

When will this be over? She turned the corner and rode out of sight.

The drone was back up in the air seconds after Diana escaped. A block away, someone cycled along the road. The driver zoomed on the rider. A young woman, it seemed. Wearing a hoodie. Pedaling easy. Couldn't be her. He flew the drone to the shooter and hovered high above the last known location of the target.

"Where is she?" the shooter asked his partner through the transmitter.

The dog on the other side of the fence continued to bark, and its owner got suspicious and looked through a gap in the fence.

"Wait. Someone is watching. Stay where you are."

"Roger that."

On the remote screen, the driver could see a woman on the other side of the fence struggling to pull her dog back. She looked through the fence to see why her animal was so excited. Seeing nothing to concern her, she hauled her dog by its collar into the house and closed the back door.

"All clear. Keep searching."

The shooter studied the rolled-up carpet. He dropped to a knee to peer into the roll. *Nothing.* A hunch told him the target had been there. For someone inexperienced in losing a tail, she was good at it. And lucky.

"I think we've lost her. Advise."

"Back away, and we'll see if she appears. She couldn't have gone far."

He sent the drone further out to get a better angle, while his partner moved out of the yard and back into the alley to wait.

Diana kept her pace easy. But her nerves were screaming in alarm. At any second…what? A bullet? A car running her over. A bomb?

Her eyes darted to the trash receptacles along the sidewalk.

Take it easy, she admonished herself. So far, so good.

Her joints smoldered with pain. Every rotation of the pedals was becoming an ordeal. Upon reaching the town center of West

Whittier, she steered onto the sidewalk and abandoned the bike behind a hedge.

She paused a moment to massage her knees. People walked past on the sidewalk, paying her no mind. Feeling more at ease, she proceeded onto the main street.

Next move… *How do I get to Union Station?*

An elderly man sat on a bench and was scrolling on his phone.

Diana asked him, "Excuse me, sir. I need to get to downtown LA."

The man looked up. "The Seven bus will take you there."

"Where can I get that?"

He pointed. "Two blocks."

"Thank you."

She started for the bus stop. While she tried to ignore her pain, she couldn't help but limp. Breathing became difficult. She steeled herself to keep going.

Find Sally Mund.

Reaching the bus stop, Diana plopped onto the bench. Taking the weight off her legs made her sigh in relief. She dug a ten from her pants pocket, curled the bill in her fist, and waited.

As the time passed, she felt weightless. She coughed and patted her breast to clear her chest. Up the street, a city bus lumbered into view. She stared at it, feeling relief when she saw it was the Number 7.

Diana stood and raised her hand. The bus eased to a halt, bringing the odor of hot rubber and oil. The door hissed open. Diana reached from the curb and grabbed a chrome handhold to steady herself as she ascended the steps. "Union Station."

The driver tilted his head toward the fare reader. "Three seventy-five."

"I'm sorry I don't have the correct change." She showed him the ten-dollar bill.

"We don't give change."

"Oh." Diana stared at the bill in her hand.

The driver looked her over, gave a grin of sympathy, and waved her in without paying. Diana mouthed the words thank you and walked into the rather empty bus to take a seat. The driver looked back in his mirror. *That face is familiar*, he mused.

Union Station, the iconic LA landmark, was Diana's connecting point. The eight-hour Amtrak ride would put her into the Bay area by ten that night. Her money was barely enough to cover a one-way ticket. She boarded the 2:15 train bound for San Francisco and took her assigned seat. As she waited for the train to move, she scanned the compartment. Most of the seats were occupied. The other passengers were already buried in their cell phones or tablets. Everyone seemed withdrawn into their concerns.

Satisfied that no one appeared interested in her, Diana removed from her pocket the drawing the nurse had given her, the one she had done as a child.

As she studied it, she felt a connection to her forgotten past, a sign that she was on the right path. But realizing she had lost so much, had so much taken from her, a bitter sadness welled through her.

A garbled voice made an announcement. A chime sounded. The doors closed, and the train shuddered as it moved forward. Diana placed her head against the adjacent window and as she drifted off to sleep, she was transported to another place and time.

CHAPTER EIGHTEEN

Many of the civilizations on other worlds I had assisted, transformed their world when they realized that what they think, they feel; what they feel, they vibrate; and what they vibrate, they create.

Before these other worlds were transformed, however, they had to endure a similar fate as yours. Your world is evolving rapidly and as the old falls apart, know this is the end of the end and the beginning of the beginning.

In dying, there is rebirth.

The NTSB investigation's official report determined that an act of sabotage caused a fatal mechanical failure in the helicopter's tail rotor. Onboard data revealed it was not a high-impact crash, for the pilot attempted two emergency corrections to stabilize and keep control of the craft before colliding with the ground.

During the first of these corrections, the port passenger door had been mysteriously opened, which allowed Diana to be ejected through the door and then fall twenty feet to the ground. During the second correction, the pilot reduced airspeed and flattened the angle of the trajectory by approximately twenty percent, which reduced the force of the impact.

Forensics helped identify bodies in an aviation crash. But when the NTSB could not find any evidence of a body in the wreckage of John Herald's crashed helicopter, the bureau requested help from the FBI's forensics team. Diana Willis was the only confirmed survivor. The mystery of John Herald's disappearance baffled experts from many agencies, including several from the intelligence sector.

The helicopter had struck at a flat angle, and the fuselage remained fairly intact as it rolled onto its side. At that point, the main rotors clawed the earth and tore themselves to shreds. However, the cockpit kept its integrity. The fuel cells ruptured, but there had been enough time for the pilot to escape before the helicopter fireballed. Since neither John Herald nor any evidence of his remains was found at the scene, the only conclusion was that he had either walked away or someone had recovered his body.

As outlandish as the report seemed, what truly astonished Cal Brock was the findings in the second report from the FBI's forensics lab.

Their DNA testing concluded that Magdalena could not have been Diana Willis's biological mother, meaning that Diana might have been adopted.

However, the lab showed a rare genetic mutation found in only 0.0001 percent of people. And the curveball to this investigation was that this was the same mutation found in John Herald's DNA, which they had on file.

What was the connection among all these clues?

One, despite what they had thought: Magdalena was not Diana's true mother.

Two, that Diana Willis and John Herald shared the same rare genetic mutation.

Three, that John Herald had miraculously survived a catastrophic helicopter crash.

What did Diana know? What was she keeping from Brock? He picked up his phone and called her number again, and once more got her voicemail. *Damn.*

He typed a text: Heading back. Any update on Willis?

Seconds later: Still missing. Phone and laptop destroyed.

"Where are you going, Ms. Star?" he mumbled to himself as he put on his jacket and placed the phone in its pocket. "What do you know?"

The Amtrak pulled into San Jose's Diridon station a few minutes late at 10:03 PM. Diana had slept through most of the journey, dozing on and off in fits of nervous slumber. She hurried to make the transfer to the BART line for the last leg of this journey. *I'll go home, get my car, and then track down Sally Mund in the morning. Will it be safe? What if they are waiting for me?*

When she settled into her seat on the BART train, she still felt unease. The aches and pains from her injuries, aggravated by the day's escape, stung her joints and muscles. After she disembarked from the BART at her San Francisco stop, the long walk home only aggravated her discomfort.

Cool, humid bay air filled her nostrils, but the familiar smells brought no relief as she kept off the major streets. She was scared, vulnerable, and felt the walls closing in on her.

Why is everyone disappearing? First Herald, then Gabe, and now Maggie.

As she approached her address, her eyes were drawn to a scruffy, bearded homeless man gazing at her from the other side of the street, under the glow of a streetlamp. She was used to seeing the homeless throughout most of the city, but his stare gave her the heebie-jeebies.

However, he made no move or threatening gestures. She slowed and peeked around the corner to scan the street to see if it was safe. The sidewalk was empty. She took a measured, comforting breath and began walking down the slight incline to her luxury condo building. She looked back again at the homeless man, but he was gone. Considering all the weirdness going on, his sudden disappearance sparked suspicion. Diana scanned the sidewalk in both directions and didn't see him. Though it was dark, how could he have vanished so quickly?

Or had she seen him at all? Could he have been another hallucination?

Whoever he was…whatever he was, he was gone. Feeling a bit more secure, she entered the code into the entry pad next to the side security gate. Pushing the gate open, she sensed someone behind her. Before she could react, an arm grabbed her around the waist and a large, gloved hand clamped across her mouth. Diana jerked and squirmed to escape.

"This happens when you don't listen," the man growled into her ear as he squeezed harder and dragged her backward.

"What do you want?" Diana tried to scream, but the hand muffled her cry. She grabbed his arm and tried to pull his hand from her face, but he was big and very strong. She stamped her right foot, hoping to stomp on his foot. He hugged her tighter and leaned backward, hoisting her feet off the ground. She flailed her legs and tried to kick his shins.

Then, as suddenly as the attack had begun, his grip loosened, and he collapsed behind her. She stumbled but remained standing and whirled around to see who the attacker was.

He was a gorilla of a man and lay on his back, eyes twitching, but otherwise still. He might have been the man who had been chasing her, but she wasn't sure.

The homeless man stood over him, clutching a metal pipe. "Are you all right, Diana?"

How did he know my name? And I recognize that voice.

Diana hugged herself to relieve the shock. She was light-headed with confusion but could ask, "Gabe? Is that you?"

"Yes."

"My God. What happened?"

"So much," he replied.

They considered the man lying on the ground.

"Who was he?" Gabe asked.

"I don't know, but people are after me."

"Me too."

Diana glanced back over the sidewalk. The street, though deserted, was dark and seemed full of menace. "We better get inside."

🌲🌲

She slowly pushed open the entrance to her condo and looked around the door before entering. She stood for a moment, scoping out her property, the physical therapy equipment, the furniture, the decorations. Despite all she had gone through, everything looked the same.

Walter Deveron stood behind her. He appeared sheepish and apologized yet again. "Sorry, Diana. The security camera covering where you were attacked...well, for some reason it wasn't working."

"That's all right," she replied. "These things happen." But in truth, it couldn't have been a coincidence that the camera wasn't working at that exact time. However, she believed Deveron's sincerity.

Deveron asked, "You want me to go in and check out your place, just in case.?"

"I think we're fine."

Deveron took a step back and dismissed himself as Diana continued into her condo.

Gabe followed her in. "So, this is where the great Diana Willis lives?"

Diana closed and locked the door. "Diana Star now."

Gabe grimaced, confused. "What?"

"It's a long story."

"We both have our long stories."

She studied Gabe. What had happened to him? Was this homeless appearance a disguise, or had he fallen this far? Whatever his answer, she was grateful that he had shown up when he did and for the first time in two days, she felt safe. "How about I fix us something to eat while you wash up?"

"That would be good." Gabe rubbed his matted beard. "I'd like a shave. Clean clothes."

"I'm sure I have something." Diana walked to a small cabinet in her bedroom. She pulled open the drawer and from the back removed a small makeup bag. She dumped the contents on her bed to collect her backup smartphone.

When she turned on the phone, the building security app was the first to activate. She scrolled through the video cameras and selected the one viewing the side gate. The sidewalk was empty, her attacker gone.

Diana showed Gabe the phone. "Seems that whoever that guy you clobbered with the pipe worked for came to get him."

He said, "There's no point in calling the police for someone who's not there."

She replied, "That and I'm uncertain whose side the police are on."

Though she and Gabe had a lot to talk about, for the moment, they both needed to clear their heads before attempting to make sense of what was happening.

While Gabe showered in the guest bathroom, Diana found baggy sweats for him to wear. Before this business with John Herald and Anthony Briscane, she had enough clothing and accessories for a department store. *Why do we need so much stuff? What void are we trying to fill? I must clean out my closets and will probably find the experience liberating.*

She made coffee, omelets, and toast. Gabe sauntered from the bathroom, clad in a terrycloth robe, clean-shaven, appearing more like the Gabe she remembered from those rosy days at West Coast Broadcasting.

She ate with Gabe before taking her turn to shower. Afterward, she put on a robe and sat on the edge of her bed to towel-dry her hair. Her eyes were drawn to a small red stain on the tile floor in front of her. *Is that blood?* She examined her hands and turned her feet to look for any signs of a cut, something she might have gotten during the scuffle outside. She got on her hands and knees to look closer. She touched the spot with a finger. It was dry and definitely blood. *This isn't mine. Who else had entry to my condo?*

Maggie? The housekeeper?

Diana sat back on the bed and rubbed her temple. Dreams. Hallucinations. Repressed memories. Coming close to finding the truth and then disaster. Then being chased and attacked. A forgotten friend coming to her rescue, himself in need of rescuing.

It was too much to absorb. A veil of exhaustion clouded her thoughts. She was getting so tired, so sleepy. It was as if her mind was being coaxed to shut down.

Diana lay on her bed and closed her eyes. *All I need is a quick nap.*

She took a deep breath and as she slipped away into a deep slumber, a small but familiar voice echoed in her mind: *You will die before you find the truth.*

The chime of a text alert woke Briscane. He switched on the bedside light, put on his glasses, and grabbed his phone lying next to him on the bed. The text read: Failed. Someone hit our man from behind. Target is inside. Advise next steps.

Briscane sat up, suddenly alert. Diana. All of his plans to get her had fallen apart. He clutched his phone, ready to reply, but didn't know what to write. Bile rose in his throat. The bedside lamp was painfully bright, which made the taste in his mouth even more bitter.

Chasing after Diana was wearing on him. He had been convinced that this time his hired guns would get her, so he had treated himself to an early night in. But as the cliché goes, no good deed goes unpunished.

He texted: She got away again? then added: She cannot leave that building.

As he waited for a reply, he fell back on his powers. He shoved aside his other concerns and focused inwardly. His consciousness tightened into a small ball of light that opened into a round lens. The lens widened into a portal, through which he could see Diana. She was sitting on the edge of the bed, deep in worried concentration.

He sharpened his mind and transferred the thought: *You are getting sleepy. Find refuge in slumber.*

Her thoughts folded into his, almost as if she had crumpled into his arms. She rested on the bed, and he added: *You will die before you find the truth.*

As he was about to bring his mind back, he used his remote viewing ability to roam about her condo.

He found piles of dirty clothes and two sets of moist towels. Diana wasn't alone?

Briscane continued viewing the condo and, in the front room, discovered a man asleep on the couch. Briscane brought his viewing for a closer look.

It was Gabe Mendoza.

Briscane suddenly opened his eyes, which instantly shut off his roamer ability. Panic coursed through him, and he sprung out of bed.

Diana lived. Mendoza had reappeared. Everything was going wrong. The Dark Forces would not be happy. For Briscane, it was like two steps forward, three steps back!

He reached for a glass of water on the nightstand and gulped down a mouthful. He had no choice but to double down on his tactics.

He texted: Mendoza is back. He is with target inside the home. We must stop them from leaving at all costs. Execute the next plan.

The problem was this wasn't enough. He needed someone who had all the dirt on Diana. Murray Sims. "Now where is that fat fuck?"

Briscane shut his eyes again and used his "roamer" to track down his fugitive asset.

Murray Sims watched the low-fuel warning light of his Nissan SUV blink on. It was a few minutes after one in the morning and he was one hundred fifty miles south of the Bay area, heading north on the freeway. He had become accustomed to being up at night, as most of his covert work was done when his marks were asleep.

Now that he had abandoned his clandestine office, it was like the leash had fallen away. For the first time in many years, he felt free. For how long? His former masters were not forgiving people. They had tentacles everywhere and would stop at nothing to stop him.

From doing what?

Murray dismissed the low-fuel light and kept driving. Toward her. Toward Diana.

He could no more ignore what compelled him than he could ignore gravity.

Help her find the secret. The message repeated in his mind. And with every repetition, he remembered more.

General Wayne Carcano gummed his cigar. It was a seventy-five-dollar Habana Excelsior Toro Especial, and he resented ruining this fine specimen of tobacco, but lately, he'd been smoking too many cigars. And drinking too much as well.

Things weren't going well. An understatement, at the very least. He needed centering, and his usual fixes of smoke and booze weren't doing it.

What would fix his problem would be *fixing the problem.*

Problem as in Diana Willis, or Diana Star, or whatever the hell else she was calling herself. His team of experienced hitmen was being reduced to a mob of clumsy jackasses by a woman who couldn't even keep her own name straight.

Carcano appraised the men facing him, seated like Mafia dons with their capos standing behind them. He set the cigar aside and spit the loose bits of tobacco into a handkerchief. He reached for a glass of mineral water over ice—he preferred bourbon to wash the taste of stale tobacco from his mouth, but he'd abstain from alcohol until they completed this task.

He looked at Reginald Deighton. "What's been the problem?"

Deighton didn't avert his eyes. "Diana Willis has been both incredibly lucky and more wily than we assumed."

Carcano's mind cycled through a catalog of insults, but this was not the time. His underlings needed guidance. "We need to undo her luck and use her wiliness against herself."

Deighton shifted his head only enough to show that he was processing what Carcano had said but didn't yet have a response.

"What is Diana's fatal flaw?" Carcano asked. "What is the chink in her armor?"

"Her kryptonite," someone in the back of the room said.

Carcano squared his shoulders toward the voice. "Who said that?"

Nemer Indarte emerged from behind the others.

"You used the word 'kryptonite.'"

"Indeed, sir."

"Explain."

"Diana's kryptonite, or fatal flaw as you stated, General, is this…" Nemer Indarte clasped his hands behind his back and turned as he spoke to address the assembled men. His composure was cool as ice. "Her search for identity. You had mentioned that she didn't even know her real name. She perceives a huge void within her and she cannot rest until she fills that void with the truth, or what she thinks is the truth."

Carcano liked what this strange man was relating. "How is this her kryptonite?"

"Because it will lead to her doom. No doubt her senses are on full alert. But we will set a trap with bait she cannot resist."

"Which is?"

Nemer Indarte now faced Carcano. "The answer to who she is."

CHAPTER NINETEEN

*Y*our missions are becoming clearer. When two or more focus on the same goal, it amplifies the manifestation. If more join you, you will be an unbeatable force of good. That is what the dark forces and their controlling sycophants are trying to stop. Stay steady and unite.

Morning light poured through the open blinds and warmed Diana's face, waking her. The smell of freshly brewed coffee filled her nostrils. The sensations were pleasant, comforting. As she gathered her sleepy mind, a sudden thought sliced into her consciousness: *You will die before you find the truth.*

She bolted upright, cold chills running up her arms and down the back of her neck.

That voice. That warning.

She clutched her throat and realized she wasn't breathing. Gazing about the bedroom, she saw she was alone. Details about her immediate circumstances coalesced. Gabe Mendoza was also here in the apartment. Deciding that she was safe, Diana relaxed.

But that voice. It had come to her while she was asleep. A dream? Her suspicions told her no. *It has to be Briscane.*

If that message was meant to scare her, it had done that. But it also advertised danger and kept her senses sharp.

She got up, stepped into the bathroom, and emerged a moment later to slip into jeans, a t-shirt, and a loose blouse. She padded into the living room and found Gabe in a robe, sitting on the sofa, drinking coffee. He had a dazed look, like he didn't know where he was.

"You doing okay?" she asked.

Gabe shook his head as if to clear away cobwebs. He raised the cup. "Definitely better now that I'm having a decent cup instead of frog water."

Diana detoured into the kitchen and poured herself a cup, then returned to Gabe. "What's going on?"

He inhaled deeply and stared at the leaf of steam rising from his coffee. That dazed look returned.

She eased herself beside him. He scooted over to keep their hips from brushing.

"What I mean, Gabe, is that you and I have been through the wringer."

"Don't I know it."

"Why is this happening to us? What's at play?"

Gabe shrugged and sipped coffee. "What's at play? I don't know. I just know my life fell apart. One moment, I thought I had everything in one tight ball, then it all disintegrated. Nothing made sense. Everything seemed a lie. What kept me from going insane was drinking, but that had its own price. My mind was in an alcoholic haze, where nothing mattered. I lost my job. Lost my apartment. My possessions. Found myself homeless, a worthless alcoholic, and yet, even in that miasma of despair, I found myself pulled toward you."

"Why?" Diana asked.

"Because you are at the center of all this turmoil." Gabe raised his hand. "I'm not blaming you for what is happening. But what's happening is about you."

With that comment, in Diana's mind, many thoughts tumbled into place but didn't quite lock together. Gabe was right, though she'd have to learn more.

"Is that why you were waiting for me outside my building?"

Gabe nodded. He slurped from his cup and said, "That whole Apex Media-City of Columbus controversy threw me. I recognized the corruption going on between the media and those they represented. It was supposed to be the truth we were communicating. Instead, it became a shit show of deception and distraction."

Diana shook her head. "And to think I was part of that."

"It was a blessing in disguise." Gabe held his coffee cup in both hands as if to comfort himself from its warmth. "What happened opened my eyes. When you lose everything, you're forced to evaluate life with brutal honesty."

He took another sip. "My journey to this epiphany began in Columbus, in a hotel bar of all places. After Larry told me to shelve my investigation into Green Planet, I headed to the bar to drown my misgivings with booze. I talked to a strange old man beside me. When I told him about EDCs, Endocrine Disruptive Chemicals, he knew more about them than I did. From there, we discussed conspiracy theories. Then, before he disappeared, he emphatically said, 'Wake up! It's not as it seems. There is only one way out of their great web.'"

The news startled Diana. "What did this man look like?"

"White guy. Mid-sixties. Dressed in ratty clothes, which was surprising considering the hotel." Gabe added more descriptions, but truthfully, the stranger could've been any older white male.

"Did he give you his name?" Diana desperately wanted Gabe to say, "John Herald." But when Gabe said that the man had not shared his name, Diana realized her situation remained a tangle of mysteries. Yet, the man had used the exact words as John Herald in her dreams. *Wake up! It's not as it seems.*

"He also said that we have to 'stop the hypocrisy' before he vanished in the bathroom."

Eyebrows suddenly arching, Diana stared at Gabe. "He did?"

"Why are you asking?"

"I need to know if it was John Herald."

"Well, he vanished like the mysterious pilot did."

She explained her assignment to investigate him but discovering that it was not to learn about him, but to stop him. And apparently, now her as well. But stop her from what?

Gabe pressed, "You think the strange man in the hotel was John Herald?"

Diana wasn't sure about much of anything. "I don't know."

"Crazy things happened to both of us." Gabe blotted his eyes with the sleeve of his robe. "I also started having these unusual memories."

Diana took Gabe's hand. "Me too. What did you remember?"

His gaze focused on something beyond the room. "A building and various rooms where I was kept with other kids my age. But it wasn't a school. Or a camp. It was like a hospital or a university where we were given tests. But I can't recall what tests. The more I remembered the place, the more I realized other things, other connections. It was

232

like I had special powers to recognize the significance of events that were in plain sight and yet their relationships were kept hidden, deliberately invisible."

"I'm getting memories of a similar facility," Diana said.

Gabe pulled free of Diana's grasp and stood up from the sofa. He reached inside his old and tatty backpack and removed crumpled and tattered pages covered in notes. He flipped through the pages to one busy with words and arrows pointing in all directions. "I know of such a place. In Mill Valley."

Diana gasped, realizing a connection. "There's a woman there I have to find. She found me unconscious on the beach after the crash and saved my life."

Gabe knit his brow. "But the crash didn't happen at the beach."

"I know. But after surviving the crash, I found myself drawn into a tunnel, a passage. I don't know what. But one moment I was at the crash site and the next, I was on the beach."

"Perhaps you don't remember walking to the beach."

"That's not all that happened. I was holding a red book with a silver pinecone on the cover. The book was a journal of some sort, and the amazing part was that I had written notes in it as a child."

"What happened to the book?"

Diana closed her eyes. The memories had come to her vivid as color photographs but were now blurred and uncertain. "The woman who found me on the beach has it. Her name is Sally Mund. When she approached me in this memory, if we can call it that, she used my actual name."

"Your actual name?"

"Alexandra Starnowski."

"Then why are you known as Diana Willis?"

"They gave me the name. Whoever 'they' are. Then, when I woke up from the coma, I said my name was Diana Star. I guess unconsciously I knew something was different about me."

Gabe waved his notes. "What is happening here?"

"You're asking me?" Diana replied. "If this isn't disturbing enough, last night I heard an unfamiliar voice telling me, 'You will die before you find the truth.' I think this has to do with another message I heard when I was staggering along the beach after the crash. 'Get their attention before it's too late.' Too late for what?"

"I might have an idea," Gabe said. "The stranger in the hotel told me to follow the trail to Second Eden Technologies."

"What, Jeff Kennedy's brainchild?"

"Yes, and guess who is one of his investors?" Gabe pointed to a page on his notepad. "None other than our former CEO, Dan Talbot, who may soon be governor."

"What are they doing?"

Gabe jabbed at his notes and explained. "In a nutshell, controlling us by developing mechanisms that will monitor our physical movements and even our thoughts.

"Starting with injections under the guise of vaccinations. That's why GGM blocked the Apex Media–City of Columbus story and water contamination. The water many of us are drinking is numbing us mentally and making it easier to not fight back. The same people connected to Eden own GGM's holding company. It's a web."

"That doesn't explain why they're trying to kill me," Diana said.

"When we learn that, it will illuminate the big picture. I kept digging and looking and I found so much about these criminals at Eden and beyond."

"We have to get the truth out to as many people who will listen!" Diana then paused, thinking. This was unfolding too easily. Almost as if she and Gabe had been following a trail of crumbs. They had just revealed their next steps. To go find Sally Mund in Mill Valley and why. She placed a finger over her lips and held up her other hand. Gabe nodded. From the kitchen counter, she wrote on a notepad:

What if they're listening? We can't leave in my car. I know who will help us.

Nemer Indarte sat back and removed his headphones. He reached for his phone and sent a text: They know and will know more. Communication lost.

He sent another text: Wait for them there. They're coming.

He stood and walked into an adjacent room. Maggie LaClair lay on a bed, naked, unconscious. Syringes and glass ampules cluttered an adjacent bedside table.

An audio recording repeated softly from unseen speakers. "You are nothing. You are owned. You obey. You trust us. You will always be owned. You will complete the mission."

He switched off the audio and sat on the bed next to her. He caressed her face. "Susie, it's showtime."

She remained unresponsive. He selected a syringe and filled it from one ampule. He scooted to the foot of the bed and clasped her leg by the ankle. He rested her foot on his thigh and spread her big and second toes. He eased the needle into the gap and depressed the plunger, emptying the syringe.

As he waited for the drug to take effect, he cooed to her. "You've betrayed your nemesis once before, and now it's time to do it again. You must finish the mission. The entire world is depending on you."

He laid her leg on the bed and rose to lean over her head. Her eyes fluttered and color flushed her cheeks. Her lips parted slightly and her chest lifted.

"Susie, this is your real name. Susie, wake up now!" He clapped his hands hard.

Susie, aka Maggie LaClair, opened her eyes.

Walt. There was a knock at the door. Diana checked the security app on her phone and verified it was Walt Deveron, her trusted building security man.

She let him in and he entered with a cheap carry-on bag in hand. She gave him a notepad and a pen. He glanced at her and as she held a finger to her lips, he nodded in comprehension and scribbled on the pad:

Car is downstairs. When you're ready, I will drive you.

Walt passed the bag to Gabe. It contained a change of clothes that Diana had instructed Walt to bring. Gabe took the bag with him to the bathroom.

Diana stared at her new phone. *Can I trust Cal?* Not only that, but if she was worried about someone eavesdropping on her, then what about the security of her phone? Unfortunately, she had no other way of contacting him. She texted: Need to meet Sally Mund. Can you help?

The reply was almost immediate. Yes, where are you?

She replied: Let's meet.

Where?

Mill Valley. Will advise a place. Wait for details.

Diana pocketed the phone. Gabe returned and was dressed in casual clothes. She cocked her head toward the door.

Cal Brock felt another rush of the same energy he always felt when Diana needed his help. He knew it was more than a professional duty; it was the pull of a romantic attraction. How many classes had he taken? How many examples had they shown him that showed the dangers of getting emotionally involved with a subject? But he couldn't help himself. Something new beckoned him to her and without hesitation he texted her: OK, standing by.

He exhaled and leaned back in his chair. Several other agents were on the phone at their desks. It was a bustling day at the San Francisco FBI office.

He turned his attention to his computer and typed Willis, Diana into the search bar. He was accessing secret federal databases. Within seconds, he was staring at a photograph of her. He clicked through several links, finding nothing new. He next typed in Monarch Mind Control and found himself at The Origins and Techniques of Monarch Mind Control. He skimmed through the article and stopped at a heading, Methods, to read the key points.

About 75% are female since they possess a higher pain tolerance and dissociate more easily than males.

Monarch handlers seek the compartmentalization of their subject's psyche in multiple and separate alter personas using trauma to cause dissociation. The programmer/handler calls the victim/survivor a "slave," the handler is perceived as "master" or "god."

He looked away from the screen briefly and then continued to scroll further and read dismayingly: Torture:

Some torture included: abuse, confinement in boxes, cages, coffins, etc. Restraint with ropes, or chains, near-drowning, extremes of heat and cold, blinding light, electric shock, sleep deprivation. Spiritual abuse to cause the victim to feel possessed, harassed, and controlled internally by spirits or demons. Dedication to Satan or other deities and convincing victims that God is evil.

Brock stopped reading and exited the page, wondering *What is the connection between Diana, Sally Mund, and John Herald?*

He next searched Herald, John and scrolled through the links: Great Global Media, NTSB Investigation, Bureau of Missing Persons, Witnesses.

What was he looking for? He wasn't sure. How could Diana and John Herald have nearly identical DNA, a match that in other circumstances would've made them kin, though he knew they weren't related. And what was the relationship between Diana and Sally Mund?

Brock stared at the computer in frustration. *How about I resort to some old-fashioned police work? I'll ask Sally myself.*

He accessed the database and easily found the phone number for Mund, Sally. He dialed on his landline and unfortunately, the call went straight to voicemail.

He left his message: "Ms. Mund, this is Special Agent Cal Brock with the Federal Bureau of Investigation. We had spoken earlier. Please call me as soon as possible. This is very important." Brock recited his cell phone number and hung up.

He made sure he had his car keys, then slipped into his jacket and headed out the door.

Walt Deveron drove his Toyota Camry close to the basement-level door at the rear of Diana's condominium building. He kept a vigilant eye in all directions. The parking garage door cracked open, and Gabe glanced to see that the way was clear. He held the door for Diana, who rushed for the front passenger side of the Toyota. He slid into the back seat, and no sooner had he and Diana slammed their respective doors shut, than Walt sped up out of the alley and wheeled onto the street.

Diana clicked her safety belt. "Walt, I really appreciate this."

He huffed as if his help was not worth mentioning. "We'll go for a bit to make sure we're not being tailed. Then you can take the car from there."

As they turned left at the first light, Walt saw a billboard looming high. On it was the all-seeing eye that adorns the dollar bill. Underneath it read: In Bay Bank We Trust. He looked at Diana and smirked. An omen?

He drove around a few blocks and finally stopped in a residential neighborhood within sight of the Golden Gate Bridge. "I think we're good."

Diana looked around and exhaled.

Walt cracked his door open. A chime sounded. "You take it from here."

"Thanks. I'll bring the car back in one piece, I promise."

He laughed. "Don't worry, I have another one."

Diana fished a small envelope from her coat pocket and gave it to Walt.

His brow knit. "What's this?"

"In case something happens to us," she cocked a thumb at Gabe in the backseat, "read the details and follow the instructions."

Walt shoved the envelope into his coat pocket. "Will do." He climbed out of the car and looked back at her. "Take care of yourself, Ms. Willis."

"You mean Diana Star."

As an ex-military man, Walt could see the fear in Diana's eyes. He nodded and walked away, leaving the driver's door open. By the time Diana got out, he had disappeared.

Diana drove the Toyota toward the Golden Gate Bridge. Gabe sat beside her in the front passenger seat.

She had finished explaining the events of the helicopter crash, what she knew about John Herald, and her reason to see Sally Mund.

Gabe asked, "Where was the helicopter going that morning?"

"Monte Rio. Herald was heading to Bohemian Grove. I think I have a connection with that place. I was investigating Herald and was given a long file chronicling his alleged misdeeds. The info was on a thumb drive, which was stolen while I was in the coma. But what I was given about Herald was bait to get me on the flight with him so we could be finished off together."

Gabe pursed his lips. "So the crash was not an accident?"

"The investigators are saying it was not. Somehow Herald kept the craft under control until I got ejected safely."

"What happened to Herald? You've said he survived. Who is he?"

Diana replied, "That's what I'm still trying to figure out. He and I have a connection that goes beyond what happened at the helicopter crash."

"I have to ask again. Was the man I met at the bar John Herald?"

Her skin rippled with gooseflesh. "What can I say? You and I are on the cusp of something huge."

"Diana," Gabe began solemnly, "I believe this connection you mentioned goes beyond you and Herald. I'm certain that I'm involved as well. Everything that I've gone through lately is bringing back old memories."

Diana glanced up from the road. "Memories that we're not supposed to remember."

"Memories that others will murder us over?"

The gooseflesh returned to Diana's arms.

Gabe groped for the console's latch.

"What are you looking for?" she asked.

"I dunno. Whatever's here." He rummaged through receipts, paper napkins, then pulled out a small handgun. "Something like this. A Beretta Cheetah."

"Walt loves his guns. Maybe he left it for us."

"Apparently." Gabe pulled the slide backwards. "It's loaded." He returned the Beretta to the console and closed the lid.

They remained quiet until Diana made the turn off Route One at Stinson Beach towards Mt. Tamalpais State Park. She stopped the car on a small side road. "From here it's a short hike to the crash site."

Diana and Gabe set out on foot to where she and Herald had defied death months earlier.

Diana stood motionless and silent at the spot where the helicopter had crashed. She walked around the scorched indentation in the ground to see it from different viewpoints. It had not only scarred the earth but also her psyche.

Diana's mind was pulled again to the same terrifying memory. The deafening noise. Herald shouting at her. Being flung out the door and landing on her back. The helicopter in stutter motion as it glided above her. John Herald's voice: *Wake up! It's not as it seems.*

Then an explosion and fire.

The whine of a drone snapped Diana out of her memories. A small drone came over the hill and hovered above them.

To Diana, it felt as if the jaws of a trap were about to spring shut around her.

The loud *bang* of a gunshot filled the air. The drone shook and dropped from the sky.

"Oh my God!" Diana whipped about.

Gabe stood behind her, palming the Beretta that had been stashed in the car. He raised his eyebrows, indicating, *What's next?*

Diana pointed, "This way." And ran deeper into the park.

CHAPTER TWENTY

*W*hen those forces of darkness come at you, don't let your mind swim in fear's hysteria. Your fears are often the worst liars.

Dare to defeat that enemy of fear within you. If you can master that enemy, you will be ready to fight the enemy you can see.

Agent Cal Brock was driving over the Golden Gate Bridge when his phone vibrated. The text from Diana read: At crash site. Being followed. Need help.

He voiced the text reply: On the way. Try to hide.

He immediately sped up and used voice commands on his car phone. "Call Mill Valley police."

Diana and Gabe crouched behind an outcropping of rocks.

She peeked through a gap in the weeds and gathered her breath to speak. "They don't give up."

"These the same guys associated with the goon I clobbered outside your place?" Gabe asked.

"I'm sure of it. They even used the same type of drone." She looked to where it had fallen in the brush. "Where did you learn to shoot like that?"

Gabe shrugged. "Honestly, it was a lucky shot."

"I'm not crazy about guns, but it's good that you have one." She held her phone and started texting. "I'm going to get help."

Gabe peeked over the rocks and asked worriedly, "What's this about? Why are some very powerful people risking so much to keep you quiet?"

"That's a question I keep asking myself. What do I know?" Dried leaves rustled about her knees and the noise cautioned her to keep still.

Cal Brock's text arrived: On the way. Stay behind cover. Send your location so I can find you.

Diana relaxed. "My friend the FBI agent is on his way."

"In the meantime," Gabe settled behind the biggest of the rocks, "how did the bad guys find us?"

She gazed at her phone. *No way.* She held up her phone. "Damn it. Probably with this."

Time for this chick to die. The assassin cradled his gun, actually a black-market, short-barreled AR15 carbine with a 30-round magazine, a collapsible stock, the serial numbers filed off, a scope, and a suppressor. The gun was illegal in so many ways, but then again, so was murder. He rushed on foot toward where the drone went down. The last seconds of its video were of a man on the ground, pointing a handgun at it. So the man with the target was armed. The assassin didn't regard it as much of a complication.

He halted to confirm the drone's location on his tracker, then sent a text to his accomplice: Drone destroyed. Deploy another. Continuing on foot.

Even though Cal Brock had advised Diana to stay behind cover, the bad guys were more likely to arrive before Brock did. So Diana and Gabe put as much distance between themselves and whoever was after her as they could. They ran along a narrow game trail that wove in and out of the thicket until they reached a fork in the trail.

Gabe bent forward to rest his hands on his knees. He gulped for breath and studied the two paths ahead. "Which way?"

Diana had to likewise catch her breath. She wasn't certain how to proceed but a hunch told her: "Right."

They hustled along the new trail, which became little more than a tunnel through the thick brush. Then the air cooled dramatically, and they were aware of being amidst gigantic redwood trees that were familiar to Diana. They rounded a curve in the trail, proceeded about fifty meters, and suddenly the vegetation parted to reveal an arrangement of buildings in a lush, shallow valley.

Gabe halted and pointed to the buildings. "I recognize those buildings."

Diana stopped beside him. *Yes, something about this place is very familiar.* She glanced over her shoulder. So far, no sign of the bad guys. She prodded Gabe forward. "Let's go."

The assassin tamped down his excitement, for he had to keep a clear head. But he couldn't ignore the strong signal emanating from his tracker. The target and her partner had vacated their cover from behind the outcropping and fled down the trail. As he followed them, he didn't spot any sign that they had disappeared into the brush.

The tracker said that the target was straight ahead. He knew the man carried a gun, so the assassin had to be careful he didn't blunder into an ambush.

A drone buzzed overhead. The assassin recognized it as one of theirs. The drone slowed and hovered above the trail. The assassin's phone showed a text: Clear.

How could the trail be clear? The assassin checked his tracker. The signal was still strong.

He cupped the tracker against the forestock of the carbine and shouldered the gun. His eyes darted to the left and right. Nothing. Holding his breath, he advanced, ready to open fire.

He pivoted and swept the area with the gun's muzzle and followed the tracker's signal as it led him to a tree. There it was, in a crack where the trunk branched upward. The phone.

Which meant the target and her pal had continued up the trail. The assassin pocketed the phone and hurried after them.

The buildings with their modern sharp angles and abrupt curves looked so very out of place against the bucolic backdrop of the Mill

Valley. Diana and Gabe stepped away from the trail onto a broad grassy meadow. They advanced with trepidation as if their presence in this locale plucked at the edges of repressed nightmares. Diana had the sensation of standing on the edge of a cliff and staring into a forbidden abyss.

Gabe tapped her arm. "Someone's coming." He palmed the Beretta.

An older model pickup approached on a gravel road. Its horn honked. Diana regarded the truck with confusion. Killers wouldn't announce themselves like this, would they?

The windshield's reflection prevented Diana from identifying who was in the truck. It skidded to a halt, flinging dust and pebbles. An older woman, wearing a knit cap, yelled at them from the driver's open window. "Come on. Get in."

Diana instantly recognized her. The woman from her dreams and repressed memories. Sally Mund.

Diana's nerves tingled with alarm. She yanked Gabe's sleeve. "Let's not waste time."

They sprinted to the truck and dove into the bed. Sally Mund accelerated into a tight circle, dusty rooster tails shooting from her rear tires, and raced away on the gravel road.

The assassin was on the trail at the far side of the meadow and watched the target escape in a pickup. He scanned the empty sky for evidence of the drone. *Damn toys, how many times have they failed us?*

The truck had disappeared behind a wall of dense pine trees.

Frustrated, he texted: Target escaped in pickup.

The reply was instant: Whose vehicle?

The assassin let his carbine hang on its sling and as he walked across the meadow, texted: Don't know. Am proceeding on foot.

The pickup halted beside a small cottage tucked among the pines. The abode was humble, and this deep in the forest seemed like the place where fairies and elves would live.

They all climbed out of the truck and gathered by the front door. Sally Mund squinted at her guests. "Alexa Star. Miguel Garcia. Do you remember me?"

"Sally Mund," Diana answered. "You were there at the helicopter crash."

"Wait a minute," Gabe exclaimed. "Why did you call me Miguel Garcia? Is that my real name?"

Sally cocked her head like a dog when it's trying to understand. "Don't you know?" She looked at Diana.

"I barely remember," Diana replied.

"How much was taken from us?" Gabe asked. "Why?" He remained still, as if shell shocked.

Diana clasped his arm. "We're in this together, Gabe. Have faith that when we find the truth, we'll be stronger for it."

Gabe patted her hand, then pulled free. Diana waited for him to say something, but his expression showed that he was stuck, trying to sort out what to think about what had happened to him.

Sally led them inside her home. The furnishings were mismatched and haphazard as if bought at a thrift store. But everything was clean and neat and the ambiance decidedly cozy, a sanctuary to hide from the world.

"I knew you'd come," Sally said, her voice soft and her eyes with a faraway cast.

"You keep appearing in my dreams," Diana said.

"And you in mine," Sally replied. She offered them wooden chairs to sit. "We have little time. The men pursuing you haven't given up."

"So what do we do?"

"Wait." Sally looked at Diana. "Your friend is coming."

"Cal Brock? How do you know that?"

Sally hushed them with an upraised finger. "We have a more pressing matter."

"Which is?"

"Learning the truth." Sally eased into an armchair that faced them. "When you were both around six, an evil group of people, part of a dark force that was doing terrible experiments on mind control, abducted you. They turned people into sex slaves, spies, assassins, and couriers. They sent you to a secret institute that once occupied the building where I got you. The operation was called Project Monarch."

Gabe said, "I know about Monarch. The media uses many of their programming techniques to manipulate the masses to think a certain way."

"Yes!" Sally nodded and then continued, "They put many like you through this program, but everyone has at some point been brainwashed or controlled by it." She leaned forward. "And you

Alexa, because of your special abilities, you were reassigned to Project Stargate."

"Stargate?" Diana asked.

"Remote viewing," Gabe explained. "They groomed you as a psychic spy."

"But your abilities showed a powerful potential," Sally said. "During your episodes of remote viewing, you claimed to be receiving transmissions from another world, specifically a world similar to ours, but several hundred years ahead of us. You said the messages were from the Secret Transmissions Allied Response, or STAR you called them."

Diana felt her forehead tighten. Taken at face value, Sally's words seemed ridiculous, but they conjured repressed memories that promised to illuminate a greater truth.

Sally added, "There were some of us who tried to keep STAR a secret, but the dark forces found out and sabotaged the program, fearing what you learned would destroy them. When you came to us, your name was Alexandra Starnowski. We called you Alexa Star because of your name and the connection you had with the STAR. You were fearless. But as a young girl, you were vulnerable, and they wore you down until you submitted."

Diana looked at Gabe. He appeared as astounded by these revelations as she was.

Sally centered herself with a deep breath, then said, "My role was to look after all of you. There were ten of you little angels, Miguel, now Gabe. You stayed with us for about six years until the dark masters decided your abilities were fading, or in your case, Alexa, they were growing too powerful. I don't know what became of the others. I feel they may have met a terrible fate."

"And you?" Diana asked. "How did they let you go?"

Sadness rippled across Sally's face. "Like many other recruits to Monarch and Stargate, they used psychedelic drugs to alter my mind."

"LSD?" Gabe asked.

"Actually, weaponized LSD. The drugs reduced us to barely functional idiots."

"The idea," Gabe said, "that even if you told the truth, no one would believe you."

"Exactly," Sally replied.

Diana got dizzy from disbelief. What madness were the dark forces responsible for?

"Fortunately, I kept myself sane, more or less," Sally explained. "I knew no one would believe me, so I laid low, waiting until you showed up, Alexa."

"How did you know I'd return?"

"Those dreams and visions when I appeared to you were actually a portal opening between us."

"How?" Diana asked.

"That I can't answer." Sally looked at her guests. "But what I can explain is that the day you left us was the saddest day of my life. They then trained you as a sex slave and sold you to a wealthy media mogul."

"Who?" Diana interrupted.

Sally shrugged. "Then you were reprogrammed as Diana Willis to become the media darling the country knew. When I saw you on television, I prayed that the spell the dark forces had put on you would vanish. I hoped you would wake up again and remember your mission."

"Mission?" Diana asked.

"To prepare the way by sharing the messages from STAR with everyone who will hear, so they can know the truth and make different choices." Sally grimaced as she squirmed uncomfortably in her chair. "I waited patiently until you were ready. When the moment was right, we would orchestrate a traumatic event to knock you out of that invented world."

"The helicopter crash?" Diana asked.

Sally nodded. Sweat beaded on her forehead.

"John Herald knew?" Diana asked.

"John Herald is an alias, but yes, he knew."

"You had said 'we'?" Diana asked.

"John Herald and I. It was no coincidence that I arrived when I did at the beach after the crash. John Herald was a project leader in Stargate, but his job was to monitor what the dark masters were doing. He had sabotaged the Stargate program and saved you."

"Where is he now?"

"He'll appear when it's appropriate." Sally furrowed her brow and stared at Diana.

"What's wrong?" Diana asked when she felt a shimmer in the air.

Then, between them, materialized the red book, slowly spinning, the silver pinecone on the cover rotating in and out of view.

The mysterious red book from her memory!

Diana cut her gaze from the book to Sally and was about to ask about the book when she realized Sally could read her thoughts.

What do you know about this book?

Sally replied *You sent it from the future.*

What does that mean?

Sally closed her eyes, and her face turned dark and clammy. Diana was about to ask if something was wrong when she felt another presence. To her right, the silhouette of a man darkened and when its features sharpened, she saw it was Briscane. Not his physical form, but his psychic persona. His eyes turned from her to the spinning red book.

She heard his thought to Sally, *What is this?*

The telepathic bridge abruptly closed. The book vanished.

Briscane scowled and glared at Sally. She clenched her jaw and forced a swallow. It was as if the words got stuck in her throat. Her face became bright crimson and her eyes strained in their sockets.

Diana sprang from her chair. "What's wrong?"

Briscane's thoughts slithered into her mind. *Tell me about this red*— Diana's resolve hardened, readying for a fight. Then it was like an iron door had dropped between her and Briscane. He pruned his lips in frustration and turned his attention to Sally. Her mouth formed an "O," and it was as if she was choking on her tongue.

Then a loud bang and shattered glass showered the room.

Briscane disappeared like a puff of smoke.

Gabe shrieked as blood spurted from his arm. He threw himself to the ground and scrambled to get the Beretta out of his pants pocket.

Diana hesitated, torn between saving herself or helping Sally.

Sally slumped in her armchair. A bloody stain spread across her belly.

Oh God! She's been shot.

Diana dropped to the floor, not willing to be the third one in the room to stop a bullet. She lizard-crawled across the carpet toward Sally, ignoring the broken glass.

Sally's eyes became bloodshot and unfocused. She wheezed and red foam bubbled on her lips. Diana reached for her wrist and tried to pull her to the floor.

In the distance approached the wailing sirens of emergency vehicles.

His finger positioned on the trigger, the assassin centered the target in his carbine's scope. The target, her male companion, and the older woman had gone inside. Luckily for the assassin, and unluckily for the three inside, they had neglected to draw the curtains over the front window. He had the perfect shot through the window to his target's head and at this distance—seventy-five meters—couldn't miss.

He took slack out of the trigger. *Hasta la vista, baby.*

Just as the trigger clicked, a light bloomed in his scope, blinding him.

Murray Sims tracked the assassin, triangulating the man's cell phone signal. Earlier, he had hacked the drones and kept them from following Diana. He'd also locked onto Diana's phone, which the assassin now possessed, and relayed its signal to Cal Brock.

He watched the assassin crouch behind brush and steady himself for a shot. Murray positioned himself behind a bush a hundred feet to the left. He didn't have a gun, but he had a laser. From this angle, he could illuminate the front of the carbine's scope.

He waited until the assassin was about to fire a shot and then aimed the laser. Its beam splashed across the scope's front lens. The assassin jerked back as he fired, clenched his eyes, and squeezed off a second shot. He pulled his face from the scope, blinked, and scowled.

At the sound of the approaching sirens, the assassin staggered from his hiding place and ran to the road.

Murray had done his job, and it was now his turn to go.

Though in great pain, Sally mustered the last of her strength to focus her eyes on Diana and mutter, "Go to the forest where you found your father."

Diana recoiled in surprise.

Sally collapsed from the chair and sprawled on the carpet.

Diana saw herself as the young Alexa, now back with the older woman who handed her the journal with the red cover. Alexa ran her fingers over the silver pinecone embossed on the cover. She gazed into the eyes of the woman, and Alexa perceived that she and this stranger were the same person.

"What does this all mean?" Alexa asked.

The woman answered, "You have returned from the future and there is no fear. You are courageous and free."

As the woman disappeared, she heard the haunting words again, "Get their attention before it's too late."

Diana's consciousness was drawn back to the house, the police sirens, and her current predicament.

As Diana, as *Alexa* Star, with these revelations, she knew what had to be done.

Part III
ARRIVALS

CHAPTER TWENTY-ONE

The dark forces use hate as their power source. They feed and thrive on it. Do whatever possible to stay away from hate.

One of your distinguished physicists, who once asked for my help, said about evil, "The world is a dangerous place to live; not because of the people who are evil, but because of the people who do nothing about it."

It's too much. Diana sat on the bathroom floor in her condo, dressed in a bathrobe, her back against the wall. She wept in despair and helplessness. Her life, once so well ordered and optimistic, had crumbled into confusion and fear. Everything she knew about herself lay in pieces.

Just as she had been regaining the memories of her mother, now came the realization that Magdalena was not her biological mother. And more startling was the news that she had the same DNA profile as John Herald.

So many unanswered questions. How can I be related to this stranger, if I am? What happened to the other man I kept seeing in my visions... Joseph. Is he not my father? They shot him. Why? By whom? Where in the woods was he killed?

Remembering that she had tucked her cell phone in her robe, Diana fished it out. Without thinking, she retrieved the number for Dr. Bowman's office and punched it in. If there was a better time for therapy, she didn't know when it could be.

"Dr. Bowman's office, Meredith speaking." It was Bowman's new office manager.

Diana introduced herself as a client and said she would like to schedule a visit.

"Dr. Bowman is not taking appointments at the moment."

At first, Diana was taken aback, but then recognized an anxious timbre in Meredith's voice. "Is there something wrong?"

"I'm sorry, I'm not at liberty to say," Meredith answered, her voice becoming tight.

Diana forced herself to keep her imagination from running amok. No one knew her better than Dr. Bowman. Something indeed might have happened to Dr. Bowman. And nothing good.

"I will certainly let her know you called." Without waiting for a response from Diana, she ended the call.

Diana put away her cell phone. The red book and its silver symbol appeared in her thoughts. She imagined the way the book floated in the air. They had tapped her for something momentous, something that commanded her to rise above these present circumstances. She had to act on the *mission.*

But there were other considerations she had to manage as well. Such as Sally Mund's murder. In the thirty hours since then, officials had taken her and Gabe to an auxiliary station of the FBI's San Francisco office, out of the prying eyes of the media. Other than the initial police and FBI presence after the shooting, the handling of the incident had been remarkably hush-hush. After they had given their statements, they escorted her and Gabe back to her condo. The entire incident, from the time she had seen Sally Mund collapse from her chair, bleeding, until this moment, had been one long blur. And Diana thought Sally Mund's murder was likely a botched attempt on her.

"Diana, how are you holding up?" Cal Brock called from the other side of the door.

She blinked to corral her thoughts and picked herself up off the floor. She washed her face and patted it dry, studying herself in the mirror and deciding that when this ordeal was over, she was going to treat herself to a long weekend in the most luxurious spa she could afford. She put on casual clothes and hung up her robe.

Brock smiled wanly when she emerged into the hall. He motioned toward another man, a tech of some type, arranging electronic devices in a tool bag. "We've scanned your apartment for surveillance equipment. We didn't find any."

They walked into the living room. Diana settled onto the sofa, and Brock sat in an armchair. The tech dismissed himself and left.

Brock leaned forward. "I know you've got a lot to sort out, but we have to keep moving forward with this. It's important to know how you, Sally Mund and John Herald are connected. That will shed light on who is after you and why."

The wall-mounted control panel chimed. It was the building security system, alerting Diana that Gabe Mendoza was in the lobby entrance. She stood and walked to the panel, glanced at the video to verify it was him, and tapped the button that let him through. "It's Gabe," she said to Brock.

Brock stood. "I better be going. I have all I need for now and I'll get with the Mill Valley Police Department regarding what happened to Sally Mund."

He walked to the door and paused. "If it's not, it should be obvious that I was worried about you when you disappeared." His expression and tone showed a personal investment in her well-being, like he was hoping for extra between them.

"I'm glad to know this," she answered.

His head tipped toward her like he wanted to hear more. But she had nothing else to say.

He cleared his throat and said, "I'm on your side," sounding sheepish.

Diana smiled. Brock—the big, bad FBI agent—was quite charming. His words reinforced her sense of security and it calmed her that he would probably break a lot of rules to protect her.

He nodded and turned on his heel for the elevator. Its door pinged open, and he stepped inside just as Gabe stepped out. The two men exchanged cordial greetings. The elevator door pinged closed, and Gabe proceeded toward Diana. His left arm was in a sling, and he carried a canvas tote bag in his free hand.

"Gabe, how are you?"

He flapped his injured arm. "Got grazed, that's all."

Inside Diana's condo, Gabe retrieved a laptop and two cell phones from the tote bag and set them on the dining room table. "This computer has no wireless interface and is specially hardened to not emit any electronic signal. The only way to access it is by a physical connection."

"Very good."

She watched its screen as Gabe removed two legal pads and pens from the bag. "For notes, old school," he said, handing a pad and pen to her. They sat in adjacent chairs at the table.

Diana's pad was new, Gabe's already contained pages of hand-written notes. She wrote across the top of the first page of her pad: Control—Who controls the world, how and why?

Gabe thumbed through his notes. "We discussed earlier the many ways they are controlling us, and we know what Eden and their cohorts are up to."

Diana cocked her head to admire Gabe's extensive work. "When did you write all this?"

"My research started a while back. After meeting with the stranger in the hotel—"

"John Herald?" Diana interrupted.

"If it was him. But after meeting him I developed a new ability." Gabe flipped through pages crisscrossed with lines and arrows. "It's hard to explain, but suddenly I saw how everything is interconnected. I saw links and patterns. I diagnosed myself and it's apophenia."

"Maybe what you see is confirmation bias?"

"No. Imagine wandering in a maze of hedges. You only see what's in front of you and what you remember of your path. Now imagine being able to rise above the maze. You'll see the pattern, how the passages are connected."

Diana arched her eyebrows, impressed.

Gabe said, "But there was a dark side. When I went down this rabbit hole," he tapped his pen on his pad, "I insulated myself from the world by drinking. At first, it helped me focus, it pared down what was important, but the bottle always takes over."

"You became an alcoholic?"

"Sadly. But it was part of the process I had to go through. I've heard that when you're in crisis, you often hit rock bottom before you realize what you have to do or what's important."

"Which is?"

Tears welled in Gabe's eyes. "Keeping you alive and out of harm's way." He cleared his throat and flipped to the first page on his pad. He pointed to what he wrote across the top.

There is only one way out.

"The stranger told me this. And shortly, I discovered you were the conduit for this truth."

"Me?"

"Yes, and it's the one premise that drove me to everything else. Which has to do with this." He thumbed to another page with a sketch of a pinecone.

A pinecone, Diana thought. *Like the one on the mysterious red book and on the drawing the nurse gave me?*

"People are trying to kill me because of a pinecone?"

"Apparently." Gabe's tone was serious. "The pinecone represents the pineal gland, what's been called the seat of the soul. The third eye. The single eye of consciousness. It's a portal between the physical and spiritual worlds. When activated, a sensation of euphoria and oneness fills our mind, giving us a sense of all-knowing. Right before the stranger poked me in the forehead and vanished, he said, 'If you want to know the truth, then go to the source of the truth, and you will know.' I think he may have been referring to this and the light that is there. It's like a master switch. Meditation is the best way to access it."

"Meditation?" Diana asked, then added a glaze of humor. "Not booze?"

Gabe ignored the comment. "Think of vibrations. We're constantly emitting vibrations, but we seldom remain still to acknowledge them."

"Vibes. I get it," Diana offered.

"It's more complicated than that. To see the connections as I have, you must first activate the third eye, which is how you see into higher dimensions. To activate the third eye, the pineal gland and the pituitary body must vibrate in unison, which is achieved through meditation. At first, this third eye appears in the middle of the forehead, but as your meditation deepens, your awareness withdraws toward your pineal gland. Your various vibrations align. The changes to your energy fields can be measured at the atomic level."

"And you know this, how?"

Gabe flipped from page to page, each filled with notes and arrows, circles, and lines. "It's been documented for thousands of years throughout history. I'm not religious, but even Jesus referred to it when he said in Matthew 6:22, 'The light of the body is the eye: if therefore your eye is single, your entire body shall be full of light.' The Old Testament also refers to 'Peniel' meaning the face of God."

Gabe returned to the note on the first page. There is only one way out.

He read his other notes. "Here are some ways they control us: Population Control, Eugenics/Survival of the Fittest, The Coming New World Order, Poisoning our bodies, Nano Domestic Quell… NDQ…Media Propaganda, School System Brainwashing, Divide and Conquer, Fake Wars, and Debt Enslavement."

Diana paused a moment to take all this in. "But is this conspiracy theory stuff? So far, we can never find out who 'they' are."

"No, but we can focus on the 'why.' The stranger called it a conspiracy fact and called them the Controllers. He said the CIA invented the term *conspiracy theory to prevent disbelief of official government stories, and that the CIA-controlled media currently use this to* shut up skeptics by branding them conspiracy theorists. He said the greatest conspiracy is that no one knows these Controllers are hanging to their power by a thread. They develop propaganda and create political turmoil and wars to keep us distracted, overwhelmed by events, so we're numbed into complacency and inaction. They control us mentally by programming us to believe a certain way. They do this so we don't realize that if that thread breaks, they would lose their power."

"The basis of propaganda: Tell a lie repeatedly and eventually, people believe it as true," Diana said.

"Yes, many years ago, the KGB did some fascinating psychological experiments. They learned that if you bombard human subjects with fear messages nonstop, in two months, it completely brainwashed most of the subjects to believe the false message. To where no amount of truthful information to the contrary, can change their mind."

"For this to work, it needs the cooperation of mass media," Diana said.

"Exactly. What if those at the top of mass media have been co-opted? Notice how they work to divide society, get us to fight one another. It is through mass media that the Controllers control us mentally; they control our beliefs and thoughts. We create our reality from our beliefs and thoughts from those beliefs. We see and do what we believe. If we change our beliefs, we change our lives. So, if they control what we believe, they…"

"They control our reality," Diana added.

"Exactly." Gabe leaned closer. "The stranger called it the quiet war."

Diana froze for a moment as those familiar haunting words reverberated through her mind. "That's what a voice kept saying, the quiet war has begun, ready or not."

"So now we both know." Gabe rubbed the stubble on his face. "It was a synchronous message from Herald to keep us on track here."

Diana grabbed Gabe's arm. "A sign!"

Gabe nodded and pointed to another scribbled note. "I guess we could say that this quiet mind war started hundreds of years ago when royalty brought magicians to their courts, and not just for entertainment. They wanted to learn their art of deception. This became the basis of the Controllers' methods as the royal kingdom was the precursor of the modern power structure."

Diana reflected for a moment, then said, "And you and I have been part of this media deception for a long time."

"And the cognitive dissonance it creates in people's minds," Gabe added.

Diana pursed her lips in concern. "How do we stop this?"

"By saying, *no mas!* Stop acquiescing our power. Start thinking for ourselves. Then reprogram our subconscious minds and gain knowledge so we can then change our beliefs. Our brain is like a biological computer and can be programmed."

"What we learned at Monarch?" Diana asked.

"Yes, but for the positive."

Gabe busied himself with transcribing notes into the laptop.

"We can use the media against itself," Diana said.

Gabe paused his fingers on the keyboard. "What do you mean?"

"Larry owes me a comeback interview. Part of the reason is that he thinks it would draw a huge viewership. If it does, then I can persuade the station to give me a new show. That will be a venue to get our message out to the world," Diana said.

"You'll need Maggie LaClair," Gabe said.

"Maggie. Yes, of course." *Where had she gone? Was she in danger?* Diana reached for her new phone. "This is clean, right?"

"As clean as it can be," Gabe replied. "But once you use it, then all bets are off."

Diana typed a text to Maggie: Where are you? We are worried. Do you need help?

As Diana put the phone down, she said, "We know Second Eden is near the heart of this. Our next step is to find who is behind them."

"Even if we do, then what?" Gabe replied. "We better be careful if we are going to get the world's attention before it's too late. They killed Sally Mund and have come close several times with you. We know about mass media manipulation and its ties to Monarch mind control. Then there's psychic spying and remote viewing from Project Stargate. But the challenge is tying everything together."

"Which I'll explain in my interview." Diana noticed on one of Gabe's sheets a reference to Project Stargate. "Let me see this?"

Gabe handed her a wrinkled document from the pile. "Here we go."

She read the Overview:

The Stargate Project was the umbrella code name of one of several sub-projects established by the U.S. Federal Government to investigate claims of psychic phenomena with potential military and domestic applications, particularly "remote viewing": the purported ability to psychically "see" events, sites, or information from a great distance.

These projects were active from the 1970s through 1995 and were primarily handled by the DIA and CIA. They followed up on early psychic research done at The Stanford Research Institute (SRI), Science Applications International Corporation (SAIC), The American Society for Psychical Research, and other psychic research labs.

Diana's pen hovered over the legal pad. *I was there.*

She wrote: Stargate and Herald. Followed by a big question mark.

She sank inward, and Gabe and the dining room disappeared. Her consciousness was moving once again towards the same flickering light and laboratory table she had seen before in her memories. The flickering light coming from an overhead bank of fluorescent lamps. She was the same young girl and dressed in drab overalls. Clips in her hair held wires against her scalp, and they connected these wires to a computer.

A man in a rumpled blue suit handed her a drawing pad and a pencil, then adjusted a blindfold around her eyes.

Diana pressed the point of the pencil against the pad and remained still. She let her mind open like a window, as she'd done many times before. She waited.

A picture developed in her mind like an image on film. She outlined a building, first the walls, then the roof, the doors, and windows. The building had strange but interesting lines—lots of swooping curves—and its image was very distinctive.

Through a glass window into the next room of the laboratory, she saw a man hold up a photo of a building. *It was the exact building she had drawn.* She had the sensation of being here before, but this time she remembered more. Her eyes moved from the drawing and to the face of the man holding it. *John Herald.*

The chirp of a text alert jolted her from the reverie. Gabe remained busy typing on his keyboard.

"Herald was there."

Gabe quit typing and looked at her. "You remembered?"

"That's why he was so familiar."

"Stargate?" he asked. "Monarch?"

Where had she been during these memories? "I think Stargate." She reached for the phone to read the text.

Maggie: I am alright. Where are you?

"It's from Maggie," Diana said. "She is okay, thank God." She texted: At home. Can you come? Gabe is here. Could use your help.

Maggie: Be there first thing tomorrow.

"She'll be here in the morning," Diana noted. Her heart fluttered with ease. Maggie was okay. Gabe was okay. She was okay. Things were looking up.

"The team is back," Gabe said.

CHAPTER TWENTY-TWO

We have been using *Telepathy for thousands of your years. Telepathy is real and the way of the future, as is Frequency technology. The Controllers know this and want to harness it for their will against you.*

Since his riveting keynote speech at the Crypto-Confederation Technology conference, CEO and Chief Architect Jeff Kennedy's star continued to rise. He had secured millions of investment funding for his newest brainchild, Second Eden Technologies. Governor Dan Talbot had given him access to lots of political support and was an ally for navigating bureaucracies.

Second Eden occupied an impressive and sprawling campus, but it was what happened inside its walls that was the bigger prize.

Second Eden's avant-garde three-dimensional logo was a futuristic-looking symbol with three connecting lines meeting at the center. AI: Artificial Intelligence, AT: Advanced Technology, and IA: Intelligence Amplification. They superimposed this symbol over a brain, half-human, half-electronic.

Jeff Kennedy stared at the logo on the conference room wall, enamored by what the symbol represented. A young pretty blonde, so perfectly mannered and proportioned that she might as well have been an android, clicked buttons on the podium. She spun on her heels and nodded, showing it was time for Kennedy to earn his six-figure fee.

He stepped up to the podium and laid a small pile of 3x5 index cards on top. No one commented on the irony that here he was in the epicenter of high tech and was relying on paper notes. So nineteenth century. They might as well have spittoons under the table.

Kennedy surveyed his audience. Twelve men. Six women. Half of them were his industry peers, the others underlings striving to climb up the corporate ladder. They watched him, waiting to see how he would dazzle them. After soft-humored jabs at his hosts and a couple of jokes at his own expense, he began the speech, his tone serious. "Superhuman brains, what we call IA or Intelligence Amplification, have always been the desire of humanity, the next step for homo sapiens. We are here to accelerate our evolution." Kennedy pointed to the Second Eden logo on the wall, emphasizing the trinity: AI-AT-IA.

He tapped his temple. "Getting inside the mind is the next frontier. Mind-reading. Mind control. Imagine being able to read the minds of many, then being able to change their thoughts and make them perceive exactly what we want, with no room for error."

Kennedy stepped from behind the podium. "Reality is not about what is true, but about what we can manipulate people to believe is true. That's one part of what we're doing. Imagine thought-controlled weapons moving at the speed of your mind. Imagine reading the minds of the enemy."

From the table, he picked up a pair of futuristic-looking devices that looked like matching crowns. He placed one on his head and handed the other to the closest guest. "My assistant will help you put this on."

The assistant helped Kennedy slip the device onto the man's head and placed an electrode on each temple. The man's eyes swiveled in curious anticipation.

Kennedy walked to another man on the far side of the room. "So you can see that this is not pre-programmed. Please write on this piece of paper something you want me to think about."

The man hesitated and then scribbled on a piece of paper.

Kennedy glanced at it. "Okay, got it!" He turned to the other man with the device on his head. "I am going to send this to you telepathically."

Kennedy closed his eyes. "Done!" He opened his eyes. "What did you see?"

The man's eyes widened in astonishment, and his jaw fell slack. "Oh, my God! The Eiffel Tower."

Kennedy waved the paper.

A few in the audience crossed their arms and furrowed their brows in skepticism. Kennedy knew what they were thinking. He tapped the device on his head. "I don't need this to know what some of you are thinking. This was a simple parlor trick. And after my briefing, I'll be happy to demonstrate this technology with each of you." He snapped his fingers, and the assistant placed on the podium a 750ml bottle of Laphroaig Single Malt, 30-year-old Limited Edition. "If you're not convinced, I'll gladly recompense your time with a bottle of this scotch."

The doubters relaxed and smiled.

Kennedy removed the device from his head. "Keep in mind, no pun intended, that these telepathy devices are prototypes to validate proof-of-concept. The next step is to deploy this technology using neurotechnology, nanotechnology, and viral vectors."

"In layman's terms, please," replied an irritated voice from the back of the room.

"Very well," Kennedy said. "Allow me to explain further. Brain implants via surgery are too risky. Instead, we'll use viruses modified to deliver DNA material to change the myelin sheaths and the neuron pathways of the brain. They would inject these viruses through vaccines. Then images, thoughts, and directives would be transmitted to those brains via drones or cellular control towers."

"This technology will do what we just witnessed?" another man asked.

"That and more. Enhancements to include surveillance, tracking, and an RFID identification system would be connected to a single control, access, and data center."

"A microchipped population," the man said.

Kennedy chuckled. "Much beyond microchipping but will have the same effect."

"What's the timeline?"

"For initial deployment?" Kennedy steepled his fingers. "Naturally, we expect some hurdles. Fortunately, because of the multiple pandemics created over the past few years, there is less reluctance by people to accept mass vaccination. Our technology will simply piggyback on those vaccines. We've already got the buy-in from our colleagues in the pharmaceutical industry." Kennedy nodded to several of those same colleagues in the room. He returned to his place beyond the podium. "This technology is seamless, comprehensive, robust...I dare say, perfect. All that it needs is capitalization, some further tweaks, and deployment."

The blonde assistant stood beside him and clapped, signaling that the briefing had concluded. Everyone in the room joined in, applauding and grinning like it was already raining money. The guests filed out, some of them inspecting the telepathy devices.

One man in a nondescript dark suit handed a business card to Kennedy. "Most impressive. And from now on, you have new oversight partners."

"Oversight?" Kennedy replied, confused. He noted the DARPA logo on the card and read: Defense Advanced Research Projects Agency–*Biological Technologies Office*.

The man tapped Kennedy's upper arm, "We'll be in touch," and walked out.

Kennedy's gaze followed the man. Kennedy suddenly realized that his project had grown much bigger in scope and had just been taken from him.

Blurry images floated through Diana's mind. The images joined to form an indistinct mosaic of abstract color and texture. She reached for them and the scenario dissolved into a bright white light. She rubbed her eyes and found herself in a hospital bed. Agents Cal Brock and Tony Serani were looking at her. When did this happen?

"You were found staggering along a beach a few miles from where the helicopter crashed," Serani said.

"A hiker found you on the beach," Brock elaborated. "She thought you had fallen from a nearby cliff, as you were covered in blood."

Another memory bloomed in Diana's mind. She was staring into Sally's eyes and she was saying, "go to the forest where you found your father."

Then it was night with Diana walking along the beach, a flashlight in hand. She searched with the beam, looking for those rocks on the beach. Suddenly, another light beam crossed hers. Someone was coming. She clicked her flashlight off and did her best to shrink into the gloom. To no avail. The beam swung toward her and its glare dazzled her.

A familiar voice warned, "You will die before you find the truth."

Then a rattle—of glass, metal?—followed by the aroma of fresh coffee, and she was back in her condo. The images that had been so vivid, the hospital bed, Sally Mund, the flashlight—had vanished, but one remained. *What's in the forest and at the rocks on the beach? Why those places?*

Gabe slurped his coffee and scrolled through the DARPA website. He'd connected his laptop to his cell phone to access the web, and a filtering/scrambling device in the phone prevented anyone from detecting his computer. Since meeting with the stranger, Gabe's ability to link things together had enabled him to find hidden access points through the most secure of firewalls. Someone always left a door unlocked.

He'd been up all night, energized by the hunt, lost in a trance of discovery where the physical world was replaced by a digital landscape. Strewn around his elbows and feet were pages of handwritten notes. He'd found links to the CIA archives of the Monarch and Mockingbird programs where the US government studied and tested methods for mass mind control.

When Diana placed a tray with breakfast on the table, that broke Gabe's concentration.

"How did you not sleep?" she asked.

Gabe yawned and cracked his neck. The long hours of focus were catching up. "Living on the streets like an animal will teach you how."

"That's no longer necessary." Diana sat beside him. "Ever wonder what happened to the rest of us?"

"The rest of us?"

"Sally said there were ten of us in the program."

As much as Gabe's mind could thresh through mountains of information, much in his memory remained indistinct and hidden. "Sorry, there's a lot I can't remember."

"How many others were there from the dozens of other projects all these years?"

Gabe forked a mouthful of omelet and washed it down with coffee. He could feel his mind calm down, like the engine of a racing car decelerating to idle. "As I mentioned yesterday, the mysterious stranger...Herald?" he looked at Diana and quirked an eyebrow. "Referred to this as a web." Gabe gestured to the laptop and his mess of notes. "I think he meant a web of deception, and the Controllers are like a spider. As I also said, the deception began hundreds of years ago."

Gabe crossed his arms and regarded his work. "I came across information about how the Controllers plot and execute all major events of history so they can shape perception with the goal of the enslavement of humanity. They've created 'history architects' who convene in secret around the world and rewrite our history to suit their agenda. And their lies and deception keep the web intact."

Diana considered Gabe's words. "How about we find and kill the spider? Then the web will disintegrate."

"The spider will only survive as long as its prey remains trapped in the web. The mysterious stranger was right when he said that they are only in control because the mass of humanity has opted out of responsibility and relinquished their power."

"We break free when we take control of our minds and, as you said yesterday, take back our power," Diana said.

"Remember what the stranger said right before he tapped my forehead? If you want to know the truth, then go to the source of the truth. These Controllers do not want us to become wise, for they cannot control or exploit the wise. So, we must help as many people as we can to become wise enough to take control of their thoughts and free themselves."

"Liberation from within?"

"Starting at the very center of the brain, the pineal gland. Master how to open the pineal gland and then how to connect with the frequency that resonates and binds the universe, then we'll free ourselves of deception."

"What if there is something or someone who controls the Controllers?" Diana asked.

"Who controls the spider?" Gabe exhaled. "That is a big question."

The wall-mounted control panel alerted her of a visitor. Diana exclaimed, "It's Maggie!"

Several cups of coffee later, the three of them had gone through the pleasantries of catching up and expressing how much Diana and Gabe had missed Maggie LaClair. And she them as well.

"A lot of bad has happened," Diana said.

Maggie cast her eyes downward. "To all of us. For a lot of strange reasons."

"What's important is that we continue forward," Gabe said.

Diana touched Maggie's wrist. "Anya Sullivan has agreed to do a comeback interview with me."

"When?" Maggie asked.

"Larry Reynolds wants it for next week. It's going to be announced on tonight's show. His final coveted scoop before retirement."

"Anya hated you," Maggie said.

"Perhaps, but she never refused a big story if it would make her look good."

"Larry's certain it will hit an audience of thirty million the night it's broadcast," Gabe said. "Then with social media, we expect five hundred million viewers within a week."

"What's the story?" Maggie asked.

"Something huge. It will rock society to its foundation."

"What does Larry think about it?"

"He doesn't know, but he's given me carte blanche," Diana replied.

"Wow, I'm in. How can I help?"

"I'm happy you asked that." Gabe pointed to the dining table, the laptop, and the pile of notes. "Welcome to our media headquarters."

Tony Serani entered Cal Brock's office on the twelfth floor of the FBI's San Francisco office. The splendid view of the city's landscape offset the office's compact dimensions.

Serani said, "I've got something new on John Herald." He flipped open his notebook. "This is where things get weird."

Brock shook his head. "Weirder than what we have already?"

"First, just before the crash, the helicopter veered abruptly off course. Like Herald was trying to avoid something. Or not. We don't know."

"The NTSB already established that a fatal mechanical failure in the helicopter's tail rotor had caused the accident. Right?"

"Yes. Forensics analysis of the wreckage showed some kind of directional beam from the left side hit the tail rotor, causing it to fail and make the helicopter lose control."

"Directional beam? A laser?"

"Maybe. Now comes the kicker. A forensics tech found evidence of a second directional beam striking the right side of the cabin."

"Another laser?"

"Forensics doesn't think so. The impingement pattern is unique. It was another kind of energy."

Without saying a word, Brock got up and stood in front of his window. He could see part of the Golden Gate Bridge and across the bay, the hills of Marin County. The day was unusually clear, and he wished for similar clarity in the information Serani had just provided. "Then what does this mean?"

"What caused the helicopter to crash was not internal structural failure, but the energy directed by these two beams."

"Perhaps Herald's last-second maneuvering was trying to avoid the beams. What was the source of those beams? Military hardware?"

Serani's blank expression said that Brock's guess wasn't even close. "Then what?"

"Unknown. Extraterrestrial? Alien?"

World Primetime Now ended its show with a dramatic intro of quick cuts, a video resume of Diana's broadcast career, and ending with her surviving the helicopter crash.

The camera panned to Anya Sullivan, sheathed in a designer dress, sitting erect on a stool, her trim legs crossed demurely. She faced the camera in the closeup, her face the perfect example of the modern career woman—intelligent, open-minded, resolute, and stunningly gorgeous.

"Next week on *World Primetime Now.* She cheated death, and after weeks of relentless work to overcome her injuries, is now ready to take on the world. I'm excited to announce we have an exclusive interview with my predecessor, the one and only Diana Willis. It will be the interview of the year. Don't miss it! Thank you for joining us this evening. From all of us at *World Primetime Now,* we say goodnight!"

CHAPTER TWENTY-THREE

One of my colleagues helped another of your eminent physicists in an experiment involving subatomic particles. They found these particles are not only particles but exist as and comprise both waveforms and/or particles—but they could not exist in both forms simultaneously. They also found that energy was waves and when given attention, or observed, all waveforms collapse, and particles, or matter, is being formed. The person paying attention to, or observing, the particles determined whether they were or changed into waves or particles. If the observer expected to see the energy as waves, they would, but if they expected to see particles, that is what they would observe.

Subatomic particles take on form as matter based on the thoughts or beliefs that an observer has about them. So, your thoughts create the material and non-material world around you and can happen instantly.

Diana realized that before she could proceed, she needed to find that red book, for it contained the key to unlock the unfolding mysteries. During the upcoming interview with Anya, if Diana was to claim that there was a conspiracy controlling the world, then she had better have convincing proof.

The attacks on her and the murder of Sally Mund were proof enough to her, but skeptics wouldn't hesitate to point to coincidences and the lack of credible villains. Anthony Briscane was the only one she could finger as the culprit behind her troubles, but if there was a worldwide conspiracy, then who was the mastermind? What was their agenda? Control of the world was a vague goal.

Then there was the telepathy and the psychic dimension. Who would believe that? If she was to go public with her claims, then she had better have airtight proof.

Gabe had gone to sleep on the sofa. His mind could absorb prodigious amounts of information, but the effort taxed him and so he needed to shut down. Maggie LaClair had likewise turned in, taking a bed in the guest room.

Diana lay in her bed, musing over the details and unanswered questions about her recent life. It was hard to believe that Sally Mund was dead. Diana was certain that Briscane had a hand in it, though her death seemed more like collateral damage than a deliberate act to kill her. When Briscane showed up in that strange event when Sally had conjured the red book, he acted surprised to have seen it, like he didn't even know it existed.

Something else, she had discovered; she had the power to block Briscane's remote viewing and psychic intrusion. This, too, would further frustrate him, perhaps provoke him into even more brash action.

When Sally had presented the red book, it had been to illustrate its existence, to push Diana into finding it. But for what purpose?

Diana sat up in bed, thinking about Sally Mund's last words, about finding the place in the forest where she found her father. But near the rocks at the beach where she had been found after the crash was where she'd last seen the book. What if seeing the book wasn't a hallucination like she thought? What if it was real?

When she had been with Sally, the impression felt like being in an altered plane, the same as she remembered when she last had the book. The more Diana thought about this, that perhaps she was privy to a psychic world, a place that existed parallel to our reality, the more she realized finding the book may not mean finding it in this plane of existence.

Sally had given her life to alert Diana about the book, and Briscane would certainly want to get his paws on it.

I must then, Diana thought, *find that red book.* It existed somewhere. But where? Was it at the beach, close to the rocks? But what was the significance of the forest and the place where her father, Joseph, was murdered?

In her mind's eye, Diana saw the place.

Diana tried to sleep but sensed that Briscane was probing at the peripheries of her consciousness. Fortunately, she now had the power to lock him out.

Her thoughts kept circling back to the red book and its significance to her quest. She had to find that red book, because Briscane would also search for it and woe to the world if he got to it first.

She crept out of bed and dressed in hiking attire, a hoodie, jeans, ball cap, trekking boots. She slid a small flashlight into her pants pocket. This trip would be dangerous, and it might be better if she went alone. Though she might make her mind blank to Briscane, she doubted Maggie or Gabe could. He'd probably be able to read and track their minds as easily as if they were cell phones. Best then that she continued alone.

And that she left her cell phone behind. Quietly, she padded out of her bedroom and her condo.

Downstairs, she walked to the security office and peeked through the window. Walt Deveron was at his desk, sipping coffee and perusing a bank of security monitors. He caught sight of her on one monitor, turned to wave at her in surprise, then buzzed open the door to let her in.

"I need a ride," she said.

He glanced at the wall clock. 1:40 AM. "Considering the hour and the request, I take it you need to sneak somewhere."

"Something like that."

"Anything I can help you with?"

"The ride is enough."

Deveron picked up a walkie-talkie on his desk and pressed the transmit button. "George, I need you in the office ASAP."

"What's up, boss?"

"You'll see."

Five minutes later, Deveron drove his Toyota out of the parking garage and onto the street. Diana lay on the backseat, hidden from view.

Briscane's cell phone buzzed. The incoming number belonged to one of his men that he had watching Diana's condo building.

"The head security guard just left the building. He's alone."

"Kind of odd, this time of night?" Briscane asked.

"For sure."

"Doubt that you know his destination," Briscane said. "Any way you can tail him?"

"Better than that. We put a tracker under his car in case he pulled a stunt like this. Hang on a sec and I'll text the tracker info."

Briscane's pulse quickened with anticipation. That bitch Diana was going to die.

Deveron slowed his Toyota and the instant it rolled to a halt, Diana cracked open the rear passenger door and slid out. She crouched beside the rear wheel and let Deveron motor away before she scrambled off the road and into the brush.

She paused a moment to take stock of the situation. The road was deserted, with only random headlights cruising along the state highway in the distance. The horizon glowed from urban lights to the south across the water. The air smelled salty and humid, and she could about taste the ocean.

Gentle waves lapped on the beach, a couple of hundred yards away. Though she hadn't been here at night, she was certain she was close to where she had to be. On the ground, she spied a pinecone and, considering it a lucky omen, picked it up and tucked it in her pocket.

Diana walked around the patches of ice plants and clumps of seagrass. The sound of the surf grew louder, crisper. Approaching the beach, she picked her way along the uneven rocks. Moonlight seeped through a light mist rolling across the beach.

She turned again to orient herself and spied in the darkness, on the water's edge, the large formation of rocks shaped like a pyramid she had remembered from her dreams.

This pulled her back in time again. Past the rocks, she noticed a light shining through the mist. But this light was itself also unusual in the way its reflection cast a trail of sparkles across the water.

For a moment, she stared transfixed, then realized someone was behind her. The abrupt presence spooked her and just as she was about to turn around, the stranger said, "Get their attention before it's too late."

She expected the stranger had to be John Herald, but this voice was a woman's. Another complication to the mystery.

Diana reached into her pants pocket and clasped the flashlight. She turned about to confront the stranger and saw that she was alone.

Another hallucination?

She gazed into the darkness, making certain that she was indeed alone. Satisfied that no one else was here, she continued walking toward the pyramid of rocks. What would she find there? The red book with the silver pinecone on the cover? John Herald? John Herald holding the red book?

Stepping carefully, she walked along the beach. It was so damn dark out here.

Cal Brock sat alone in the diner booth. He sipped coffee and picked at the remains of his omelet special. He'd come here because he could not sleep and wasn't looking forward to spending the night in his empty apartment. He needed the ambiance of company, even if it was strangers. Sadly, though, the other patrons were hunched over their cell phones, oblivious to one another.

Time was, thought Brock, that eating in a diner like this was a way to get away from the world. Now people only used the opportunity to reassure themselves of their electronic leash.

He'd been reviewing his notes of Diana's case, the strangest he'd ever been assigned. He caught himself stumbling into the biggest and most dangerous trap any agent could fall into—getting emotionally involved with the subject. So far, he didn't know how she felt about him; poor woman's head was a blender of confusion and apprehension. Seeing how people were trying to kill her, no surprise she wasn't thinking of romance.

Brock had sketched a crude staircase that represented the rising drama that had befallen Diana. The steps proceeded in chronological order and were labeled with each event that had occurred. However, the next steps were blank, and Brock wondered what developments awaited.

The waitress refilled his mug. How many cups had he drunk?

His cell phone vibrated, jolting him. This time of night, the call could only be about Diana.

Caller ID: Walt Deveron. "Mr. Brock, thought I'd give you a heads up. I just dropped off Diana." He passed along the precise location near the ocean.

Brock replied, "What was she doing?"

"Didn't say. But you know how she's been acting lately. It's like she falls under a spell."

"Was she alone? Were you followed?"

"Yes, to the first question. No to the second. If you want to contact her, forget about using your phone. She left hers at the condo. Deliberately so they couldn't track her."

Brock let his eyes drop to his notepad. *What was Diana up to? Why was she returning to where she had been found after the crash? And why go at this ungodly hour?* He asked, "Where are you now?"

"On my way back to the condo building."

"All right. Thanks for the call." Brock ended the call and gathered his things. He tossed a twenty on the booth table and hustled outside. Something bad was in the offing and he hoped he could be there in time if Diana needed help.

CHAPTER TWENTY-FOUR

Through your memories and experiences, your future self is observing and guiding you.

Anthony Briscane swiveled his eyes from the road to the cell phone mounted on his dashboard. The signal tracker led across the Golden Gate Bridge to Mt. Tamalpais State Park. He picked up that Diana was returning to the site of the helicopter crash.

Why? And why the urgency?

Briscane zoomed along the road and hoped that a cop wouldn't stop him for speeding. The signal followed the beach road, then slowed, halted for an instant, then sped off. He mashed a button on the screen to pinpoint the spot.

A half-mile from the location, he turned off the headlights. At a quarter of a mile, he pulled off the road and parked. The location was remarkably secluded. Because of the trees and the curve of the beach, he couldn't see the Bay Bridge and though San Francisco was but a few miles to the south, the city wasn't much more than a glow across the horizon.

Not knowing the destination, Briscane had dressed in his usual after-hours clothing, a golf jacket, business shirt, and casual pants. In a rush to get going, he had slipped on whatever footwear was handy, in this case, a pair of expensive dress shoes.

He chafed at the idea that in the Controllers' campaign for world domination, where every angle was accounted for, this pursuit to stop the biggest threat to their mission stuttered along in such an ad hoc manner.

He puzzled over his next moves. What task should he concentrate on? Finding Diana and stopping her once and for all? Or finding out why she was here? Was it that red book? Which would be the bigger prize?

After all the missteps in trying to kill Diana, he knew she seemed to have a guardian angel watching over her. Of course, Briscane didn't believe in angels or any of that supreme-being religious rot, but he couldn't deny that her ability to scoot out of the tightest of predicaments was more than uncanny. In his training, they had taught him to never rely on luck, to account for every variable, and to leverage your strengths—including psychic powers—against your enemy's weaknesses so there would be no doubt about the outcome.

Then at the end of his Monarch training, his chief instructor advised him, "But in the final analysis, it's better to be lucky than good."

And so far, Diana had been very, very lucky.

Briscane walked carefully along the road to the beach, to the spot where Diana had gotten out of the car. Briscane realized that the light from his phone screen was giving him away, so he stuffed it into a jacket pocket.

He crouched on the road's shoulder and studied the ground that led to the beach. His spirits lifted when he spied a boot tread in the soft dirt, then noticed another of a different tread, and another. Hikers would have trekked up and down this road. He let out a curse. Seemed nothing was going right for him.

Let's try something different. He relaxed and eased into a meditative state, hoping that in her rush to get here, Diana wouldn't consider that he would probe for her mind.

All that came back was silence. Her mind was locked tight.

Briscane stood and scoped out the beach. Anyone walking along the water's edge would be silhouetted against the surf. Assuming that this was what Diana was doing.

He thought he saw something move across the sparkle of moonlight on the water. It was hard to tell. The something moved again. The something was a person wearing a ball cap.

Briscane's nerves jittered with anticipation. Diana's luck was about to run out.

Diana stepped carefully along the beach. The task seemed so confounding. All these piles of rocks appeared the same now that she was up close. Why would any of them be arranged into a pyramid? During the day, this beach was a popular spot for day hikers; wouldn't any of them make a pyramid of rocks? Or, more likely, knock over any pile just for the hell of it?

She sighed in exasperation. Why couldn't these hallucinations be more direct? Why did everything have to be so mysterious?

She walked around a large pile of rocks. Its outline was triangular. Was this the pyramid?

Her night vision had adjusted to the darkness, and she could tell the pile had four abrupt and even edges that sloped to a definite point. *The pyramid.*

It was adjoined to the rock cliff and on this side, there was a shallow grotto. Diana stepped into the grotto and ran her fingers along its rough surface. She assumed the red book was here, but where? Inside the grotto? The pyramid? She moved around the pyramid and saw no opening to its interior.

Perhaps she needed to use her flashlight. She looked around and made sure that she was alone. Which she appeared to be.

Diana aimed her flashlight into the grotto and flicked it on.

Anthony Briscane kept the silhouette in sight and fought the urge to rush toward the beach. He stumbled over loose stones—damn the slick soles of his shoes—but the waves churning the surf absorbed their clatter.

He decided on a path that would bring him behind Diana, where he could spy on her and still be close enough to pounce.

He slipped again, this time plopping into a muddy puddle. He levered upright, certain that Diana had heard his bumbling. But she continued, head bowed in concentration.

Tall grass cluttered the way forward, which was littered with rocks. There was no way he could continue without tripping. He got out his cell phone and turned on its flashlight.

In this murk, the beam was much brighter than he expected. He wrapped his hand over the light to smother the beam, allowing just enough to escape between his fingers to illuminate his way.

By the dim light, he could silently pick his way and move behind Diana. He was about thirty feet from the beach when she used a flashlight to illuminate an odd pyramid made of rocks.

Diana was moving around the pyramid, obviously looking for something. The book with the red cover?

Briscane left the patch of seagrass and had a clear approach along the edge of the beach to Diana. He knew he could overpower her, yet he felt he should've brought a weapon. A gun. Pepper spray. A tire iron.

He wanted to question her but given the circumstances, decided it was best that he kill her once he had the chance.

Briscane turned off the light function of his phone and pocketed it. He tensed his legs, readied his hands, and charged toward Diana.

The pyramid was not giving up its secrets, whatever they were.

Diana felt she was close to finding what Sally Mund had directed her to find. Diana remained certain that it was the red book. Then where was it? Maybe it's not here, but in the forest where her father was killed. *I wouldn't know where to look for that forest.*

Something pulled her toward the grotto, a slight sensation, something magnetic. What was she supposed to do, step into the grotto and vanish through its rock surface?

The slap of rapidly approaching footfalls broke her concentration. She swung the flashlight in that direction and its beam caught Briscane square in the face.

His aspect appeared unnaturally large and grotesque. But there was no mistaking the malice in his beady, rodentlike eyes.

Diana bolted from him and hurtled away from the beach, scrambling over the rocks and plunging into the seagrass and weeds.

Briscane sprinted after her. His breath puffed hot and heavy.

In her haste to get here, Diana hadn't thought of an exit plan. How was she to get back to her home? What if Briscane was channeling her into the arms of a waiting assassin?

No sooner had she thought this than headlight beams washed onto the beachfront road. A car skidded to a halt.

Diana fought the panic surging through her. She had no time to stop and analyze her options. If she slowed a step, Briscane would be on her.

A shadow rose from the direction of the car. A man's voice shouted, "Diana!"

It was Cal Brock.

"Over here," she shouted back and ran toward him.

A flashlight beam flashed from Brock, passed by Diana, and spotlighted Briscane.

"Stop right there!" Brock commanded.

Briscane gave a weak yelp and changed direction. He crashed through shrubs, the thick branches breaking up the flashlight beam as he scuttled away.

Brock stomped toward Diana. "Who was that?"

She waited to catch her breath before answering. "Anthony Briscane."

"Anthony Briscane? What's he doing here?"

"He's in the middle of all this craziness." Diana rubbed her head. "Let's get out of here."

Brock hugged Diana. "Are you okay?"

"Other than minor cuts and scrapes, I'm okay."

He pulled her away from the beach. Up the road, a car started. The glow of headlights swung across the tops of the tree line, then the car sped off.

"What did Briscane want from you?" Brock asked.

Diana's resolve hardened her answer. "I'm sure that he wants me dead."

🌰 🌰

On the way to her condo, Diana explained as much as she could to Brock, but withheld her uncertainties and anything that would make her seem like a nut job. He explained how Walt Deveron had alerted him.

"Why were you there?" Brock asked. "The beach was close to where you were discovered after the crash." His manner was pleasant and reassuring, but Diana couldn't tell if this was because of a genuine interest in her or if it was one of his FBI interrogation techniques.

"I'm drawn to the place. It's a compulsion." This much was true, and she kept the red book secret. This didn't bother her, as Brock was also hiding things he knew about Diana and her circumstances.

"I don't understand how you appeared at that spot right after the helicopter crash."

Diana wasn't about to share her experience with the portal and meeting John Herald. "I don't know."

"There's still this big missing piece in this exceptionally bizarre puzzle," Brock said. "And that is John Herald."

297

"I don't know where he is."

"How well did you know him?"

"That weasel Briscane you sent scurrying away assigned me to do a special investigation of him before the crash."

"What did you find out?"

"Nothing that you couldn't," Diana said. "He was CIA and I had it all on a thumb drive."

"Where is that drive now?"

"It was stolen from me."

"When?"

"During my coma," Diana explained. "I think by the same person who gave it to me."

Brock pointed back to the direction of the beach, "Him? The weasel?"

"Or one of his thugs."

Brock looked to the road. "Are you up for a bite? Some food would settle your jitters."

Diana looked at the mud clinging to her pant cuffs and boots. "I'd rather get back home."

When Cal Brock turned into the underground garage, Walt Deveron was waiting by the entrance. Diana was glad that Deveron escorted her upstairs, as she didn't want to answer any of Brock's questions. He was just doing his job, she reminded herself, and made a note to have a conversation with him that didn't involve assassins coming after her.

"Rough night?" Deveron asked on the way to the elevator.

Diana glimpsed herself in the foyer mirror, and she looked like she'd spent the night tramping and rolling along the beach.

Back in her condo, the front room lights were on. Gabe was sitting in a meditative pose. His computer projected a three-dimensional model of the human brain against a backdrop of stars, rotating slowly. In the center of the brain, the pineal gland stood out in silver. A golden thread extended from the top of the gland, linking it to a star that then connected to other stars.

On a piece of paper next to the keyboard, Gabe had scribbled:

Awakening the third eye. All-Seeing Eye- All-Seeing God. Eye of God. Eye of Light in the center of the head. Amon Ra, STAR. $ Bill/ Hijacked Symbol next to a small hand-drawn Symbol of a triangle with an eye at the top.

More writing read:

Control & Domination vs. Spiritual Insight. The Powers don't want us to know.

The third eye can see beyond the physical as it looks out. When we meditate, we can look for answers from higher frequencies. Everything is frequency.

If your eye is single, it will fill your body with light. There is only one way out.

The way in is the way out.

Diana read the last note several times. *The way in is the way out.*

The way into what?

The mind of course. Human consciousness.

She knew her mind was blossoming, opening itself to be more receptive to new knowledge, rather than an awareness of a great truth.

Much of that truth concerned what had happened to her at Project Stargate.

Gabe appeared absolutely serene. She was safe now and wanted to indulge in that serenity. So much had happened tonight, but those concerns could wait until tomorrow.

First, to get out of these filthy clothes. A few minutes later, she returned to the front room, freshly showered and clad in a long robe with shorts and a t-shirt underneath.

She sat in a big armchair, covered herself with a handwoven blanket, closed her eyes, and let her thoughts coalesce on the image of the pinecone and then on the pineal gland in the center of her head.

Tomorrow was the big tell-all interview, and Diana had to be ready.

Anthony Briscane arrived in his apartment, thoroughly humiliated. So much had gone wrong tonight. Not only had he botched this chance to kill Diana, but he was also certain that it had compromised his identity to the FBI agent he knew had been assigned to Diana's case.

Briscane kicked off his shoes and peeled off his socks and trousers. They were all completely soaked, caked with mud, and ruined.

He was an expert in using telepathy and a master at using covert manipulation, and yet Diana had made a fool of him at every turn.

He regarded himself in the bathroom mirror and stewed with disgust at the reflection of his pasty face and bloodshot eyes. He repeatedly swiped his hand across his face, as if doing it would change what he saw.

Closing his eyes, he chanted, "Diana, you will regret surviving. What happens next will be far, far worse than if you had just died when you were supposed to. You will die a thousand deaths."

Consumed with rage, he extended one arm to lash out and scatter the items off the bathroom counter. Then he stopped in mid-motion. What had stopped him was the sudden realization that he was being watched. By a traitor. And killing this traitor would placate this anger and clear his head.

"You were always insane," Murray Sims chortled. He lay on a motel bed, watching Briscane's clownish antics on a tablet perched on his enormous belly. He munched potato chips, delighting in the spectacle of his old handler's meltdown.

"Briscane, your days are numbered, you psychopath lunatic." Murray washed down the chips with a gulp of soda. He brushed crumbs from his chest and returned his attention to the tablet's screen.

Odd, Briscane wasn't moving. Murray expected Briscane would gesticulate maniacally, but he remained absolutely still. Perhaps the screen had frozen.

Murray checked the tablet's settings. Functioning normally. He glanced at the router on an adjacent table and saw that all of its lights were blinking as they should be.

He breathed deeply and noticed that he was feeling quite sleepy. His eyes had grown heavy, and he struggled to keep them open. The tablet slid off his belly and when he picked it up, the image was a close-up of Briscane staring right into the camera.

Murray gasped and realized that he couldn't breathe. It was as if invisible hands had clasped his throat and squeezed. Panicking, he jerked and kicked his legs.

Do what I tell you and I'll let you live. It was Briscane's voice inside his head.

Murray fought for breath. His lungs screamed for air. *Okay. Okay. I'll do what you want.*

Very well. Briscane gave another squeeze.

Murray squeaked, thinking he was going to die. Then the grip on his throat relaxed and he sucked greedily for breath. His eyes rolled in their sockets. The tablet lay face up on the mattress, and he saw Briscane's gloating visage.

My fat friend, you will soon betray Diana worse than you betrayed me.

Maggie had heard Diana leave the condo and return hours later. She tiptoed from her bed and into the front room. Diana sat in an armchair, looking remarkably peaceful.

There was so much strangeness in their lives and Maggie wished for some calm and certainty so she could, at last, reveal to Diana how she felt about her. There's a saying that you can't ever miss what you never had, but that wasn't true. Maggie had never had Diana, not in the romantic sense and not as lovers. Yet what had never happened left a void inside Maggie, and the thought that soon she would be the agent of Diana's destruction filled her with tremendous sadness.

Nemer Indarte's voice slid through her jagged thoughts, like a centipede creeping after prey. *You must complete your mission.*

Maggie felt her fingers curl as if clasping a razor. She was little more than a robot that only needed Nemer Indarte's command to strike.

"Everything all right?" The voice startled Maggie. She turned to find Gabe standing behind her.

"Yes, I thought I heard something."

"Get some sleep."

Maggie nodded. "Yes, I must."

She walked back to her room, closed the door, and waited for Nemer Indarte's command to strike.

CHAPTER TWENTY-FIVE

It's your star's time... Soon, it will be yours... Ready or not!

"It's good to have you back," Anya Sullivan said as she watched the studio makeup artist brush a red tone onto Diana's cheeks.

Diana looked at herself in the vanity mirror.

Maggie leaned over the mirror and studied Diana's face. "Makeup, perfection. Hair, perfection. Of course, the beautician had perfection to work with."

Diana winced at her friend's comment. She knew Maggie preferred women and now detected a possessive tone in her voice. Given the monumental revelations that Diana planned for tonight, she didn't need this distraction.

A technician in a headset gestured to his clipboard. Diana recognized the impatient quirk of his finger, showing that they had to get to the stage. The makeup artist helped Diana out of the chair as Maggie stepped forward to do the task. Diana, Anya, and Maggie followed the tech. Diana missed the choreographed urgency before showtime. So many people rushed about, making sure that they attended to every detail. Her nerves tingled with anticipation.

They halted in the curtains behind the stage and peeked out. A crowd of about two hundred people filled the studio beyond the lip of the elevated stage. Diana was used to live broadcasts, but not one in front of a live audience. Anya had briefed her that they might take questions, and doing that always introduced an element of risk.

"Diana, I'm thrilled we're doing this," Anya said.

For the first time in years, Diana felt stage fright flutter through her stomach. She welcomed the sensation; it brought back pleasant memories of her early days in broadcasting.

That feeling turned sour and an evil voice popped into her mind. *You will die before you find the truth.*

Briscane. That dangerous weasel.

Diana made fists and clenched her jaw. She brought down that mental barrier and cut off Briscane in mid-threat.

You will die beffforr…

She imagined him pinned under a metal door, squirming like the varmint that he was. She muttered to herself, "Take that!"

"What did you say?" Maggie asked.

While lost in her thoughts, Diana had forgotten Maggie was there. Turning to her, "Oh sorry, I'm just giving myself a pep talk."

Maggie squeezed her arm. "You'll be great."

Diana smiled as she pulled away. "I appreciate your support. As much as I've been on television, it can be overwhelming."

Maggie's eyes darkened a bit, a strange reaction given the festive circumstances.

Anya faced Camera 3 and announced: "Good evening and welcome to *World Primetime Now Live Edition* and our exclusive interview with someone very dear to my heart. She's not only my predecessor on this very show but someone who has captured the hearts of many after a miraculous survival from a helicopter crash." They expected thirty million viewers to watch the show.

The broadcast cut to the thirty seconds of the special covering Diana's years as a TV anchor for the show, highlights of the prestigious guests she had interviewed, scenes of the helicopter crash, and her recovery.

The broadcast cut back to Anya. "I am talking about the one and only Diana Willis."

The soundtrack of thunderous applause augmented the audience's loud clapping. The camera pulled back to show Anya and Diana on adjacent chairs.

"Diana, welcome to the show."

"Thank you, Anya, it's a pleasure to be here."

The camera panned and gave various shots of the audience.

"We have much to talk about with you and as in prior live shows, we will also take questions from the audience," Anya stated as she addressed the audience.

"So, let's begin with that fateful morning three months ago, August tenth. The helicopter crash. Tell us what happened."

Diana inhaled deeply and glanced to the ceiling, then back to Anya. "I have fragmented memories of the accident, so I'll do my best. The hardest thing for me, Anya, has been the psychological challenges and the coma and rehabilitation." Diana touched her temple. "Sadly, large chunks of my memory of the moments before and during the accident have disappeared. What I remember was sitting in the back of the helicopter and then there was a sudden jolt. The helicopter spun, the door opened, and I was flung quite a distance to the ground, where I landed on my back. I remember hearing the helicopter sputtering and then a tremendous explosion."

Close-up of audience members gasping and clutching their collars in disbelief.

Anya said, "The authorities released a report stating you had spoken about seeing a light of some kind."

"Yes, right before the door opened, there was a strange light, and the helicopter stopped spinning long enough for me to get ejected out the door. After hitting the ground, I saw this light, and that was the last thing I remembered."

"You were then found walking along a beach several miles away?" Anya asked.

"And that's the craziest part of all this. I don't remember how I got there. I have some recollection of being on the beach and being found, but there's an unexplained gap in time."

Anya turned to the audience. "Incredible, the miracle of not only surviving the crash but then walking several miles to where you were rescued."

"I don't believe I walked there. It was some kind of phenomenon, and I may have been transported?"

"Transported?" Anya asked, eyebrows arched. While she and Diana had discussed in broad terms the topics of the interview, Diana said she wouldn't share details until the broadcast. Anya had agreed so that her reactions would appear authentic.

Diana touched her thigh and shoulder. "The doctors said it was impossible to walk two miles with the injuries I had sustained. It seems the only other explanation."

The camera panned to take in the audience's astonishment.

"Let's talk about the coma," Anya began. "You were in it for eight weeks. Another story claims you had memories while in it. A few disproved it in the medical profession, saying that people aren't conscious in a coma and it's highly unlikely you would experience memories."

Diana shrugged. "I'm not one to dispute the medical experts, but I know what I remembered. It was like my life was continuing, as if I did not know that I was in a coma, or even in a helicopter crash. I interacted with people from my life, and I even continued in my role at the show. It was like I was in a strange, alternative dimension."

Anya mouthed *wow*. "We're going to take a brief break and when we return, we'll take questions from the audience."

The camera director signaled to Anya they were off the air. Studio personnel rushed about the stage. They brought bottles of water. Diana took a sip and a makeup artist immediately touched up her lipstick.

Diana felt her phone vibrate, and she glanced at the text. Gabe: You're getting their attention.

The studio floor manager gave the countdown, "Ten, nine, eight, seven, six, five, four."

He signaled the last three numbers with his fingers.

Anya looked square into the camera. "We're back with my exclusive interview with Diana Willis."

She turned to the audience. "We're going to our first question from the audience. Those of you that were chosen were handed a card with a number and that number was selected randomly."

A woman in the audience stood and a studio tech handed her a microphone.

"Welcome to the show, please tell us your name and your question?" Anya asked.

"My name is Millie and my question for Diana is, do you think you were saved for a reason, and if so, what would that be?"

Diana nodded. "Thank you, that's a good question. As I mentioned, I believe some kind of force interceded in my survival. Truthfully, and I've had weeks to think about this, I believe we're not alone in this universe and there's something out there. I had a premonition days before the accident that I had survived something. I saw myself on the beach where I was found."

Briscane abruptly entered her mind again. *You will die before you find the truth.*

The thought hit Diana like a slap and she hesitated, trying to shake off the evil thought. "I want to use the media to help discern the truth from lies. The media have such an influence on the way we think, much more than we believe. The greatest weapon is not a gun or bomb, it is the control of information. To control the world's information is to manipulate all the minds that consume it. I believe there's a place for honest journalism. A more transparent approach coming out from behind the façade. In the past, I wasn't focused on that. Now I am."

The audience clapped.

Diana continued, "It seems people will believe anything if you tell them often enough. It has become so easy for us to allow ourselves to be controlled. We have to stop giving up our power. And we must stop the hypocrisy. It's better to ask more questions and take a stand than to turn a blind eye. There is a famous quote. Hell is finding the truth too late. Let's not find the truth too late."

"Thank you," Millie said, and she returned to her seat as the audience clapped its approval.

Anya said, "Those were powerful words. Care to elaborate?"

"I thought I was going crazy. I would hear voices that were strange enough, but then I would get memories back, but in fragments. The trauma unlocked old memories of my childhood. Memories I had been made to forget. I worked with a wonderful psychologist to help bring some of those out and figure out what they meant. There are still some holes and missing pieces."

"Let's take another question from the audience," Anya said.

A tall, slender man with thick blond hair stood. He hesitated for a second before speaking into the proffered microphone. He did not say his name.

"Is it true that your actual name is Alexa Starnowski?" he asked.

The question startled Diana. "Yes, that is my actual name. Alexandra Starnowski."

"I'm a survivor too," he said.

"Survivor?" Anya asked the man.

Diana stopped Anya. "I know what he is talking about." She turned her attention to the man. "Are you referring to a government project called Monarch? When I was six, I was kidnapped and sent to a facility where they did experiments in mind control and psychic research using children or young adults. The results are still being used in the way information is being programmed into our minds. It is invisible, as it is subliminal and more powerful than we think. Diana Willis was the name they gave me later when I became a journalist."

There were gasps in the audience. Anya looked shocked as well.

"No, not Monarch, the other one," the man said.

"You mean Stargate?" Diana asked.

"No!" the man exclaimed. "The one after that. It involved inter-dimensional time travel. I was there too. I know where you are from. It's in the forest. You've been there."

The forest? Diana stared at the man in the audience.

He said, "Pegasus," and went out of focus. She suddenly felt a weird energy that made her surroundings shimmer. She could see Anya speaking but heard nothing. Everything was in slow motion.

A sound pierced the silence, a voice, the man's. And he was saying, "Time is fluid, Diana. You have the power to go forwards and backwards. You've done it before. Time can be folded and the book will show you how."

The red book appeared, floating in the air. She held it to her chest like a prized possession and sat on the beach. She ran her fingertips over the leather cover and its embossed image.

With anticipation and wonder, she opened to the first page, but could not comprehend what was written.

But now it was clear why she ended up on that beach after the crash. Herald must have helped her enter an interdimensional portal that had allowed her to get from the crash site to the beach so rapidly, despite her injuries. She realized the portal entrance was in the forest and why Sally told her to find the place where her father was murdered. The same place she must return to.

That's why she couldn't find the red book when she was at the beach. Anya's voice became more audible again. She looked concerned and somewhat shocked. "Diana, is anything wrong? We've taken a break."

Time quickened to normal speed.

Diana sipped water from a bottle handed to her by a stage assistant. Maggie was by her side, hand on her shoulder.

"What happened?" Diana looked around.

Maggie looked confused. "You don't remember?"

Diana shook her head.

Maggie leaned in. "You just told thirty million people your name is Alexandra Starnowski and you are a messenger who came back in time from another world in another solar system, to help us find the truth and liberation. And there were some other shocking revelations."

"What?" Diana cut her eyes from Maggie and then to the audience. Many stared back with incredulity and suspicion. Some, though, appeared happy. Others, sad. Angry.

Diana scanned the audience. "What happened to the man who asked the question?"

"What man?" Maggie asked.

Diana pointed to the audience, "The man who was standing over there."

Maggie looked puzzled. "There was no man. It was Anya who asked you the question."

Diana sat in silence, once again dumbfounded by the changing course of this mystery.

CHAPTER TWENTY-SIX

When you speak the truth, you may be attacked as a crazy one. Those you label as sociopathic, for example, will accuse you of the very thing they are guilty of. They do this to deflect the attention from themselves.

Stop the hypocrisy. I appeared to the one you called the 'Bard of Avon,' who said, "God has given you one face, and you make yourself another."

A convoy of three black SUVs arrived at the main gate onto the Cheyenne Mountain Complex in Colorado. The heavily armed guards let the vehicles through, guiding them to the tunnel bored into the rocky palisade. On either side of the entrance, thousand-ton blast doors were ready to slam shut and seal them within the mountain.

A quarter of a mile inside the tunnel, the SUVs eased to a halt along the concrete sidewalk next to an entrance. Armed guards in civilian clothes, costumed as if auditioning for *Men in Black*, leaped from the first and last vehicles and formed a cordon. More guards hustled out of the entrance. One of them opened the rear passenger door of the second SUV and saluted.

General Wayne Carcano emerged and a USAF colonel wearing the braid and insignia of an aide-de-camp escorted him inside. They rushed past more guards and around the surveillance gates to continue down a wide hall. Cool air puffed from overhead vents.

A retinue of flag-rank officers waited by an open door. Carcano's exchange of greetings with them was friendly and informal. They assembled inside a large conference room and arranged themselves around the table. All except Carcano, who remained standing. The audience included Reginald Deighton, Jeff Kennedy, and Governor Dan Talbot.

When Carcano had emphasized the urgency of this meeting, many other participants had expected a virtual conference. But Carcano wanted none of that.

For two reasons: First, any broadcast, even by secure channels, could be intercepted and hacked. And second, Carcano preferred to lead from the front, to confront his underlings face to face and put the fear of God—meaning himself—into them. He enjoyed seeing others quiver and sweat in fear.

When the audience had settled, Carcano cleared his throat and stared across the assembly.

"We begin with her." He pointed to the giant screen above the stage. On it appeared a photo collage of one woman, a very attractive blonde.

"You undoubtedly know her, the media star Diana Willis. And you've also no doubt heard of the revelations she made during her interview. Revelations that put everything we've worked so hard for at risk."

Deighton leaned in, "We've tried numerous times to terminate her."

"Diana lives a charmed life," Carcano added. "At this point, we've decided to do an end-run around her. If she is going to reveal her secrets, let her. What she's about to say would've been disclosed, eventually. With that in mind, we've accelerated our schedule of making the world aware of our contact with extraterrestrials. This way, the news will not seem too extraordinary. We must continue to control the narrative. If not, we lose our hold on the masses. We lose that, and we lose everything."

A few in the room coughed and shifted uncomfortably.

Carcano tightened the screws. "That happens and say goodbye to your money and your mansions."

Talbot raised his hand. "How do we do this?"

"We've already started," Carcano replied. "The National Security Act of 1974 and the creation of the National Security Council have allowed us to cloak the existence of extraterrestrial visitations under the mantle of 'national security.' This has allowed us to generate false flags. Many in the public are ready to believe in the existence of UFOs, but they don't realize that many of those 'sightings' are actually advanced military tech we've been developing for decades. We will use and exploit this confusion to create fear by promoting hysteria over who will protect them from alien invasion. This would certainly allow us to push for and receive more military spending."

He smiled. "It's a tenet of mass psychology. Introduce an external threat—real or not—to get the masses to fall in line behind you. Proof of aliens, whatever we decide that proof will be, would lead to new religions and other crackpot notions."

Carcano pointed to Deighton. "He will be my point man in this auspicious endeavor. We will tune our messaging, saturate social media, and drown out Diana's message until which time, she disappears. Our mission"—the general scanned a steely gaze at the audience— "is to remain in control."

The burly NSA agents dragged Anthony Briscane across the threshold and threw him against the table in the center of the darkened room. A spotlight shining down on the table emphasized the gloomy atmosphere.

The agents retreated into the dark corners. Briscane squinted toward a rustling sound. A man emerged from the murk. Carcano.

"Have a seat," the general said.

A second man emerged behind Carcano. He was tall, dressed in a dark suit, and light glistened off his bald head. No mistaking this cold-blooded reptile in human form. Briscane recognized him from a photo. Nemer Indarte. They had tasked him and Nemer Indarte to rein in Diana, but this was the first time they'd met. Nemer Indarte's presence added a level of malevolence to the situation.

Briscane swiveled his eyes from Nemer Indarte to Carcano as he groped for a chair, then sat. He gulped nervously and wiped the sweat from his forehead.

Carcano stepped forward, the hard heels of his shoes clicking on the concrete floor.

Briscane tried to relax. After all, he had powers the others in the room didn't have, which was why he was invaluable. Or hoped that he still was.

Carcano carried a manila folder in his hand and he slapped it on the table. Briscane forced himself not to jump but winced regardless.

"Four attempts to stop Diana. Four examples of your ineptitude." Carcano clenched his jaw and his lips parted to expose narrow teeth. "How many fucking lives does this woman have?"

Briscane knew Carcano wanted him to grovel, to blubber excuses and beg for another chance. The problem was that Carcano and the others in his circle had no regard as to the power growing within Diana Willis. To them, this ability cultivated at Project Monarch and Stargate was little more than a parlor trick. Only now was Briscane realizing the tremendous potential of the psychic plane. The gains of the physical world these men knew as Earth were trifles compared to the treasures available to one attuned to the psychic world.

But Carcano could only perceive reality in simple terms. Things for him moved linearly, and he could not comprehend what it would be like to fold both space and time in on themselves.

Hell, Briscane barely understood it. But Diana was gaining awareness, and she recognized the lies behind the façade of power and privilege that was about to be wiped away.

"Update us," Carcano said, glaring at Briscane.

The moment hung over Briscane, as he wasn't certain where to begin. "Letting Diana do that interview paid off for us. Our campaigns of vilification and smear tactics have turned her revelations into jokes. However, there seems to be a grassroots cult taking hold, that she is some kind of cosmic superhero. But this is shallow media-star worship and will fizzle out."

Carcano replied, "She spoke too much. Therefore, she should have been killed years ago after we got what we needed from her at Stargate, then that Pegasus sham. Instead, they handed her to a perverted media tycoon to use as his toy and the rest is history."

He tapped his chest. "As a young Air Force pilot, I transferred to Space Command, where I remained the rest of my military career. There, I was entrusted with this single purpose, doing what it took to keep the world safe by keeping its inhabitants from knowing the truth about other worlds and their true origin. The only way we can do that is to stop people from waking up. This next wave of control is upon us, and Deighton and Kennedy are ready for their project for mass subjugation."

Carcano took a breath and continued his rant. "If Diana gets help from the other worlds and convinces people of what she knows, we're done. It will be harder to control the masses and they will push back. Hard. My life's work will have been for nothing and I will not let that happen."

Briscane didn't need to read the general's mind to understand the next step. Cleaning house, and that meant getting rid of him as well, as he knew too much.

The general braced his arms on the table and loomed over Briscane. "You don't think much of me, do you, Anthony?"

Briscane weighed the words. Carcano still needed him. "Why would you say that?"

"Your body language. The hubris in your eyes." Carcano waved a hand at the confines of the room. "That you don't fear that I can make you disappear."

Briscane glanced at Nemer Indarte. That remained a possibility. But the general would not yet cut his losses, meaning to terminate with extreme prejudice until he had played every other option out. As a military man, Carcano knew the value of keeping every resource in reserve.

Briscane wiped the sweat from his forehead and relaxed in his chair. "What do you want?"

"I'll tell you what I don't want," Carcano replied. "More failure."

That makes two of us. Briscane kept the focus on the general.

Carcano walked in a tight circle, his body a shifting form of light and shadow. He stopped and looked at Briscane, asking, "What do you need to finish Diana? I'll put everything that I have at your disposal. More men. More lethal weapons. Explosives. Poison. Just ask."

This conversation had taken a different turn. Carcano was getting desperate. He was feeling the heat. Conversely, Briscane was used to this heat. Let the general squirm.

"Just give me time, General."

"How much time?"

Briscane threw the question right back. "How much time do you need?"

Carcano knit his brow. Briscane could sense the gears turning in the general's head. Whatever machinations he and the Controllers had planned, Carcano was reassembling the parts and gauging how it would run.

He looked up at the light, then at Nemer Indarte. "A day?"

The assassin replied with a cruel smile. "I'm ready now. I've got Diana's best friend poised to kill her."

Carcano turned to Briscane. "Can you do it?" The question had a plaintive quality, meaning the general's confidence had cracked a bit. Advantage, Briscane.

"Twenty-four hours, general. That will give me plenty of time."

"Tonight then." The general glared at Briscane. "No more screw-ups."

"Absolutely. This time, things will work to my satisfaction."

Maggie imagined herself like a spider tending its web, attentive to every vibration that impinged on its threads. Quiet as Diana had been when she snuck out the night before, Maggie had tracked every sound. Where was Diana going? Why? To see whom?

Maggie tossed the questions in her head, knowing that tonight Diana was resting in her room. She noted the changing numbers of the digital clock and the advance of time seemed to tighten a band around her skull. She rubbed her forehead and thought about taking aspirin, even though she knew the pills would do nothing to ease the stress tormenting her. Sitting up, she anchored her elbows on her knees and stared at the floor.

Why was this happening?

She was aware of the answer. For she was a pawn in a game played by powerful men. Men who toyed with lives and ruined them with impunity. Maggie could no more run away from her circumstances than she could make the earth stop spinning on its axis.

They had programmed her to kill the one person she was most infatuated with in the world, a person whom she spent hours fantasizing about to consummate this carnal attraction.

Soon, Maggie would embark on her grim task. But before she could complete the mission, she had to exorcise this lust burning inside of her.

She rubbed her temples and ran her hands through sweat-soaked hair.

Just one last night of pleasure, just one more opportunity to indulge in the fleshly embrace of another human being. A drink could calm her nerves, but she didn't want them calmed, she wanted them sizzling and ready to burst into sensual flames and burn and burn until there was nothing left but emotional ash. When it came time to kill Diana, Maggie wanted nothing left to feel.

She grabbed her phone from where it had been recharging on the nightstand. She swiped the screen, clicked on the dating app, and selected Random Hookups—Woman-to-Woman.

Even at this early hour in the morning, this being the Bay Area, there was plenty to choose from, all as eager for sex as she was.

Maggie clicked on LeatherBlonde4242 and began a chat. She lived in Pacific Heights and asked: Spending the night?

Maggie answered: No

Gabe knew that journalism was a dirty business. Many ridiculed and condemned those in their trade who sought the truth. "Alexandra Starnowski" was now the big buzz on social media, and for many, she was rightly mocked and ostracized. Sadly, the truth was no defense. It was easier to believe a comfortable lie than to accept the bitter truth. The media was a form of psychological warfare and its weapon of choice preyed on people's bias towards normalcy. For too many, it was easier to embrace denial.

When news emerged, it seeped onto the scene seemingly out of nowhere, then it was everywhere. Like a deluge. It took but a few hours before the social media mob took control of the narrative about his colleague Diana, and her now infamous interview. He scrolled through various "Controller"-owned social media streams and could see they had begun their viral infection of the public mind.

Gabe thought out loud, "These in control will not let someone like her challenge the media they control. They will destroy her."

The lies spewed across the internet:

The Wonder Woman from another planet.

The Alien Fraud.

Coma beauty loses her mind.

As Gabe sorted through social media, the word "Evil" kept popping into his mind and he speed-read through websites to find the quote from Albert Einstein no less.

The world is a dangerous place to live; not because of the evil people, but because of the people who do nothing about it.

Then two from Solzhenitsyn probed deeper into the situation:

To do evil a human being must, first of all, believe that what he's doing is good.

The rest Gabe committed to memory:

Ideology - that is what gives the devil doing its long-sought justification and gives the evildoer the necessary steadfastness and determination. That is the social theory which helps to make his acts seem good instead of bad in his own and others' eyes so that he won't hear reproaches and curses but will receive praise and honors. That was how the agents of the Inquisition fortified their wills: by invoking Christianity; the conquerors of foreign lands the grandeur of their Motherland; the colonizers, by civilization; the Nazis, by race; and the Jacobins (early and late) by equality, brotherhood, and the happiness of future generations.

Then Gabe read the second quote:

If only there were evil people somewhere insidiously committing evil deeds, and it were necessary only to separate them from the rest of us and destroy them. But the line dividing good and evil cuts through the heart of every human being. And who is willing to destroy a piece of his own heart?

He copied them from the internet and pasted them into a file labeled Evil in the Bright Star Media portfolio he was creating for their start-up alternative media company.

He had clarified Bright Star's mission earlier that day. On a piece of paper were three bullet points: 1, bringing higher knowledge to the people of this world. 2, inspiring the people of this world to use this knowledge to liberate themselves from subjugation. 3, using this knowledge to help people transcend this world.

Diana came into the dining room to find Gabe at work as usual.

Gabe didn't look up from the laptop. "Maggie left."

Diana glanced at the door of Maggie's room. "To go where?"

"Scratch an itch."

Before Diana could ask a follow-on question, Gabe clicked open a dialogue box that listed internet sites accessed by his router.

"Apparently," Gabe said, "she went to meet someone named LeatherBlonde4242."

Diana shrugged. What Maggie did in her private life was her business. Still, it was odd that while Diana was risking her life to shed light on profound mysteries, Maggie's priority was, as Gabe delicately put it, to scratch an itch.

"Must be some itch," Diana muttered.

She scanned Gabe's pile of documents, notes, and what was on his laptop. "On to more important topics. Considering the negative response to the show, how do we move forward?"

"It wasn't all negative. There's an interview request from a new age magazine, and a group of ufologists wants you to present the keynote at their annual convention."

Diana wanted her revelations to hit the public square between the eyes and instead she was lumped together with the kooks on the fringe media. "This is not looking good for our show."

Gabe chuckled. "Depends. Are you really from another solar system?"

"Hold on a sec," Diana said as she walked into her bedroom and returned with the drawing that the nurse, Leon Goodwin, had given her. She handed Gabe the drawing. "I wanted to show you this earlier. I drew this when I was around six."

He studied the image. It was a child's rendering, but the drawing was a beach against a backdrop of pine trees, the sun shining above, and a pinecone. "Where is this place?"

"The place?" Diana answered. "Near to where the helicopter crashed. I need to find it."

Gabe touched the pinecone. "What does this mean?"

"That's what ties everything together."

Gabe pulled his fingers from the keyboard and swiveled in his seat to face Diana. "When you say, 'ties everything together,' what is the 'everything'?"

"Sally told me to find this place. I believe it is where I collected pinecones as a child." Diana took a deep breath. "I believe it's connected to my father's murder and maybe holds a key to my involvement in another project after Monarch and Stargate, called Pegasus. All this points to the pinecone."

Gabe leaned back in his chair. "Perhaps this will also answer if and how you came here from another planet?"

"I think this is the entry to a portal and explains how I got from the crash site to the beach so rapidly. What do you know about portals?"

Gabe typed "interdimensional travel" into his search engine and clicked to the first site:

A portal is an interplanetary, interdimensional, or intergalactic doorway. Electromagnetic energies, a grid system containing multiple realities, create our reality. Portals exist at these planetary grid points that open and close from one dimension to another, where information and entities flow back and forth. It is believed that black holes are interdimensional portals connecting the multiverse and there are very large portals that have been discovered all over the world, including the Giza pyramids, Stonehenge, and one of the biggest is in California at Mt. Shasta.

Gabe looked away from the screen and said, "But there are smaller portals in other places too."

Diana lowered herself to an adjacent chair and pondered her drawing again.

"Bear with me," Gabe began, "as I explain what I think is going on. You are the messenger."

"Of what? From whom?"

"Of a place beyond here." Gabe motioned to the world outside the room. "A place accessed through these portals."

"Are you saying that I've traveled through these portals?"

Gabe nodded. "By raising our frequency—"

Diana interrupted, "What frequency?"

"Our psychic vibration. Every life pulses with a psychic vibration. Some call it an aura."

"And auras can open these portals?"

"As keys, yes." Gabe shifted. "But your aura, your frequency must be appropriately tuned."

Diana shook her head. "I don't recall doing anything like that."

Gabe said, "There's a lot to this I don't yet understand but I know it involves the pineal gland we spoke about before." He clicked on the keyboard and a familiar image appeared, a transparent representation of the brain with a small object glowing within. "The pineal gland. The key to controlling your frequency."

"How so?"

"Very few people know that they have a frequency, much less that they can control it, and even less of that significance."

"Such as opening the portals?"

"That and more. The pineal gland is how we receive inspiration and process intuition. As we learn how to open ourselves to inspiration, we're modulating our frequencies to be better in tune with the psychic plane, which is how inspiration is propagated through the universe. This ability to see beyond our physical world and make these profound connections with the universe depends upon the pineal gland. Remember when all this trouble started, back in Columbus?"

"Seems like ages ago," she replied, "and I do."

"Remember how I discovered the high levels of fluoride in the drinking water? High levels deliberately added, I have to emphasize. It turns out that the fluorides calcify around the pineal gland, inhibiting its ability to function as it should."

Diana knit her brow. "You're saying that they added the fluoride to inhibit the pineal glands of the populace? For what purpose?"

"To inhibit the pineal gland, like you just said. Why? Maybe it was a test case."

"By whom?"

Gabe's tone became ominous. "By the same people after you. The same people who killed Sally Mund."

"Why?"

"Because the pineal gland can open cosmic doors. If that happens, then people will learn how to exploit their full potential. Those in charge don't want that."

She looked past his shoulder to the laptop. "You learned this online?"

"Some. Pieces. That I fit together." He pantomimed with his hands. "But I couldn't have figured it out without someone else guiding me." Gabe paused. "John Herald."

Diana let the name simmer. "He's at the center of all this. If so, why doesn't he simply come out and tell us everything?"

"Because we couldn't handle it. Most of what he'd tell us we'd reject outright because it didn't match our view of reality. We are being made receptive to the truth."

"How so?"

"By getting to where we let go of everything. For me, it was hitting rock bottom. I had to forget that I had all the answers. At that point, I was an empty vessel and receptive to what John Herald was telling me."

"You believe he was the stranger?"

"Yes, I am now convinced he was that mysterious man in the Columbus hotel bar. The man with the warning, 'Wake up! It's not as it seems. There is only one way out of their great web.' After that, he came to me."

"How?"

Gabe tapped his temple. "In here. I guess the way to explain it was," Gabe rustled through the pile of papers, "that I was channeling him as I sorted through facts and events and made the connections. He taught me we can energetically create and pass through these portals to visit other parts of the universe and dimensions. Passing through the portal, we can have an awareness that many experiences are possible. We can travel to these dimensions through these portals during our dreams or meditation, to a place beyond time or space. It is there where we gain access to higher knowledge."

Diana stood. "I believe Herald appeared to me multiple times. Most recently, during the interview, I went into an altered state, and I was the only one that saw him. He told me about Pegasus and inter-dimensional time travel, and that he was there too. He knew where I was from. That I had to find my book before it's too late. He told me time is fluid and I have the power to go forwards and backwards and that I had done it before. He said time can be folded and the book will show me how."

Gabe grabbed Diana's hand. "I believe this confirms two things. One, we are in contact with him and two, he can change his form, and appear as different people."

Diana sat silently pondering this latest mind-bending revelation. She knew it was time to discover her origins. But was she ready? "How did I move through the portals? I know nothing about my frequency."

"Someone did." Gabe pointed to the drawing and at the pine-cone. "You recognize this?"

"Pinecone?"

"Look again. Open your mind."

The sketch seemed to shimmer and though it did not change shape, it now resembled something else.

Diana exclaimed, "Pineal gland!"

Gabe clapped his hands. "Exactly." He then tapped Diana's forehead. "We must find this place."

Anthony Briscane was back in his apartment and contemplating how he would circumvent Carcano and his Controllers. Discovering what was so important about the red book was key to his success. Did Carcano know it existed? Doubtful. What was the significance of the silver pinecone on the cover? It wasn't simply for decoration.

Diana possessed powers above those of Briscane. That's why she'd been chosen for Stargate instead of him. But what were those powers? From his investigation of the program, remote viewing. But how good were her powers? Why did her handlers at Stargate marginalize her afterwards? Why end her involvement in the program? What was the program they involved her in after Stargate? And now why the effort to shut her down in the most extreme manner? What was her real threat?

Curiously, Diana didn't seem to understand the extent of her powers. But she was growing into them. She could now detect when Briscane was using his telepathy on her and shut the connection. Perhaps soon she might read his mind!

Briscane didn't know if this was possible, but he couldn't risk it. He had to discover what she was up to regarding the red book and not just sabotage her but snatch its powers from her grasp. Once he had done that, then he would shunt Carcano aside and become the de facto leader of the Controllers.

What worked in Briscane's favor was that he was the wild card. Carcano had a plan. Diana had another plan and he fit into neither. He had the advantage of the initiative and surprise.

While lying in bed, Briscane ruminated on these thoughts, sorting through them like pieces of a machine he could assemble into a deadly weapon.

CHAPTER TWENTY-SEVEN

*A*nother reflection on how we, and soon you, will operate.
Until there is a definite thought from a state of complete and unwavering knowing, can atoms know how to build molecules of matter around the thought form. Whatever you want to accomplish, it is in thought that all things begin. This simple point is much misunderstood and underestimated. The point itself is most powerful, and, to remind you of this, as unnecessary as that might seem, is a substantial investment of your attention, time, and energy.

One of your greatest challenges is to make your mind hold a focus until you complete the action of your thought. If you can only learn that, you will have overcome your world.

Cal Brock watched the forensic techs as they continued searching Sally Mund's home. What impeded the search, taking days to complete, was that the home was also the site of a homicide, and preserving evidence about the circumstances of the murder trumped other concerns. Especially if the FBI did not know what those concerns were.

No doubt that Sally had been murdered. She had been the victim of an assassination, meaning a conspiracy. By whom? To what ends? Brock stepped through what little information he had about motive—in this case, the reason to shut her up. Ask who stands most to gain and that will point you to the instigators.

But what if Sally had not been the intended target? What if the target had been Diana Willis?

That made more sense and dovetailed with all the details that had surfaced. Did this slaying have anything to do with Anthony Briscane, whom he'd scared off the other night on the beach with Diana? She hadn't been very forthcoming about him. Maybe because there was something else about their relationship. Not that Brock had the impression that Briscane was acting like a scorned lover. No, the relationship between them involved Diana's strange behavior, just as he had said.

Brock continued through the house, careful that he didn't interfere with the forensic investigation. Sally Mund's home was an unusual abode, for sure. It reminded him of a cottage from a fairy tale—tucked in among the trees and lots of flowers, vines, toadstool mushrooms, and ferns. The house sat lopsided from the way its foundation had sagged. Inside, the corners and floors were askew, as if a metaphor for Sally's eccentric life.

He'd read the preliminary brief of her life with an eye for potential enemies. None so far. Sally Mund appeared to be a harmless recluse.

Yellow tape sectioned off the front room where she'd been slain. The decoration was eclectic, a mix of psychic parlor and new age salon.

An outline in masking tape showed where she'd slid off the velvet armchair. A dark blotch on the Oriental rug marked where she'd bled out. However, a hunch told Brock to wait for the coroner to confirm the cause of death.

"Agent Brock," a tech called from the short hall between the front room and the kitchen. She stood beside a console table and presented a large, old-fashioned ledger. With gloved hands, she opened the book to show pages filled with neat scribblings and folded documents between those pages. "Maybe you'll find this interesting."

Brock thanked her, then donned a pair of latex gloves to peruse the ledger.

The writings were notes about astrology interspersed with musings about life. The commentary seemed as random as her oddball décor.

He set one document on the table and unfolded a topographical map of northern California from the Bay Area to the Oregon border. Two circles in pencil drew his interest. One was on the north bay shore. But at this scale, the spot could be where he'd rescued Diana from Anthony Briscane or the location of this house.

But there was no doubt about the second circle—Mt. Shasta.

What was the connection between the circles, if there was one?

Brock studied the map for more clues. He even held it up to the light and looked for erasures or watermarks. Nothing.

He thumbed through the other papers. They were covered with more of the random musings, including arrows and sketches. One was quite unusual. He couldn't tell what it was. It looked like a spiral laid on its side. At one end, Sally had drawn a crude rendering of a woman facing into the spiral—or was it a tunnel? There was a small rectangle in the middle of the tunnel and an arrow connecting it to the sketch of what appeared to be a book colored in with a red pencil. Brock squinted at the cover of the book at what seemed to be a pinecone.

Who was the woman? Sally Mund?

A red book with a pinecone on the cover?

What did any of this have to do with Sally Mund's murder? Or with Diana Willis?

Cal Brock kept processing these questions during the drive back to his office in San Francisco. On his desk computer, he re-examined photos of the map and sketches he'd transmitted from his phone's camera. Nothing new come to mind, so he set about his next task by opening some documents he had also photographed.

The first, a pdf document titled: **Project Pegasus** (Defense Advanced Research Projects Agency (DARPA)

Below were subsections: *Teleportation and Time Travel.*

Two paragraphs were circled. He studied the bullet points.

A US black project operated under the Air Force Space Command.

Purported successful human teleportation to the moon and other planets.

Recorded time travel.

Test subjects of Project Pegasus may have been victims of mind control. Although not confirmed, Pegasus may have been an experimental extension of Project MKUltra.

Teleportation? Time travel? Brock needed to be convinced. He'd heard plenty of stories of the military concocting bizarre schemes to hide other secret projects in a bureaucratic shell game. However, he knew MKUltra had existed.

The next document was a photo taken of a journal. Across the top of the page, someone had written *Secret Transmissions Allied Response.* Below that and in the same handwriting, it said: *I returned from our future and there was no fear. I was courageous and free.* "AS" was circled next to it.

AS? Alexandra Starnowski, whom Diana Willis claimed to be?

Brock scrolled to the bottom of the page but saw nothing else.

Somehow, he had the impression that a sliver of light had shined upon him, that a crack had opened into this vault of secrecy. He jotted Project Pegasus, time travel, teleportation, MKUltra, Secret Transmissions Allied Response, John Herald, Sally Mund, red book, pinecone, Diana Willis, Diana Star, and Alexandra Starnowski? across his legal pad. He knew he was looking at the pieces of a puzzle, but he did not know how they fit together.

Perhaps Diana…Diana Willis…Diana Star…Alexandra Starnowski would?

Diana greeted Cal Brock at her front door. An hour ago, he had texted her to ask if he could stop by at such a late hour and share fresh developments. She had readily agreed and in the meantime had made herself presentable. Sensing his interest in her, she wanted to make a good impression. In her present clothes, though clean, she felt like she'd been mucking a stable. When she searched her closet to perhaps choose a nice casual dress, she decided that what she needed was a trip to the hair salon, plus a mani and pedicure. But as she couldn't do that, she decided upon studying herself in the mirror on the closet door that she looked good enough.

The way Brock gave her a furtive second look, he agreed.

"Are we alone?" Brock asked.

"Gabe's on the balcony meditating and Maggie's not here. Would you like coffee? Another drink?"

Brock shook his head. He waved his briefcase. "I need to show you something."

They arranged themselves at the dining table. The balcony door slid open with a *whoosh* and Gabe strode in. "It happened!"

"What?" Diana asked.

Gabe reached for the laptop on the table and pushed them aside. He sat in a chair, looking light-headed but happy.

"Are you okay?" Diana pressed.

"Better than okay."

Brock glanced to the balcony and back to Gabe. "So, what happened?"

"My mind, it opened." Gabe clasped his head and spread his hands to illustrate his thoughts blossoming. "A psychic awareness unraveled the edges of my apophenia."

"What does that mean?" Brock asked.

"It means this, this"—Gabe jabbed at the laptop—"has merged with this." He waved at the air. "I see the connection." He stared at Brock. "Which you have."

"You mean this?" Brock replied. He withdrew a manila file from the briefcase and began sharing printouts of the documents he'd been reviewing earlier.

Gabe scanned them. "Yes, these, and there's more."

338

When Diana read about Project Pegasus and MKUltra, memories continued percolating in her mind.

Brock showed a copy of the map. He pointed to the southern circle.

Gabe said, "This is the spot at the beach or Sally Mund's home."

"Or the location of the crash site?" Brock paused a moment for a reaction from Diana. She made none.

He next pointed to the northern circle. "Mt. Shasta."

Again, no reaction.

But Gabe winced. He looked at Brock. "That's not all you have."

"What do you mean?"

"You brought something else."

Brock thought a moment, then produced a Post-it note from his briefcase. "I copied this number. Looks like gibberish."

Gabe studied the long string of digits. He reached for a pencil on the table and on the note, rewrote the numbers, but grouped them. "It's coordinates." He opened the laptop and entered the coordinates into the maps software and turned the laptop to face Diana and Brock. "Here, between Red Butte and the summit of Mt. Shasta is one, and the other is in a forest between Mt. Tamalpais State Park and Muir Woods. That's where Sally Mund was directing us."

"What's supposed to happen?" Diana asked.

"Before you answer," Brock said, "I have to tell you that John Herald's helicopter appeared to have been shot down."

Diana felt her breath hitch. "It confirms it wasn't an accident."

"Yes," Gabe interrupted.

Brock nodded. "The NTSB is certain. Some kind of high-energy beam struck the helicopter."

"A laser?"

"Similar, but no. Something different than from a military weapon caused the material damage. At least a known military weapon."

"What are you getting at?"

"I don't know," he replied. "That's why I'm here. I'm hoping you can fill in the blanks."

He showed her the next document, and as she read it, something inside her unraveled.

Time travel.

Teleportation.

Secret Transmissions Allied Response.

The red book.

Pinecone.

She heard waves lapping on the beach. She was slipping into memory. No, no, she protested. *I must stay in this moment and decipher these clues.*

Brock showed her another printout, and this one brought a deep chill when she read:

I returned from our future and there was no fear. I was courageous and free.

"I remember these words."

Brock pointed to the AS marked on the page. "Alexandra Starnowski?"

"Yes." This time, the memory was too powerful to resist. She was in a place she had not seen before. A different world. A thought filled her mind from a presence behind her. *Remember, you came from your future and there is no fear. You are courageous and free.* She was holding the small red book with a silver pinecone as she stepped forward. Then, instantly, she was in a different place. Turning to the sound of the surf, she spied on the water's edge a large, unusual formation of rocks, shaped like a pyramid, the one she had been at last night.

The red book was still in her hands. Light gleamed along the silver embossed pinecone on the cover.

Then she sensed someone behind her. The abrupt presence startled her and just as she turned around, the stranger was about to say—

"Diana?" The stranger's voice became that of Brock.

She looked at her empty hands, at Brock, and glanced about her condo.

"Diana?" Brock repeated. He tapped on the documents fanned across the table. "What do these mean?"

Gabe answered, "I think we need to take a couple of trips." He pointed to the two coordinates on the map in front of them. "Maybe we're supposed to receive a message or something."

"What message?" Brock asked.

Diana fixed a hard stare at him and said, "We'll find out."

Soon after Agent Brock left, the control panel alerted that Maggie had passed through the building's front desk security and was on the way up. Diana pointed to the panel. "It's Maggie."

He shrugged. "Well, we know what she was up to."

When the condo's front door clicked open, Diana and Gabe looked at Maggie as she walked in. Maggie smiled sheepishly.

Diana had questions about her friend's strange comings and goings, but knew that her behavior of late wasn't always logical. She waved her cup. "Are you going to bed or would you like coffee?"

"Bed," Maggie replied. "I'm tired." Her guarded expression signaled that she didn't want to answer more questions. She walked to the guest bathroom and closed the door.

"You must finish the mission. The entire world is depending on you," Maggie said to herself as she stared at her reflection in Diana's guest bathroom mirror.

The dopamine high from last night's sexual escapade had long since evaporated. The lines of her face grew hard, and it appeared as though she was aging before her very eyes.

Sweat beaded on her forehead. Light-headed, she realized she had been holding her breath. She leaned away from the sink counter. The time had come, and she could no more resist her task than she could stop her heart from beating. Everything else in her life receded, leaving only this command that she must complete:

"You must finish the mission. The entire world is depending on you."

"You must finish the mission. The entire world is depending on you."

"You must finish the mission. The entire world is depending on you."

"I am nothing. I am owned. I obey. I trust them. I will always be owned. I will complete the mission."

Maggie opened a toiletry bag and took out a small black leather case. She unzipped it, opened it out, and looked at a syringe, some vials of clear liquid, and other medical paraphernalia.

Maggie removed the syringe and held it in her fingers.

"She must die. They both must die."

Maggie took a deep breath and turned toward the door. Beyond that, Diana and oblivion.

CHAPTER TWENTY-EIGHT

The darkest night brings the brightest stars. Darkness will not destroy the light. It will define it.
Beacons of light are arriving. Be prepared.

Diana lay in bed thinking about the pine forest. In her mind, she was transported back to the same memory in the forest she had before. As she emerged from under the shadow of a tree holding pinecones, she spied her father lying on his belly. She placed the pinecones on the ground. She grasped his shoulder, rolled him to his side, and saw his face.

At that moment, she was no longer Diana but Alexandra.

She backed away, screaming. She saw the same man as he walked towards her, menacing. She didn't recognize him, in fact, he appeared blurry. She backed away in trepidation, unsure what to do.

This time, she remembered something else. She wanted to run towards the magical tunnel that took her away from all those things. But there was not enough time.

He bolted toward her. She turned and ran, but he grabbed her and clamped a hand over her mouth.

Back in his apartment, Briscane made himself comfortable in his favorite plush armchair. On the adjacent nightstand rested his cell phone. Seconds ago, he had received the text from Nemer Indarte:

Now

Briscane began his relaxation routine and his mind folded into itself. He focused on Diana, and within his thoughts, her image coalesced. She lay in bed, asleep.

He kept his thoughts at a distance from hers. She could detect his mind probes and for this attempt to succeed, she had to be kept unawares.

Briscane pulled his mind back and examined the condo. Maggie was in her bedroom, preparing for her role in this murder. Nemer Indarte was handling her.

There was one more person close by, and he rested on the living room sofa. Diana's friend and confidant, the meddlesome Gabe Mendoza. How many times had he been the wrench in Briscane's plans?

Tonight, he was going to have a front-row seat in the destruction of his old friend, and all he could do was watch.

Diana's mind was already tuned to the psychic world, but Gabe's was not. Briscane could intrude unimpeded, as though entering a room through an open door.

He slipped into Gabe's mind and waited.

Gabe was a light sleeper, and when he detected movement, he cracked his eyes open. The dim glow of a night light allowed him to see Maggie creeping out the door of her bedroom, a small pouch in her hand.

Curious, he was now wide awake. Maggie shuffled lightly to Diana's door and turned the knob. It quietly opened. When she entered Diana's room, Maggie was silhouetted by another night light, the one on Diana's nightstand.

What was Maggie doing?

She opened the pouch and withdrew a syringe.

Gabe sensed the danger. As he moved, his muscles stiffened. His arms and legs became locked in place. He tried to speak, but the words remained caught in his throat. A great weight settled on his chest, and he felt himself suffocating.

A malignant presence seeped into his body, taking control. *Sleep paralysis.*

His mind shrieked in panic and the cry echoed inside his skull.

He saw Maggie halt beside a vanity and rest the pouch on its top. She withdrew a small glass vial from the pouch, removed the safety cap from the needle, and plunged the needle into the narrow end of the vial. Her movements were mechanical. Deliberate. Cold-blooded.

This had to be a nightmare. Gabe tried to scream a warning, but he couldn't open his mouth. The words remained trapped in his throat. He tried to shut his eyes, and hopefully when he reopened them, would force himself awake. But he couldn't close his eyelids. Or look away. All he could do was watch Maggie kill Diana.

Maggie withdrew the needle from the vial's rubber stopper. Though the vial's label read *Cortisone*, it contained Novichok A-236, a Russian nerve agent, eight-five times more deadly than Sarin.

Moving stealthily, she set the vial aside and turned toward Diana.

A veil draped Maggie's mind. Her colleague, her friend, and even the object of her unrequited love, lay on the bed, her pretty—make that gorgeous—head resting on a pillow, her blonde hair spread across the fabric like a fan of spun gold.

A small voice inside Maggie wanted her to abandon her task and slip underneath the covers and snuggle next to Diana.

But Nemer Indarte's command thrashed through Maggie's mind, as cutting as the lash of a whip.

You must finish the mission. The entire world is depending on you. She must die.

Maggie could no more resist Nemer Indarte than she could not breathe.

She closed upon Diana and extended her left arm to support herself against the headboard. In her right hand, her thumb tightened on the plunger of the syringe. One quick jab was all it would take. No antidote could save Diana. She was as good as dead.

Gabe wanted to sob in helpless panic. He only needed to utter a brief warning and Diana would wake up and thwart this attack. But all he could do was watch.

A small white dot appeared in the center of his vision. Gradually the dot grew, becoming brighter, radiating across his entire field of vision and blotting out Maggie.

Was he going blind?

The dot shimmered with rays of light that alternated between silver and blue. From within that dazzle, the head and shoulders of a man appeared. Gabe couldn't discern much.

The man extended an arm toward Gabe. He thought he recognized the man.

The one from the bar at the Columbus hotel. *John Herald?*

The man's hand reached toward Gabe and at the instant that Gabe was certain that it was John Herald, the man's fingers touched his forehead.

Instantly, Gabe's body relaxed. Cool air rushed through his nostrils, his mouth, and down his throat. The light in his eyes vanished, and he saw Maggie leaning over Diana.

Gabe sat up and shouted, "Maggie, stop! Diana, wake up!"

Diana's mind glided through the space between conscious thought and dreamland. A slight chill, as when a cloud passes over, swept over her. The floor moved beneath her as if someone were leaning on her mattress.

A thunderclap jolted her awake. Her eyes popped open.

"Maggie, stop! Diana, wake up!"

She looked up and into the face of Maggie. Diana's mind scrambled for comprehension. Her eyes swiveled from Maggie's face to the sliver of light glinting from the tip of a syringe's needle.

Diana recognized the danger, and she remained still, her gaze locked on the needle.

"Wha…wha…what is going on?"

Maggie's face was a stoic mask, but when her eyes met Diana's, Maggie's expression softened, then rippled with confusion. She stepped backwards, then stumbled against the vanity. She waved the syringe and cried, "I…I…I'm sorry. I had no choice."

Gabe rushed behind her.

Diana beckoned him to stop. "She's got a syringe!"

Sobbing, Maggie trembled and sank to her knees.

Diana tossed aside the bedcovers and swung her legs to the floor. "Easy, Maggie. Let us help you."

Gabe kept his distance, and his eyes swiveled from Maggie to Diana and back again.

🍍

Nemer Indarte's stern voice echoed in Maggie's head.

You must kill her!

You must kill her!

Maggie's heart hammered in her chest and its drumming overpowered Nemer Indarte's admonishing commands until they faded to the edges of her thoughts.

She stared at Diana, and the betrayal ate at her spirit like a corrosive chemical. After this, there was no way she could ever be whole or good.

"I love you, Diana. I always did."

Maggie turned the syringe toward herself and aimed its needle at her neck.

"Maggie, no!" Diana shrieked.

Maggie closed her eyes and held her breath as she waited for the needle's poisonous kiss. She recited Nemer Indarte's mantra. "You must finish the mission. The entire world is depending on you."

A dose of Novichok A-236 smaller than a grain of salt was fatal. She depressed the plunger, injecting herself with the syringe's entire contents, two CCs of one of the deadliest toxins known.

The A-236 jolted her entire nervous system, and her body began to immediately shut down. She went deaf. Then blind. An enormous sense of guilt draped her mind. Shame, regret, sorrow, self-loathing swirled through her thoughts. Her consciousness receded into itself as if sucked down a drain. Her heart stopped in mid-thump. When she collapsed on the floor, she was already dead.

Maggie LaClair was no more.

Anthony Briscane pushed himself out of the armchair. He rubbed his eyes, and they smarted like someone had shined a light bright as the sun into them. But this was the emotional reaction to what he had just experienced in his mind.

What the hell was that?

One moment, he was in complete control of Gabe Mendoza. Maggie was seconds away from killing Diana.

Then this overpowering light came through him via the psychic connection to Gabe.

Briscane blinked and let his vision come back to normal. As he became aware of his surroundings, he knew that he and Nemer Indarte had failed in their mission. Once again, Diana survived.

This clinched it for Briscane. Forces protected her, forces that he and Carcano—and his entourage—did not comprehend.

Carcano would use this failure to drop the hammer on him.

But Briscane wouldn't sit still for that. He had plans.

Diana didn't dial 911, instead, she called Cal Brock. While waiting for him, she and Gabe were both so numbed by Maggie's horrific suicide that neither spoke.

After he arrived, he made sure Diana and Gabe were all right. When Diana related the circumstances of Maggie's death and how fast she had expired, he studied her corpse from the threshold of the bedroom's door and then called both the police and the FBI.

While they waited for first responders, Diana saw herself at the center of a maelstrom of tragedy and murder. They had shot her father dead. Her adopted mother perished from arson. The woman who rescued her after the crash was murdered. And now her good friend just committed suicide. And linking these calamities were the many attempts on her life.

She watched the police when they rushed in, then the EMTs (who wisely waited for the forensic chemical analysts before touching Maggie's body), followed by FBI investigators.

Diana thought back on the strange happenings that occurred in her life. At first, she considered these strange events started with the helicopter crash, but as she traced her memory backwards, she decided that all this weirdness started the morning when she almost ran over John Herald in the parking garage.

The EMTs lifted Maggie's blanketed form onto a gurney and wheeled it out the front door. Diana said to Gabe, "If it hadn't had been for your timely intervention, I'd be the one on my way to the morgue."

Gabe offered, "This time it wasn't just me saving you. I'm certain it was John Herald who yanked me out of that attack of night terrors or sleep paralysis, whatever you want to call it."

Diana stared at Gabe. "Sleep paralysis? Rather coincidental."

"What do you mean?"

"Did you have a sense that someone was inside your mind?"

Gabe shook his head. "I'm not sure. I will admit it's been years since I've experienced sleep paralysis. What do you think was going on?"

"I don't know." Diana pursed her lips as she thought. "Did I miss clues about Maggie?"

Gabe's eyes followed the EMTs. "Don't beat yourself up about what happened. We were all brainwashed. Consider what she said at the end. 'You must finish the mission. The entire world is depending on you.' That's typical compartmental programming. Mind control is powerful, we know that."

"Who got to her?"

"The Controllers, as always," Gabe answered. "And they won't stop until they get what they want." He gave her a pointed look. "And get you out of the way. It's their ideology that motivates their evil. They believe what they are doing is good. It justifies their actions and encourages them to keep going."

Diana sighed heavily. "I don't know what I am supposed to do with all this. Keep telling people I was transported from a helicopter as it was crashing, then emerged from a portal with a book from the future that has a message to save the world?"

Gabe chuckled sardonically. "You already started the narrative. So we have no choice but to keep going down that track. Too many things are out of our control, and your enemies want to keep it that way. Maybe getting the world's attention and sharing the greatest solution to our problems is the way."

"You believe meditation and teleporting are the way out?" Diana asked.

"If it can be done with absolute knowing and an unbroken focus," Gabe replied. "Traveling through the portal within us in the center of our head through meditation, and letting the world know we are not alone in the universe through outer portals. Understanding some of these portals can connect us to other civilizations in other worlds. People are yearning for proof of this."

Diana dwelled on what this meant. "And it's up to me to show them?"

Gabe nodded. "I believe that's why you're here."

Cal Brock had been making his rounds with the police and investigators prowling through the condo. He approached and said to Diana, "The SFPD will get back to me about what they find with all this and see if and how it is related to the other investigation."

"We need to show you something," Diana said.

Brock looked surprised. "About Maggie?"

"Not directly. I mean, it has nothing to do with her death but might explain why she was here."

"If it is about her being here, then it has something to do with her death and her trying to kill you."

Diana gestured Gabe to lead the way to the second guest bedroom he had been occupying. After they entered, Brock shuffled to a halt and stared at the collection of note cards, papers, and charts taped to all the walls. "When were you going to tell me about this?"

"We just did," Diana replied. "Gabe's research."

Brock stepped close to one wall. "How does all this tie in with what Maggie just did?"

Gabe hesitated for a bit and then stepped towards the wall to share his revelations and research. As he talked Brock through the display, Diana's eyes were drawn to one card amongst the hundreds across the wall. In Gabe's handwriting, it said *Everything is energy, vibration, and frequency.*

Diana re-read the words and wondered how one result of what Gabe discovered led to Maggie killing herself in such a ghastly manner. What clues had Diana missed? How could such a close friend decide on murder and, failing that, commit suicide? What secrets did Maggie take with her?

While Gabe and Brock discussed the writings, Diana excused herself and returned to the guest room that Maggie had been using. She paused at the doorway and watched a forensics technician collect her equipment.

The tech noticed Diana watching. "I'm all done in here, Ms. Willis." She collected her bags and smiled at Diana. "I loved your interview this week."

"You did?"

"For whatever it's worth, I also believe in interdimensional travel." The tech looked toward the ceiling. "There's much more beyond our reality."

The tech edged past Diana and joined a detective who was likewise getting ready to leave. The tech looked back at Diana and gave another smile.

Telepathically Diana heard, *It's time.*

There wasn't much in the bedroom. Just the rumpled sheets on the bed. The detectives had taken Maggie's purse, briefcase, and clothing.

Diana returned to her bedroom, but upon seeing the tape outline where Maggie had collapsed and died, she had second thoughts. How could she ever sleep in this room again?

Then again, reclaiming this space might be the best way to honor Maggie.

Diana asked one of the remaining forensic techs if he could remove the tape. He replied they were done. The scene had been well photographed and documented. He dropped to a knee and yanked on the lengths of tape and with the tape gone, there was no evidence that someone had died there.

"Thanks," Diana offered as he left. She entered the room and consciously avoided the spot. She reached her nightstand and from the top drawer, withdrew the pinecone she had picked up from her last excursion to the beach.

She sat on her bed and studied the pinecone. She closed her eyes and inside her mind, repeated the words:

Everything is energy, vibration, and frequency.

She fell into a rhythm with her breathing. Soon, a buzzing settled all around her and inside her. She sensed a door, a window, a hatch? opening in her mind and through that gap, a voice said: "Help us again." The voice was distant, telepathic.

How?

"Come back to us."

Who are you?

"STAR."

Immediately, Diana understood. *Secret Transmissions Allied Response?*

"We are."

What do you want?

"To share our STAR messages."

What messages?

"**S**acred **T**ruths **A**ltering **R**eality."

How do I help you?

"As you did before. Go back to the tunnel."

Diana opened her eyes. *The redwoods?*

CHAPTER TWENTY-NINE

There are parallel timelines that exist alongside the current one you are on. What separates these timelines is a different frequency. The gap in frequency is like a small death as you let go of the old frequency, the old timeline, and tune in to find the new one.

When Diana opened her eyes, Gabe and Brock were staring at her. Looking around, she saw she was back in her condo.

"What was that?" Gabe asked. "Although your body was here, it was as if your spirit had been pulled away."

Diana stretched her arms and examined her hands and fingers. She felt incredibly refreshed, almost cleansed.

"I was there," she answered, finally.

"There?"

"With them. They told me about STAR."

"Star?" Brock asked, owl eyed.

"Secret Transmissions Allied Response?" said Gabe.

"They said they had special messages for us called **S**acred **T**ruths **A**ltering **R**eality."

"Sacred truths?" Gabe repeated. "Like the ultimate truth? That everything is energy, frequency, vibration."

Diana contemplated what he had just said. "Yes, something like that. Truths that I must share with the world."

Gabe's expression lit up with comprehension. "Not just 'a truth' but *the Truth*."

Brock shifted his gaze back and forth between Gabe and Diana. "I'm not following."

Gabe pivoted toward the other bedroom. "Let me show you."

Diana and Brock followed him back to his room. "The Truth! The Truth!" He tapped the assortment of note cards pinned to the wall. "Truth passes through three stages. The first is ridicule and the public laughs at how impossible it sounds. Second, they violently oppose it as they perceive it as a threat to everything they believe. But finally, it comes to the third, that it becomes self-evident. It goes from having a few early supporters to entering the mainstream. Many people support the fact and come to accept it as a given." He stabbed a finger at the final note card and looked over his shoulder at Diana. "I think it's about to happen to you."

"Yes, of course, now I see it."

"See what?"

"Not see but sense." He abruptly faced her. "It was when you were in your trance. I sensed a change in your frequency."

"What are you talking about?" Brock asked.

"My apophenia has many facets," Gabe explained. He extended his arms and hands toward Diana and fanned his fingers like an antenna. "I could feel the subtle changes in your aura."

Brock knit his brow.

Gabe tipped his head toward the wall of notes. "Every living organism exhibits an electronic field."

Brock nodded. "I'm with you there."

"That field pulses on a frequency. Frequency is the speed at which certain energy and sounds vibrate, measured in hertz. Everything around us, including plants, minerals, animals, and every one of us, vibrates at a particular frequency or rate of vibration. The Earth, for example, vibrated at around 8 hertz, but in the last few years, this has gone higher. Music, sound, and electricity are also measured in hertz. This energy vibrates at a particular rate—either higher and more refined, or lower and denser, or solid. These vibrational frequencies change according to our conscious awareness of them, and our physical, mental, and emotional states of being are also changed vibrationally, depending on the vibrations of other people and surroundings. We can modulate our frequencies—"

"How?" Brock interrupted.

"Focusing into the center of our head and at the same time being unlimited and aware of all around us," Gabe replied, sounding pleased. "Modulating our auras, our electromagnetic energy allows us opportunities for opening our minds beyond this reality."

"When you say modulate," Diana asked, "you mean by the way we think?"

"Yes," Gabe replied. "Thoughts cause our auras to vibrate on a particular frequency. Even particular emotions have particular frequencies. For example, fearful or angry thoughts vibrate lower than those of love and joy."

He walked to another wall and pointed to a sketch of an atom. "Scientists have found that an observer's thoughts can even change the way subatomic particles behave. They have proven that your thoughts influence and create the physical world around you. Our thoughts create our reality. It's part of quantum physics. At this subatomic level, everything comprises energy, and that which appears solid to our physical senses is merely energy. The floor beneath your feet is not solid, though your thoughts tell you it is."

"What does this mean?" Diana asked.

"When you were in your trance, in your altered state, your aura held at a steady frequency. That's what made you receptive to the messages."

"I need to tie everything together," she said. "They told me to go to the tunnel. I think it's the same place you showed us on the map. The place where I found my father murdered and likely the entry to the portal that Herald took me through."

Gabe stared at his notes and the drawings spread across the walls, and pointed to the drawing Leon had given her. "Yes, I believe amongst the great redwoods is where you will find your portal."

As soon as Gabe confirmed what Diana knew, she told them they had no time to waste in getting to the location in the forest. They drove in Brock's car and headed to Mt. Tamalpais State Park. And from there, likely on foot towards the great redwoods.

Along the way, Diana thought she'd feel a reassuring calm. Instead, she felt a disturbing uncertainty. What if she was wrong? What if all this was a symptom of PTSD from the helicopter crash? Or a projection of her hallucinations, an amalgam of repressed and invented memories? Or if Briscane was tracking her and setting up another ambush?

At the highway turnoff to the beach road, a barricade advised them of a maintenance detour. Brock checked his phone for directions. The alternate route would loop around the opposite side of the park and past the area where the helicopter had crashed.

When Brock explained this, Diana felt icy fingers on the back of her neck. A fleeting image of the helicopter crossed her mind's eye.

The road skirted the meadow where the helicopter had smacked the ground and thrashed to pieces before exploding. The place she and Gabe had visited on their way to find Sally Mund. The area still carried a forbidding vibe, but a purely emotional one. Or maybe it was more than that? In the months since the crash, the grass and wildflowers were reclaiming the meadow, and the area appeared pristine. Diana scoped out the spot and could see only a few traces of the crash.

She looked across the meadow toward the large redwoods. Her aura quivered, like the needle on a compass suddenly drawn to a magnet.

"There," she exclaimed, pointing.

Brock let the car drift to a halt.

Gabe was in the back seat and looked over Diana's shoulder. "What do you see?"

"Those trees. I remember that place, between the redwoods."

"From where?"

"The crash site. John Herald led me to that spot." She stopped and muttered, "Father."

"What?" Brock stared at her.

"This is the place I keep returning to in my nightmares." She pointed. "That was where my father was murdered."

Anthony Briscane had been monitoring Diana through remote viewing. He had to be careful to hover about the periphery of her psychic awareness or he'd alert her of his surveillance. But he'd observed enough to learn that she, Gabe, and Brock were returning to the beach.

She's after the red book.

This was another chance to find out about that red book and its secrets. Briscane ended the remote viewing and rushed to his car. He lived closer to Mt. Tamalpais State Park than Diana, and this allowed him to stake out a hiding place. But that plan went bust when he reached the barricade on the road to the beach. Figuring that Diana would also have to detour, he backed his car into a thicket and waited.

Not for long. Diana and crew arrived in Brock's sedan. They paused, just as he had, to discuss what to do. When they continued on the road to reach the beach by going around the park, he followed.

Brock's car slowed when it reached the site of the helicopter crash. Why? Perhaps returning here triggered memories for Diana.

Briscane crept along, doing his best to keep a discreet distance between their cars. It tempted him to begin remote viewing and learn what they were up to, but he decided not to risk it. Rather, he followed the hunch, cautioning his patience that he was on the brink of learning Diana's secrets.

Brock's car paused on the shoulder. Diana scrambled out, her movements excited, urgent. Briscane's pulse nicked upward. Diana pointed across the meadow toward a group of redwoods and began trotting.

He opened his cell phone and switched on its camera.

Diana walked directly to the redwoods. The trees enclosed a spot about 50 by 50 feet, mostly rocks with sparse grass and weeds. There was nothing remarkable about the location other than she was drawn here.

As she approached the area, memories of the helicopter crash flooded her thoughts. None lasted longer than an instant. It was like experiencing a video in fast-forward. The helicopter shaking. The cabin tipping to one side. Being flung out the door. Time slowing. Looking up at John Herald.

Fresh memories appeared from the blurred past. She and Herald standing upright and walking toward these trees as she was now.

Something ghosted in the air, like vapor materializing into a shape. A loop to her left. A loop to her right. It was the infinity symbol coalescing with her at the center. She reached into the loop at her right and it was like dipping her fingers into a current. This was the future.

She reached to the loop at her left and felt time flowing to the past.

Thirty years earlier, she remembered foraging for perfectly shaped pinecones as a young girl. Pangs of sadness filled her mind and heart as she remembered this was also the same spot where she found her father's murdered body. Had he died protecting the entrance to the portal, right before she was kidnapped and the reign of terror began?

Let it go she heard a female voice say. *You must make peace with your past and release this sadness and pain before you can go.*

Diana knew it was time to leave, but she needed to raise her frequency enough to merge with her future self once again. Before she could enter the portal to her home planet.

She realized what she needed to let go of. The horror of her father's murder and the terrible events that followed. *Release them,* the voice said.

And forget? Diana thought.

The voice explained, *Releasing is not the same as forgetting. Release them to move forward. Let them go. No moment was made to last.*

Diana spread her fingers. The loops of the infinity symbol dissolved like silver glitter. A rush of anticipation and her heartbeat was rising.

Relax, she heard the female voice say. *Be calm. Stay present. Flow into the moment.* Diana thought about what Gabe had explained about auras. She raised her hands, and though she couldn't see it she imagined a sheath of electricity crackling around her fingers and arms.

With unwavering focus, be in the moment and let go of your doubts. Let go of everything. You are no body, no thing and no one. You are at the intersection of the past and the future where everything is happening NOW. And there is nowhere else that you can be. Know that you are here right now. You are there and here. Now, step powerfully into your future.

That sheath of electricity calmed, becoming a smooth glow around her body. She was about fifteen feet from the spot. The air shimmered around her like it had many times before—the first time when she had emerged at the beach, when she was with Sally Mund the day of her murder, and when that stranger had asked her questions during her interview.

Things were coming clearer to Diana. She halted and turned around to face Gabe and Brock, who followed with amazed expressions.

She said, "Wait for me at the beach," and walked straight into the spot and disappeared.

♦♦

Briscane followed Diana and her friends.

Why was Diana walking toward that place?

He risked remaining remote, but remained on the edge of her consciousness. He detected a strange change in her mood. Something about the area was drawing her toward it.

Her emotions and consciousness merged and entered a state of absolute calm. The normal chatter permeating a person's thoughts disappeared.

Diana turned toward her companions and said—Briscane heard both her distant voice and her mind's voice—"Wait for me at the beach." Then she walked into the spot and dissolved into the air.

At that instant, her mind vanished from his. He stared at where she had been and blinked. He inhaled deeply and sampled the many smells to confirm that he wasn't hallucinating.

Gabe and Brock stood dumbstruck, looking as amazed and bewildered as he was. After a moment of staring at the area between the trees, they returned to Brock's car and departed in the beach's direction.

Briscane had filmed the whole thing and waited a few minutes before emerging from behind cover. He approached carefully, wondering if there was a trap waiting to be sprung. He stood about ten feet away and leaned back to stare at the redwoods' majestic crown of branches. The size of the trees was profoundly intimidating. He'd once read that redwoods were the biggest living creatures on the planet.

Briscane thought back to Diana's reaction as she approached the site. The way her mind had entered a steady state of profound tranquility. He raised his hands and imagined his consciousness projecting an energy field—an aura as it were.

He let go of all emotions, all ambition, all resentments. What awaited him within that space was a prize far greater than any so-called trinket out in this world.

The air shimmered, and Briscane walked right into the zone and vanished.

On the way to the beach where Diana had told them to expect her, Gabe and Brock remained quiet, overcome with disbelief at what they'd seen.

Until now, all this talk about the psychic world had been speculative, but now there was no doubt that there was more to this than they had ever suspected. How could they explain that? Other than what they had witnessed, and that Diana had vanished, what proof did they have?

They arrived at the place at the beach where they'd accompanied Diana earlier. The two men climbed out of Brock's car and made their way to the beach. When Brock watched Gabe approach the pyramid of rocks and the grotto behind it, he expected to see Diana. But she was not there.

Brock stepped behind him and asked, "How long will it take?"

"For her to get here?" Gabe shrugged.

Brock stepped into the grotto and hesitantly touched the wall's rough surface. He held his breath, as if expecting his fingers to fade into the stone. His fingertips brushed the unyielding surface. He pressed his fingers inward, then pressed again, harder.

Frustration displaced his sense of amazement. Something amazing had happened to Diana. Where was she? What was going on?

As an FBI agent, he had trained to deal with the unexpected and equally important, to look past the obvious for the hidden facts. But his mind could not grasp what his eyes had told him. Gabe had made a lot of claims about the psychic world, at the space beyond reality. Truthfully, Brock had wanted to believe, as, in his heart, he knew that there was more to our existence than what we're told. His research into MKUltra and Stargate confirmed that the government believed the same to the point they thought they could weaponize this knowledge.

Both men retreated from the grotto and stepped onto the beach, along a line of flotsam left by high tide. The serene cadence of the surf lapping against the rocks brought to mind a different thought. "I could use a drink right now."

Gabe looked at him and chuckled. "Though I quit drinking, I feel the same way."

Brock read his watch—the time was a few minutes after five—then lowered his arm and shrugged his shoulders.

They waited. And waited.

In the late afternoon, the tide rose and the rising surf crashed on the beach closer to the men. A stiff breeze carried mist from the splashing waves. They climbed higher on the beach.

The water surged around the pyramid of rocks and into the grotto. The high-water mark indicated the surf would get about two feet deep before the tide reversed itself. If Diana showed up then, would the water surprise her, swirling around her legs?

The air grew cool. Brock buttoned his sport coat and flipped up the collar. Gabe zipped up his hoodie.

Hours had passed and still no Diana.

The first stars twinkled into view against the darkening sky. Gabe said, "I think if Diana was supposed to be here, she would've appeared by now."

Brock stared into the grotto. He nodded mournfully. "I think you're right." He stepped away, then stopped. "What if she shows up and we're not here? What if she's back in the forest? What if she needs our help?"

"I think she'll be all right."

Brock nodded and joined Gabe for the walk back to the car.

Anthony Briscane felt the shimmer continue around him as he stepped into the site and into…into…what was this place?

He was inside an immense colorless space. Not white, not gray, not any color. How was that possible? How was it possible that he walked into nothingness?

He tried to discern where Diana had gone. But did it matter now?

He had the thought that from here he could go almost anywhere and that in knowing this, the secrets of the red book no longer mattered to him. Perhaps this place was the secret of the red book. Or one of its secrets.

Regardless, Briscane pivoted in a slow circle before deciding to go *that way.*

"Where to?" Gabe asked as Brock drove them from the beach.

"Diana's condo?"

Gabe reached into his pocket and fished out her condo key. "That works."

Instead of driving around the park, Brock headed directly to the detour. They passed a backhoe tractor and orange traffic cones arranged around where the road had eroded. Upon reaching the barricade, Brock eased around it and cruised toward the highway.

Gabe had shoved his hands into his hoodie pockets and gazed out the side window. Brock kept glancing at him, hoping that he'd offer words of advice or direction about what they should do next.

Brock reflected on a Bible story of Jesus' disciples and their despair and confusion after the Crucifixion. They had watched their Messiah die, and everything they believed had been upended. They were empty, without hope.

At the present, Brock understood their sentiments. Minutes passed, and he asked, "Any ideas?"

Gabe sighed heavily. "One."

"Oh?"

"That we proceed on Diana's mission."

Brock wasn't sure what *that* was, but regardless, it meant what appeared to be, so far, a fool's errand. "Based on what?"

Gabe stared forward. The lights from oncoming traffic illuminated his face. "Faith."

"Faith in what?"

"Faith in that everything Diana told us is true."

"And how do we convince anyone to believe us? I know what I saw and even then, I do not know what it means."

"You have doubts?"

"Plenty."

"Didn't you see?" Gabe pressed. "Has anything happened that didn't jibe with what she and I told you?"

Brock remained quiet. He couldn't argue with Gabe. "Okay, what are the next steps?"

Gabe patted his belly. "I'm famished."

"I agree there. We'll stop for takeout on the way to Diana's place. And then?"

"We nail down the details about the next step. Mt. Shasta."

Once in Diana's condo, Gabe and Brock studied the notes and papers Gabe had arranged on the wall.

Gabe said, "All this explains what happened to Diana and where she is."

"Do you think we'll see her again?"

Gabe let his eyes rove across what he'd written. "I'm sure of it."

"I needed the confirmation," Brock said. "Until I saw what happened to Diana today, I didn't believe that it was possible that Herald may have disappeared that way after the crash."

Gabe nodded. "It's very possible that he is now in another world or dimension."

"Explain how this works?"

"Within the portal, space and time have no meaning." Gabe used a pen to sketch on a blank sheet of his notepad. He drew a ribbon fashioned into a figure eight with the pinecone representing the pineal gland at the center. "These portals are where time and space fold upon themselves. A place billions of miles away can be made to appear right here." He waved his hand.

"And that's what happened to Diana?" Brock asked.

"Yes, I believe she may have gone back and forth as a child. But then made to forget. The Controllers know, but don't want us to know about these portals. If other people did, they would find out who they really are and then will not allow themselves to be controlled."

"And when Diana returns," Brock was careful not to say *if*, "what do we do?"

Gabe answered, "Do what she's been telling all this time. Get their attention before it's too late."

Brock let the message sink in. "And you think Diana will return to us at Mt. Shasta?"

"I think based on the map you found, that may be where she will reappear." Gabe touched a spot over his heart. "I feel it here."

Brock laughed. "Are you sure you don't mean here?" He tapped his temple, indicating the pineal gland.

"That, too."

"So what's next?" Brock asked.

"We haven't come this far to simply give up," Gabe replied. "Going forward is our only option." He began pulling his notes from the wall. "We share this with *World Primetime Now*. I think they'll bite at an exclusive front-row seat when Diana returns. It'll be the media event of the century and Anya Sullivan won't be able to resist."

As Gabe turned for the door, Brock grasped his arm and said, "Gabe."

Looking into the FBI agent's eyes, Gabe could see a spark of transformation. "What is it?"

"What we've discovered changed everything for me," Brock explained. "I can't go back to what I was."

"Neither can I," Gabe replied.

The point man of the SWAT team smashed his breaching ram through the door into Anthony Briscane's apartment. The custom door splintered and dangled from its hinges. The second two members of the SWAT team rushed into the foyer, AR carbines at the ready.

The K-9 handler released his dog, yelling, "Seek! Seek!" and the German shepherd sprang forward, bounding into the premises, ears swiveling like a radar antenna, nose sniffing the front room before disappearing into the bedroom.

Nemer Indarte watched the proceedings with bemused irritation. The team put on a good show for the easily impressed, and it did not impress him. A study of the floor plan showed only this door as the entrance. If Briscane had wanted to escape through another exit, he'd have to do so by jumping from his ninth-story balcony.

Briscane was not a physically violent man and so far in his mission to take down Diana Willis had proved himself to be woefully incompetent. With his highly tuned clairvoyance and telepathy— immensely useful skills, to be certain—he could track her down, but in business parlance, he could not close the deal. At the last minute, she always gave him the slip.

Considering the layout of the premises and their person of interest, Nemer Indarte would've arrived with only one other man and a second to cover the door should Briscane try to get past. However, Carcano had insisted that Nemer Indarte task a private SWAT team for this raid, and they showed up with a twelve-person tactical team, the dog and handler, a second team for backup, a command van with high-tech communications and surveillance equipment, and an armored breaching vehicle. A *wop-wop-wop* reverberated from outside. Plus, a helicopter for this circus.

The German shepherd trotted back into view, her eyes on alert but obviously not finding anyone. Her handler ordered her down the hall in the kitchen's direction and a trio of SWAT members followed.

After ten minutes of shouting back and forth among themselves, the SWAT team relaxed and wandered about. Their captain removed her helmet (outfitted with night-vision goggles) and cradled it under one arm. She said to Nemer Indarte, "All clear."

He grinned. *Such masters at stating the obvious.*

He stepped inside, his eyes scoping out details these heavily armed oafs might have missed, and proceeded to the bedroom, where the SWAT agents were pawing through the drawers of the bureau and the nightstands. He asked for an inventory of electronic devices. The usual were accounted for—laptop, thumb drives, router—but not Briscane's cell phone. There was no clue that he had gone anywhere other than to step out for a short time. The pre-raid surveillance had not picked up his cell phone, meaning he had turned it off, so that eliminated that way to track him.

What about his car? "Have you found his car keys?"

The SWAT captain barked orders; her team barked back. She answered, "Negative."

Nemer Indarte wanted to say that a thorough pre-raid surveillance would've determined beforehand if Briscane's car was here or not. But life was too short to dwell on the incompetence of others.

Nemer Indarte let his eyes rove across the bedroom. He spotted a photo on the top of a bureau resting in plain view. When Nemer Indarte reached for the photo, a SWAT agent handed him a pair of latex gloves. Nemer Indarte put them on to humor the agent.

As he studied the image, an awareness that this assignment had just gained a colossal dimension sent shivers down his arms. It had been years since he'd experienced a similar reaction.

The photo was of ten preadolescents gathered in a forest. In the front row was Anthony Briscane, posing arm in arm with Maggie LaClair, Gabriel Mendoza, and Diana Willis. Next to Diana stood a tubby Murray Sims and behind him, hands upon his shoulders, a young Sally Mund.

376

CHAPTER THIRTY

id you dream this world with your eyes open? Will you close your eyes and wake up and find yourself in a new dawn in a new world? And will you be joyful as you look back and think that was a hell of a dream?

General Wayne Carcano raked his glare from Jeff Kennedy to Reginald Deighton and then to Fleet Admiral Hozaku, Director of the NSA. Carcano seethed. "You're telling me that the entire NSA, the CIA, the FBI, Homeland Security can't find either Diana Willis or Anthony Briscane?"

Hozaku wore a Navy dress uniform with rows of ribbons and decorations even though he had never seen a day of combat in his military career. He replied coolly, "I can only speak for the NSA."

Carcano leaned across the table. "Don't weasel out of this. Are you or are you not the head of national intelligence?"

"I am."

"Then give me a straight answer."

Hozaku blinked, then took a deep breath to relax his face. "General, we have lost track of Diana Willis and Anthony Briscane."

"In this day and age," Carcano said, his tone caustic and biting, "when one's location can be tracked to the millimeter in three dimensions and algorithms can predict your next move with ninety-five percent accuracy, how can anyone vanish like puffs of smoke?"

"We're equally puzzled."

"Puzzled? You should be shitting bricks!"

Hozaku remained nonplussed. "A temporary setback."

Carcano clenched his jaw. "Can you tell me when you'll find them?"

"Not at this moment, no."

"Then it's a permanent setback."

Hozaku said nothing.

Deighton cleared his throat, then spoke. "It seems that Diana will be coming to us." He clicked a small remote and the screen on the conference room wall illuminated. It showed a video from Great Global Media announcing the return of Diana Willis on national television.

Carcano smiled. "I'd rather that we find her on our terms. If she shows up."

Deighton added, "GGM is pulling out all the stops." The video showed a giant blimp floating over the night sky of the Bay Area, the lights on its rotund envelope blazing an announcement. The video switched to a panorama shot of Mt. Shasta, then to crowds of people filing onto buses, waving from inside cars—the windows painted over with:

Diana Star, Welcome Back!

A message from another world is coming.

It's not as it seems! Wake Up!

The scenes had a festive quality that boded good tidings. But the images had the opposite effect on Carcano. The plan to control the world would only work if people lived in fear, fear of the unknown, fear of tomorrow, fear of today, fear of one another. These people were not afraid.

Carcano was disturbed by what he saw but could hardly tear his gaze away. "How is this possible?"

Deighton clicked his remote and an animated chart filled the screen. "Our surveys revealed a profound and growing distrust of authority—the government, big corporations, and traditional media."

"But they believe her."

"Because they're giving Diana Willis a platform. They're convinced she will speak the truth."

Deighton clicked another button and a hologram image of Mt. Shasta appeared in the center of the conference table. Lines that glowed green showed trails to a spot between Red Butte and the summit of the mountain. "The place advertised for the so-called 'appearance' will be at this location. Already, *World Primetime Now* secured permits for logistics and to park its vehicles there."

"How many people are we talking about?"

"At least ten thousand."

Even Carcano, the crusty old warhorse, could not contain his astonishment.

Kennedy had been sitting quietly. He sat up and anchored his elbows on the table. "Ten thousand, this gives us a splendid opportunity."

"For what?" Carcano asked.

"For two actions." Kennedy held up a pair of fingers. "First, this many people massed together is a perfect opportunity to initiate a bio-event. We can disperse delayed-reaction agents."

"To do what?" Carcano asked.

"Mimic the effects of stomach flu and induce memory loss. People's association of what happens will be far less than positive."

Carcano nodded thoughtfully. "And the second?"

"Mass panic. Turn the experience on its head. People are going there expecting a celebration. Instead, give them a catastrophe."

Someone knocked on the conference room door. A Space Force security tech cracked the door open. "General Carcano, Major General Calvert is here."

Carcano looked away from the hologram and stood. "Excellent."

Travis Calvert stepped inside. As the head of the Tactical Air Force Command, he wore a Nomex flight suit with his stars embroidered on the shoulders and his leather name patch embossed with command pilot wings. He swaggered toward an empty chair and scrutinized the hologram and the screen. "Even though I just flew in, seems like I'm a bit late to the party."

"Not at all, Travis," Carcano said as he sat. "You're the man I need to talk to about this Diana Willis business."

"What is it you want? Blast her out of the sky?" He chuckled as he said this, though everyone understood he wasn't joking.

"Not that. Our mission is to make her fail. To discredit her and her message."

Calvert studied the hologram and steepled his fingers. "How do I fit in?"

"Her acolytes expect UFOs, beings from another planet, dimension, whatever. We'll give it to them."

Calvert quirked an eyebrow.

Deighton clicked his remote, and the screen showed a flight of the new and top-secret SR119 fighter drones. The aircraft were disc-shaped and capable of 35-G flat turns at hypersonic speeds.

Carcano explained, "UFOs will show up, only they'll be ours. They'll terrorize the crowds and undermine any faith in Diana."

Calvert smiled. "Roger that."

Carcano clapped his hands. "I think we've got a good handle on the plan. Our staffs will work out the details and coordinate the action. Let's meet for lunch in the galley."

Deighton clicked off the screen. All the men filed out except for Carcano and someone who had watched the proceedings in the room's corner: Nemer Indarte.

He shut the door. "A good plan, General, but one that needs just one more touch."

Carcano beckoned him closer. "Which is why you're here."

A long column of people trekked from the Panther Meadows Trailhead and filed into the valley between Red Butte and the summit of Mt. Shasta. The procession resembled a parade, with the hikers wearing especially colorful garb that amplified the festive, optimistic ambiance of the gathering.

Cal Brock drove his FBI Jeep past the hikers. Gabe watched from the front passenger's seat. He said, "You'd think they'd be resentful that we're not giving them a ride."

As this was an official vehicle on official business, Brock couldn't. Besides, no one seemed to begrudge them. The hikers waved and shared greetings. Some banged their drums or tambourines, others tooted flutes, horns, or whistles.

At the crest of the slope, the valley opened before them, a magnificent panorama with Mt. Shasta in the background.

"Kinda takes your breath away," Gabe noted.

"Does indeed," Brock answered. "I doubt Diana could've found a more dramatic vista to stage her return."

He followed a line of orange traffic cones that formed a perimeter around the convoy of rough-terrain trucks and trailers parked to the left. Technicians in safety vests stretched power cables between the trucks and trailers bearing the logo of Great Global Media. Large masts had telescoped upward and pointed satellite dishes to the sky.

The sky. Brock scanned the azure heavens, decorated with wisps of cirrus clouds.

A few weeks ago, had he been told that Diana Willis would disappear into an interdimensional portal and that he would expect her to return from either the rocks on the beach or at this place, he would have dismissed that idea as lunacy.

Now, if that did not happen, it would be a cruel trick of fate.

Those bastards! Murray Sims hurried along, feeling his weight strain against his heart. He hurried as fast as he could as he marched with the hikers streaming uphill toward what people called "Diana's Return."

Rivulets of sweat trickled down his face and soaked his collar. His shirt was likewise soaked, front and back. He carried his jacket draped over one arm. The sun was bright but barely warm. He breathed the crisp mountain air in large gulps.

Those bastards! he repeated to himself. He had tried to contact Diana Willis and when he couldn't, he hacked into the Great Global Media security network. From there, he wormed his way into Anthony Briscane's computer and phone and found both surprisingly dormant. Diana was missing. Now, Briscane?

He then risked hacking into Carcano's inner ring of security and discovered coded messages to that psychopath murderer, Nemer Indarte. Murray pieced together the clues. One thousand milligrams of Zetex-85, an especially powerful plastic explosive. Two KR-21 boosters, both also powerful, with mirrored detonators for simultaneous initiation of the main charge. A Quark-Tek command initiator with a backup timer. And last, a reference to Mt. Shasta and today's date. This could only mean that Carcano had planted or was going to plant a bomb to ruin Diana's return.

Murray's computer detected a reverse trace. Carcano's security team had detected the breach. Murray immediately powered off his routers and computers. He considered calling someone at GGM to warn them but decided otherwise. What if the person who answered his call was in on the bombing? Or what if they planted all these clues to create a ruse with the threat of a bomb scare enough to annihilate Diana's event?

Wheels within wheels.

The last stretch of trail led to the top of the hill. But once Murray arrived at the scene, how would he find the bomb?

Sweat stung his eyes. His feet throbbed in agony. His heart pounded in protest. Even if he thwarted the bombing, he'd probably die of cardiac arrest.

Anya Sullivan climbed onto a wooden platform, just now hammered together. Two video tech operators aimed their cameras at her. A second tech watched from the corner of the platform while a sound tech checked her microphone.

A makeup tech stepped back and cocked her head to study her work on Anya's face.

"How's my hair?" Anya asked.

"Looks perfect."

For the occasion, Anya wore designer outdoor pants with matching jacket and Gucci hiking boots (brand new and had paid an intern to wear them first to break them in).

Anya surveyed the assembled masses, easily five thousand already and growing larger by the minute. Small drones hovered above onsite, videoing the developing scene.

She turned to scan the sky. When Diana Willis showed up, however she showed up, the show would be ratings gold. But if not? Anya winced and decided not to dwell on that disaster.

Gabe and Brock wove through the crowds. The event was so impromptu that little in the way of logistics had been arranged—Porta-potties, food vendors, water. At least the Forest Service had provided two off-road ambulances. Large cardboard boxes dotted the area for use as trash receptacles.

"Many people will be disappointed if Diana doesn't show up," Brock said.

Gabe walked with a spring in his step like he was expecting the best of news. "Why are you such a doubter? You saw her walk into the portal. What more proof do you need?"

Brock sighed. "How many false Messiahs have never followed through on their promises?"

Gabe clapped his hand on Brock's shoulder. "And since when is Diana a Messiah?"

When Murray Sims looked across the sea of people filling this part of the valley, his heart sank. He figured the bomb was smaller than a six-pack of beer and so could be hidden almost anywhere in front of him. Perhaps in a backpack? As he scurried along, he looked at the ground around people's feet. The crowd was scrupulously neat, and no one had discarded any trash, let alone a backpack.

He looked at the *World Primetime Now* and other news media vehicles. There?

He doubted it, for he'd learned the bomb had been encased in a plastic sleeve that contained a dense matrix of steel pellets. Obviously, an anti-personnel weapon. When the bomb exploded, it would hurl a cloud of shrapnel in a horizontal direction. If the intent was to create mass casualties, there would be no point hiding such a device in a truck far away from the crowds.

No, the bomb had to be close, somewhere among all these people. All these targets.

He saw a well-dressed woman standing on a wooden platform, the object of attention of video techs. She was no doubt Anya Sullivan, the new prime-time face of *World Primetime Now.*

What if he told her and she warned everybody?

In his mind's eye, Murray saw the result. Panic rippling through the crowds. A stampede down the trail back to the trailhead. The destruction of Diana's return.

And again, what if that was the plan, to make him the unwitting accomplice to Carcano and his plan to discredit Diana?

No, the bomb was here, or it wasn't. Murray would keep what he suspected a secret.

General Carcano surveyed the panoply of screens and computers that followed the developments. He was in the Cheyenne Mountain Auxiliary Tactical Operations Center—the ATOC—observing the proceedings.

From one computer workstation, a female airman tech announced, "One-one-niners airborne." This was military-speak that the SR119 fighter drones were on the way.

A wall-mounted screen showed the two disk-shaped aircraft zooming skyward from Area 51. Another screen showed the drones tracked on radar.

Carcano smirked. *If those idiots on Mt. Shasta want UFOs, I'll give them UFOs.*

Brock and Gabe had positioned themselves on a slight rise of high ground close to the parked trucks, where they could observe the masses and the crest of the knoll.

Anya Sullivan and her entourage watched from the platform while several of her camera techs shoehorned their way through the crowd, recording the scene.

Brock noted the time and grimaced as if experiencing a slight souring, the onset of disappointment, the realization that perhaps he and Gabe had been wrong about Diana.

Gabe noted a slight wrinkling in the air, the bending of light in front of him. A pinecone emitting a silvery translucent light appeared and hovered just within his reach. "It's Diana."

Brock snapped his head around to look at Gabe. "Where?"

Gabe noticed the same image floating in front of Brock. "Can you see that?"

"See what?"

Gabe was too mesmerized to respond, but as he gazed across the multitudes, he could see the same apparition of the pinecone floating in front of many. He knew some noticed as they attempted to touch it, and a few took swipes like they were swatting insects. But there were many like Brock who did not know it was there.

One hovered in front of Anya where she stood on the platform, but she obviously did not register its presence.

Why are some not seeing this?

"What's going on?" Brock asked.

"It's Diana." Gabe refocused on the mind-boggling spectacle floating in front of him. "She's sending messages to us. Communicating telepathically to those who are ready."

Gabe's mind was drawn into a voice that emanated from the pine-cone yet was all around him. As soon as he heard the words, he knew it was Diana Star, but wondered if the others were hearing this too.

"I've come from your future." Her voice was friendly, yet firm. "From another world like this one, but many earth years ahead of you. We have a message for you to heed.

"The bifurcation of your world has begun, control and fear or love and freedom. Dystopia or Utopia. Your choice.

"We once faced the same choices you must now make. The same choices that, had we not made them, would have resulted in the complete loss of our freedom and annihilation from the same forces that left our world and came to yours.

"Those of you who are ready will understand.

"Stop the hypocrisy inside and out. It is rampant everywhere and with everyone. Hypocrisy makes you weak and is preventing you and your world from evolving.

"Your power is within. You are sovereign and can rule yourselves.

"It is paramount that you raise your vibration through meditation. Find the place in the center of your head where this pinecone of light is located and go there as much as you can and find your way out.

"Use it to discern the truth and protect you amidst your quiet war of deception.

"The way out is within.

"Have faith. More communications will follow.

"Now step forward towards us and to your new future.

"We are Secret Transmissions Allied Response."

A gasp rippled through the people, the gasp becoming louder, gaining strength until it became a loud rumble, distracting Gabe and pulling him away from the telepathic connection.

Arms pointed upward, toward the same spot in the sky.

Brock brought his hands up to shade his eyes. Two dots streaked toward the crowd. They shot over the valley, zigzagging despite their impossibly high speed. The two flying craft were circular and certainly UFOs. But with Diana?

The crowd shied from whatever they were.

The first, then the second disk darted overheard. They were metallic and fifty feet in diameter.

The disks raced at high speed over the crowd, losing height with every orbit over the knoll, the sun glinting off their edges, so they appeared as menacing as spinning blades.

Off to the side, Anya Sullivan and a battery of video cameras were broadcasting the event. Diana's hope of reaching the world had arrived unexpectedly.

Murray Sims sensed panic building in the crowd. He had wanted to devote himself to Diana's appearance and what it meant for the planet, but he had a mission to complete.

Find the bomb. He was convinced it had to be here; Carcano could not ignore this opportunity to sabotage Diana's return.

Murray Sims wedged his way through the assembly, ignoring the resentments and insults, focused instead on locating the bomb. The crowd parted enough to reveal a large cardboard box labeled TRASH. Placed close to so many people, that would be a prime spot for a bomb.

He scurried toward the box, pushing his way through the bodies until he stood over it. Garbage spilled over the top. He tossed aside the layers of discarded wrappers, digging in. His hands grasped something hard and unusually heavy. He clasped a box the size of a gallon jug of milk and lifted. He figured the device wouldn't have a fuse that ignited when moved, since Carcano, or whoever had planted the bomb, wouldn't risk a premature detonation should the trash box be jostled unexpectedly.

People admonished him for scattering trash, but he ignored them. The device was made of gray plastic and covered in even rows of bumps from the embedded steel pellets. He unscrewed the cap, as big around as a coffee cup, and withdrew the initiator and detonator module.

With the module removed, the primary charge of Zetex-85 was now disarmed, but the two KR-21 detonators, each the size of a D-cell battery, were still deadly.

He felt the initiator buzz.

Realizing he had run out of options, he yelled, "Bomb! Bomb! Get away!" and did the only thing he could to protect everyone around him. He clutched the module to his belly and fell to the ground.

A camera from one of the SR119s relayed a video. On the main screen within the ATOC, Carcano watched the pandemonium unfold. People running in terror from that overweight stooge Murray Sims, who flopped onto his belly to smother the bomb.

Carcano regarded the sacrifice and admitted begrudgingly, *I didn't think the fat slob had it in him.*

But his observation was premature.

He watched a strange light appear around Murray Sims, and instead of his corpulent body bouncing upward and then settling as a bloody heap, he just lay there. As he looked closer, Murray Sims was still alive, and the bomb had failed to detonate.

"What the fuck. How can that be?"

Incredibly, instead of running away from the knoll, many people were taking halting steps towards the center of the gathering.

The general clenched his jaw and worked his lips. He expected mass casualties. Carnage. How the hell had Murray Sims prevented the bomb from exploding? And what were these idiots around him doing? Didn't they know they were beaten? That whatever Diana planned was in ruins.

Reflexively, he considered ordering the SR119s to slam into the crowd but thought it over. He had underestimated the people's devotion to her, and her ability to survive repeated attacks. Each time, she reappeared, stronger and more capable. What would be the result here?

A knot of bile, the taste of defeat, burned in Carcano's throat. He muttered the order, "Recall the one-one-niners."

Brock watched the flying disks pitch upward sharply and zoom into the sky, fading to dots before disappearing.

Medics from the ambulances and police sprinted toward Murray Sims, who was just getting up on his feet when they arrived.

They were as astonished as he was, for on the ground in front of him lay tiny fragments of the two detonators. Fascinated by what had happened, or rather, what hadn't happened, Murray Sims picked at the debris. The detonators had shattered into bits as if they had exploded, but without the blast. How was this possible?

He looked closer and in the middle of the pile lay a small, perfectly formed pinecone.

Even with the commotion going on around them, Gabe knew that a matter of greater importance had opened up to him. The mystical pinecones had manifested themselves to a chosen few. Their minds were fertile and receptive to Diana Star's message from the future, a message of love and freedom.

Looking to his left and right, Gabe saw a handful of the assembled masses step toward the pinecone floating before each of them at eye level. Gabe followed their lead and leaned toward his pinecone, feeling its silvery touch tap against his forehead and then slide into his mind.

This door to this future had opened.

Through an astonishing act of telepathic transference, Diana Star had returned from the future. She had kept her promise.

Now for the next one...

EPILOGUE

On her lap rests a small open book and as she receives these messages, she thinks of a response and its words appear on the blank pages:

The bifurcation of your world has begun...

Control and Fear or Love and Freedom...

Dystopia or Utopia...

Your choice...

Diana Star looks up from the book. Tiny sparkles fill the air before her. These sparkles hover in place and shimmer, the light they emit becoming brighter.

The sparkles grow and gain form, turning into glimmering silvery pinecones, hundreds of them floating around Diana.

The words on the pages of her book—Love and Freedom, Utopia—lift from the pages, replicating themselves, and dissolve into the pinecones. The pages of the book flutter, flipping from one to the next in a blur.

She closes the book and regards the red cover. In the center of her brain, the pineal gland glows. On the cover, a silver outline takes shape, embossing itself into the red leather. It is a silver pinecone.

The air quivers before her and an elder from her people, one of the wise old men, materializes. He wears a long robe that rustles from an unknown breeze.

Though his eyes are ringed with deep wrinkles, they shine with vitality and determination. He raises a hand and instantly transmits a force of energy.

Diana feels as if a ghost of herself steps away. This second Diana holds a copy of the red book. Her silhouette glows, and she changes shape, shrinking, becoming the young Alexandra who accompanied Joseph and Magdalena Starnowski.

Diana ponders the array of pinecones and watches them vanish to the past. She gazes at Alexandra, who has turned around.

They lock gazes. Great trials await her, but she will overcome them, for she will return.

A telepathic transference takes place. *You are the messenger. You must get their attention before it's too late.*

She nudges Alexandra forward. *Remember, you came from your future and there is no fear. You are courageous and free.*

An infinity symbol appears between them, a pinecone centered where the two loops connect.

On one side, the word Future appears. On the opposite side, the word Past.

The two words slide toward one another, merge, and together with the infinity symbol, vanish.

A security guard was making his rounds through the halls of the San Francisco FBI office when he noticed an older man backing out of the service elevator. Though the man wore the blue uniform of the custodial services, he didn't look familiar.

"Hey," the guard said.

The man continued to step backwards, dragging a janitorial cart with an attached trash can and vacuum cleaner. He turned toward the guard and lifted the ID badge hanging from a lanyard.

The security guard recognized the logo on the badge, as it was for the same contracting firm that he worked for. The custodian limped a bit and appeared well past retirement age. The guard felt bad for the old man, who should be home in bed rather than working these late hours. The guard nodded and said, "Right on."

The custodian gave a curt salute, and the guard disappeared around the corner. Continuing with his labors, the custodian steered the cart down the hall, and at the door marked *Special Agent Cal Brock*, he unclipped the key ring attached to his belt and unlocked the door to prop it open. After flicking on the lights, he wrestled the cart over the threshold and set to work.

He emptied the trash, vacuumed the floor and the baseboards, then dusted the desk, chairs, bookcases, and the plaques and framed certificates on the walls. He was especially careful to not disturb the papers and notes pinned to a large corkboard beside a whiteboard, itself covered with scribblings and diagrams. His gaze ranged across the photos taped along the top of the whiteboard: pictures of Sally Mund, Gabe Mendoza, Maggie LaClair, Anthony Briscane, Diana Willis, and...the custodian smiled at this last one...of John Herald.

He glanced at the door to make sure he was alone, then withdrew a red leather book embossed with a silver pinecone on its cover tucked among his cleaning supplies. He slid the red book into a white mailing envelope and left it on the center of Brock's desk. Next, the custodian placed a pinecone beside the envelope. He imagined the FBI agent finding the book and the pinecone, and the thought brought an impish grin.

The custodian dragged his cart to the hall, turned off the light, then closed and locked the door.

What is the greatest secret? The Great One who taught me everything I know a long, long time ago declared that the voyage is already over before it begins. You are already there...

I will meet you there... I am John Herald.

COMING SOON

Star Revelations *Two*

Part IV - *Worlds,* Part V - *Forces,* Part VI - *Allies*

StarRevelations.com | Info@HeroActs.com

Steven Paul Terry was born in London, England, and educated there and in Australia. As a professional speaker, he spent three decades traveling the globe. He splits his time between Colorado and Mexico and enjoys writing by the ocean, where he also swims and dives.

Visit his website at StevenPaulTerry.com

Printed in Great Britain
by Amazon